# THE
# BURNING
# GIRLS

BOOKS BY RITA HERRON

DETECTIVE ELLIE REEVES SERIES
*The Silent Dolls*
*Wildflower Graves*

# RITA HERRON

# THE BURNING GIRLS

bookouture

Published by Bookouture in 2021

An imprint of Storyfire Ltd.
Carmelite House
50 Victoria Embankment
London EC4Y 0DZ

www.bookouture.com

ISBN: 978-1-83888-983-8
eBook ISBN: 978-1-83888-982-1

*To my mother, who taught me to appreciate all things Southern.*
*May she rest in peace.*

# PROLOGUE

Her father would kill her if they found out what had happened.

Isabella had to run away. Save herself. Save them from the shame.

Fear and nausea clawed at her as she threw some clothes in her backpack. She snatched the cash she kept in the shoebox and stuffed it inside the bag, then grabbed her toothbrush and hairbrush and… oh, God, what else did she need?

Panic caused her heart to pound. Summer break had just started. She'd been so excited about starting college last year and returning in the fall. She was the first in her family to do so. But now…

She couldn't go back. And she couldn't stay at home. Where could she go? How would she get by?

A noise outside. She looked through the window and spotted headlights down at the holler.

The picture of her mother and her in their matching Christmas pajamas taunted her, and tears stung her eyes. She'd yelled at her mom that she was too old for such silly nonsense. "You'll always be my little girl," her mother had said.

The love in her mother's voice had gotten to her, and she'd caved, putting on the reindeer hat and pjs, even though she'd been frowning in the picture.

Her mother would be devastated when she left…

She'd be even more devastated if she learned the truth.

Eyes clouding over, she jammed the picture in her backpack, then grabbed her pink jacket and tugged it on. Slinging her backpack over her shoulder, she eased open the window and crawled through it. Grabbing hold of the nearest tree branch, she climbed down, just as she had so many times in high school when she'd snuck out to see her friends.

She would miss them, too.

But she had to go.

Tree bark scraped her palms, but she bit back a cry, maneuvered down and dropped to the ground. Nausea twisted her stomach, but she swallowed it. Poised like a cat, she turned and peered through the darkness. Trees rustled in the wind.

Brush parted as something—or someone—pushed through it.

Terror seized her, and she glanced at the street and her yard. Deciding it was safer to cut through the woods, that maybe she could make it to the bus stop in town, she darted around the side of the house and sprinted into the thicket of pines and cypresses backing the property.

Not far from Moody Hollow, where vacationers hiked up to the waterfalls, she might even be able to hitch a ride.

Her feet skidded over pine straw and she stumbled over a tree stump, but she raced through the brush, grateful she'd run track last year. Just as she veered onto the trail that would take her to the falls, she heard the sound of footsteps crunching, closing in on her. Suddenly someone jumped from behind a boulder and grabbed her.

She kicked and screamed and tried to bite, but something jammed in her neck, and then she felt her body go numb. Unable to move or fight, she hung limp and terrified as the man dragged her deeper into the forest.

# CHAPTER 1

*Winding Rock*

The bones of the body were charred so badly they looked like ashes.

Detective Ellie Reeves had never seen anything like it. Her own family's house had burned down a few weeks ago, blazing away her childhood room and all her memories. Her parents were starting to sift through the ashes now and rebuild their lives.

But this… this person had died a miserable, painful death.

And the stones… a circle of them stood around the body like a monument. So different from the rocks that had skidded down the hill into the ravine and lay in a natural pile.

These stones resembled giant arrowheads and had been driven into the ground with their tips pointing toward the sky. Her pulse jumped. She was sure she had seen something like this before, but she couldn't quite place where.

She turned to scan the area, looking for clues to tell the story. Something to identify the body.

There was no ID in sight. No wallet, purse, jacket or backpack. The clothing was scorched, light-gray fibers had caught on a patch of briars.

Pulling her bandana over her nose to stifle the stench, Ellie leaned closer, noting a chain hanging loosely around the brittle ankle bones. Scattered by the water's edge, she spotted tiny pearls from a necklace. A lone black shoe dangled from a thorn bush, the kind of shoe a woman might wear to an office or to dinner, not to hike in the rocky terrain of the Appalachian Mountains.

"It's a woman," Ellie mumbled, half to herself, half to Cord McClain, a ranger who worked Search and Rescue in Bluff County. As a teen, she'd had a crush on the brooding tough guy. Years ago, after a harrowing rescue mission, they'd slept together. Afterwards, he'd been distant and she'd been trying to prove herself as a cop, so romance was not in the picture. Although occasionally she glimpsed a spark of interest in his eyes, and felt it, too.

Recently they'd been thrown together investigating murders on the trail, and she'd hurt him by questioning his involvement in the crimes. One day she hoped to repair the damage. She had no idea if that could ever happen, though.

A squawking bird drew her attention back to the case, and questions rattled through her head. What exactly had happened here? Was the woman out here alone? Had she been meeting someone for a romantic rendezvous?

Ranger Cord McClain wiped sweat from his forehead. The heat was oppressive, magnified ten times by the brush fire that had rippled through the woods earlier in the day.

The third in the last few days. Trouble was they didn't know if the fires were accidental or if they'd been intentionally set. So far, they had no clear evidence and, with the recent drought, a campfire or a match accidentally dropped could have set the dry brush ablaze.

A frown tugged at Cord's chiseled face as he shined his flashlight across the blackened ground. "She could have been hiking but got caught out here and didn't see the fire until it was on her. But what do you make of those stones? It looks like someone arranged them that way."

"Which means this was no accident," replied Ellie. "According to folklore, standing stones represent social circles where people gathered to mourn the dead."

"How do you know all that?" Cord asked.

"My dad used to fill me with stories when we went camping," Ellie said. "After that, I checked out books on the area and read about the folklore."

Cord's voice was gruff. "Bodies are burned during cremation to symbolize that we are nothing, that we'll be turned to ashes after death."

Ellie shivered, his comment reminding her of Cord's troubled past. As a foster kid, he'd grown up above a funeral home. Worse, his foster father had defiled the bodies he was supposed to take care of. That dark time still haunted his eyes and had made him a suspect in the last case she'd worked, where the killer had buried the bodies in a ritualistic pattern. He was cleared, but their relationship was far from repaired.

She pulled at her T-shirt, desperate for relief from the heat and the suffocating air.

Instead, a breeze stirred the sickening scent of burned flesh and bone, and her stomach roiled.

Reining in her repulsion, she scanned the area again. It was odd for females to hike alone, but it happened. God knows she'd gone off into the wilds of the mountains by herself when she'd needed space and time alone to think.

"Looks like she was by herself," she said. "But why? The news and park service have issued warnings for people to stay away until we get a handle on these brush fires." With the steep cliffs, wild animals, and endless miles of forest, hiking alone was dangerous at any time. But especially now. The fires were robbing the precious land of its beautiful greenery, killing forest animals and destroying the natural order on the Appalachian Trail.

As the fires raged, the local prayer group known as the Porch Sitters met daily, sending pleas up to the heavens for much-needed rain and the safety of the firefighters and park rangers who protected the land. They also prayed for the adventure seekers who tackled the treacherous 2,200-mile trail that started in Georgia and stretched all the way to Maine.

But until today, the fires hadn't taken a life.

Voices echoed, and she glanced up to see the medical examiner, Dr. Laney Whitefeather, pushing through the mass of pines and oaks, the crime scene investigators close behind.

"God," Laney said as soon as she spotted the burned body.

The CSI team paused, expressions pained as they absorbed the gruesome image.

Laney recovered first. "Who found her?" she asked.

"Firefighters," Cord responded. "They were trying to extinguish the blaze and called it in." He gestured toward a tall, broad-shouldered man in a firefighter's uniform combing the area.

"That the arson investigator?"

Cord nodded. "A newbie to Bluff County Fire Department. Name's Max Weatherby. He's looking for signs it was a campfire that got out of hand, and for the point of origin."

Ellie nodded. The blaze had cut a path through the woods about six feet wide, destroying the dense weeds and eating at the trees, the dry land prime for spreading it. She studied the spot where the woman's body lay for indications that the fire began there, but with nothing but ashes and charred debris, the expert would have to make a call on that. But if the fire had been set intentionally, the point of origin could be some distance away. In that case, there would have been smoke, heat and flames shooting into the sky, so why hadn't the woman seen it and gotten out of there? Because she'd been killed first? The stones pointed to that theory.

Ellie rubbed her chin. "Who reported the fire?"

Cord shrugged. "Another ranger."

"I guess you can't tell cause of death or time yet?" Ellie said to the ME.

Laney rolled her eyes. "You know I can't. I'll have to request an expert forensic anthropologist on this one. Bones aren't my specialty. With the body being burned so severely, we'll have to rely on PMCT for identification and to determine what caused death."

"PMCT?" Cord asked.

"Postmortem computed tomography," Ellie explained.

"Exactly," Laney confirmed. "It's complicated, but analyzes toxicology, looks for traumatic fractures, surgical dissection of foreign bodies and state of carbonization."

"You're way over my head. Can you do that?" Ellie asked.

"The specialist will handle it."

Ellie's stomach clenched again as the hollow eye sockets of the woman's face stared at her.

# CHAPTER 2

*Crooked Creek*

Bone-tired, Ellie wanted a hot shower and a chilled vodka. The stench of smoke, her own sweat, and burned flesh clung to her every pore. Laney had finally been able to transport the bones to the morgue, but the forensic specialist wouldn't be in until tomorrow. Analysis of the soil and burned brush would also confirm if an accelerant had been used. The team had not found any sign that the victim had been camping. No gear, no food, no supplies. If there had been evidence of another party there, the fire had probably destroyed it. The only item of interest found by the arson investigator was a discarded lighter a few hundred feet from the woman's body, which was also sent to the lab.

Before she went home, Ellie wanted to check on Deputy Shondra Eastwood. Just six weeks ago, Ellie's friend had been abducted by the Weekday Killer, a serial killer who'd targeted women in the area because of a vendetta against Ellie. Years back, when she was at the police academy, she'd reported him for sexual harassment. Her claims had started a wave of others and he'd been dismissed from the academy. Then his wife left him, and he'd lost her and his daughter in a tragic accident. An accident he blamed on Ellie. That rage had transferred to his victims.

Shondra had barely escaped alive.

Guilt for her friend's torture kept Ellie awake at night. Ever since she was a child, she'd struggled to sleep, but now night was even more her enemy. Sometimes she didn't sleep for days on end and could barely function. Other times she slept fitfully, her nightmares filled with the horrors of her past, the cases that haunted her.

Work was her salvation. Having a new case to focus on, horrifying as it was, would stop her from spiraling.

Parking her Jeep at Shondra's apartment, Ellie killed the engine, then glanced at her own reflection in the mirror. God, she looked ragged. Her ash-blond hair was a mess, soot stained her cheeks and dark circles rimmed her blue eyes. Licking her fingers, she wiped away the dirt and redid her ponytail, but she couldn't do anything about the permanent shadows under her eyes.

Just as she felt helpless to erase Shondra's. For a moment, she sat staring at the cinder-block building. Ever since the attack, Shondra had shut down and hadn't wanted to see her.

Who could blame her? The monster who'd abducted her had done so to get revenge on Ellie.

Sucking in a breath to steady her nerves, she climbed out and walked up the sidewalk. The recent tornado had completely destroyed Shondra's mobile home, so she was staying here instead. But the brutal weather had also wreaked havoc on this property. Although the concrete building was still standing, the sidewalk needed patching, the building painting, and Ellie smelled the acrid scent of pot as she made it to Shondra's door. Hopefully this ramshackle place was just temporary and her friend could find a more suitable home soon. That's if she didn't leave altogether—Shondra had mentioned that she wasn't sure she'd be staying in Bluff County.

Ellie understood the need to run and start over. She'd felt that way a few weeks ago herself. But her ties to Crooked Creek ran deep, and she'd finally decided she couldn't run far enough to escape her past. She had to stay and face it.

A quick knock, then she called Shondra's name. Seconds ticked by. She knocked again. "Shondra, please open up. I need to see you." The image of the woman's blackened bones taunted her. "Please, let me in," Ellie said. "I'm worried about you."

Shuffling could finally be heard, and the door creaked open. Shondra's face, pale and gaunt, appeared. The bruising and swelling from the beatings she'd taken were fading, but Ellie knew that the emotional scars were still raw. "Ellie, go home. It's late and I'm tired."

"I know, but… I wanted to make sure you were okay."

Shondra's curly black hair was pulled back with a clip, her eyes almost as hollow as the sockets of the dead woman. "Go away."

"I'm not leaving without making sure you're all right."

Tears blurred Shondra's eyes, and she released a wary sigh, before opening the door and motioning for Ellie to come in. Except for a few boxes in the corner of the kitchen, the apartment was bare. She'd lost most of her belongings during the twister.

And more of herself during the kidnapping.

"I'm sorry," Ellie said, her heart churning. "I know it was my fault Burton took you. I don't know how else to say I'm sorry or how to make things right."

"You can't make it right," Shondra said, her voice low and defeated. "Nothing will ever be right again."

"Burton is dead," Ellie said, with conviction. "That's a start. He can't hurt you anymore. And I'm sorry he came after you because of me." She'd said it again. She'd say it a hundred times more if it helped.

Shondra's face crumpled. "I don't blame you, Ellie," she said, her voice cracking. "I'm a cop, supposed to catch a killer, not be a victim."

Ellie guided Shondra to the faded green couch, the only piece of furniture in the tiny, threadbare living room.

"Listen to me, you're a good cop," Ellie said. "Burton was cunning, smart, devious. He used everyone in his path and would have found a way to get what he wanted."

"I tried to be so strong when he had me," Shondra whispered, swiping at tears. "But since then, I… just fell apart."

"You are strong, Shondra, but it takes time to process trauma. You will get through this."

Shondra twirled the end of her hair between her fingers.

"This is about Melissa, isn't it?" Ellie said softly. It had turned out that Shondra's ex-girlfriend had been involved in the Weekday Killer case, helping him lure his victims. "You love her and you feel betrayed that she helped Burton."

Emotions streaked Shondra's face, and her chin quivered. "I do. But I realize she was victimized too. We all were."

"Maybe talking to her would help."

Shondra pushed to her feet, angry lines slashing her eyes. "You've seen her, haven't you?"

"I had to, for the case. And… for you."

"Go, Ellie. I'm done talking right now."

"Shondra, please—"

"I asked you to go."

Tears burned Ellie's eyes, but she blinked them back.

"Think about it," Ellie said as she turned and walked toward the door, but she was only met with her friend's resounding silence.

# CHAPTER 3

*Crooked Creek*

Ten minutes later, Ellie parked in front of her bungalow. The mountains rose behind it, steep and strong in their glory, the colors of summer flowers and greenery a reprieve from the long winter months.

Having grown up in these parts, she'd hiked the AT—the Appalachian Trail—for as long as she could remember. But the mountains weren't the safe place they used to be. A series of serial killer cases had left behind clouds of lingering fear, neighbors looking at one another with suspicion. Her father, Randall, had been disgraced since his retirement as sheriff, and Ellie was doing her best to prove herself to the small community. The negative press surrounding her and the revelation that Randall had withheld important information about a murder had taken its toll on all of them. She and her father had both received hate mail and the town had protested when the prosecutor dropped the charges against her father due to lack of evidence.

She'd thought once the Weekday Killer was caught, the residents would settle down, but this blasted heatwave seemed to be making everyone restless. Now the Fourth of July was upon them, too, with tourists flocking to town.

As Ellie entered her house, soft moonlight slanted its way through the blinds in the living room, the wood floor creaking beneath her boots as she crossed to the kitchen.

Still shaken by the image of those charred bones, she flipped on every light in the house. She'd made great strides in conquering her fear of the dark and enclosed spaces but needed to manage triggers in times of stress.

Body wound tight with tension, she poured herself a shot of Kettle One and inhaled the crisp citrus scent, swirling it around in her glass before she took a long slow sip. It wasn't enough to settle her mind though.

Exhausted, she walked to the bedroom, removed her gun and stored it in her nightstand. She turned on the shower and left the water to heat up, then peeled off her sweat-drenched, smoky clothes. The hot water felt heavenly as she stepped beneath the spray, desperate to cleanse her skin of the acrid odor of death. By the time she got out, her captain had called, saying he'd received the update she'd sent him, and they'd talk in the morning.

Even freshly showered, her skin still felt clammy from the heat, and she checked the dial on her air conditioner. It made an odd clicking sound, the air in the house stifling, the old unit working furiously to cool the interior and failing. She found a fan in the closet, set it up to face her bed, and flipped it on.

The humming helped to drown out her thoughts, yet her gaze fell on the phone number beside her bed.

That number held the key to her past. For years, Ellie's parents had kept her adoption secret, never telling her that she used to be a little girl called Mae. The night before her adopted mother Vera went in for open heart surgery, she'd given Ellie the name of the social worker who'd handled her adoption.

Ellie had been debating what to do with the information ever since.

Nerves drew her belly into a knot. Punching her pillow, she climbed beneath the sheets. But as she closed her eyes, voices whispered inside her head.

*Where do you belong? Do you have any real family?*

With trembling fingers, she dialed the number.

The phone rang and rang then went to voicemail, so she left a message. If the woman didn't return her call in the morning, she'd go by her office.

But despite her determination, she couldn't help asking, if her biological mother hadn't wanted her when she was born, why would she want her in her life now?

# CHAPTER 4

*Pigeon Lake*

Eighteen-year-old Katie Lee Curtis slung her backpack over her shoulder as she jogged toward the park. Tears blurred her vision. All she'd ever wanted to do was make her parents proud. Make her mama smile. Make her daddy love her.

But for some reason she didn't understand, he didn't. And she'd realized tonight that he never would. It was getting harder and harder to take.

He was nicer to her brother Marty, but he shut down when he looked at her, as if the sight of her disgusted him.

Tonight, she'd run to her room, but she heard her parents fighting again, her daddy telling her mother to pray for forgiveness. To keep her mouth shut and a tight rein on their daughter. She didn't stay to hear the rest.

A noise behind her startled her, and she ducked behind a bush, peering around her to see if she was being followed. Two joggers ran past, their feet pounding the trail leading through the park.

Katie Lee waited until they disappeared between the rows of pines then veered toward the river where she planned to meet Will. If her daddy found out she was out here, he'd kill her.

But she needed a friend, and she and Will had bonded at the church.

Night settled over the land, making the trees look like monsters with arms reaching out to grab her. Her breathing puffed out as she ran faster, twigs cracking behind her.

She froze, eyes searching the woods, but the trees were so thick the moon was lost in them. At the sound of more crackling, certain they were footsteps, she dodged a fallen limb and picked up her pace. But she was disoriented and lost her footing. She slid, grabbing for something to break her fall, and slammed into a tree. Pain shot through her arm, but she pushed away and turned in the direction she thought was the river.

The footsteps had died, leaving only the sound of critters rustling through the weeds.

Heart hammering, she shoved ahead, running past a cluster of wild mushrooms. But suddenly she heard the footsteps again. Brush being crushed, loud breathing.

Whoever it was, they were getting closer. She forged on as fast as she could but tripped over a root and went down. Seconds later, a big shadow loomed over her. Then his hands closed around her.

# CHAPTER 5

His finger stroked the glass surface of the watch as the click echoed in his head. *Ding. Ding. Ding.*

The world blurred with the memories. The horrible things he'd done. The cries of the women. Their hands clawing to get away from him. The dull, sightless eyes staring blankly at him. The quiet sound of their breathing.

Then nothing.

Except the evil inside him and an echoing voice in his head.

*Ticktock, Ticktock. You'll be dead by one o'clock.*

Rising from the shadows of the ravine, he shuffled toward where she lay nestled among the hemlocks. She looked so peaceful.

But she had been a fighter.

Remorse clogged his chest, making it hard to breathe. She was so young. So pretty.

Murmuring her name, he cradled her body in his arms then rocked her back and forth, stroking her soft hair with gloved fingers.

He was tempted to kiss her goodbye, but he knew that would be foolish. A kiss would leave DNA. DNA could lead back to him.

So he settled for another stroke of her hair before carrying her to the edge of the ridge. Looking down at the steep drop-off, he felt dizzy for a moment. The images of the women swirled behind his eyes, as clear as the raging water below.

*Ticktock, ticktock.* There was no turning back time.

No taking it all back.

She had to die.

So he dropped her into the river, watching her plunge into the swelling water.

# CHAPTER 6

*Stony Gap*

The bitter odor of charred bones still haunted Ellie the next morning as she parked at the ruins of her family's old homestead. She could still see the thick plumes of smoke curling into the sky as if it was yesterday, the flames shooting higher and higher, a bright orange, red and yellow blaze. The fire had destroyed most of their belongings, burning the mementos of her childhood. Although some memories were best left in the ashes and rubble.

Though the fire had been extinguished long ago, the memory of her mother and father emerging from the blaze still made her shudder. Vera had had a heart attack afterwards and was still recovering. Now she stood by their truck, leaning against it, looking weak and pale and small. The woman who'd always been immaculate in her clothing and makeup, who'd wanted Ellie to be a girly girl and trade her police badge for a wedding ring, now wore a simple cotton shirt and black slacks, and her usually stylish bob needed trimming. The less coiffured look made her seem less… daunting.

Ellie liked her better that way.

Her father, having lost weight himself under the stress of the last weeks, shifted his hat to shade his eyes from the blistering morning sun.

Ellie climbed from her Jeep, ignoring the twinge of emotions warring in her chest. She loved her parents, but after learning they'd lied to her all her life, she was struggling to find forgiveness. "What are you two doing here?" she asked as she approached them.

Her father's intense frown faded slightly, and Vera's eyes held the wariness of a mother who didn't know what to say to her child. Although sorrys had been said, their relationship was still tentative.

"We've made a decision about this place," her father said. "About whether or not to stay in Stony Gap."

Ellie braced herself. "What did you decide?"

Her father clasped her mother's hand and they both lifted their chins. "I know half of the town hates me," her father said. "But I'm not running."

Vera dabbed at the corner of her eyes. "Ellie, we want to recreate our family home. And we want you to be with us every step of the way."

Ellie's lungs squeezed for air. Instinctively she shook her head and backed away. "I'm sorry… you can't do that."

"This is our home," Vera whispered. "The only home we've really ever had. We made a life here."

A life full of lies.

"Look, honey," said Randall, "we know you've been through a lot. But we want to prove to the town that we're not bad, that we care about the people here."

He had his work cut out there.

"We want to prove it to you," he said gruffly.

"You can't go back and recreate something that wasn't real," Ellie murmured.

"Then we'll start over and build something new," her father replied. "With the house. With the town. And… with you."

Ellie chewed the inside of her cheek. It took courage for her parents to stay. Her father had lost his job, the respect of the people he'd served as sheriff. Vera had lost her friends and her coveted position on the social ladder. Running would be easier for both of them.

With a thud, she realized they were staying for her.

Emotion built inside her, making it difficult to speak, and then her phone buzzed on her hip. Checking it, the number for the social worker appeared on her screen.

"I'm sorry, but I have to go," she said. "I caught a new case."

She didn't have the heart to tell them that she'd called the social worker to start the hunt for her birth parents.

# CHAPTER 7

*Crooked Creek*

Needing coffee before returning the call that could open Pandora's box, Ellie stopped at the Corner Café.

The parking lot was full of locals and tourists filling up on breakfast and preparing for the day. Canoes and kayaks sat strapped to the tops of SUVs, mingling with RVs, pickups and cars gearing up for outdoor adventures. A group of motorcyclists were clustered together, and a biking club veered from the parking lot as she pulled in. A van emblazoned with the logo of a rafting tour company reminded her of whitewater rafting with her father.

Loyalty to her adoptive parents warred with her need for the truth about herself. How could she know where to go in life if she didn't know where she'd come from?

Inside the café, noisy children and excited families filled the tables. She spotted Vanessa Morely, a former classmate and the only real friend she'd had in elementary school, seated across from her daughter Mandy. A flicker of sadness washed through Ellie that they'd parted ways. At ten, Vera was pushing Ellie toward the Little Miss Bluff County pageant, but she'd balked. Instead, she had been infatuated with mystery books and the history of the area. When Vanessa's grandmother entered her in the pageant, Vera commented that the girl wasn't pageant material. It not only caused a rift between the families, but it hurt Vanessa. After that she wasn't allowed to come to Ellie's, and their friendship had fallen apart.

She considered saying hello, but Mandy slammed her fork down, rattling dishes, and Ellie realized the mother and daughter were arguing.

Turning away, she focused on her surroundings. In contrast with the morbid scenes of the day before, red, white and blue streamers adorned the interior and a sign detailed the upcoming Fourth of July parade festivities. Flyers advertising a book called *Mind Games* written by a local author sat on the counter, highlighting that the bookstore had just gotten in copies.

Lola, the owner of the café, pushed a cup of coffee in front of her and handed Ellie her standing order, a bag with a sausage and cheese biscuit. The ladies from the local garden club, Carol Sue from the Beauty Barn, and the Stitchin' Sisters who owned the quilt shop, had gathered at a round table to the left.

Knowing they were friends with Meddlin' Maude, who'd run a smear campaign against Ellie for not stopping the Weekday Killer before he murdered her granddaughter, Ellie handed Lola cash, then took her bag and headed back outside.

*We have to prove to the town we care about them*, her father had said. *This is our home.*

It was hers, and she had to remember that. Had to keep her head high and do her job.

Impatience tugged at her as she slipped into her Jeep, sipped her coffee and wolfed down her breakfast. Taking a deep breath, she called the social worker's office. A woman answered on the second ring.

"This is Analise Hoberton. Detective Reeves?"

"Yes, I was calling for Gillian Roach," Ellie said, clenching the phone.

"I know. I'm her receptionist and listened to your message." Her voice cracked a notch. "I thought maybe you had news about her."

Ellie frowned. "What do you mean? You thought *I* might have news?"

The woman's breath rattled out. "Well, I've been worried about her. Last Thursday, she packed up her things and hurried out of here and I haven't heard from her since. I tried calling her home number, but she didn't answer. That's not like her. She had several appointments scheduled this week and hasn't bothered to cancel or reschedule them."

The hair on the back of Ellie's neck prickled. "You said she left suddenly?"

"Yes, she'd just gotten off the phone, and she looked upset. She grabbed her computer and some files and ran out the door like something was wrong."

"Does she always take files with her?"

"Never."

"Does she have family?"

"No, she lives alone. Once, she commented that dealing with the troubled families we work with disturbed her too much to have one of her own."

Families just like the one Ellie had come from.

# CHAPTER 8

*Cleveland, Georgia*

Ellie's gut instincts warned her that Gillian Roach was in trouble. Ellie had done her homework on the agency. Raintree Family Services offered counseling, respite care, foster care and adoptions. And dealing with troubled families meant dealing with questionable characters.

Questions nagged at her as she maneuvered the curving mountain road toward the social worker's address. Fruit stands, signs for boiled peanuts, and outbuildings hosting flea markets dotted the rural landscape. The small town of Cleveland was nestled in the North Georgia mountains and decorated with ribbons, banners and signs about its own upcoming Independence Day celebration.

She almost missed the turn-off for the cabins where Gillian lived, and had to swerve at the last minute, skimming the edge of the road as she swung left. Gravel spewed from her tires as they chugged over the rutted road, which seemed to disappear into the overgrown foliage. The sharp switchbacks slowed her, and her ears popped as she climbed the steep mountain.

Three miles in and she spotted a sign for the cabins built along the Chattahoochee River, where wildflowers sprang up amidst the greenery.

Passing three log cabins, Ellie reached the end of the dirt road and turned down a mile-long drive. The A-frame house looked old and weathered. An old ringer washing machine had been turned into a planter, filled with red, purple and pink impatiens, and birds flitted through the trees.

Ellie shivered at the sheer isolation of the house and the crows circling above the chimney. Why had Gillian chosen to live out here alone?

Slowing her Jeep, Ellie pulled to a stop, the uneasiness inside her intensifying.

Once she opened that door, she could never go back.

# CHAPTER 9

*Moody Hollow*

Seventeen-year-old Jerry Otterman and his buddies had been looking forward to summer break all year long. Now the Fourth was almost here, he and Will Huntington had decided to celebrate by hiking to the waterfalls at Moody Hollow.

His backpack on his back, a six pack of beer tucked inside, Jerry hiked through the woods, batting at mosquitoes and scratching at the bug bites he'd gotten last night sleeping on the ground. He could smell smoke, which meant there had to be a fire burning a couple of miles from them.

The heat was a bitch, but the ice-cold Chattahoochee River would feel great. They'd already dived into the swimming hole where teens gathered in the summer to jump off the high cliff into the water below.

His mama said he was a thrill seeker. His daddy said he was a loser.

They'd both warned him that no good came from being out after midnight, that dope was like the apple Eve had picked from the forbidden tree, and that he better keep his dick in his pants. Well, his mama hadn't used those exact words, but her hellfire and damnation speeches warned him he'd be down under with the devil if he didn't toe the line.

His daddy had bought him a pack of condoms and told him he'd better not knock some girl up or he'd end up like him, working a job he hated, listening to a wife who despised him, and living in a trailer with barely a pot to piss in.

But he was young, and this was his time, and he was damned well going to do what he wanted.

And today he was meeting Jaylee Morris at the falls. He hadn't told Will though, knew he'd rib him if he did.

"This heat sucks," Will complained as he lit up a cigarette.

Jerry huffed and wiped sweat from his chin as he reached the top of the ridge, then looked down at the sharp angles of the steep overhang.

Will offered Jerry a cigarette, but he shook his head. Jaylee didn't like smoking. He trudged ahead, and they hiked another half-mile toward the falls. Will finished his smoke, then tossed the butt onto the ground. The orange embers crackled and popped against the dry, brittle pine straw, and smoke curled upward.

"Better put that out," Jerry warned. "The po-po are asking questions about those wildfires."

Will cut him a scathing look. "You sound like your old man."

"Just don't be stupid," Jerry said, throwing him a dark look.

The sound of a scream echoed from somewhere below.

He and Will halted and peered over the edge of the ridge. Smoke hung in the air, a trail of it twisting into the sky. Thick pines, cypresses, and oaks clogged the view, and patches of honeysuckle blended with poison ivy. Water crashed and ebbed over the jagged rocks, the shrill scream boomeranging off the mountain walls.

Jerry spotted the screamer standing at the edge of a lower ridge and took off running. It was Jaylee, the girl he'd planned to meet. Sweat dribbled down his back, soaking his shirt, and he tripped over a tree stump and stumbled. Righting himself, he flew between the trees, weaving between rocks and shoving at the weeds as he negotiated the path.

When he finally reached her, she was staring wide-eyed and shaking.

His stomach clenched into a sick knot. There was a circle of rocks, and inside it was a charred body, smoke coiling into the air surrounding it.

# CHAPTER 10

*Cleveland*

Hot air barely stirred around Ellie as she knocked on Gillian's door. The cabin appeared dark inside, the quiet almost eerie. Tapping her foot, she glanced down at the stoop and noted the newspapers piled on the porch floor. Their dates went back several days.

Another knock, and silence again.

Senses alert, Ellie called the woman's name, then twisted the knob. Surprisingly, the door creaked open, and instantly the scent of something rotten assaulted her. Pulling her flashlight from her pocket, she shined it inside.

"Gillian?"

The interior of the house was as stifling as the outdoors. No sounds of an air conditioner or a fan. A faucet was dripping from a back room, and the floor squeaked as she crossed the living room.

She flashed the light along the wall until she found a switch and flipped it on, then spotted the source of the rancid odor. A bowl of decaying fruit sat on the kitchen counter, fruit flies swarming. A vase held lilies that had wilted, the dead petals strewn across the pine table.

Ellie took a quick look around. A worn, outdated country sofa, faded from the sun slanting through the windows. The dark wood-paneled walls were from the seventies and scratched from wear and tear.

Down the hall, she found a bath and two bedrooms. The first room was stacked with bins of miscellaneous items, as if the woman had been collecting stuff for a garage sale or a charity. Swatting at a fly, she moved onto the master bedroom. A black iron bed, a chair in the corner, and a rickety dresser. A peek inside the closet revealed conservative slacks, blouses, and shoes, all nondescript. The suitcase on the floor, her car outside and the toiletries in the bathroom suggested that the social worker hadn't taken a trip. Wondering about the files she'd taken from her office, Ellie searched the closet, the dresser and beneath the bed, but found nothing.

Returning to the living room, Ellie rummaged through the coat closet, the desk in the corner then the kitchen drawers, but saw no sign of the files. No computer, cell phone, or personal notes scribbled on the writing pad. No photos of friends or coworkers or pets. Nothing to indicate she had a relationship with a partner or significant other.

A sunroom connected to the French doors of the dining area. More and more curious about this woman who helped other families yet seemed to have no one in her own life, Ellie stepped into the room, surprised at the airy feel compared to the rest of the cabin. Sunlight flooded the space through the floor to ceiling windows and offered a view of the gurgling creek out back. She imagined Gillian sipping coffee as she looked out the window in the morning or enjoying a glass of wine at night, listening to the sound of trickling water.

There were no files but a paint canvas in the corner drew her eyes, and she noted other canvasses stacked against the wall. Ellie walked over, expecting to see landscapes of the woods beyond the house.

Instead, it was an eerie black and white sketch of a small child, tears trailing down the little girl's cheeks.

Ellie's breath caught. Was this a child who'd come through the system? The look in her eyes was so haunting that Ellie wondered if Gillian had her own share of nightmares at night.

Her hand shook slightly as she bent down to look at the other canvasses. Her unease mounted at the images of the small children and babies, all looked heartbreakingly alone, their eyes filled with sadness.

Although there was no sign of foul play here, a shudder coursed up Ellie's spine. Pulling her phone from her belt, she called Deputy Heath Landrum. The young cop was a whiz with technology and research and had been an asset on the last two cases they'd worked together.

"Heath, I need you to find out everything you can on a social worker named Gillian Roach. She works with Raintree Family Services."

"What's up?" the deputy asked.

She wasn't ready to share that Gillian might hold the answers to her own past. "Her receptionist called and said she thought Gillian might be in some kind of trouble, that she hasn't been to work in several days. I'm at her house now and she's not here. I need to know if she has any friends who might know her whereabouts. Also, run this license plate and verify the car belongs to her." She stepped back to the front porch and read him the tag number.

"Anything else?"

"She worked with troubled families and domestic cases. It's possible a disgruntled parent or family member came after her. Check hospitals, emergency rooms, and urgent care facilities. I'll talk to the receptionist about her cases and find out if there's a shelter she might have gone to or an underground organization that would have helped her disappear if she was in danger."

If Gillian was running from someone, she might not want to be found. But if she was in trouble, Ellie was determined to help.

"Hang on, Detective Reeves," Deputy Landrum said. "The captain just got a call. Some teenagers found a dead girl at Moody Hollow."

Ellie's pulse jumped. "I'm on my way. Please just look for Ms. Roach."

"Copy that."

Ellie's gaze fell on the sketches of the children again, tears pricking her eyes. If Vera and Randall hadn't adopted her, she might have been one of them.

# CHAPTER 11

*Moody Hollow*

The midday sun beat down on Ellie, creating pockets of blinding light that flickered off the stream as she negotiated her way across the makeshift bridge. The wooden slats were half-broken and rotting, and mud had dried, caking the bank.

Teens flocked to this place, their backpacks loaded with snacks, sodas and beer. High schoolers and college coeds dared each other to swing from the tree ropes and drop into the ice-cold water at least thirty feet below. Jumping off the ridge and plunging into the swimming hole below had been the highlight of her summer when she was a kid. She and Vanessa had come here dozens of times with Randall before their mothers had that falling out.

Flies and gnats buzzed around her face as she followed the trail straight downhill to the base of the falls. The scent of smoke from another wildfire drifted through the air, making the woods look foggy.

On the drive over, she'd talked to her captain, who'd already phoned the ME. The forensic anthropologist had arrived to analyze the bones of the burn victim, freeing Laney to join her here. They'd met at the entrance to the park to hike to the scene together, and a recovery team was on its way.

Ellie spotted Cord in the clearing where two teenage boys and a teenage girl sat hunched on a bunch of rocks. The girl was crying into her hands while an ashen-faced blond boy was trying to console her. The other boy looked pale and shaken, sitting silently, as if too stunned to speak, his gaze latched onto the ground.

She'd thought she was invincible at that age and these kids probably thought they were, too. Being faced with a young person's death opened a chink in that innocence.

Ellie's gaze dropped to the ground by the water, her gut clenching at the sight of the female body lying face down against the rocky ground in the middle of what appeared to be a makeshift firepit. The body was partially burned, although the fire had sizzled out before completely destroying her.

Her left arm was twisted sideways, the bone sticking through the skin of her elbow. Her left foot was bent as well, turned completely sideways, obviously broken. The scene read as if she'd fallen, jumped or was pushed off the ledge.

Then Ellie realized the stones were not a firepit but were standing stones in a circular pattern, like the ones at Winding Rock. *Damn.* This was not an accident or a suicide.

Her mind replayed the grisly image of the victim she'd found the day before. Her first instinct was that they had to be connected, but this body was not completely destroyed by the fire as if it had been snuffed out by something—or someone.

"Poor sweetheart," Laney murmured as they approached. "She's just a baby."

Ellie swallowed back a response. Cord stood by the teens, somber, his body blocking the view of the girl as if to protect the teens from the grisly image. Even after all he'd been through, he was still a protector.

Laney stooped to analyze the scene, gently examining the girl's burned hands and arms, then easing the hair away from her face, exposing bruising and dried blood on her battered cheek.

"She's in full rigor," Laney said. "Contusions to the face, broken arm and ankle." She gently rolled her to her side and even with soot and ashes covering her face, Ellie saw her nose was crushed, lips bloody as if teeth were broken. Was the damage caused by falling or had she taken a beating?

"I won't know exact cause of death until I do the autopsy, but she suffered a severe head injury and may have internal injuries that aren't obvious," said Laney.

Ellie scanned the area. Footsteps marred the brush and dirt near the girl, but the prints might belong to the teens who'd discovered the body. CSI would take plaster casts and run comparisons to the kids' shoes for elimination purposes.

Suspicions stirring in her gut, Ellie gestured toward the ridge above. They needed to look for footprints up there as well. "My guess is she was pushed or fell while running to escape an attacker."

"Judging from her injuries, she was a fighter," Laney murmured.

"What about the fire?" Ellie asked. "Postmortem or did he set the fire while she was alive?"

Laney's gaze locked with hers, her brow furrowed, silent understanding passing between them. "I'll let you know once I finish the autopsy." She gestured toward a silver chain necklace the victim was wearing. The letters KLC were engraved on the oval pendant.

Footsteps echoed from the woods and a minute later the recovery team arrived, along with an evidence response team.

Ellie pointed out the area where she wanted them to search, then the ridge above. "Look for anything to tell us what happened here. Also search for footprints, skid marks or drag marks to indicate whether she jumped or was pushed."

One of the investigators began roping off the area while the other tech started combing the brush and snapping pictures of the girl. Ellie walked over to Cord who gestured toward a backpack tossed into the weeds. "I haven't touched it, but the kids said it's not theirs."

Pulling on gloves, Ellie picked it up, then checked the tag on the outside. The name said Katie Lee Curtis. She unzipped it and found a hairbrush and rain jacket along with a small wallet. Flipping it open, she found a photograph of Katie Lee, a pretty dark-haired girl. Her ID put her at eighteen years old. KLC—Katie Lee Curtis.

Bag in hand, she approached the teens, identified herself and asked their names.

The blond kid consoling the girl was Jerry Otterman. The black-haired kid was Will Huntington. Will smelled like cigarette smoke and looked at her warily, as if he thought he was in trouble.

The girl looked up at her with swollen eyes, shivering as if in shock. Burned victims were always the worst.

Ellie gave her a sympathetic expression, then stooped beside her and patted her back. "I know this is bad. Can you tell me what happened?"

The girl dropped her head into her hands and began sobbing again.

"Will and I camped out last night and were on the way to the falls when I heard a scream," said Jerry, straightening and clearing his throat. "I looked downhill and saw Jaylee. She was hysterical. I knew something was wrong, so I took off running. I saw smoke, and… then when I got here, I… saw the… body."

Ellie gestured toward the wallet and ID. They'd need to verify her ID but judging from the photograph she was pretty sure it was her. "Do you know the girl?"

"It's Katie Lee." Will leaned over, head in his hands, as if he might be sick.

Ellie patted Jaylee's back again. "Jaylee, were you friends with her?"

Jaylee shook her head, wiping at her eyes with the back of her hand. "Not really, but she goes to my school." Jaylee accepted the tissue Ellie pushed into her hand and blew her nose. "Why would someone do this to her?"

"I don't know," Ellie answered softly. "But I promise you I'm going to find out. Did you see what happened to Katie Lee? Was someone else here?"

"No, I found her just like that," Jaylee said on a whimper.

She darted a look at Jerry and Ellie raised a brow. "Let me guess. Were you meeting these guys?"

The girl swiped at her tears with the tissue. "Just Jerry," she admitted.

Jerry straightened, his expression defensive. "We were just going to hang out and go swimming."

"Listen to me," said Ellie, "we need to know what happened here, so if you're holding back something, speak up. Did any of you see her on the ridge? Or did you see anyone else out here?"

Jerry and Will shook their heads in unison.

Jaylee gulped. "Do you think she fell from up there?"

"Maybe," Ellie said. "But we're going to need to talk to her parents and everyone who knew her. Did she have trouble at home or at school with anybody?"

"I didn't really know her that well," Jaylee said. "We had trig class together last year, but she was really quiet and kept to herself."

"Who were her friends?" Ellie asked.

Jaylee scrunched her nose in thought. "I don't know. I never saw her hanging out with anyone."

"She was kind of a loner," Jerry interjected.

Will hunched his shoulders and rubbed his hand over his pocket as if in search of a cigarette.

"Will?" Ellie asked.

"She went to the same church as my folks," he admitted.

She noted that he didn't say it was the same church he attended. She had a feeling that Will was the rebellious type. "And what church was that?" Ellie asked.

"Ole Glory," Will mumbled. "But she hated it as much as I did. Bunch of holier than thou judgmental assholes."

One of the Weekday Killer's victims had been found in the grave-yard at Ole Glory. The Pentecostal church had primitive beliefs, with rumors of snake handling and exorcisms being performed behind closed doors. Others whispered that it was a cult, and there was talk of a Manson-type leader and that they had plans to move to a more remote location, totally isolated and closed off from outsiders.

Then it suddenly struck her—that was where she'd first seen the standing stones. Several of the graves in the Ole Glory cemetery had monuments of stones exactly like this. Was the killer someone who belonged to that church?

"So, you *did* know Katie Lee, Will?" Ellie asked, the hair on the back of her neck prickling.

His jaw clenched. "Not like that," he said with a shrug of his thin shoulders. "I just saw her at one of the revivals. But her old man was mean to her. Heard some ladies whispering one time that he might be hitting her."

Questions mounted in Ellie's mind. "I'm going to need your parents' names and phone numbers," she told the teens.

"Do you have to tell my father I was here?" Jaylee asked, panic flaring in her teary eyes.

"I'm sorry, honey, but I do. I'm sure he'll understand."

"You don't know him." Jaylee began to cry again, seeming to fold within herself.

Ellie would feel him out when she talked to him, make sure the girl's fear wasn't founded on some kind of abuse. Either way, the kids were minors, and she had to speak to their parents. Nightmares had a way of sneaking up on you once the initial shock wore off.

Laney stood, gesturing that she wanted to speak to Ellie. Leaving Cord to take down the kids' contact information, Ellie joined Laney by the body.

Laney's dark eyes looked serious. "We're ready to move her. But I thought you'd want to know. It looks like there's some kind of fiber or skin beneath her fingernails. I'll scrape and send to the lab."

"Dirt? Tree bark? Resin?" Those would mean the girl might have grabbed at a tree root or branch to keep from falling. "Or maybe skin cells from her attacker?"

"I won't know until I get the lab results," Laney said. "But I think she was killed last night… or at least in the night."

Ellie glanced back at the teens who were fidgeting and looking at each other warily. What exactly had happened here?

# CHAPTER 12

As much as Ellie despised working with Sheriff Bryce Waters, he was head of the county. But she still didn't trust him. He drank too much, had a big mouth and had unwittingly fed the last killer information about her and Shondra.

But finding two bodies in two days warranted extra manpower. It was necessary that they work together.

Still, she was edgy. During the last investigation, it was obvious that Bryce wanted to push her into leaving the force, but Ellie Reeves was no quitter.

She escorted the teens to the parking lot, where Bryce was waiting.

"I'm going to drive the girl home," Ellie said. "She's anxious about her father finding out she was here, and I want to make sure she's okay. Then I'll notify Katie Lee's parents."

"I'll follow the boys home and speak to their folks," Bryce said with a nod.

Ellie turned to the kids. "Let me see your phones."

"Why do you want them?" Will asked as the teens traded wary looks.

"To make sure you didn't take pictures of the scene." It would be a shitshow if the Curtises learned of their daughter's death from someone else or social media. "We don't want you telling anyone about this or posting anything online. When we drive you home, we'll explain that to your folks, too. We have to respect how difficult this will be for Katie Lee's family."

Jaylee hunched inside herself, and Jerry put his arm around her as if he needed to hold her up.

"You aren't going to keep them, are you?" Will asked, his tone anxious.

"Do we need to, or can we trust you not to get on the phone with this news the minute we give them back?"

The boy kicked at a clump of dirt. "You said not to talk, so I won't. But my mom will be pissed if she thinks I lost that phone. I have to check in or I get in trouble."

"We'll return them. But if you leak this before we have a chance to talk to Katie Lee's folks, I'll haul you in for interfering with a police investigation." She hoped to hell she put the fear of God in them.

Bryce muttered something beneath his breath, but she ignored him as they took the phones. They quickly scrolled through the photo libraries, texts, calls and social media. Thankfully none of them had posted, a sign they had been in shock. She thanked them before returning the phones.

Bryce gestured toward the sheriff's car. "Do you have cars here?"

"That's my Honda," said Jerry. "Will rode with me."

Bryce nodded. "I'll follow you to your house, then drive your friend home."

The boys' eyes widened, as if they knew being escorted home by the police would land them in hot water but shuffled silently toward Jerry's dark green vehicle.

Ellie addressed Bryce, "Ask the parents if they knew Katie Lee—"

"I know how to do my job," Bryce said sharply.

He also knew how to run his mouth.

"Just listen, for cripes sake. I was going to suggest you focus on Will." Ellie glared at him. "He and Katie Lee attended the same church, Ole Glory. Said they both hated it. I want to know just how well they knew each other. Maybe they dated in secret or something." And if her parents imposed strict rules on the girl, that could have been a problem.

Bryce glanced over at the boys. He was probably thinking about himself as a teenager. Popular, cocky and eager to get into girls' pants. Having been on the receiving side of that agenda, Ellie would be less sympathetic to the boys than he would be. But that might prove to be an asset in persuading the teens to talk.

He walked over to the Honda and asked Will to ride with him, while Ellie turned to Jaylee. "How did you get here, Jaylee?"

The girl twisted her hands together. Her eyes were practically swollen shut from crying, her face splotchy, her lower lip quivering. "A friend dropped me off."

Ellie arched a brow. "And how did you plan to get home?"

"Jerry was going to drive me."

"I'll take you home," Ellie said. "Then I have to notify Katie Lee's parents."

Jaylee's face crumpled. "They're gonna be so upset."

Ellie squeezed the young woman's shoulder. "Yes, they will. And I'm sorry you had to find her."

"It's awful," Jaylee whispered. "Just awful." She climbed in the passenger side of Ellie's Jeep wiping at more tears. In spite of the unbearable heat outside, the girl shivered the entire ride home.

# CHAPTER 13

*Crooked Creek*

"Tell me about your family," Ellie said as she parked in front of the small brick ranch house where Jaylee lived. The yard was mowed although the flowerbeds were empty, the house void of any character or decorative touches. A jacked-up, dirty white pickup truck was parked beneath the carport, fishing poles propped against the wall, and three lawnmowers that looked in disrepair cluttered the corner. And an old rusted Chevy sat on cinderblocks in the side yard.

"Daddy is a mechanic," Jaylee said. "Business has been slow, but we scrape by."

"What about your mother?" Ellie asked when the teenager got a faraway look in her eyes.

"She died last year, cancer," Jaylee said with a catch to her voice. "Daddy took it hard. I try to cook and keep house for us, but we both miss her."

The weight of the world seemed to have landed on that girl's shoulders. "I'm sorry about your mother," Ellie said, thinking of Vera and how close she'd come to dying. "That has to be difficult. Come on, I'll explain things to your father."

The girl sucked in a deep breath then the two of them walked up to the house together. As soon as she opened the door, a big burly man with a thick beard came at her. His gray eyes narrowed as he looked at his daughter, then up at Ellie.

"Where have you been, Jaylee? I've been calling your cell phone for an hour." Although anger sparked in his eyes, his tone sounded more worried than mad.

"I'm sorry, Daddy," Jaylee said. "Something's happened."

He folded his beefy arms and glared at Ellie. "Who is this?"

Ellie flashed her shield. "Hello, Mr. Morris. My name is Detective Ellie Reeves."

"What's going on, Jaylee? Are you in trouble?"

"No, she's not," Ellie cut in.

He arched a brow towards his daughter. "Jaylee?"

"I just went to meet some friends at Moody Hollow, Daddy. I'm sorry, I should have called you first. But I don't have that many friends and I wanted them to like me."

Emotions thundered across the man's face before he softened. "Honey, you have friends."

"Not really," Jaylee said in a broken voice.

The man ran his hand over his thinning muddy-colored hair. "I don't understand," he said.

Ellie gently squeezed Jaylee's arm as another onslaught of tears flowed from the teen. "Mr. Morris, another girl from your daughter's school died at Moody Hollow today. I'm sorry to say that Jaylee was the one who found her." She curved her arm around the girl's shoulders. "It was pretty traumatic for her, so I drove her home."

"What? Who was the girl?"

"Katie Lee Curtis," Jaylee said in a whisper. "I was heading toward the waterfall when I saw her. She was just lying down in the dirt, her body all twisted up and bloody. And... she was burned."

Shock turned the man's eyes glassy. "Good lord. How did that happen?"

"I don't have those answers yet," Ellie said. "In fact, when I leave, I have to inform the family." Dread curled in her gut. "I've asked

Jaylee and the other kids not to talk to anyone about this until we have a chance to notify the family."

"Of course, of course," he mumbled. "God, I'm so sorry for them."

Jaylee's body began to shake with emotions, and her father reached for her, wrapping his arms around his daughter. Relief filled Ellie.

"Aww, honey," he said, his own veneer cracking. "It's okay, I'm here."

Ellie swallowed against the lump in her throat. "If you think of anything else or remember seeing someone around the area, please call me, Jaylee." She pushed her business card toward the father, and he took it, hugging his child harder and rubbing circles over her back.

Ellie could just imagine what was going on inside his head. He'd lost his wife. He didn't want to lose his daughter.

# CHAPTER 14

*North Georgia State Hospital*

Her baby was crying. The precious little one needed her.

Mabel could feel the child in her arms, the soft weight of her pressed against her chest. She heard the whispery sound of her breathing, inhaled the scent of baby powder and sweetness and knew she'd never love anything more than she loved her daughter.

But her eyes felt so heavy, her dreams pulling her so deep into the darkness that she couldn't open them.

The anguished cry broke through the haze again. Her heart began to pound, the need to comfort her baby intensifying.

Where was she?

She'd rocked her to sleep the night before, sang "Rock-a-bye Baby" to her until her tiny eyelids slipped shut and her cries quieted.

But something was wrong. She was too quiet now.

Mabel had to wake up. Get to her daughter. Feed her, soothe her and tell her how much she loved her. But her limbs were so heavy it was hard to move, and her head felt fuzzy.

Confused, she shoved the covers off her, raking her hands across the bed in case she'd fallen asleep with her child in her arms.

But there was nothing there.

The crying again… except it sounded far away, faded. Panic built inside her chest, and she forced her legs over the side of the bed.

Her legs buckled, and she grabbed the bedrail to keep from falling. *Get it together. Your daughter needs you.*

Motherly determination fueled her strength, and she pushed away from the bed and staggered across the floor, towards the bassinet in the corner… One step. Two. Another and she swayed, so dizzy she didn't think she'd make it.

The soft wail again, growing louder this time. A hungry cry. How long had it been since she'd fed her?

She would feed her now. Hold her and soothe her and never let her go…

Another step, and she grabbed the wall and fumbled toward the bassinet. One more step and she reached it. Hands shaking, she leaned over to pick up her child, but the bassinet was empty.

A scream lodged in her throat and she lifted her head and searched the room. But she was alone, the room blurry and gloomy.

Tears flooded her eyes, and she staggered toward the door and banged on it. "Help me!" she cried. "I want my baby! What did you do with her?"

Footsteps echoed outside the door. Then the lock turned, and two nurses appeared.

"It's okay, Mabel," the gray-haired woman said softly. "Your baby's right here. We just took her to give her a bath."

Tears clogged Mabel's throat as the other nurse helped her back to bed and then the nurse carrying her infant placed her in Mabel's arms. Her daughter was swaddled in a pale pink blanket, and Mabel inhaled the fresh scent of baby shampoo. Her heart swelled with love, and she traced her finger over the little one's pudgy pink cheek, cradling her close and looking into her daughter's trusting eyes.

Mabel held her tighter. She had to protect her. Keep her close or they'd come and get her. And then there was no telling what they'd do to her…

# CHAPTER 15

*Pigeon Lake*

Pigeon Lake had been named after a wave of dead pigeons had been found in the trees when the man-made lake had first been carved into the soil. Some believed the birds were an omen of death, and others thought they symbolized the end of pain or suffering.

The developer had since gotten the pigeon problem under control, although occasionally more flocked to the area.

With the heatwave, the lake was down and muddy looking, with patches of briars and dead bushes surrounding the water. Several people had reported finding dead fish washed up on the bank, and Ellie thought she detected the stench of them as she wound up the drive to Katie Lee's home.

Ellie clenched her phone as she sped toward the Curtises. "What can you tell me about Katie Lee's family, Deputy Landrum?"

"Father's name is Josiah, mother is Agnes," said Deputy Landrum. "One son, Martin, fifteen months younger than Katie Lee. He just turned seventeen last week. Josiah works for a feed store, mother stays home. They belong to Ole Glory, where the father is a deacon. No arrest record or domestic calls. I talked to the preacher at Ole Glory who claims the couple are good Christians who abide by the law and the Bible and run their house accordingly."

"Yeah, where the women have no voice," Ellie muttered. "Once I notify the family, we'll need to talk to people at the school." She pulled up outside the ancient, weathered Victorian, which resembled something out of a haunted-house movie. "Gotta go. I'm here now."

The knot in the pit of her stomach grew rock hard as Ellie climbed out and walked up to the door. Pigeons flew across the turrets of the house, late-afternoon shadows casting a gothic gray over the sharp angles and the tiny attic window. For a moment, Ellie thought she saw a face there, but then the image disappeared as if a ghost had just passed.

Eula Ann Frampton, an old local lady who was legendary for talking to spirits, would say that the face was Katie Lee's ghost. That she was lost between life and death, unable to find peace until her killer was caught. Ellie shook off the eerie sensation.

*Focus, Ellie, focus. A girl died today. Her parents need to know.*

Ellie stood on the welcome mat and stabbed the doorbell, startling at the sound of the gong-type ring. A minute later, a pale-faced woman answered the door. She looked around forty, with long, straight rust-colored hair drawn back in a bun at the nape of her neck. She wore a plain back skirt that fell to her ankles and a white blouse buttoned to her chin, which looked like it was choking her. She had to be smothering in the ninety-something heat.

"Yes?" the woman said, a puzzled look on her face.

Ellie identified herself. "I need to talk to you and your husband," she said. "Please, it's important."

The woman's thick eyebrows pinched together, accentuating her stark angular face. At one time in her life Agnes Curtis might have been young and vibrant, but over time something had drained the spark out of her. Now she looked like a shell of a person.

Regret made Ellie's chest throb. She was just about to add to the woman's pain.

"Who is it, Agnes?" A man Ellie assumed was Josiah appeared behind Agnes. His long beard was scraggly, and he was wearing a black shirt and black pants.

"She says she's a detective." Agnes instantly stepped behind her husband, as if that was her place.

"May I come in?" Ellie asked. "I really need to speak to both of you."

The man was tall and thin, his chin as pointed and severe as his narrow eyes, with cheekbones that pushed against his leathery skin. Both of them looked older than their years.

Josiah led the way through the foyer, which was filled with dusty antiques, into a living room heavy with a cloying, musty odor. Through the doorway, she saw pots of dried herbs on the kitchen counter, along with a pot on the stove boiling something that smelled like collard greens.

"Why are you here?" Josiah folded his arms as if he didn't like another female, much less a cop, in his house.

Ellie inhaled a deep breath. "I'm afraid I have some very bad news," she said quietly. Neither of them reacted, so she forged ahead. "A body was found earlier this morning, and we believe it's Katie Lee."

The woman's pallor faded to a ghostly white. Josiah stiffened, a muscle ticking in his jaw.

"No… you… have to be wrong," Agnes whispered. "Katie Lee… she'll be home soon. She just went… went out for a while."

"I wish I was wrong but I'm afraid I'm not," Ellie said, her heart aching. She walked over to a side table, picked up a photo of Katie Lee then turned to the couple. "This is Katie Lee, correct?"

"Yes," the father said through clenched teeth.

"I'm so sorry, but I saw her myself. In fact, I just came from where she was found at Moody Hollow."

"Moody Hollow?" Josiah snapped. "My daughter wouldn't go there."

"I'm sorry, but she was there, Mr. and Mrs. Curtis."

Suddenly a noise sounded, and Ellie looked up to see a dark-haired boy at the bottom of the stairs. The son, Martin. "You found Katie Lee?"

Ellie nodded and offered him a sympathetic look. "I'm afraid so. I have reason to believe she wasn't home last night. Is that true?"

Tension stretched between the family for a long minute.

"She was here," the father said. "But she stayed in her room all night."

"Apparently she didn't," Ellie said, gauging their reactions. "The Medical Examiner thinks she died sometime during the night."

Martin gripped the stair rail, emotions darkening his face. "This is your fault, Dad. All your fault she's dead."

# CHAPTER 16

Ellie maintained a calm expression as she studied the family dynamics. She silently reminded herself not to make snap judgments. People reacted to the news of the death of a loved one in different ways. Sometimes, in shock and grief, they blamed a family member or even themselves.

Katie Lee's brother opened his mouth to speak again, but Mr. Curtis cut him off with a scathing look. "Go to your room, Marty. Now."

"Why?" Marty said through clenched teeth. "She was my sister. I have a right to know what happened to her."

Mrs. Curtis stepped over to her son and placed her hand on his back as if to calm him, but he stiffened.

"Mr. Curtis," Ellie said, "I understand this news is a shock and you're grief-stricken. But I want to find out exactly what happened at Moody Hollow and I need your help."

Mrs. Curtis used an old-fashioned needlepoint hankie to dab at tears that streaked down her pale cheeks like a river. "How… can we help?"

"By telling me what was going on with your daughter," Ellie answered.

"Nothing was going on with her. Katie Lee is a good girl. My son is just a hothead," Mr. Curtis said.

The fact that the two were at odds sent red flags waving in Ellie's mind.

"When did you last see her?" she asked.

Mrs. Curtis looked down at her hands. "Last night, when she went to bed."

"What time was that?"

Mr. Curtis responded, "Actually she went upstairs right after supper and locked herself in her room."

"What about this morning?" Ellie asked.

The couple exchanged an odd look. "She didn't come down for breakfast," Mrs. Curtis murmured.

"Is that unusual? Did you check on her?"

"She's eighteen years old and moody," Mr. Curtis said. "Sometimes she locks herself in her room for hours. We assumed that was the case, that she'd come out when she was ready."

"I want to see her," Mrs. Curtis cut in, her voice a shaky whisper. "Please, where is she?"

Ellie held her breath for a moment. The poor woman did not need to see her daughter in the condition they'd found her. But she couldn't deny them, and they could confirm the ID. "Of course. She's being transported to the morgue for an autopsy. I can arrange a visit."

"We don't want you cutting up our daughter," Mr. Curtis said harshly. "We just want to bury her."

"I understand, Mr. Curtis," she said softly. "But when there's a sudden or suspicious death, an autopsy is required by law. We have to make sure we know exactly what happened to Katie Lee. I'm sure you want that, too."

The man folded his arms, and his wife released a pained breath.

"You mean it wasn't an accident?" Mr. Curtis asked.

"That's what I'm trying to determine, but no, I don't believe it was," Ellie said. "I'll be speaking to her friends and teachers. Anything you can tell me might help. Did she have a close girlfriend or maybe a boyfriend?"

"Katie Lee did not have boyfriends," Mr. Curtis said staunchly. "She wasn't allowed to date."

The girl had probably snuck out last night—or had she been lured out?

"Please just leave us alone." Mr. Curtis gestured toward the door. "Our family needs time to grieve."

Ellie dropped her business card on the side table, then followed him to the door. When she looked back, Mrs. Curtis was sobbing into her hands. She saw Martin slumped on the staircase, watching her leave. His troubled gaze suggested he longed to say more.

# CHAPTER 17

Ellie met Dr. Whitefeather at the morgue, knowing that every hour the family waited meant another hour of suffering.

Bracing herself for the gruesomeness of the autopsy, she inhaled several deep breaths before entering. Although the ME kept the autopsy room immaculately clean and organized, the scent of chemicals, blood and body waste permeated the walls. The horrible odor of charred flesh and the age of the girl made this one even worse.

Laney looked up from Katie Lee's body as Ellie entered, the doctor already well underway in the process of conducting the autopsy.

The Y-incision marking the teen's chest made it difficult for Ellie to breathe. Katie Lee had had so much to look forward to in her life. Her petite body was now purple and black due to bruising sustained from the fall, and what skin was left was tinted blue with death.

At first glance Ellie saw no tattoos or piercings, but judging from her family's strict religious beliefs, she didn't expect to.

Laney pushed her face shield up, a frown streaking her eyes. "I'm almost finished."

"Time of death?" Ellie asked.

"I'd say sometime between ten p.m. last night and one this morning."

Laney pursed her lips and motioned for Ellie to move closer. Sorrow for the teen welled in her chest as she looked down at the youthful face. Scrapes and bruises darkened her scorched cheeks and forehead, and her nose was smashed in. There was no way to repair the damage and make her look peaceful for an open casket. That would compound the family's agony.

"She died from internal injuries caused by the fall, and blunt force trauma to her head, meaning her brain bled out." Laney lifted the girl's head, angled it sideways and parted her hair. Blood matted the dark strands, then Ellie saw the spot Laney referred to. "She fell face forward," Laney explained.

"Then how did she get the injury on the back of her head?"

"Good question. My guess is that someone hit her on the back of the head with a hard object. The force caused her to pitch forward and fall."

"So, she was pushed and fell to her death. And the fire?"

"After she died, so postmortem."

Had the killer then created the circle of burial stones around her to indicate she was never coming back?

"There's more, Ellie." Dr. Whitefeather stepped over to the board where she'd displayed the X-rays. "There are other injuries, old ones. A fractured wrist, scarring around her ankles. A torn rotator cuff."

Ellie's eyes widened as she followed the markings Laney pointed out. "Her ankles and wrists were also restrained at some point. And she fought to escape."

# CHAPTER 18

*Stony Gap*

Anger burned through Ellie as she thought of poor Katie Lee. What had that girl suffered, and at whose hands?

As she parked at the sheriff's office, she spotted the news van from Channel 5. Local reporter Angelica Gomez had been dogging Ellie for a tell-all about her family. Angelica had confronted her about her adoption, making that public knowledge, and Ellie had redirected, determined for her private life to remain private. But the reporter was nothing if not persistent.

Had Angelica already heard about the young girl they'd found today?

Drained from the day, she mopped her forehead with her hand as she entered the sheriff's office.

"Sheriff Waters," Angelica said as she tilted the microphone toward Bryce. "What can you tell us about the recent wildfires spreading across the AT?"

Bryce spotted Ellie, a twitch of his eyes his only response before he squared his shoulders. "The sheriff's department is working in conjunction with the National Park Service to determine if the fires are caused by the dry weather conditions or if arson is involved. A warning has been issued to all campers and hikers forbidding campfires and brush fires of any kind, and violators will be prosecuted." He gestured toward Weatherby.

"This is arson investigator Max Weatherby," the sheriff said. "He's heading up the investigation into the fires." Bryce angled his head toward the other man. "Do you have a report for us, Mr. Weatherby?"

The big guy's brows furrowed as he spoke. "At this point, we're still exploring possibilities. At least two of the five fires appear to have been started by campfires left unattended or not properly extinguished. At a third, we found cigarette butts, which are not often strong enough to start a blaze, although an empty can of lighter fluid like one might use on an outdoor grill was found in the woods nearby. Forensics are analyzing them for prints."

Angelica turned back to Bryce. "Sheriff Waters, you released a statement yesterday stating that a burned body was found at Winding Rock. This is the first casualty due to the fires. What can you tell us about the victim?"

Bryce's eyes met hers, his posture stiffening. "At this point, all I can say is that the body belonged to a female," Bryce said. "We don't have an ID yet as we're awaiting autopsy results." He paused. "Anyone with information regarding the fires or this woman should call the sheriff's office immediately."

"Is it also true that the body of a young woman was found at Moody Hollow?" Angelica didn't miss a beat.

"That is correct," the sheriff said then raised a brow in question to Ellie.

Ellie stepped in front of the microphone.

"Detective Reeves, have you identified the young woman?"

Sucking in a breath, Ellie said, "Yes, her name is Katie Lee Curtis, and her family has been informed. At this point, we are treating her death as suspicious. If anyone has information regarding her or her death, please contact our police department immediately."

"What was cause of death?" Angelica pressed.

"That won't be determined until after the autopsy." She gave Angelica a warning look, not to probe. "I'll keep the public updated as soon as we have more information."

"Sheriff, there were two bodies found less than twenty-four hours apart," Angelica said, determined to get one of them to talk. "Are these deaths related?"

Ellie's heart thumped as she waited on Bryce's response. "It's too early in the investigation for me to speculate. But I'll be sure to keep the public apprised as details become available."

Frustration flickered in Angelica's eyes, then she smiled at the camera. "Look for updates at WRIX Channel Five News. But folks, please be careful. The Appalachian Trail has been chocked full of danger the last few months, and these fires are not to play around with. And ladies, be careful. There may be another murderer out there."

# CHAPTER 19

"What happened with the boys?" Ellie asked as she followed Bryce into his office.

The sheriff took his desk chair, swiveling to face Ellie while she claimed the seat across from him. "Jerry Otterman was upset. His parents seemed concerned. He plays baseball and is working towards a scholarship to play in college. I don't think he had anything to do with Katie Lee's death."

"I got that impression, too, although I think he has a crush on Jaylee," Ellie said. "Her father was okay, too. Mother died of cancer. He seems protective, but not in an overbearing way. I think she's a good kid." She crossed her legs. "What about Will?"

"He claims he and the girl weren't going out, but his mother shut him down from talking. The minute I asked, she yelled at the boy that he wasn't supposed to be out goofing off, that he should have been home doing yardwork, not messing around with girls."

"Did Will mention why exactly he and Katie Lee hated Ole Glory?"

"What teenager these days likes to go to church with their parents?" Bryce gave her a sardonic look.

Ellie sighed. He had a point. "That may be all it is. But there's something off about it. And the killer stacked stones in a circle just like they do at Ole Glory cemetery."

"What do the stacked stones mean?"

"They represent places of burial or gathering places to honor the dead." Ellie rubbed her forehead. "I've heard that church borders on cult-like behavior. That there's talk of them becoming an independent entity."

Bryce grunted. "I guess it's worth looking into them more."

Ellie refrained from rolling her eyes. She had a feeling the sheriff conceding to her on any point got in his craw.

"What about Katie Lee's folks?" he asked.

"As expected, they were broken up. There's a lot of tension in that household. The mother is clearly repressed by her husband. Father insisted his daughter did not date. The brother, Marty, looked shaken up and instantly blamed his dad."

"Why?" Bryce asked, raising his brows.

"I don't know, but I'll dig deeper into the family. I can tell you one thing—the parents were strict. When Marty sounded off, Mr. Curtis ordered the boy to go to his room. There was no attempt to console him. I wouldn't be surprised if he got punished. And Will did mention that he'd heard whispers that Mr. Curtis might be hitting Katie Lee. I'll ask the school counselor about the possibility of physical abuse in the family." Her conversation with Laney echoed in her head. "By the way, Dr. Whitefeather finished Katie Lee's autopsy. This was no accident, Sheriff."

A flicker of surprise lit his eyes. "Tell me about the report."

Ellie explained about the bruising on the girl's upper arms and the contusion on the back of her head. "It appears someone hit her with a blunt object, causing her to pitch forward. Then whoever it was pushed her over the ridge."

Bryce cursed. "One of those kids may know more than they're telling us. None of them admitted to inviting Katie Lee along."

"It's possible Mr. Curtis didn't like the fact that his daughter was rebelling. He could have followed her to the hollow to keep her from meeting up with the other kids. If so, they could have argued and in the heat of the moment, struggled. Then she could have tried to get away and…"

Bryce shrugged. "Sounds like a leap."

"I still think we have to consider it. He could have set the fire to make it look like the same person who killed the lady at Winding Rock—our statement was on the later bulletins last night."

"Katie Lee's body wasn't burned nearly as severely as our first victim."

"Maybe he had remorse and extinguished the fire himself," Ellie suggested. "Except we didn't release news about the circle of stones to the press, so he couldn't have known about that unless he was involved in both murders."

"You don't think we have another serial killer on our hands, do you?"

Ellie bit her lip. "I don't know yet, but my instinct is saying so. Even if the fires don't match exactly and the victims' profile is different, the standing stones are similar."

Bryce sighed, running his hands through his hair. "Do the Curtises know their daughter was murdered?"

"I told them we suspect foul play. That's when they asked me to leave."

# CHAPTER 20

*Stony Gap*

Vanessa Morely watched the sheriff's report on the local news in horror. Another murder in Bluff County.

Just like high school, Bryce was full of himself. Years ago, she'd thought it was appealing. Now, she avoided him. She had to.

Mandy was all that mattered.

Mandy gasped as she walked into the den with a bag of chocolate chip cookies. "Oh, my god, Mom," she said, seeing the headline. "Katie Lee goes to my school. Did the sheriff say what happened to her?"

Vanessa shook her head, her stomach churning. She didn't know the girl, but she did know her mother.

Thankfully Ellie Reeves was working the case.

She would dig for the truth no matter what it cost her. When she'd seen her at the Corner Café, for a minute, she was swept back to childhood, when they'd played hide and seek and built forts in the woods. Then things had changed. Would her life have turned out differently if they'd remained friends?

"Do you ever go to that place Moody Hollow?" she asked her daughter.

"Everyone goes there," Mandy said, giving her the *are you for real?* eyeroll.

"Well, I don't want you there or on the trail at all."

"But, Mom…"

"No 'but Mom'." She was tired of arguing with her daughter. "You're staying home until the sheriff figures out what happened to Katie Lee and that other woman."

Mandy slammed her fists into the sofa and jumped up. "That's not fair."

"I don't care," Vanessa said sharply. "There are bad people out there, Mandy. And it's my job to protect you." After all, she knew about bad people, how quickly they could pounce when you let down your guard.

"You're a hypocrite," Mandy shouted. "You let men crawl all over you at that bar, then you lock me in the house like I'm a little kid."

"I have to work to make ends meet," Vanessa said, ignoring the jab. "And I mean it, Mandy. Do not go anywhere tonight. Whoever killed Katie Lee is still out there. And I don't want to have to bury you like the Curtises are about to bury their daughter."

# CHAPTER 21

*Crooked Creek*

Before confronting the Curtis family again, Ellie decided to research Katie Lee. If she was going to imply the father harmed his daughter, she needed to be armed with facts.

Summer break made it difficult to know which students to question. So far, the teenagers at Moody Hollow had painted a picture of a loner. First, Ellie checked with the principal, who knew barely anything about her family. He sent a list of Katie Lee's classmates the previous year, so she spent a couple of hours calling and leaving messages.

According to the three she reached, Katie Lee was studious, quiet, and conscientious. She didn't participate in any extracurricular activities. No sports or clubs, although her English Lit teacher said she'd briefly worked on the yearbook, but her father forbid her from doing it when he found out.

Ellie was liking Mr. Curtis less and less.

Finally, she got in touch with the school counselor, a woman named Letty James. She sounded truly upset when Ellie broke the news about the teenager's death. "Her parents must be devastated," the woman said, her voice warbling.

"They are," Ellie said. "Did you know Katie Lee?"

"Yes, I do programs with the homerooms to get acquainted with all the students so they'll feel comfortable if they need to talk."

"What was your impression of Katie Lee?"

"She was a sweet girl, a people-pleaser. She did her schoolwork and kept to herself. From what I gathered, her parents were pretty strict with her."

"That's what I've gathered, too," Ellie said. "Did she ever mention any problems she was having?"

There was a moment of hesitation. "I value my students' privacy and confidentiality."

"I understand," Ellie said. "But there are suspicious circumstances surrounding her death, so if she had problems with anyone, a friend, boyfriend, if she was being bullied or had issues at home, I need to know. Katie Lee can't speak for herself right now. But you can speak for her."

The sound of Letty shifting carried down the line. "What do you mean, suspicious circumstances?"

"I'm afraid that's all I'm at liberty to say at the moment. But please tell me anything you know. Even if it was just a feeling or a sense that something was wrong."

"Well…" Letty released a wary sigh. "She came to my office for information about local colleges and scholarship applications. According to her, her father did not approve. He said college was for men."

Ellie bit her tongue to keep from voicing her opinion.

"What about boys? Did she date someone from school or have a crush on anyone in particular?"

"Not that I know of," Letty said. "Although I saw her talking to Will Huntington a few times in the hallway."

So, Will was cropping up again. And he hadn't mentioned that they'd talked at school.

"When I notified the Curtises of Katie Lee's death, her brother Martin got upset and blamed his father. There was a lot of tension between them."

"That doesn't surprise me."

"Why do you say that?"

Letty's breath rattled out. "This is just between us, Detective. But Marty has had problems with his father's control issues and was also protective of his sister. He stood up to Mr. Curtis, which didn't sit well in that household."

"Was there any specific reason he felt he needed to protect her? Was someone bothering her?"

"No… he didn't say."

"Let me ask you another question," Ellie said. "Do you think the father could hurt Katie Lee if she disobeyed him?"

Silence stretched between them for a minute. "That's a difficult question. He was tough on Marty, but even more so on the daughter. Martin never specifically described physical abuse, although once he commented that his father barely spoke to or looked at Katie Lee. Marty said he didn't understand it. I thought it had to do with the church, but I just don't know… I think strange things go on there."

She wasn't the only one in town who thought that. "What kind of strange things?"

"Exorcisms, social isolation from others who aren't in the group. They're veering away from religion and are almost worshipping the leader, Reverend Ike. He sees himself as some kind of prophet. Everyone is encouraged to give up worldly belongings and donate their money to him." She paused, taking a sharp intake of breath. "I know one young woman who finally got out. Said he tried to marry her to a man old enough to be her father, that he arranged for other girls to be given to older men in his group. Anyone who disobeys or tries to leave is ex-communicated."

Ellie's head spun. What punishment might Mr. Curtis and Ole Glory have had in store for Katie Lee if they found out she was rebelling?

# CHAPTER 22

*Pigeon Lake*

Thirty minutes later, Ellie was knocking on the door of the Curtis house again. Now the dreary atmosphere of the house and its isolation painted even more of a sinister picture.

Dusk shadows crept over the murky lake, the sound of frogs croaking mingling with the song of crickets. The temperature had climbed to the mid-nineties with no relief or rain in sight. Flies and gnats swarmed the humid air around her face, the heat plastering her damp ponytail to her neck. Already locals were joking about it being so hot you could crack an egg on the pavement, and it would fry. Ellie wouldn't doubt it.

Mr. Curtis answered the door, dressed in all black, his expression closed.

"It's awfully late, Detective."

"I apologize for the hour, but it's urgent."

His eyes sharpened as he looked down at her. "Did you come to tell us we can finally see our daughter?"

"Yes, but I also need to speak to you and your wife and son first."

"What for?" he asked, his bushy eyebrows knitting.

"Please, just gather your family. It's important that I talk to all of you together." The family dynamics would probably tell her more than their words.

He clamped his lips tightly together but stepped aside, leading her through a small entryway to the living room. Furnished in eighties style, the plaid couch and ruffled curtains were faded, and crosses and pictures of Jesus adorned the walls, along with a family picture on the mantel she hadn't noticed when she was here before. She couldn't see a TV or computer anywhere.

She quickly glanced at the kitchen and noticed a tin milk can holding black-eyed Susans on the primitive pine table. An old-fashioned butter churn sat in one corner and fruit flies danced above a bowl of overripe bananas.

"Wait here while I call my family down." He gestured toward a chair in the living room, but she didn't sit quite yet. Instead, she studied the photo on the mantel while he hastened up the staircase. In the picture, the family was all dressed in Sunday clothing. The father in a dark jacket and white shirt, the mother in a long black skirt and white blouse with her hair pulled back into a bun so severe that her skin looked stretched. Not a hint of makeup on her face and no jewelry. The son wore black pants and a white shirt, his scowl as dark as his clothing. Then there was Katie Lee.

She had on a white blouse and skirt like her mother, as if it was a uniform. Her dark hair was braided and hung over one shoulder, her body slightly slumped.

A shiver chased up Ellie's spine. None of the family members were smiling.

The sound of shuffling feet drew her to the doorway, and Mr. Curtis appeared, his wife and son beside him. It was clear the mother had been crying and Marty's eyes looked red-rimmed.

"Can I go see my daughter now?" Mrs. Curtis asked.

Ellie took a slow breath. "If you'll give me the name of the funeral home, I'll arrange for you to visit."

Mrs. Curtis dabbed her eyes with a handkerchief. "We'll use the funeral home associated with our church. It's called Glory Days."

"I'll take care of it. Now, let's all sit down."

The woman and son headed to the couch, Marty helping his mother while the father remained standing. "Just say what you have to say," he said curtly.

"I spoke with the Medical Examiner," she said. "Your daughter's death was definitely not accidental."

Martin jerked his head up, his jaw tightening. Shock and something else streaked his eyes—suspicion? Mrs. Curtis gasped and wrapped her arms around her waist as if to hold herself up.

"What do you mean it wasn't an accident?" Mr. Curtis asked, outraged. "I thought you said she fell off a ridge."

"Actually, I did mention that the circumstances were suspicious. The Medical Examiner found bruising on your daughter's upper arms and a contusion on the back of her head consistent with blunt force trauma, as if she was struck by an object from behind."

Mrs. Curtis made a strangled sound. "You think someone killed her?"

"Katie Lee was murdered?" Marty asked in a whisper.

Sympathy for the family mingled with the need to objectively analyze their reactions. "That is how it appears from her injuries."

"Who would hurt our Katie?" Mrs. Curtis cried. "She was sweet and smart and a good girl."

There was the "good girl" comment again.

"I don't know who did this, ma'am. But I promise I will find the answer to that question," Ellie said with conviction. "Can you think of anyone who would hurt Katie Lee? Someone at school or church she had problems with?"

"Everyone liked her," the girl's mother said, wringing her hands.

"My daughter was well behaved," Mr. Curtis interjected. "She didn't make enemies."

Ellie turned toward Marty. "How about at school? Did she have a confrontation with another student? Was she being bullied?"

Marty ran his fingers through his short hair, his hand shaking. The kid looked as if his mind was spinning.

"She didn't have many friends," he muttered angrily. "She was a pleaser. I never saw anyone mad at her or bullying her. It was almost like she was invisible."

That was the saddest thing they'd said so far, Ellie thought, her heart sinking.

"What about a kid named Will?" she asked. "I believe he attends your church."

"You mean Will Huntington?" Marty asked.

Ellie nodded. "He was one of the teens at Moody Hollow who found her."

"I warned her to stay away from him," said Mr. Curtis, anger flaring in his expression. "And I told him to stay away from her."

"Do you think he hurt our daughter?" Mrs. Curtis asked.

"That's not what I'm saying. I'm just gathering information at the moment, trying to get a picture of Katie Lee's life. Will was at Moody Hollow today, but he was with another boy—they'd been camping. Your daughter also had old bruises on her. Do you know how she got those?"

"She was a clumsy girl," Mr. Curtis said. "Always having accidents."

Ellie gritted her teeth. That sounded like a typical excuse for an abuser.

"Maybe Will hurt her and she was too ashamed to tell us," Mr. Curtis continued.

Ellie gave him a cold stare. Katie Lee had probably been ashamed to tell. But she didn't think it was Will that had hurt her.

"Where were you when Katie Lee snuck out to go to Moody Hollow?" Ellie asked the couple.

"Here all night," Mr. Curtis said curtly.

Ellie glanced at his wife, who gave a little nod of confirmation, although the poor woman seemed to wilt deeper within herself.

"Mr. Curtis, what was your relationship with your daughter like?" Ellie asked.

Pure contempt flared on his face. "What are you implying?"

"I'm not implying anything. Again, I'm just gathering background information. And I'll need a DNA sample from you." She feigned a smile to soothe his feathers. "Just for elimination purposes of course."

But if he'd killed his daughter, she would cook the bastard.

# CHAPTER 23

"You are out of your mind, lady," Mr. Curtis snarled. "You have a lot of nerve coming into my house and suggesting I'd hurt my own daughter."

"I don't mean to offend you, Mr. Curtis. Honestly, I'm just doing my job. As I said, the sample is for elimination purposes." Ellie pulled some paperwork from inside her pocket. "This is a subpoena for it and a search warrant for your house."

Wide-eyed, Mrs. Curtis covered her mouth, but a pained sound came out anyway.

"Just what do you expect to find here?" Mr. Curtis asked, his eyes blazing.

"I don't know, but I'd especially like to see Katie Lee's room. Teenagers have a way of keeping secrets from their parents," she said, aiming a look at Martin. "If Katie Lee was seeing someone you didn't know about, maybe there's something in her room to tell us who it was. And if someone was bothering her, stalking her even, she might have written about it in a notebook or journal." The parents traded skeptical looks, but seeing they had no choice, Mr. Curtis clamped his jaw and gave a consensual nod. "Thank you so much, Mr. Curtis. I know you want to get to the bottom of this as much as I do."

"You do, don't you, Dad?" Martin said, earning him another warning look.

"I will pray for your forgiveness for this," Mr. Curtis said.

Ellie didn't need or want his prayers, but she contained her reaction, then removed swab kits from inside her jacket. She pulled on gloves and ripped open the first package, taking some small measure of joy in the hateful man's discomfort.

"Open your mouth," she said.

He balled his hands into fists by his sides, then did as he was told, and she swabbed his cheek. Then she stowed it in the baggie, sealed it and put it in her pocket.

After she'd taken samples from Mrs. Curtis and Marty, she angled her head toward the son. "Marty, why don't you show me Katie Lee's room?"

As the boy escorted Ellie up the short staircase, she heard Mr. Curtis reading from the book of Matthew about the unforgiveable sin of blasphemy.

Martin seemed shaken but cooperative as he directed Ellie to his sister's room.

Before she went in, she paused. "Marty, if you know something you aren't telling me, if Katie Lee confided in you, or if something happened at the church, please speak up. I know you cared about your sister and you tried to protect her."

"I didn't do a very good job of that, did I?"

Emotions choked his voice, and Ellie wanted to comfort him. Instead, she pushed a business card into his hands. "You can call me anytime, day or night. I'm so sorry for your loss. I can't bring Katie Lee back, but I want to help find whoever hurt your sister and get justice for her. That much I can do."

He nodded, tears filling his eyes, then he ducked into the room next door which, judging by the model airplanes on the shelf, was his bedroom. Maybe he collected them because he wanted to fly from this place. She felt suffocated just being inside, and she couldn't imagine being a teenager and living under this kind of control. They made her family look like saints.

If she had a child, what lengths would she go to in order to protect them?

# CHAPTER 24

Ellie stepped into Katie Lee's room, not surprised that the furnishings were minimalistic. The bed was an antique white iron with a solid black comforter. There were no colorful decorations, frilly girly items, posters of her favorite band, movie star, or sports team, or pictures of her and her friends. She didn't see a single stuffed animal or the usual remnants of childhood.

The room looked sad and lonely, which only confirmed everyone's description of the girl. Pulling on gloves, Ellie looked inside the closet. Jeans, sweatshirts, and three identical black skirts and white blouses. Her church clothes. Tennis shoes, a pair of winter boots and plain black flats to go with the church outfits.

Ellie checked the top shelf for a shoe box or anything that might be a hiding place but found nothing.

The desk held school notebooks, along with pencils and pens. Curious, she flipped through the notebooks. Past assignments in math and English, a history paper about the Trail of Tears, but no notes or doodlings of a boy's name, no hearts or mentions of a crush.

She tucked them back in place, then moved to the bed, checking underneath. Nothing but dust bunnies and a pair of socks the girl had kicked off. Lifting the mattress, she raked her hand underneath it.

Her fingers brushed something hard, and she realized it was a small notebook. She pulled it out, opened it and flipped through the contents. Not exactly a diary, but it appeared to have short stories Katie Lee had written along with scribbled notes.

A noise brought her gaze to the door, and she saw Mrs. Curtis standing in the doorway, looking forlorn and grief-stricken. Ellie's heartstrings twisted.

"Did you find what you were looking for?" the woman asked, her voice sharp.

"Did you know your daughter wrote short stories in here?" Ellie asked, lifting the book.

The woman's face wilted. "She talked about wanting to be a writer one day. But Josiah told her that was nonsense."

No wonder she'd hidden her musings.

"I'd like to take this and look through it," Ellie said. "Maybe she wrote something inside that might help us."

Looking shell-shocked, Mrs. Curtis gave a little nod. "Can I have it back when you're finished?"

"Of course," Ellie said.

But she wanted to see what was inside first. Maybe somewhere in the girl's writings, she'd mentioned something that would lead them to her killer.

# CHAPTER 25

*Haints Bar, Bluff County*

The locals filled the tables and stools at the bar. Drinking and carrying on about the bodies that had been found. Wondering if that detective, Ellie Reeves, was capable of solving yet another crime and how many people would die first.

That sheriff was here, too. He was boozing it up as if he didn't have murders in his county.

Too bad he wasn't on the list to die.

A smile curved his mouth as he mentally ran through the names in his mind.

One he would take tonight. The woman had her secrets. But she'd been asking too many questions. Nosing around.

She had to be stopped.

*Ticktock, Ticktock.*

The chime on his watch sounded and his brain clicked.

He slid onto a stool, intrigued by the bar that had been built overlooking White Lilies Cemetery.

The waitress smiled hesitantly as she delivered drinks to a table of horny retired cops. This bar was a watering hole for the police force. Coming here was risky, but he knew how to sip his whiskey without being caught on camera, and no one knew who he was. With the booze flowing, no one cared. They certainly wouldn't remember him. With the way he was dressed, he fit right in.

At a nearby table, the retirees were discussing the wildfires that had been raging across the trail, speculating on who had set them and why. One was sure it was teens. Another suggested a thrill-seeking pyromaniac. A third thought they were a smokescreen for other crimes, like the bodies left at Winding Rock and Moody Hollow.

Katie Lee's face flashed behind his eyes. The fire hissing around her body. The circle of stones erected to honor her.

He closed his eyes, the flames sweeping him back in time. To his childhood. The gatherings. The crackle and spitting of the fire. The stone markers circling the ground.

He'd prayed for forgiveness for what he'd done back then. He'd prayed for it when he lit the match and set the girls on fire.

Cheers erupted from a table to the left. Apparently, some dude had proposed to his girlfriend. Not a chance in hell it would last. They never did.

The waitress flitted through the crowd to the bar where she picked up a tray of IPAs then delivered them to another table, her cleavage spilling over her low-cut top and drawing ogles from the patrons. She seemed jumpy tonight, her hands shaking as she set the beers on the table. She kept looking over her shoulder as if she knew she was being watched.

Her shift ended in a few hours.

All he had to do was sip and wait. Make sure she didn't leave with one of the other men.

She was a sweetheart. Pretty and flirty and full of life.

But that would end soon.

He motioned that he wanted another whiskey, then sat back and watched her work the room. The sound of the chime taunted him, and he glanced at his watch again, murmuring her name to himself.

*Ticktock, Ticktock. You'll be dead by two o'clock.*

His fantasies consumed him as his fingers curled over the matchbook on the bar. He could already hear the sound of her screams mingling with the sizzle and popping of the fire as it began to eat her hair and bones.

# CHAPTER 26

*Crooked Creek*

An hour later, Ellie couldn't shake the image of Katie Lee's parents' agony as they'd stood by their daughter's body at Glory Days Funeral Home. Although it was late, the father had insisted on seeing her before the mortician worked on her, which had been horrible for his wife. He had stood by silently, his body rigid, his eyes filled with an icy brittleness that was hard to understand.

Ellie struggled not to be judgmental as he shed no tears. Neither did he touch his daughter while the mother bowed her head against Katie Lee's bruised and burned face, sobbing her heart out. Marty's body shook with anguish, and he clung to his mom.

No mother should see her child like that, and Mr. Curtis was cruel to insist his wife be present. She couldn't help wondering if it was his way of punishing her for something.

It had been all Ellie could do to rein in her own emotions. Disturbed by the tension in the family, she'd called her mother on the way home just to hear her voice, as if the cracks in Katie Lee's family made her anger toward Vera dissipate slightly. The house plans for the rebuild were under way, and Vera wanted her to come by and look at them when she had time.

But this murder case took precedence. She was still waiting on news about the charred bones found at Winding Rock. Identifying them was a complicated process.

Too restless to sleep, she'd called Gillian Roach's number again, but nothing. Determined to focus, she made a cup of decaf, then settled on the couch to study Katie Lee's journal.

As a teen, she'd kept a diary and would have been furious if anyone else had read it. On the door of her room, she'd hung a sign that said 'Keep Out', and written 'PRIVATE' on the front cover of her journal. She had a feeling Katie Lee had kept this one tucked beneath her mattress for the same reason.

She'd kept her secrets stored in here.

Opening the journal, she skimmed the first few entries and found short stories scattered throughout about a young girl leaving her home for great adventures.

Interspersed between the fantasy stories, she found a common theme—the girl in the stories was repressed by her family, desperate to soar on her own.

But in a separate section she'd forgone the fiction and documented her personal reflections.

*My father hates me. He won't even look at me at the table. He just ignores me like I'm not even there.*

Ellie's heart squeezed, and she flipped the page.

*I heard Mama crying tonight in the bedroom. Daddy said something about what happened years ago, but I couldn't hear what it was. Then he said he wished they'd never had me.*

Anger tightened Ellie's body. Why had Mr. Curtis felt that way? Curious, she turned another page.

*Today Reverend Ike told Daddy that he found the perfect place for the commune. That if I strayed or kept talking about college, he*

*would take me there and show me the way. That he could get the*
*evil out of me and break me.*

Was that how Katie Lee had gotten those bruises on her wrists
and ankles?

# CHAPTER 27

"*Rock-a-bye baby, in the treetop*," Mabel cradled her baby close as she sang. "*When the wind blows, the cradle will rock…*"

The child whimpered, and she patted her back, rocking her back and forth and doting on her tiny face and that dainty chin that quivered when she cried. Her baby was perfect. A small round head, pink coloring, button nose, and a mouth that worked vigorously to drink milk from her breast.

"What did I ever do before I had you?" Mabel whispered.

The baby cooed and looked up at her as if she knew her voice. A deep love swelled in her heart. "Yes, I'm your mommy," she murmured as she planted a soft kiss on the little one's cheek. "I'll love you forever and ever and always."

The door opened and the nurse came in, her expression so austere that a shudder coursed up Mabel's spine.

"It's time," the stern woman said.

Mabel shook her head back and forth. "No… don't take her… I love her."

"I'm sorry, Mabel, but this must be done."

She cried out and clung to her infant, but the woman pried Mabel's hands from around her child and lifted the baby away.

"No!" Mabel cried. "Please, I want her."

But the nurse ignored her, stepping away. Tears streamed down Mabel's face as the woman carried her sweet little princess out the door. The baby's scream echoed in her head, and she curled into a ball on the bed, a hollow emptiness opening inside as pain engulfed her.

# CHAPTER 28

*Haints Bar*

The waitress kept her eyes peeled as she finished her last table and went into the staff restroom to change out of her work outfit.

All evening she'd been ill at ease. She didn't intend to accept any offers for a cocktail or rendezvous tonight. She couldn't shake the memory of Ellie Reeves's statement. If a murderer was stalking the mountains, she wanted to get home as fast as possible.

Just as she stepped outside, she spotted a shadow lurking beneath the awning.

Nerves on edge, she ducked back in and decided to exit through the front door. Maybe the owner would walk her to her car. She'd never asked before, but with two bodies being found lately, surely he wouldn't mind. He was behind the bar, finishing counting the register. But the sheriff was still on his favorite stool, polishing off another whiskey.

He looked up at her and grinned, that gleam in his eyes. The one that she'd succumbed to the summer she'd graduated high school.

She didn't intend to fall into his bed again.

"Hey," he said with a wink. "Want to join me?"

"No, I have to get home to my daughter," she said. "But I was wondering if you'd walk me to my car. I… thought I saw someone lurking outside."

His flirtatious smile faded, his eyes going dark. He tossed cash on the bar and motioned that he'd follow her. Relieved, she walked beside him to the door, then he looked around outside, searching the parking lot as he escorted her to her Honda.

He paused at her car and she unlocked it, offering him a smile. One that made her stomach churn. She'd stayed away from him for a reason.

"Thanks, I guess the news about those two bodies got me spooked."

Bryce's gaze locked with hers, his eyes flaring. Was he remembering the past too?

She jammed the key in the ignition, started it and reached for the door. Drunken voices from the alley by the parking lot, sounded like an argument escalating. Bryce glanced that way, his body tensing before he turned back to her.

"Do you want me to follow you home?" he asked in a gruff tone.

"No, but thanks." Her hand trembled and she shook her head, then closed the door and pulled from the parking lot.

A black pickup pulled from the lot in front of her onto the street, and she slowed, giving it time to go on, before turning the opposite direction to take the shortcut back to her house. A few cars were still out, but most of the stores were closed for the evening. The sky was gray, her breathing wheezy as she struggled to stay calm. She was just being paranoid. No one was after her.

Except… She had made that phone call. Had been asking questions…

Car lights suddenly appeared behind her, nearly blinding her. She gripped the steering wheel so hard her hands ached and maneuvered onto the road leading to her house. The car followed, closing in on her.

Anxiety tightened her shoulders, and she sped up, taking the curves too fast but desperate to get home. Another car raced toward her, and she swerved to avoid it as she crossed the line. Her tires skated on the shoulder of the road, and she swung a sharp right onto a side street.

The car behind her did the same.

Suddenly terrified, she braked quickly, causing them to do the same. Then she hit the gas and floored it.

By the time she reached the turnoff for her house, the car appeared again.

She raced up the drive, threw her vehicle into park, and snatched her phone and purse before running to her front door.

The car slowed, the beams still blinding. She peeked back to see the make and model but all she could tell was that it was a dark sedan of some kind. He flashed his lights as if to send her a message.

She fumbled with the keys, dropped them on the porch, then snatched them up. Clumsily she opened the door and practically fell inside. Slamming the door behind her, she locked it and went to the window.

The car was still there. Watching. Waiting.

# CHAPTER 29

*Crooked Creek*

Nightmares always came for Ellie. And now there were new grisly images to add to the dreams that consumed her. Charred bones. A dead teenage girl. The flames shooting into the sky. A family that might be responsible.

After tossing and turning, stewing over the questions in her head in search of the truth until 5 a.m., she finally got up, showered and poured herself a cup of coffee in her to-go mug. Grabbing a bagel on the way out the door, she phoned her captain, requesting a meeting with the ME, the arson investigator, and the sheriff.

Two hours later, they convened in the conference room to review the two cases. Except for both bodies being burned and the circle of stones, they didn't have a connection between the victims. They needed more information on victim number one to make a determination.

Everyone shuffled in with coffee and situated themselves around the table while Ellie drew a column to distinguish the information for each victim on the whiteboard. She started with the charred victim found at Winding Rock and turned to Laney. "Dr. White-feather, do we have an ID on body number one?"

"Not yet," Laney replied. "Our forensic specialist is still working on her. But I can tell you that she didn't die of smoke inhalation. This woman was dead before the fire."

That means they had another homicide. She couldn't say that she was surprised. "What was cause of death?"

"She was strangled."

"So the killer set her on fire to cover evidence," Ellie surmised. She turned to the arson investigator. "Do you agree with these findings?"

Max Weatherby gave a nod, his deep brown eyes somber. "The fire's point of origin was the spot where the woman's remains were found. Meaning she wasn't caught out in the wildfire and couldn't outrun it. Her body was intentionally set on fire."

"So now we have a homicide and ritualistic behavior. But until we ID her and know about her family, there's not much we can do except check missing persons reports. See if someone is looking for her." Ellie placed Katie Lee's photo on the whiteboard then wrote her name below it. "Now for our second case, the death of eighteen-year-old Katie Lee Curtis." She summarized all the information she had learned so far, then added the names of the family members, the church, and the teens who'd discovered the girl's body.

"I spoke with her parents, who were understandably upset." She described the family dynamics, the fact that everyone she'd interviewed about Katie Lee described her as quiet, bookish, with no real friends.

Dr. Whitefeather filled them in on the autopsy report. "It's my opinion that the girl was struck from behind then pushed. Again, the fire was set after her death."

"Any persons of interest?" Captain Hale asked.

Ellie gave a noncommittal shrug. "The teens we talked to at the scene didn't suggest anyone, and the counselor at school only mentioned her being friendly with Will Huntington. Her father insisted she didn't date. But his relationship with her was strained, and he'd warned her off Huntington."

"How about a girlfriend? Or possible female love interest?" Heath asked.

Ellie chewed the inside of her cheek. "So far, nothing, but we should keep an open mind."

"Maybe some girl's boyfriend showed an interest in her and that girl got jealous," Bryce pointed out. "Could have been a cat fight."

"That doesn't fit," Ellie pointed out. "This killer planned the murder. The symbolism of the stones and the fact that he had to carry them with him suggests he's smart and methodical. This was not spontaneous or a crime of passion." Ellie gestured toward Katie Lee's journal. "Katie Lee kept a diary. The entries are short, but she felt like her father hated her. The school counselor said she'd inquired about college scholarships, so she wanted to pursue her education. Apparently, her father didn't approve."

"Geesh," Captain Hale muttered. "Hard to believe some people still have that mindset."

A chorus of mumbled agreements floated around the room.

"Mr. Curtis was extremely strict with his daughter," Ellie continued. "It's possible she turned outside the family for affection. Will Huntington is a possibility, but we have nothing to confirm that yet. He attended Ole Glory Church just as the Curtises did and knew Katie Lee from there, although so far, he hasn't been very helpful. But the circle of stones we found around the two bodies mimic the ones in the graveyard at Ole Glory."

"Then we may be looking at someone who attends that church," Deputy Landrum said. "I heard the reverend sees himself as some kind of god. Apparently he has cameras around his house and there are whispers that he has people watching his followers to make sure they toe the line."

Ellie grimaced. "Go over that list of parishioners and run background checks. Maybe you can talk to some of them, too." She paused, clearing her throat. "We can't rule out the father at this point. Something was going on behind closed doors, something that feels wrong." And her gut was telling her that it had everything to do with Katie Lee's death.

# CHAPTER 30

"I obtained a sample of Mr. Curtis's DNA and sent it to the lab, along with samples from Mrs. Curtis and Martin Curtis," Ellie said quietly. "Next, I'll have a chat with the preacher at Ole Glory."

"We'll do it together," the sheriff said.

"I can handle it."

Irritation flickered in his green eyes. "He might talk to me before he would you."

Ellie gritted her teeth. Bryce had a point. The good old boys in the area understood and stuck together like a pack of rats. "All right," Ellie conceded. "Let me talk to Deputy Landrum for a minute and then we'll go."

Bryce nodded, then stepped aside to make a phone call. Heath was deep in his computer, combing social media for mentions of Katie Lee and her brother.

She claimed the chair beside him and lowered her voice. "Anything on Gillian Roach?"

Heath ran a hand through his dark blond hair. "She worked with Raintree Family Services for thirty-five years. The agency started with a handful of volunteers, a counselor and two social workers and, with grant money, has grown to a staff of fifteen. They handle foster care placements and adoptions for babies and at-risk kids, connect victims of domestic violence to the Family Justice Center, and offer counseling resources.

"Gillian's coworkers spoke highly of her, said she was dedicated to helping children find loving homes although she never married or had children of her own. She talked about retiring next year."

"Good work," said Ellie. "She could have made enemies working with DV victims. Dig deeper and see if there were any threats against her or if she had any specific problems with a client lately. A disgruntled parent who wanted their child back, an abuser or stalker who'd come after his child or the mother, someone with charges filed against him."

"On it."

Apprehension slithered through Ellie. Was it possible the burn victim was Gillian?

"Focus on the Curtis murder for now," Ellie said, hoping the forensic specialist would have an ID on the other victim soon. "Her family wants answers."

And so did she.

# CHAPTER 31

*Rose Hill*

Eula Ann Frampton worried the beads around her neck as she hobbled over to the rose bushes she'd planted years ago. The beads were supposed to ward off evil, just as the dried herbs and garlic pouch she kept in her house. Yet she felt the dark forces slithering through the woods and town as if nothing could stop it from spreading.

Dried, dead petals from her prized roses lay scattered on the ground, black and crumbling among the withering grass.

Just as things were crumbling around her.

Her bones creaked as she stooped down to pull the faded blossoms from the bush. The roses had always bloomed without her tending to them, the soil rich with fertilizer. But the drought had dried the ground, turning it hard as stone.

She walked over to the side of the house, snagged the hose, turned it on and sprayed the bushes and ground, watching the water soak into the dirt.

Below lay her secrets.

Secrets she feared were about to come back to haunt her.

The minute she'd seen the news about the Curtis girl, she'd had a terrible sense of foreboding.

Maybe her death had nothing to do with what Eula knew.

After all, she thought she'd taken care of the problem long ago. Had she missed something?

No. It couldn't be.

There had been other murders on the trail the last few months, as if the devil himself hid in the dark forests with those who lived in the shadows. This one might be a new breed.

As the water drenched the ground, her tears flowed. She'd started life young and hopeful. In her mind, she saw her husband on his knee proposing. Saw the promises in his eyes and heard the love in his voice.

All lies.

Lies that had destroyed them.

# CHAPTER 32

*Ole Glory Church*

The parsonage was a brick ranch house built on top of the hill overlooking the church and adjoining cemetery. A giant dogwood stood in the middle of the yard, although the beautiful flowers had past being in bloom.

Ellie had the distinct feeling that Reverend Ike Jones liked being perched above his church so he could monitor his parishioners' every move.

"Let me take the lead," the sheriff said as he knocked on the door.

The door opened, saving her from having to pretend she didn't mind. The preacher's wife, Ruth, stood on the other side with a tentative smile, dressed in a long black skirt and white blouse similar to the ones Mrs. Curtis wore.

"Mrs. Jones," Bryce said, flashing one of his deceptively charming smiles. "I'm Sheriff Waters and this is Detective Ellie Reeves."

"I know who you both are," the woman said, her brows pinched. "And I know the reason you're here. Josiah called my husband for counseling after you were at his house. It's so terrible what happened to poor little Katie Lee, God rest her soul."

So, they'd expected the police and were prepared.

Mrs. Jones fidgeted with the top button of her blouse. "But I don't see how we can help you."

"It's routine that we talk to everyone who knew the girl and her family," Bryce said.

Mrs. Jones fiddled with her blouse again, looking wary.

"Please," said Ellie. "Since you know the family personally, I'm sure you want to do everything possible to help us find out what happened to her."

Bryce cut her a sharp look, but Ellie ignored him as the preacher's wife stepped aside and gestured for them to enter. Pictures of Jesus and the Last Supper hung on the wall, along with framed cross-stitched pieces boasting Bible verses. Wood floors, dark paneling, and heavy drapes gave the living room a closed-in feel and a musty odor permeated the space. Reverend Jones might like to know what was going on with his members, but he obviously didn't want anyone seeing in his own house.

"Your house feels warm and inviting," Ellie lied. "Do you have children?"

A flicker of sadness deepened the grooves beside the woman's eyes. "I'm afraid we were not blessed that way. But God had his plan for us."

"I'm sure he did."

Bryce was shooting her odd looks, but she wanted to establish a rapport with the wife before her husband joined them.

"Please sit down in the parlor and I'll get the reverend. He's in his private study working on the sermon for Wednesday night. We have a supper that night as well."

"How often does the church meet?" Ellie asked.

"Wednesdays and Sundays for services, although we offer special prayer times every night. Our church is always open."

Ellie and Bryce situated themselves in the hardback chairs flanking the fireplace while Mrs. Jones briskly walked from the room down a dark hall.

"Interesting that she calls him the reverend instead of Ike," Ellie commented as she noted the old-fashioned organ in the corner. Stacks of sheet music and gospel song books were piled on a small table beside it. She wondered if the wife played.

Bryce gave her a wry look. "At least she didn't call him the prophet."

In spite of her animosity toward Bryce, Ellie's mouth twitched. "True."

Footsteps echoed as the couple approached. Ellie had seen the preacher in town, and although Mrs. Jones said the church was open to everyone, he was closed-off. Judgmental. His probing eyes held accusations of sin and damnation, not forgiveness and tolerance.

Bryce stood and offered his hand, but the man simply looked at it and kept his distance, his narrow jaw clenched so tightly Ellie expected to hear bones cracking. He was over six feet, thin with wiry graying hair, and wore a plain black suit that looked worn and as austere as the man himself.

"Mr. Jones—" Bryce began.

"It's Reverend Ike," the preacher cut in. "And I know why you're here so don't bother with pleasantries."

A muscle ticked in Bryce's jaw. "Right. There's nothing pleasant about this visit. We are very saddened over the loss of Katie Lee Curtis and know you are as well."

"Yes, no family should have to bury their child," the reverend said.

"Can you tell us your impression of Katie Lee?" Bryce asked.

The man glanced at his wife for a brief second, then claimed the wing chair opposite them. His wife took his lead, seating herself beside him, her hands smoothing down the folds of her skirt.

"She was a nice girl," the reverend said. "Quiet and well behaved."

Bryce kept a neutral tone, "What about friends at church?"

"No one specific. Her parents encouraged her to attend youth group, and she came a few times, but she didn't really join in." He scratched his chin with one finger. "I saw her talking with Will Huntington a couple of times though and knew that was trouble."

"Why do you say that?" Bryce asked.

"That boy made a mockery of our beliefs," the reverend said. "He needed rules. I advised Josiah if he wanted to keep his daughter holy, he should keep Will away from her."

"And he tried?"

The reverend glanced toward the closed drapes then back with a detached look. "He did his best."

"That must have upset Will and Katie Lee," Ellie cut in. Bryce went still, but Ellie didn't back down. "Did either of them ever come to you to talk about the situation?"

"If you're asking if I counseled the teens, no. I offered my services, but both declined." Anger glinted in his eyes as his gaze met Ellie's. "But if they had, I would have warned them they were on the wrong path. That if they dishonored their parents and God, they would go to hell for eternity."

*Just what every teen wanted to hear.*

"Mrs. Jones, can you add anything?" Ellie asked. "Maybe Katie Lee or her mother talked to you?"

"My wife has nothing to say." The reverend stood, buttoning his jacket. Mrs. Jones had dropped her gaze to her hands and twisted them together.

"If Katie Lee had listened, maybe she wouldn't be dead," the reverend finished. "Now, it's time for both of you to go. I have a sermon to prepare. Mr. Curtis wants me to speak at his daughter's funeral, and my loyalty is to him."

Without another word, he left the room, dismissing them entirely.

# CHAPTER 33

*Somewhere between Pigeon Lake and Stony Gap*

"Fuck, Ellie, what was that about?" Bryce bellowed as soon as they drove away from the parsonage.

"I was trying to get some answers. And that man is hiding behind a bunch of archaic beliefs."

Bryce pinned her with a look of contempt. "Does everything have to be about your feministic ideals?"

"It's not about me. It's about Katie Lee and who killed her. I think the reverend knows more than he's telling us."

"And now he probably won't talk to us again because you pissed him off," Bryce snapped.

"He wasn't going to talk anyway," she said quietly. "You heard him. His loyalty lies with Mr. Curtis and his principles, however skewed they are."

"Next time, I speak to him alone."

Ellie gritted her teeth as she passed the cemetery, and the series of standing stones, just like the ones surrounding the victims. In her mind, she could hear the gospel choir singing about the blood of Jesus. But it was Katie Lee's blood that had her worried and angry. That girl had been crying out for help in her journals. Yet no one had listened.

Ellie had to be there for her now.

A strained silence fell between her and the sheriff as they drove past farmland and several chicken houses. Bryce said nothing as he parked by her car and she got out. But she'd bet her next paycheck he'd head over to Haints for a beer, his nightly ritual.

Exhaustion clouded her brain as she climbed in her Jeep and drove the short distance home. Her phone buzzed just as she let herself in her house.

She quickly connected. "Detective Reeves speaking."

"It's Marty," the boy said in a hushed voice. "I think you should know something."

"What is it, son?" Ellie asked.

His voice was muffled when he spoke. "My father… he wouldn't have anything to do with Katie Lee. It was like he hated her for some reason."

"Do you know the reason he was standoffish with her?"

He hesitated, then mumbled no.

Tension vibrated over the line. "Is there something else?"

"Yeah, they argued night before last. It got bad. I heard Dad say he was calling the reverend to set up a time for some kind of sin-cleansing ceremony. Katie Lee started crying and said she wouldn't go."

Ellie's lungs tightened. "What happened after that?"

The boy's labored breathing rattled over the line. "He said she didn't have a choice. That he knew the minute she was born that she was full of sin. And he'd get it out of her somehow or she couldn't stay in our house anymore."

From what she'd heard about the girl, she was practically an angel. And how exactly had her father planned to get the sin out of her?

"Marty, did your father go out at all later that night?"

"I don't know," Marty said, his voice cracking. "But he came in early the next morning, when I was getting breakfast. He said he'd been to talk to Reverend Ike, to pray for Katie Lee. He seemed sweaty and his clothes were dirty, and he was upset. He went up to his room and shut himself in."

The reverend hadn't mentioned seeing Mr. Curtis. If he hadn't been at home or church, where had he been?

# CHAPTER 34

*Crooked Creek*

Two hours later, Ellie sat on the back deck of her bungalow overlooking the mountains. They looked gloomy tonight as they climbed toward the clouds, stars fighting through the haze of lingering smoke that seemed to pervade the sky long after the fires had burned out. The vibrant green of the trees was tinged with brown from the lack of rain, flowers sagging beneath the weight of the humidity.

Consumed with what might have gone on behind closed doors in the Curtis house and at that church, her mood was just as ominous.

After she and Bryce separated earlier, the sheriff had met with the town council about the Fourth of July festivities—part of which involved him riding on the float with the winner of the Little Miss Bluff County and Miss Teen Bluff County pageant. Meanwhile, she and Heath had divided up the list of parishioners at Ole Glory and paid them visits.

The interviews had yielded no insight into the killer but had intensified Ellie's suspicions that all was not right in that church. The women literally clammed up. The men exerted complete control over their households.

"Reverend Ike demands loyalty," one woman whispered. "Anyone who doesn't follow him is banned from the church."

"I don't like the way he treats the young girls like servants," an older woman named Polly had said.

Desperate for someone to bounce ideas off, but not desperate enough to do so with Bryce, Ellie called Shondra. But the phone rang four times and then went to voicemail.

Sighing, Ellie left a long message. "I think something bad happened in the Curtis house, and I thought you might have insight into the family dynamics. Maybe we can meet for coffee tomorrow and talk about it." Sensing she'd said enough for tonight, that she had to be patient, she hung up.

The air was thick and muggy, inviting mosquitoes and gnats to party in her backyard, the air so silent you could hear twigs crackling and leaves rustling as the forest creatures scampered through the rows of giant oaks, pines and hemlocks.

Shadows darted along the paths, a few stars splintering the dark skies, bringing Ellie's imagination to life just as they had when she was a child. Her father had told her about the recluses, hillbillies, and criminals who lived off the grid—he called them the Shadow People. Some nights, when the moon was full, she thought she saw a lone man standing at the edge of the forest looking up at her house. Sometimes she thought he was a spirit.

Tonight, the quarter moon hung low over the tops of the sharp ridges splintered like broken glass. The sound of vultures grunting and diving down into an area known as Death's Door cut into the heavy silence.

Her phone buzzed, startling her, and she checked the number, hoping it was Shondra. Instead, it was Angelica Gomez.

Her mind raced as she debated whether to answer. She had no more details to add about the case but decided the reporter might be helpful, so she answered.

"This is Detective Reeves."

"Thanks for taking my call. I was wondering if you have an update on the Curtis case."

"No suspects that I can name at this time. Do you know anything about the Ole Glory Church?" Ellie asked.

Angelica hesitated slightly. "A little. I've been wanting to run a story about them, but my boss hasn't approved it yet. Why? Do you think someone there is involved?"

Ellie chose her words carefully. "I don't know, but the family attends that church, and I'm trying to learn everything I can about the preacher and their beliefs. Katie Lee also had bruises on her wrists and ankles, as if she'd been restrained. If they are performing exorcisms, that could explain them."

"Sounds like a Manson in the making. I'll be happy to dig into them some more," Angelica said, an excited note to her voice.

"Thanks. Let me know what you find. But I don't want this information released yet."

"Understood." Angelica paused. "One more thing, Detective. Have you decided to look into your birth parents?"

A shadow moved through the woods, and Ellie leaned forward, peering through the bushes. "Let's just stick to the case, Angelica."

She hung up, then went inside to lie down. Tomorrow she had more work to do. Two cases to solve.

Although sleep was as elusive and fleeting as peace these days, and she was afraid to close her eyes for fear the nightmares would come for her again in the darkness.

# CHAPTER 35

*Stony Gap*

A noise jerked the woman awake. Dazed and confused, she blinked to orient herself. The stairs creaked. The window rattled. Something scraped the windowpane.

Clutching the sheets between her sweaty fingers, she held her breath as she listened.

The room and hall were pitch black. But she'd left the lights on.

Cold fear clogged her throat. A squeak of the floorboards. A breath echoing in the stillness.

And then a hulking figure loomed over her.

She opened her mouth to scream, and summoned her courage to fight, but the moment she swung her fist up, a hard hand clamped over her mouth and another gripped her wrist. Pain shot through her arm and she heard the bone crack, sending nausea bolting through her.

Her eyes widened in horror as she looked up into the face of her attacker. A face covered by a black mask, only his eyes visible. Eyes that screamed a warning.

"Do you want your daughter to live?" he murmured in a sinister voice.

Tears of terror filled her eyes. She couldn't move for the force of his heavy body on top of her, but she managed to nod her head up and down.

"Good. As long as she knows nothing, I don't have to kill her."

She had to protect her daughter. She'd been doing that all her life.

Her daughter's voice taunted her. *Leave me alone. I hate you!*

An image of her girl as a little baby flashed behind her eyes. Her tiny rosebud mouth. That sweet little cry. Those trusting eyes.

She'd made a decision then that she didn't know how to take back. What would happen when she was gone? Her daughter would be alone.

A sharp sting at her neck made her cry out, but then she felt her limbs going numb and her eyes closing.

If only she hadn't asked questions. If only she'd told her girl the truth about her daddy… If only…

# CHAPTER 36

*Crooked Creek*

Dawn barely cracked the sky as Cord McClain sat outside Ellie's house. He'd spent all night worrying about the blasted woman. Dammit, he didn't like the way she tore him in knots, shattering his calm the way he splintered wood when he chopped it.

But her pale face as she'd studied the ashes of that charred body would haunt him forever. Just as seeing her nearly dying at the hands of the Weekday Killer had.

He'd felt helpless and angry, the way he'd felt when his foster father had tried to hurt one of his foster sisters. A man's job was to protect a woman.

But Ellie *didn't* want his protection. In fact, she'd be pissed as hell if she knew he'd parked himself here half the night. The sight of her on the news triggered the past, when she'd spoken out. When it had almost gotten her killed. He didn't want to see it happen again.

Gripping the thermos of coffee he'd brought, he willed himself to be strong and leave her alone. He'd protect her with his life if he had to.

But he'd walk away, too, to make sure she was safe.

He had nothing to offer but a disturbing past that forced him to live in the darkness and the wild.

Ellie was drawn to that. But she was on the right side of good. And sometimes he questioned whether he was, whether the shadows had claimed him or not.

During the last case, Ellie had learned some of his secrets.

He hoped she never learned the rest.

She thought he was angry with her for questioning him in those murders. For doubting him. But he didn't blame her. She had reason to distrust.

He wanted redemption, but that wasn't on the cards. He'd settle for just making peace with Ellie.

As night turned into day, the light in her kitchen burned bright, and he saw the bedroom light flicker on. He forced himself to wait. Watched the sun rise over the tops of the mountain peaks. Birds twitter and soar across the lawn. Felt the sizzle of the summer heatwave as the sun blazed down on the asphalt. He made a quick run for breakfast then returned to Ellie's.

Other lights flicked on in the house, then the bathroom. Still, he waited.

Another twenty minutes, and he snatched the thermos of coffee and the biscuit and sausage he'd picked up and headed to her door.

Last night he'd thought about those standing stones and the memories had launched themselves out of nowhere. He'd kept things from Ellie in the Weekday Killer case, things that might have expedited her search.

He didn't intend to do the same again.

Even if it meant baring his soul.

# CHAPTER 37

Ellie was just about to brew coffee when the doorbell dinged, startling her. She hurried to see who would show up this time of morning.

Cord stood on the front stoop, his brooding face shadowed by morning stubble, his pacing an indication that he hadn't slept last night either.

Running a hand through her tangled hair, she tightened her bathrobe and opened the door.

His hair looked scruffy, his expression wary. "I brought coffee and breakfast," he said and lifted a bag from the Corner Café. "Lola sent your usual."

Ellie's mood softened. She'd never been able to turn down a breakfast sandwich. "Thanks. Come on in. I need caffeine."

His shoulders relaxed slightly as he wiped his feet on the mat. So at odds with the gruff mountain man she saw on the trail.

She led him to the kitchen, and they took seats at her kitchen island, both sipping their coffee before talking.

"Thanks for bringing food." Ellie's stomach growled as she tore into the warm sausage and cheese biscuit. The gooey cheese melted on her tongue, a perfect combination with the hint of sage in the meat.

He shrugged, his intense expression hinting that something was going on behind those dark brown eyes. "I saw the interview with Angelica Gomez. You had to notify the family?"

Ellie nodded. "It was rough. There's something odd happening in that household. I think it has to do with that church Ole Glory."

She ran her finger around the rim of her mug. "But you didn't bring me food to talk about them. Or did you?"

He finished his biscuit and wiped his mouth, then took another sip of his coffee. "No, but when I was a kid, my foster father took us to Ole Glory."

Ellie raised a brow. Cord never talked about his past. In fact, he'd kept his silence until he'd been forced to explain when he'd been framed for murder.

Cord ran a hand over his thickening beard stubble. "You're right about something going on at that church."

Ellie forced herself not to react, although her heart ached for Cord and how he'd suffered as a child. "What do you know?"

"Just things I saw as a kid. Whispers. There's a basement at the church where he takes women and girls. I don't know what goes on inside the locked room, but I snuck down there once and smelled some kind of drug."

That didn't surprise her. Cult leaders often used drugs to bend the minds of their followers.

"My foster father made his wife go down there once. And when she came back, she was never the same. She wouldn't talk or make eye contact. It was like she was brainwashed."

Before Ellie could reply, her phone rang.

She was tempted to ignore it, but with two murders to solve, that wasn't an option. She checked the number on the display.

"I have to get this," she said. "It's Special Agent Fox."

Cord's gaze met hers, then he stood, grabbed the wrapper for his sandwich and discarded it.

"Wait," Ellie said as he headed to the door. She wanted to apologize again.

"I gotta go. Take your phone call."

Ellie gritted her teeth and answered the call as the ranger strode outside. Her conversation with Cord would have to wait.

The two murders on her caseload couldn't.

# CHAPTER 38

*Decatur, Georgia*

Special Agent Derrick Fox stared at the replay of the interview from Crooked Creek's Police Department as he waited on Ellie to answer her phone.

He should have slept good last night. Shouldn't feel so restless. He'd ended the day by putting away a gang member who'd killed a family for retribution. But he'd been torn up over the sight of the toddler lying dead in his mother's arms. Judging from the scene, she'd tried to protect the boy but the bullet had gone straight through her to the kid.

That child's death had gotten to him bad. He'd tracked down the gang member, who still had the kid's blood on his hands and the gun on him. He'd been bragging about the kill. Bragging, for fuck's sake.

Derrick had exploded, and nearly beaten the bastard to death. His knuckles were still bruised and battered, and the urge to bash the man's head wouldn't let go.

His boss had ordered him to take some time off.

Then he'd come home and seen Ellie on the evening news. Ellie with her soft ash-blond hair and her sassy attitude. He'd noted the dark circles beneath her eyes and the slight quiver in her voice. It was so subtle no one else might have detected it, but he knew Ellie pretty damn well.

Hell, he hadn't been able to get her out of his mind since the first case they'd worked together, when she'd gotten under his skin.

Two major cases had broken in Crooked Creek in the last few months and now she had more murders on her hands.

The phone clicked, and Ellie's voice answered. "Derrick?"

"I hope it's not too early."

A tense moment passed. "No, I've been up for a while."

From the sound of her gravelly voice, she hadn't been sleeping again. "I saw the news. Looks like you have your hands full with another case. Or two." He cleared his throat. "Do you think they're connected?"

"I think so, but don't know how," Ellie said. "I'm working an angle regarding the Ole Glory Church here. People are saying it's cult-like and there's talk of drugging parishioners. The family of the young girl, Katie Lee Curtis, belonged to it and is acting strangely."

Derrick's pulse kicked up a notch. "I can come there if you need my help."

A tense heartbeat passed. "Thanks, but that's not necessary. I've got it."

She'd always been independent, but they'd become close on the first case, until their families had gotten in the way.

"I'll look into the church," he offered.

"Thanks. My captain's calling," Ellie said. "I have to go."

She hung up without saying goodbye. Derrick walked over to the window and stared at the view of the city under the morning sun. He could see the tall buildings of the Atlanta skyline in the distance, hear the loud traffic noises and the zoom of a jet taking off at the airport. Nothing like the peaceful view of the mountain ridges in Crooked Creek.

Except it wasn't as peaceful as it looked. What kind of killer was Ellie dealing with this time?

# CHAPTER 39

*Stony Gap*

Mandy Morely climbed from bed, shuffled to the bathroom, splashed water on her face, then went to retrieve her phone.

News of Katie Lee Curtis's death was all over social media. Someone had posted a picture of her when she'd worked on the yearbook, a candid shot that captured the mournful look on her face. Katie Lee had always seemed sad and lonely.

Mandy didn't know her well and had never made the effort. She was busy with soccer and schoolwork—trig and algebra sucked. They were like a foreign language she'd never use—she'd had to stay late a few days to get help from the teacher.

In the kitchen, she poured herself a bowl of Cheerios and a glass of orange juice and settled at their rickety table. Except the normal groaning of the old air conditioner, the house was still. Almost creepy. No smell of coffee or the shower running from her mother's bathroom.

She rolled her eyes. Last night her mother had bugged her with a half dozen phone calls to make sure she stayed home. She had and missed meeting up with some of her friends at the Dairy Delite. Another reason she was pissed at her mom. She'd told her that she hated her right before she hung up on her.

Knowing she'd probably get grounded for life, she'd put on her headphones and listened to music until she fell asleep. She hadn't heard a thing when her mother came in.

And now several texts from her friends said their parents had seen the news and wanted them to stay home today—last night might have been the last meet-up for a while. All for their own good, apparently. Parents were always saying that—this is for your own good. When they did whatever the hell they wanted.

Frustrated to face another boring day, she tiptoed down the hall to see if her mother might be waking up. Maybe if she was nice to her, she'd take her to the mall. Probably not after last night, but she was desperate to break out of house jail.

She pushed open the door to her mom's room and peeked inside. The bed was unmade, covers tousled. Then again, she never made her bed. The bathroom door stood open, makeup and facewash scattered all over the counter.

Her mother was nowhere to be seen.

Had she even come home last night?

Anger churned in Mandy's stomach. It wouldn't be the first time she'd stayed out with some strange man. How dare she hook up while she forced her daughter to ditch her friends?

Furious, she went back to the kitchen, grabbed her phone and dialed her mother's number. The phone rang five times then the voicemail kicked in.

"I can't believe you made me stay home and you don't even bother to come back all night!"

Furious, she ended the call, threw on her shorts, T-shirt and tennis shoes then retrieved her soccer ball. In the backyard, she set it on the ground, then kicked it so hard it hit the back of the house and she could hear the windows rattling.

She kicked it again and again, sweating and fighting off tears as her anger mounted. If her mother really was worried about her, she would have come home last night. Or at least answered her phone. She wiped at her eyes again and slammed the soccer ball so hard it sailed over the top of the house.

She must not care about her at all.

# CHAPTER 40

She struggled with the ropes around her wrist as her abductor stared at her from the mouth of the dark cave where he'd brought her. They were somewhere in the woods although she had no idea where. She'd lost consciousness from whatever drug he'd given her then awakened to find herself tied up and gagged. Then he'd dropped her on the cold ground and left her.

But he was coming back. He'd promised her he would. That he'd make her death short and quick just like he did the others.

How would her daughter handle that? Would she ever recover from her mother's brutal death?

She closed her eyes to stem the tears, but they spilled over and she began to sob. She'd cried the day she'd realized she was pregnant. Hadn't known what she would do. Her grandmother was old and could hardly get around. Her sister was off at college doing her own thing.

She hadn't been prepared to be a mother. She'd even thought about giving her up for adoption. Hadn't even told the baby's father.

But the moment the nurse had laid that pink, wrinkled, six-pound squirming infant in her arms she'd fallen in love with her. And she'd known she'd do whatever it took to take care of her.

Another sob wrenched her gut. Like a movie trailer, memories of her daughter growing up flitted through her mind. The day she'd said Mama. The first footstep when she'd learned to walk. The sweet giggles when she tickled her belly.

The Christmas she'd given her child her first soccer ball. They'd kicked and dribbled and played all day together.

But mistakes had been made. She'd failed so many times.

Just like last night. Regret for losing her temper clogged her throat. There were so many things she wished she'd said to her daughter.

She didn't even hug her goodbye last night. Now she'd never get to hug her again.

# CHAPTER 41

Meddlin' Maude and her hen club, which included Bryce's mother Edwina, were gathered outside the police station as Ellie parked. Silently cursing, she stowed her phone in her pocket and climbed out, already sweating. Tourists and locals were filling the park and sidewalks, a line had formed outside the bakery, and window washers were cleaning the storefronts to spruce the town up for the Fourth of July.

The sheriff's car was nowhere in sight. *Dammit.* He would have been able to gracefully take care of his mother. Her captain and Deputy Landrum's cars were already here, but they were probably tucked inside, avoiding the flack Maude was ready to dish out.

"Hello, ladies," she said. "If you're here for the meeting about the Fourth, I believe it's being held at the library." She prayed that was the reason for the visit.

Maude threw her shoulders back, her straw hat tilting sideways on her head. Let the clucking begin. "No, we've been discussing that news report you gave," the woman said, her voice shrill. "Ever since you started working in Crooked Creek, we've had nothing but murders."

Ellie crossed her arms and looked at the other ladies who fidgeted nervously. "And you believe that's my fault?"

"You brought trouble to us, and you know it. You and your family. I don't know why you just don't leave town and let the sheriff run this county." She gestured toward Edwina. "At least he's from a respectable family."

"Maude," said Ellie, struggling for compassion and stamping down her anger. "I realize that you're still grieving, and I'm so sorry. I can't imagine what it's been like for your family losing Honey Victoria like that."

"No, you can't," Maude said, dabbing at her eyes with a delicate handkerchief. "And she wouldn't have died if you'd done your job." The woman pointed her finger at Ellie. "Now another young girl has been killed in this town. Are you going to let her murderer go on a killing spree and slaughter more of our children?"

Ellie felt as if the wind had been knocked out of her. Maude had no idea how haunted she was by the faces of the young women who'd died. "I'm going to forgive your animosity as I know you're hurting," she said. "And I don't intend to let the person who killed Katie Lee get away. Now, unless you have helpful information about Katie Lee's death, please move so I can go to work and get justice for her."

She brushed past Maude, slipped through the door and closed it firmly behind her. Her breathing burst out in erratic pants as she leaned against the wall, closing her eyes.

But she couldn't banish the images of the burned bodies or Maude's hateful words. Because deep down inside, she was afraid the woman was right.

# CHAPTER 42

*Stony Gap*

Mandy was mad as hell at her mother. But she was sweating like a pig, and her soccer ball needed air, so she opened the garage door to get the pump.

Her mother's car sat inside.

She gaped at it for a minute, confused. If her mother hadn't come home, why was her car here? Had she come home then left with someone else?

A seed of worry sprouted inside her, and she ran back inside and looked around the kitchen. A wine glass sat on the counter. Dirty.

Her mother often had a drink before bedtime. She said she was wound up when she got home and it helped her sleep. Fumbling with her phone, Mandy called her mom and heard the faint sound of it ringing from somewhere. She searched the kitchen counter, the table, then the couch, where sometimes it fell between the cushions. It was nowhere.

The ringing was so faint she could barely hear it. She ran to her mother's room and listened. She checked the nightstand then the bed covers but couldn't see it.

Stooping, she looked underneath the bed and raked her hand around. Her fingers touched the cool surface. That was it. Pulling the phone out, she saw the battery was almost dead.

Then a spark of something red caught her eye. Droplets, crimson colored.

Blood.

Her heart jumped to her throat. She looked around the room again, then noticed the clothes her mother had worn to work had been tossed on the chair in the corner. Her shoes lay beneath the chair, and her purse… was right there.

Fear took root, immobilizing her. The blood drew Mandy's gaze again and she spotted a small spatter on the wall near the floor by the bed.

There were all sorts of weirdos who flocked to the bars, the booze bringing out their meanness. Her mom had told her that.

A tremble started deep inside her. Had one of them followed her home and done something to her?

# CHAPTER 43

*Death's Door*

He hoisted her limp body over his shoulder and began the long hike to the top of the ridge. Even though it was daytime, the cover of the trees cast the area in darkness, perfect for the privacy he needed. He swatted at bugs, sweat soaking his shirt and dripping down his neck between his shoulder blades.

But sweat could leave DNA, so he'd wrapped her in a cotton sheet that he'd brought with him, then plastic. Her arms swung down by his sides, her legs dangling like a rag doll as he walked for miles and miles, hovering in the shadows of the thick trees whenever he heard another hiker or group nearby.

Keeping watch, he waded through the creek to climb the steep incline. Dry, brittle grass, pine straw and brush crackled beneath his feet just like the embers of a fire.

Ashes to ashes, dust to dust.

The creek was so low it had almost dried up, dead fish washing to shore and creating a stench. Flies and mosquitos buzzed above the carcasses, and vultures glided above. He carried the woman over tree stumps and piles of dried weeds and bramble until he reached the top of the ridge.

"This place is called Death's Door," he whispered to his victim. Locals claimed many had killed themselves by hanging from the trees, which remained stubbornly bare all year long.

It was the perfect place to leave her body.

Slowly, he lowered the woman to the parched soil, smiling at the way her head lolled to the side. She slowly roused as he removed the rope from his bag and began to wind it around her slender pale throat.

"Ticktock, Ticktock," he murmured. The sands of time were slipping away…

Her eyes slid open, big dark orbs in her oval face, her skin almost translucent beneath the sliver of moonlight peeking through the bare branches of the surrounding pines. Confusion blurred her eyes, fear seeping into them as she struggled to regain consciousness.

He wound the rope in a noose, then lifted her head, her chestnut hair falling around her shoulders as he secured the noose around her neck. She opened her mouth in a scream, but no sound came out.

Securing the other end of the rope around the pine nearest the ridge edge, he tightened it, then returned to gather her in his arms. All the ways he'd imagined taking a life played through his mind, challenging him to make each kill unique.

"Shh, it'll be over soon," he murmured as he glanced at his watch. *Ticktock, ticktock.* The clock struck the hour.

It was time. He threw her over the edge and watched her flail and kick, her silent scream lost in the air as the rope cut into her throat and snapped her vocal cords.

Tension coiled inside him as he realized what he'd done, and the urges hit him swift and hard. He wasn't finished yet. He needed to hear the flick of the match, see the flames spark to life.

Quickly he cut the rope, watching her body fall to the ground below. Adrenaline heated his blood, and he scurried down the slope, skidding to a stop as he reached her lifeless body.

His fingers itched. A vein jumped in his neck. His breath quickened.

The scent of smoke along the trail lived within him just as it curled toward the summer sky.

Excitement built as he drew a circle in the dirt around the woman, finding stones and stacking them around her. He gathered dry sticks from the woods and used them as kindling, then removed the matchbook and struck a match. His pulse raced as he held it up in front of his eyes and watched the perfect glow of the flame as it flickered against the cloudy sky.

The rippling sound made his body hum, and he was mesmerized as the kindling burst into flames.

Once the circle of fire was complete, the calm began to wash over him. Still, he watched the fire spread, glowing off her ashen face, and trickling over to snatch her hair, the flames shooting up all around her.

# CHAPTER 44

*Crooked Creek*

Ellie pulled herself away from the door as Captain Hale shouted her name. He was rushing toward her, his cheeks ruddy, his hands waving.

"What is it?" she asked, shaking off the unsettling conversation with Meddlin' Maude.

"You have to get over to Vanessa Morely's house. Her daughter just called, hysterical. She thinks something happened to her mother."

Ellie's stomach sank. She'd just seen Vanessa and Mandy arguing a couple of days before at the Corner Café. "Why does she think that?"

"Said her mother worked late last night and when Mandy got up this morning, her mother wasn't in bed. A while ago, she realized Vanessa's car, purse and phone were at the house."

"Maybe she went for a walk or a run," Ellie suggested, grappling for some other answer than foul play.

Captain Hale shook his head and popped a mint in his mouth, chomping and cracking the candy vigorously. "She said there was blood. I want you to go talk to her."

"But the case—"

"This could be related," he said, his eyes wide.

She didn't see how. Katie Lee and Vanessa were years apart. "She works at Haints, the sheriff's favorite watering hole," Ellie said.

"Don't I know it? I called him earlier and he sounded hungover. I left a message for him to get over here and handle Maude and that bunch of busybodies outside."

"You know Bryce's mother is with them?"

Hale nodded. "I called the mayor, too. Told him to get his wife and her friends under control. They may think they're helping by putting pressure on the department, but they're doing more harm than good, inciting anger and distrust. I don't intend to put up with their bullshit."

Ellie agreed, although the mayor had power and she knew her boss was walking a fine line. If he got fired, she might be next.

"I'll get out to the Morelys'," Ellie said. "Have Heath keep digging into that church. Maybe Bryce can talk to the people at the bar. See if anything strange went down last night."

# CHAPTER 45

Twenty-nine-year-old Sarah Houston had thought the night would never end. Sleeping on the ground in the middle of the wilderness with mosquitos and flies nipping at her had kept her tossing and turning long into the lonely evening.

She shouldn't have been lonely though, not with her boyfriend beside her. Except he'd lapsed into one of his strange moods and shut down, folding within himself, setting her nerves on edge.

Last night, while Ryder Rigdon had lain snoring like a bear, she'd envisioned a different life. A life where she was planning her wedding. Her biological clock had been ticking for three years and she'd finally decided to get serious about husband hunting and stop falling for every sad sack that walked into her life with his sob story. She always saw the potential though, she always thought she could fix them.

Although with Ryder, she'd noticed a few warning signs. Sometimes he disappeared for a few days, he had a short fuse and was addicted to his damn smartwatch. But she'd dismissed them because he was a tall drink of water. He also volunteered at an animal shelter, where she saw his soft side come out. The moment when she'd seen him tend to a sick Lab, she'd fallen hard.

Last night she'd thought he'd brought her to the Lazy River Falls for a romantic night. But he'd crashed as soon as his body hit the sleeping bag, and she'd been left to sweat and fume until she'd finally taken a sleeping pill and passed out. When she'd awakened, he looked as if he'd been up for hours and insisted on hiking through the smoky mountains. They'd been at it for hours.

"Maybe we should head back," she said as the smell of burning vegetation grew stronger.

Ignoring her, Ryder slashed at weeds with his hunting knife and increased his pace until she was almost running between the massive trees to keep up with him. Was he trying to lose her?

Her breathing grew labored, her ankle throbbing as he veered onto a path pocked with briars.

Ahead, flames shot upward. "There's a fire!" she shouted to Ryder, who was several feet away.

But he disappeared over the crest of the hill as if mesmerized by the flames. Terrified and afraid she'd get lost if she turned back on her own, she followed. The charcoal-gray smoke was growing thicker by the minute, the scent of burning lumber and brush clogging her lungs.

Ryder suddenly halted, and she nearly ran into him. From the top of the ridge, she looked down and saw a charred body in the midst of the flames. River stones had been arranged in a circular pattern around the body, the tallest ones pointing to the heavens as white ashes fluttered around them.

# CHAPTER 46

Dread made Ellie's belly clench. Vanessa's white clapboard house needed a fresh coat of paint, although impatiens and marigolds added pops of color to the tiny yard and drab exterior.

A dried wreath decorated the front door and a fern that needed watering hung from the overhang of the stoop.

Memories tickled her conscience. In first grade, Vanessa's family had moved to Crooked Creek. Vanessa had been quiet and awkward, and for the first time since Ellie had been traumatized by being lost in the woods, she'd formed a friendship, someone other than Mae, her imaginary friend. They'd swung together, side by side in the playground, and made playhouses in the forest. They'd climbed trees and lain in the grass behind her house and looked up at the clouds, talking about the shapes and animals they saw in the sky.

Praying this call was nothing more than a teenager with an overactive imagination, she climbed from her Jeep and followed the graveled drive to the front door. The door swung open before she could knock and a teary-eyed Mandy faced her, the fear on her face wrenching Ellie's gut.

"My mom, something happened," she cried. "You have to find her."

Ellie hoped the girl was wrong. Gently she took Mandy's arms and rubbed them. "Hey, Mandy, I'm here to help. Let's go inside."

"But it's my fault," Mandy gulped. "I had a fight with her last night and she went to work and I don't know where she is."

"Nothing is your fault," Ellie said as she ushered her through the foyer. "And we don't know what happened yet. But I need you to try to calm down and talk to me. Okay?"

Mandy's already tear-stricken face reddened more as she rubbed at her eyes. Ellie caught sight of a photograph of the mother and daughter on the wall. Vanessa was still petite and had grown up to be an attractive woman, although she looked weathered by life. Her wavy auburn hair curled around her shoulders, highlighting her porcelain skin and a smile that broadened her face as she looked down at her teenage daughter. They shared the same skin tone and hair, with a sprinkling of freckles on their noses.

"Let's sit down and you can explain what happened."

Ellie handed the girl a napkin from the table and they seated themselves. Mandy was shaking so hard that it took her several minutes to catch her breath.

"I know you're worried and upset, honey, but talk to me."

Fear streaked the young girl's eyes. "We watched the news. You were on it," she said, her voice catching. "Talking about that girl who died."

"Yes, that was me," Ellie said softly. "Did you or your mother know Katie Lee?"

"I know who she is," Mandy said. "But we're not friends or anything. Anyway, Mama freaked over it. She had to go to work the last couple of nights, but each time she ordered me to stay home and then last night I yelled at her and she left." Another sob escaped her.

Ellie soothed her again. "Go on, Mandy. What happened after that?"

"She called me a bunch of times. I was so mad I told her I hated her." Tears choked her. "That was the last thing I said to her…"

Ellie pulled the girl into her arms. "It's okay, all teenagers argue with their mothers. But their moms know they love them anyway. Vanessa knows you love her too."

Ellie handed her another napkin to dry her eyes. "You said her car is here?"

Mandy nodded. "And her purse and her phone… Although the battery is about dead."

So if she was abducted, it might have happened late last night after she'd gotten home, before she had a chance to plug it in. Or… she could have been so tired she'd forgotten.

Ellie hugged her again, then eased away. "You said you saw blood?"

"In the bedroom by her… bed." Her nails dug into Ellie's arms as she clenched them. "You have to find her, Detective. She's all I've got."

# CHAPTER 47

The photographs of Mandy on the mantel told the story of a mother who doted on her daughter. Baby pictures, photos of Mandy with a gap-toothed smile, the little girl riding her bicycle and smiling as she held up a soccer trophy.

"Just look in Mom's room," Mandy said in a ragged whisper. "You'll see what I mean."

"Did you hear a noise or an intruder last night or early this morning?"

Mandy shook her head. "I had my headphones in when I fell asleep. And I'm used to Mom working late, so I usually sleep through her coming in."

"Okay. Let me look around. Is there someone you can call? Another family member or friend?" Or the girl's father, but Ellie had no idea who that was.

"My aunt, Trudy," Mandy said.

"Okay, call your aunt while I look around."

She left the girl and walked into the hall, then past the girl's room. It was a typical teenage room, except instead of posters of bands or teenage idols, they were of the US women's soccer team when they'd won the World Cup.

Vanessa's room held a queen-sized four-poster bed, a chair in the corner covered in clothing, a dresser and a small desk. Just as Mandy said, Vanessa's purse was there, and her phone lay on the bed. Pulling on gloves, Ellie picked it up and scrolled quickly through her recent calls. Nothing suspicious. But she would have Heath do a thorough analysis in case Vanessa had received threats.

Regret for not making more of an effort to reconnect with Vanessa washed over Ellie.

Continuing her search, she checked the wall and floor where Mandy had seen blood. Her pulse jumped when she found it. Several drops on the carpet, then some spatter on the wall as if Vanessa might have fallen or hit her head. As she bent down to look closer, she realized the blood was fresh.

# CHAPTER 48

Ellie searched the rest of the house, then Vanessa's car and the garage for signs of foul play, but if she'd been taken, her abductor had gotten in and out without leaving a trace. Somehow, they'd done so without waking Mandy. Hadn't Vanessa screamed for help?

She phoned a CSI team to come out and by the time she'd finished checking over the place, Vanessa's sister had arrived.

Ellie remembered Trudy, although she'd been a few years older and had avoided her and Vanessa at school. "I encouraged Mandy to eat something," said Trudy, meeting her in the living room, "but she won't. Says she feels sick to her stomach."

"She's beating herself up because they argued last night," Ellie said. "I tried to assure her whatever happened is not her fault."

"Oh, goodness," Trudy whispered. "I'll talk to her, too."

"Did Vanessa mention having problems with anyone lately? A neighbor? Boyfriend? Someone from the bar?"

"I really can't say. Vanessa and I haven't been close for a while."

"How about Mandy's father? Were they in touch?"

Trudy made a low sound of disgust. "I wouldn't know that either. Vanessa refused to talk about him or tell me his name."

Ellie mulled that over as she noticed the crime scene investigators arrive. Could the father have something to do with Vanessa's disappearance?

"For now, I'm going to treat this as suspicious and have a team search and take prints. Trudy, can you take Mandy to your house for a while?"

"Of course."

Ellie's phone buzzed on her hip. It was the sheriff. "I need to take this. Please tell Mandy I'll do everything I can to find her mother." She pushed a business card into Trudy's hand. "My work number and cell are on there. Call me if there's anything you think of that might help."

She tucked Vanessa's phone, contained in an evidence bag, in her pocket while Trudy went to help Mandy pack.

"Sheriff," Ellie said as she connected the call. "I assume Captain Hale told you about Vanessa's daughter's call?"

"Yeah," he said, his voice deep. She bet he was hungover. "What do you think?"

"Looks suspicious," Ellie said. "There was blood on the floor of her bedroom."

"Any evidence of an intruder?"

"Just the blood. But a CSI team is here now." Ellie walked outside to meet them. "I'll canvass the neighbors if you'll talk to the staff at Haints. You should pull security footage too in case someone was stalking her at the club."

"Don't tell me how to do my job," Bryce barked.

"Then don't drink on the job." Her phone vibrated with another call. "It's the captain. I need to take this," she said, hanging up and connecting to her boss.

"Ellie," Captain Hale said.

"I just talked to Bryce. I think Vanessa might have been abducted."

He spewed a litany of curse words. "I was afraid of that."

"Why? Did something happen?"

"Ranger McClain called. We have another body."

# CHAPTER 49

*Death's Door*

Afternoon sunlight barely bled through the tree branches as Ellie hiked to the summit to meet Cord. Smoke twisted into the sky in the distance and she heard the loud hum of a helicopter flying above. Her captain had warned her about another wildfire breakout. It was close by.

Firefighters were already on the scene, extinguishing the blaze and working to keep it from spreading.

She had been to Death's Door half a dozen times over the years. It was common practice for teens to dare and goad each other into camping out there. But she mostly remembered it for the time her father took her and Vanessa. They'd snuggled in their sleeping bags while her dad told them ghost stories.

One tale was that the gate to Satan's home was carved into the ground beneath the kudzu plants. Others claimed if you slept under the stars at the top of the ridge, you could hear the screams of the dead as they were dragged into the bowels of hell.

Stepping through the dry weeds and grass, she plowed her way up the path to the ridge. Breaking through the clearing, she saw Cord standing next to a couple. Max Weatherby was there, too, combing the area for forensics.

The young woman looked to be early thirties, her wavy auburn hair piled on top of her head in a messy bun. She sat hunched on a rock, looking pale and shell-shocked. A tall muscular man with black hair stood beside her, body taut, expression neutral as Cord spoke to him.

Brush crackled beneath Ellie's boots as she approached. Her gaze scanned the area until she caught sight of the crime scene.

A sickening feeling overwhelmed her. *Please don't let this be Vanessa.*

Cord moved up beside her, his voice thick. "You okay, Ellie?"

"Yeah. But I'm afraid of who this might be." She explained about her visit to Vanessa's. "We were friends growing up," she said, blotting sweat from the back of her neck.

"Maybe you should step away from this one."

"No, I have to work it. Stop whoever's doing this." She exhaled, tasting the acrid odor of burned wood and flesh. "Stay with the couple. The woman looks pretty shaken."

"She is."

Pulling herself together, she yanked on boot covers and gloves, then scanned the ground in search of footprints. Slowly, she made her way to the edge of the ridge.

Her stomach clenched. Another burned body lying in the center of the circle of stones.

Questions railed through her head. Three bodies, all burned, left inside stone circles, smoke still coiling up into the sky.

But this one was slightly different, the method of murder more complicated. A rope in a hangman's knot was tied around a tree near the edge of the ridge. She followed the line of the rope, which stretched about fifteen feet, envisioning the crime in her mind. This woman had been hanged, then the rope was cut, dropping the body. Then someone had arranged the stones and set the fire, watching the flames destroy what was left of her.

# CHAPTER 50

*Rose Hill*

Eula Ann Frampton felt death in the air just as strongly as she smelled the sharp odor of burning trees and leaves. She could see the smoke winding into the sky now, thick plumes of gray, the sound of burning limbs and brush forcing the forest animals to escape the blaze that had been eating up their home.

For years, the demons had laid dormant in the mountains, but a few months ago, they'd been awakened and now she saw them in her mind, skulking in the shadows, stalking human prey just as a mountain lion hunted a rabbit or squirrel.

The air felt still, barely moving, weighed down by the record high temperatures, the heat from the fire scorching her skin as she stood on her front porch. Though it was miles from her house, she feared the flames might spread to the garden, and then her secrets might be exposed.

Secrets the gossipmongers had whispered about for years, that she'd killed and buried her husband in her own yard.

Her bitter laugh cackled in the wind. No one knew what had really happened. She hoped they never would.

Her secrets were too dark to tell, her pain too deep. Both had trapped her here on Rose Hill, just as the spirits wandering the woods at night kept her from leaving.

But no amount of prayer could bring repentance for the past. The fires of hell would turn her bones into ashes one day.

She could hear Satan's laughter as he called her name, welcoming her home.

# CHAPTER 51

*Death's Door*

Denial stabbed at Ellie as she stared at the body. A memory floated to her—Vanessa in high school on the cheerleading team, doing cartwheels and chanting as she cheered the football team to the state championship.

She remembered watching and wishing they could be friends again. But she didn't know how. Vanessa fit in with the popular girls and was into makeup and boys while Ellie liked exploring the wilderness and reading crime novels.

Mandy looked so much like Vanessa had at that age. The last thing she wanted was to break that girl's heart by informing her that her mother was never coming home again.

The sound of crying broke through her shock, and she glanced at the couple who'd found the body.

Cord was talking softly to the woman, while the man standing beside her showed no emotion. In fact, his cold gray eyes almost looked past them. He made no move to comfort the young woman.

A glance down below and she saw that the victim was lying face down. It was impossible to tell from her vantage point if she might have been alive and had attempted to crawl away from the fire. But the rope suggested strangulation, or if she hadn't died from that, the fall might have killed her. She would leave it to the autopsy to confirm that.

Behind her, she heard voices and footsteps as the ME and the Evidence Response Team arrived. Hurrying over to meet them, she explained to Laney that she'd just gotten there herself.

"It's the same guy?" Laney asked.

"The circle of stones and the fire suggest that it is." She lowered her voice. "I can't be certain, but I may know who she is."

"You found an ID?" Laney asked.

Ellie shook her head, then explained about Vanessa and her daughter.

"I hope it's not her," Laney said, squeezing Ellie's arm. "But I'll request her medical and dental records for comparison."

"Of course."

While Laney pulled on gloves to examine the body, Ellie addressed the crime scene investigators. "Be sure and get photos of everything, including close-ups of the body just as she was found. Look for a purse, wallet, jewelry, anything to help identify her."

While they began working, Ellie identified herself to the couple. "Your names?"

The man stood at least six three, looked like either an athlete or ex-military, and screamed alpha male.

"Ryder Rigdon, and this is Sarah Houston. We camped out last night several miles from here and were on our way back on the trail this morning when we saw her," he said. "We called 911 right away."

Ellie glanced down at their hands and shoes but saw no indication that either had been involved in the woman's death. Both wore sneakers, and she spotted their footprints leading from the woods to where they were now.

"Did you touch the body or go near her?"

The woman shook her head vigorously. "No, but when we reached the clearing from the hill, we saw her." Her voice broke and she swiped at her damp cheeks.

"What time did you set camp last night?" Ellie asked.

"We drove to the approach trail yesterday around five," Ryder said, "then hiked to Lazy River Falls for the night. Pitched tents, grilled burgers over the fire, and turned in about ten."

"Did you see anyone out here or hear someone by the falls when you approached?" Ellie asked.

"No," the man said, his voice calm but firm.

"Sarah? Did you run into another hiker or see anyone else in the woods last night or this morning?"

Sarah tugged at her T-shirt, then wiped at her eyes. "No. It was pretty deserted."

"But you two were together all night?" Ellie asked.

"We were," Rigdon said, his eyes steely. Sarah frowned, looking as if she wanted to say something but clamping her lips together.

As she watched the interaction between the couple, something about Rigdon's demeanor bothered Ellie. Even if he hadn't killed this latest victim, she sensed he was dangerous.

# CHAPTER 52

A slight breeze stirred the scent of seared flesh and made Ellie's stomach roil. Even Laney paled and turned away for a second, while Cord left to join the firefighters, who'd radioed about a family trapped in a shelter.

Gray smoke filled the sky, filtering through the trees and making the hot air even more intense. She felt as if her skin was being singed and her eyes were burning.

"These deaths have to be connected," Ellie said, thinking out loud.

Were they personal? Did he know the victims? Or was he choosing them randomly? Sometimes a victim was simply in the wrong place at the wrong time.

But that was far less common than being murdered by someone close to home. Mr. Curtis's face flashed behind her eyes.

"Hopefully we'll have an ID on victim number one late this afternoon," Laney said, dragging Ellie away from her thoughts.

"Good. At least then I'll know where to start with the questioning. Is this vic a female?"

"Yes," Laney said, pointing to the pelvic bone. "Judging from the size of her skull and other bones, an adult woman. Petite, maybe five three. The heat speeds up the decomp process and we'll factor that in, but I'd guess she's been dead for a few hours. I'll narrow that down when I finish the autopsy."

Ellie stood and envisioned possible scenarios. The brush was mashed down, and dirt appeared to have been raked around as if to cover prints, the rocks and pebbles scattered.

Laney motioned her over. "Look at this. She was wearing a ring."

Gently, Ellie studied the ring on the woman's hand. The metal was still warm to the touch and the aquamarine stone was still intact.

Her pulse raced as she realized what she was looking at. It was a high school class ring. She had one herself from Stony Gap High with her own birthstone, an emerald. Much to Vera's consternation, she'd sold hers in exchange for money toward her first .22.

A sinking feeling swept through her as she remembered that the tradition of using the birthstones for the class rings had died out after her senior year. That meant the victim could be one of her own classmates. It could be Vanessa.

# CHAPTER 53

*Bluff County Medical Examiner's Office*

At the ME's office, Laney and the forensic anthropologist, Dr. Lim Chi, sat across from Ellie. Dr. Chi took a sip of her coffee before opening the folder she'd been holding. "I have information on the remains you found at Winding Rock."

"Who is she?" Ellie asked.

"I used PMCT, compared bone structure, medical and dental X-rays, toxicology and DNA. We had a hit. Her name was Gillian Roach. She was a—"

"Social worker." Ellie's disposable coffee cup slipped through her fingers and hit the floor by her feet, sloshing warm liquid all over the painted concrete.

"What's wrong, Ellie?" Laney asked. "Did you know Gillian Roach?"

Ellie jumped up, ran to the bathroom and gathered paper towels. When she returned, Laney was watching her with a worried look. "What is it, Ellie?" Laney asked again.

Blowing a strand of hair from her face, she wiped up the mess. "I didn't exactly know her. But I had left her a message that I wanted to talk to her."

Laney narrowed her eyes and Dr. Chi ran her fingers over the file but remained silent.

"This stays between us," Ellie said. "Understood?"

Dr. Chi nodded, and Laney murmured, "Of course."

"Gillian Roach was the social worker who handled my adoption."

Laney's mouth parted in surprise.

"I left a message for her, but she didn't return my call. I talked to her assistant the next day, though, and she was worried about her. She said Gillian rushed from her office upset and carried work files with her. I went by her house and had the impression she'd left town, so I asked one of the deputies to look into her. She has no family. But I thought she might have been threatened by someone from a case she'd worked. What was time and cause of death?" Ellie asked the ME.

"I'd estimate her death to be approximately four days ago. It appears that he snapped her neck. A quick and fast death. The fire was set postmortem."

"Just like the others. He kills them, then places them in the stone circles and sets the fire."

"There's something else that was interesting," Dr. Chi gestured toward photos she'd taken of the bones. "Look at this tiny indentation in the mastoid bone."

"The bone behind the ear?" Ellie asked.

"Yes." She used her pen to point to the exact area. "At first I thought it was a result of her injuries, but when I took another look, I realized it had been carved into the bone by a sharp instrument."

Ellie looked closely at the photo, her heart stuttering as she realized the markings formed a shape. "It looks like an hourglass." She contemplated the meaning. "An hourglass is a symbol of the sands of time, that time doesn't last forever." Just like burning the bodies meant that we are nothing, that in death we turn to ashes. "The hourglass obviously has a special meaning to the person who killed Gillian. She was out of time."

A strange expression tinged Laney's eyes. "I have to check something."

Laney pulled a file from the organizer on her desk. Katie Lee's photo lay on top, the grisly sight of her twisted and mangled body a reminder of the killer's depravity.

Laney turned the photograph so that they could see. "Look at those cuts behind her ear."

Ellie examined the picture.

"I thought those were just scratches and scrapes sustained from falling on the jagged rocks, so I didn't think anything about them, but—"

"They do look crude," Ellie admitted, her stomach plummeting. "But I'm willing to bet it's an hourglass."

# CHAPTER 54

A half hour later in the autopsy room, Ellie was still struggling to pull herself together when Laney dropped another bombshell.

"The third body is Vanessa Morely," Laney said as she compared Vanessa's dental and medical records to the body on her table, the bridge in the victim's mouth confirming her ID.

Ellie swayed slightly, emotions flooding her.

"Are you okay?" asked Laney, touching her arm to steady her.

"I knew Vanessa from school. We used to play together as kids." In her mind, she saw Vanessa chasing frogs in the creek and making mud pies, her pigtails bobbing up and down as she skipped. God, she wished she'd reconnected with her.

And her daughter… poor Mandy.

"I'm so sorry," Laney said softly.

Dr. Chi hurried to the sink and returned with a paper cup of water. "Here, drink this."

Ellie straightened and accepted the water, sipping it slowly. Questions ticked through her head at lightning speed.

Was there a connection between the victims? Katie Lee was a high-school student with an overprotective father and a family who attended Ole Glory Church. Had Gillian attended that church too? How about Vanessa? Or did Katie Lee or Vanessa contact Gillian for some reason?

Mandy's young face taunted her. "I have to notify Vanessa's daughter and her sister." She just wished she had answers to give them when she did.

Vanessa's body lay draped in a sheet. The strong odor of cleaning chemicals assaulted Ellie, mingling with the putrid scent of death and body decomposition.

Vanessa's skin was purple and black, the bruising pattern around her neck consistent with rope burns. Ellie didn't see handprints on her neck, although her upper arms were bruised. The pale, battered body before her was nothing like the Vanessa she remembered. The vibrant girl in high school who'd made the cheerleading squad. Although they'd run different paths, Ellie had been happy Vanessa had come out of her shell. She'd expected Vanessa to go on to college and be successful. Then she'd had Mandy and never left town while Ellie had gone off to the academy. Ellie had no idea what had happened afterwards.

Laney gently turned Vanessa's head to one side, using her magnifier to study the area behind her ear. "Not there." She turned her head to the opposite side and made a small sound in her throat.

"There it is."

Ellie moved closer, her heart thumping wildly when she spotted the hourglass carved all the way to the bone.

# CHAPTER 55

"I've never seen anything like it," Laney said.

"Me neither," Ellie murmured. "I don't want a word of this leaked until I have time to investigate. I especially don't want details of the hourglass carving to be revealed or that we might have another serial killer in this county. We have to withhold details from the public, so don't talk to the reporters or your friends. Not even pillow talk."

"Ellie," Laney said, her tone irritated, "you know I would never do that."

"Neither would I," Dr. Chi said. "I understand the importance of discretion."

"I didn't mean to imply you would be anything other than professional," Ellie said and meant it. "I was just thinking about our sheriff running his mouth to the Weekday Killer."

Laney squeezed her arm. "I know you've had a lot to deal with. I'll do whatever I can to help."

"Thank you both," Ellie said. "Can you determine cause of death?"

"Asphyxiation due to strangulation," Laney replied. "Set fire to afterwards."

The image of the killer tying that rope around Vanessa's neck and then dragging her across the ground blinked behind Ellie's eyes. She had probably fought, screamed… thought about her daughter.

"Ellie, maybe you should let someone else handle this," Laney suggested.

"No, I promised Mandy I'd find her mother. Now… I have to tell her I did, but she's dead."

Ellie excused herself, then walked down the hall. Her stomach was churning, so she ducked inside the ladies' room and splashed cold water on her face. She couldn't help but wonder about Gillian. Instinct told her that the missing files held the answer.

Patting her face dry with a paper towel, she decided to stop by Raintree Family Services and speak with Gillian's assistant before she went to the Morelys'. She needed time to pull herself together. Mandy and Vanessa's sister would be full of questions.

Questions she didn't know how to answer.

# CHAPTER 56

*Cleveland, GA*

Ellie entered the office of Raintree Family Services, an older two-story home on the town square. A raven-haired woman in her late thirties sat behind the desk on the phone, her gold loop earrings bobbing up and down as she moved. The building seemed quiet, the sound of the air conditioner rattling filling the room. No voices or phones ringing indicating anyone else was here.

She crossed to the receptionist. "Annalise? I'm Detective Ellie Reeves. We spoke on the phone before. Are you alone here?"

"I am. Velma's on a home visit, and Rochelle is in court with a foster care hearing." Worry knitted the woman's slender face. "Did you locate Gillian?"

Ellie hadn't yet divulged the social worker's ID to the press. But with no family to notify and needing information, her best bet was to confide in Annalise. "I'm afraid we did. And I'm sorry to report that she's dead."

"Oh, my word," said Annalise, clutching her chest. "Not Gillian… She was always so kind and helpful to others."

Ellie gave the woman a moment to process the news. "Wh-what happened?" she asked, finally recovering.

"Evidence indicates she was murdered," Ellie said gently.

The color drained from her face. "No… poor Gillian." She reached for a tissue on her desk and dabbed her eyes. "Who would hurt Gillian?"

"That's what I want you to help me with," Ellie said. "Was Gillian seeing anyone? Did she have a lover or partner?"

"Not that I knew of. She was married to this job."

"You mentioned that she carried work files home, but I didn't find them. I'm going to need a list of anyone who might have been upset with her or held a grudge against her."

Annalise gave a shaky nod. "She didn't really confide in me, but I'll ask the other two social workers. They might know more."

"Thank you. I need her computer."

"She took her laptop with her that day," said the receptionist, tapping her acrylic nails on her desk.

"It wasn't at her house or in her car. Is there a way you can determine which files she took?" Ellie asked.

"I might be able to. But that will take time. I'll get right on it." An eagerness flashed in the woman's eyes. Ellie had learned that one coping skill when faced with grief was to have something to do to feel useful.

"Thank you." Ellie swallowed. "Do you know if Gillian ever spoke to a young girl named Katie Lee Curtis or one of her family members?"

"That's the teenage girl who was killed?"

Ellie nodded. "Did you know her?"

"I don't recall her or anyone from the family being here, but I'll check when I sort through our system."

"Please do," Ellie said. "I also want you to look for a Vanessa Morely."

Annalise's eyebrows furrowed in confusion. "I don't understand. What do they have to do with Gillian's death?"

"I think they were killed by the same person."

# CHAPTER 57

*Stony Gap*

Bracing herself for the grim task ahead, Ellie walked up to Vanessa's house. Nerves bunched Ellie's shoulders as she thought about how much Vanessa would miss out on. She wouldn't be there for her daughter's prom or wedding or if she had a baby. Trudy opened the door, her face ashen and her eyes wary. As she showed Ellie inside, Mandy raced down the stairs, eyes red and swollen.

"You found my sister, didn't you?" Trudy asked, a quiver to her voice.

Ellie gave them both a sympathetic look. "I really didn't want to be here saying this, but I'm afraid so."

"Where is she?" Mandy said, tears filling her eyes.

"At the morgue," Ellie said softly. "I'm so sorry."

Trudy took her niece by the arm and guided her toward the living room, looking lost as to what to do. Mandy wrapped her arms around her middle, rocking back and forth, a wail escaping her.

"What happened?" Trudy asked finally.

Ellie didn't intend to share the gruesome details. "She was strangled."

"Someone murdered her?" Mandy cried in horror.

"I'm so sorry, honey," confirmed Ellie. "I know this is painful to hear."

Mandy choked on a sob, then turned and ran outside. Through the window, she saw the girl kicking a soccer ball, pounding it against the garage door.

"I'm sorry, Detective. She's been so distraught."

"No need to apologize," Ellie said over the lump in her throat. "Her whole world just got turned upside down."

"I can't believe this is happening, that she's gone." Trudy's gaze searched Ellie's. "Do you know who killed her?"

"Not yet."

Trudy leaned her head into her hands for a minute and Ellie gave her time to absorb the shock.

After a moment, Ellie said, "The first forty-eight hours are critical in finding a killer, so I need to ask you some questions. If that's all right, of course."

Trudy wiped at her eyes, then gave a slim nod.

"Do you have any other family I can call?"

"No. Our mother died in childbirth, so Vanessa never knew her. I don't remember much about her either."

"What about your grandmother?" Ellie said, recalling the plump older woman who always smelled of gingerbread and molasses.

"She died a few years ago."

"Was Vanessa close to anyone else, someone she might have confided in?"

"Not that I know of," Trudy said. "But I can ask Mandy."

"Thanks," said Ellie. "Did Vanessa attend the Ole Glory Church?"

"Are you kidding?" A sardonic laugh escaped the woman. "Vanessa never went to church period."

"Did she ever mention a woman named Gillian Roach?"

Trudy shook her head. "I'm sorry I'm not more helpful. You must think I'm a terrible sister."

"I don't think that at all," Ellie said.

The sound of the ball pounding against the garage door grew louder. "When Mandy is ready to talk, please ask her. Give me a call when you do."

Ellie choked back her own tears as she let herself out. She should be hardening to this, but she'd almost lost her own mother and it had broken her. Mandy hadn't even had a chance to say goodbye.

The hot, still air robbed her breath as she made her way to her Jeep. A dog howled somewhere nearby, a black hawk soaring toward the jagged mountaintops. Silence hovered over the peaks and valleys like a heavy weight, night falling and casting the sharp ridges in shadowy grays. It was a vicious reminder that another predator lurked in the hills. Was he hunting his next victim now?

# CHAPTER 58

*Crooked Creek Police Station*

"What the hell is going on, Ellie?" Bryce yelled as he stormed into Ellie's office a half hour later. "I expected an update from you on the Curtis case."

"I've been a little busy," Ellie said, her hackles instantly raised. "The ME confirmed that the latest body we found is Vanessa Morely, and I had to notify the family."

Bryce made a low sound in his throat. "She's certain?"

"Yes," Ellie said, surprised at the shift in Bryce's voice. Then again, he had taken Vanessa to prom in high school. "Have you talked to her recently at Haints?"

He hesitated a little too long.

"Bryce, what are you holding back?"

After a beat, he cleared his throat. "She waited on me a few times, but we didn't hang out or date. The other night she seemed jumpy, said she thought someone was watching her, I walked her to her car, but I just figured she was spooked because of the murders."

"Her daughter Mandy said she was nervous," Ellie admitted. "Did you learn anything from Vanessa's coworkers?"

"Only that she dated around," Bryce said. "She hadn't mentioned a problem to anyone."

"Anything on the security cams?"

"Just people coming and going from the bar. No sign of anyone stalking the vicinity."

"Dr. Whitefeather found something else," said Ellie, explaining about the hourglass carvings. "Don't go spilling that to the press. We don't want to trigger a copycat or escalate the unsub because he knows we found the marks."

"You're not going to let it go that I talked to Burton, are you?"

"It's hard not to remember it," Ellie pointed out. "Shondra and I both have scars from his handiwork." Hers weren't as deep as her friend's. The whip marks on Shondra's back might never fade but it was the emotional trauma she was most worried about.

"I said I was sorry," Bryce said.

"Have you said it to Shondra?" His hesitation told her he hadn't.

"Until you do, don't expect forgiveness from either one of us." She wiped her clammy hands on her jeans as she stormed out.

Knowing she couldn't sleep yet, she went to the conference room and added a photo of Vanessa and the crime scene to the murder board.

Standing back, she compared the details of the victims' lives, searching for something she'd missed, something to tie them together.

Nothing jumped out at her.

Next, she wrote the word UNSUB, short for unknown subject, in a separate column. What did she know about him?

That he used various methods to kill his victims. After that, he set a fire around them. He created a monument of standing stones and carved an hourglass into the bone behind his victims' ears.

Why was time significant to this killer? Had he waited with the victim for an hour after he killed her? Did it take an hour for her to die? That might have been true with Gillian or Katie Lee, but if Vanessa was strangled by the rope, her death would have been quicker.

How could she determine the perpetrator's identity when she had no idea how or why he'd chosen to murder these particular victims?

Did it all come back to Gillian Roach?

The questions spun in her mind, dizzying her.

Thinking back to the hourglass, she wondered if this unsub had struck before. Deputy Landrum could research that, but a crime like this would have gained media and police attention in the area. But if the killer had struck in a different area or state, it wouldn't necessarily have been on her radar.

One person who could help was Special Agent Derrick Fox.

Although the sheriff detested calling in the feds, she didn't have a choice. Derrick had access to resources that she didn't, and he'd already offered to help. Her victims deserved for her to do everything she could to get them justice.

# CHAPTER 59

*Atlanta, Georgia*

Special Agent Derrick Fox stared into his bourbon as he watched the evening news. This mandated time off was fucking with his head.

He'd been following the story in Crooked Creek ever since it had broken. Those mountains had gotten in his soul, and it had been hard to leave them behind for the city.

"This is Angelica Gomez for Channel 5 news, here with Bluff County's Sheriff Bryce Waters and arson investigator Max Weatherby," the reporter stated. "Sheriff, what can you tell us about the woman who was found at Death's Door?"

"We have identified her as thirty-year-old Vanessa Morely." Waters paused. "We also have identified the first victim found. Her name was Gillian Roach."

His phone rang and he saw it was Ellie. Keeping one eye on the TV, he answered. "Hey, I was just watching your sheriff on the news."

She grunted. "Then you know we have another murder?"

"Yes."

"Vanessa Morely… I grew up with her."

His lungs tightened at the raw pain in her voice. "I'm sorry. You think you're dealing with one killer?"

"Yes, and I need your help."

He swirled his bourbon around in his glass, watching the dark amber liquid as the scent of caramel and vanilla greeted him.

Hearing Ellie's soft voice brought an image of her silky hair and sky-blue eyes to his mind and made his body harden, a reminder of the night they'd slept together on the first case they'd worked on. A night he couldn't repeat. Emotions didn't belong in the job. And he had too much baggage for a relationship. "What can I do?"

"The MO varies slightly, but the scenes are all similar. After death, he places the victims in the center of a stone circle and burns their bodies."

"Overkill, or he's destroying evidence?"

"Not sure."

He sipped his drink patiently, savoring the earthiness and feeling the warmth seep down his throat.

"The killer has a signature. He carves a tiny hourglass behind each of his victims' ears."

"That's distinctive."

"I know. Can you search for other murders with a similar signature?"

"Of course," Derrick said. That was a logical first step. "I take it that you aren't releasing this information to the press."

"No, I'm not," Ellie said. "Right now, we're focusing on each individual, their lifestyles, enemies and families. There has to be a commonality between the three victims, but I haven't figured it out yet. There's something else that's disturbing."

*More disturbing than another serial killer stalking the Appalachian Trail?* "Go on."

"The first victim's name was Gillian Roach. She's the social worker who handled my adoption."

He ground his teeth. "Were you in contact prior to her death?"

"No, but I had left a message saying I needed to speak with her," Ellie said in a low voice. "But she disappeared a few days before that."

Derrick set his highball glass onto the corner desk. "I'll run that search."

She thanked him and hung up before he could ask anything personal. Like how she was doing. If she was having nightmares about the Weekday Killer. If Vera and Randall knew she was looking for her birth parents. The unspoken words were stuck in his throat, and he washed them down with more whiskey.

# CHAPTER 60

The scent of smoke lingered from the recent fire, and his eyes felt gritty as he walked mile after mile. He was best alone in the wilderness, away from the sights and the sounds he couldn't drown out. Things that tormented him and triggered the pain and the nightmares that clawed at his sanity.

Except he couldn't exactly call them nightmares. Nightmares happened when you slept, and sleep was the demon he chased at night.

But he continued to fail, spending endless hours staring into the dark, hoping it would come for him and give his body a rest. Endless hours that stretched into days where he couldn't remember where he'd been and what he'd done.

Endless moments of waking up and finding himself in strange places with blood on his hands and clothes and the nasty scent of death permeating his soul.

If he had a soul. Sometimes he didn't know.

He'd been suffering from insomnia ever since he was a child. The night terrors had started when he was five and consumed him ever since, burning into dark fantasies.

They'd gotten so bad he'd climb from bed, walk through the house like he was half dead and stand over his mother, staring into her face yet seeing nothing, screaming as if the devil had gotten inside him.

One night he'd grabbed a butcher knife and shredded the curtains in her bedroom. Even her terrified shouts had not shaken him from the trance. She'd thought he was possessed and started tying him to his bed at night, locking him in the tiny dark room and leaving him alone to imagine what he would do to her if he escaped. Maybe the fire would be real, and he'd set her hair ablaze. Or maybe he'd push her into the street until a car came along and crushed her like a bug, splattering her guts over the asphalt.

One stormy night when the wind shook the house and falling tree branches banged the windows, something had snapped in his mind. The screeching sounds had tormented him, fueling his strength, and he'd managed to yank the wooden bed post from the frame. Then he'd ripped the ropes from his hands and beaten the door with his baseball bat until the wood splintered and he crawled through the opening. His daddy had run off long ago, but he'd left his shotgun behind. His mother kept it locked in a cabinet, but he smashed the glass, grabbed the gun and slipped into her bedroom. He'd seen nothing but the fluffy white bedding and the lump beneath the covers so he'd fired the gun straight at the wall above the bed where his mother was sleeping.

She'd jumped up, screaming like a banshee, and he'd fired the gun at her head. She'd ducked, running from the room and out the front door. Still lost in the place between sleep and coherency, he'd fired one cartridge then another at her.

Before he knew it, the police showed up, and he heard his mother yelling that he was a monster. Sometime later, he'd come out of the trance and found himself locked in a hospital for *sick* boys.

The smoky odor of burned lumber and brush swirled around him, and his vision was blurring. There were weeks when he lived among the normal folks and weeks when he disappeared into his head and the woods and lived among the animals and the shadows.

His watch buzzed, and he checked the time as the chime echoed in his head, sending him back in time. He was strapped to the table, the light burning his eyes, the ticking of the clock reverberating around him. A sharp stinging pain screamed through his head. An earsplitting screeching sound took over him.

The sand began to slip through the hourglass. *Ticktock, ticktock.*

His fingers dug into his pockets and one hand brushed the knife he used for carving while the other fingered the matches.

It was time. Another woman had to die.

# CHAPTER 61

*Laurel Springs*

Sarah Houston dragged herself up from the floor, her arm hanging limply by her side, the pain so intense that nausea bubbled in her throat. Blood dripped from her lip and her eye was nearly swollen shut.

She had no idea what had happened, but after she and Ryder had come home from finding that woman's body, he'd acted as if he was possessed. She'd been upset and wanted him to hold her, but he'd shoved her away with such force she'd fallen and banged her head against the corner of the kitchen table.

At first, she'd thought it was an accident, but then he'd jerked her arm and twisted it behind her back until she heard the bone snap. Pain had ricocheted up her arm and shoulder, and she'd screamed and doubled over. His fists became lethal, and he'd hit her over and over as if she was nothing more than a punching bag.

She'd pleaded, begged him to stop, but his eyes were so glassy, it was almost as if he wasn't looking at her. As if his mind was somewhere else.

After he'd purged his rage, she'd collapsed into a puddle on the floor and he'd stalked out, slamming the door behind him. She was terrified he'd come back.

Tears mingled with the blood on her cheeks, and she struggled to crawl to her phone. She needed help.

But the room was spinning and twirling, and bile clogged her throat. She cried out, forced herself another inch. Her phone was in sight, just over there, on the kitchen counter. Her ribs ached, a stabbing pain splintering her every time she took a breath. Another inch. Another. But as she reached for the chair to drag herself up, the chair toppled over, and she fell backwards again.

Pain seared her as the world went dark.

# CHAPTER 62

*River's Edge*

Before Ellie had left the police station, Bryce texted that one of the waitresses had seen a man named Ryder Rigdon talking to Vanessa. He'd failed to mention that he knew her when he'd discovered her body. Ellie wanted to know the reason.

His home in River's Edge overlooked the eponymous river, surrounded by oaks. Ellie scanned the yard and driveway but didn't see a car in sight. The scent of smoke from the fires hung in the still, muggy air, and the lights were off inside as she walked up to the door. Hand on her weapon, she punched the doorbell.

She tapped her foot, raised her fist and knocked, listening for signs that someone was inside. Except for the buzzing of mosquitoes everything was quiet.

"Mr. Rigdon, it's Detective Reeves, I need to speak to you." She waited several more seconds, then shined her flashlight through the front window. There was no movement or lights on. She jiggled the doorknob, hoping it was unlocked, but no luck. Using her torch to illuminate the way, she walked around the exterior of the cabin, checking the windows and back door, but they were all shut tight.

She would have to get a search warrant, but she needed more evidence for that.

She returned to her Jeep, cranked the engine and headed toward Sarah's. The night sky was so black that Ellie had to crawl around the winding switchbacks, her unease mounting as she climbed up the mountain. The ten miles to the small community called Laurel Springs seemed to take forever.

A sliver of moonlight seeped through the black but quickly disappeared behind a cloud. She finally reached Sarah's small rustic house. It was set on a hill, with mountain laurel dotting the backyard. There was a white picket fence and ferns hung from the front porch, while metal yard art in the shape of sunflowers lined the cobblestone path to the porch steps.

A light was burning through a window to the right of the steps, and a white SUV emblazoned with the logo *Scents by Sarah* sat in the driveway. No other vehicle, which meant Ryder might not be here.

She parked, her senses honed as she let herself inside the gate then walked up to the porch. The wood boards squeaked as she climbed them. The door was ajar.

Instantly the hair on the back of her neck prickled. "Sarah, it's Detective Reeves," she called out. Slowly she inched inside the hall, pausing to listen, but dead silence stretched around her, thick with the sense that something was wrong.

"Sarah, it's Detective Ellie Reeves, are you here?"

The pine floor creaked as she crept toward the kitchen area where the light was burning. Water dripped from the faucet, and a low moan broke into the night.

Ellie's heart sprinted as she spotted Sarah lying on the floor, blood pooling around her head, her fingers stretched out in a cry for help.

# CHAPTER 63

*Cherokee Point*

The late-night news segment repeatedly played in Janie Huntington's mind, sending terror through her. As soon as it ended, she'd called her brother and asked him to come and get Will. She needed to save her son.

The sheriff of Bluff County was close-mouthed about the three murders that had occurred in the county. Bodies all found on the Appalachian Trail. Bodies he'd given no details on—except for their names.

Katie Lee Curtis was Agnes's daughter. And Gillian Roach… she knew that name, too.

It was happening just like she'd feared. She'd kept her mouth shut but someone else must have opened the can of worms by asking questions. Questions that would get them all killed.

Her heart hammering, she dragged her suitcase from the closet, then snatched jeans, T-shirts and underwear at random, not bothering to fold them as she shoved them into the bag. Her toiletries were piled in next, then she laid down on her belly on the floor and retrieved the shoebox where she kept her emergency stash of cash. Yanking it out, she thumbed through for a quick count. Nine hundred. She shoved it in her purse.

It was enough to get by on until she could figure out what to do.

He would be coming for her next. Some of the girls didn't remember, but his face was etched in her mind permanently. She'd never forget that musky odor. Never forget his breath on her. Never forget the sinister warning in his eyes.

*Talk and you die.*

For a second, her hand hovered over her phone, and she considered calling that detective. But that might put her son in jeopardy. And then he would find out the truth.

She'd protected him from that so far and she didn't intend to give up now.

She snagged her stuff and crept to the door. Pulse racing, she slipped outside and dashed toward her car.

In the darkness, a figure moved toward her, and she lunged for the car door. He grabbed her from behind, but rage fueled her adrenaline, and she jabbed her elbow into his chest then turned and sprayed him in the face with the mace.

Bellowing, he staggered backward for a second, loosening his grip on her. She took advantage of that second, and dove into the car. He lunged at the door, but she fired up the engine, pressed the accelerator and sped from the driveway, tires screeching as she slung gravel.

Glancing in the rearview mirror, the moonlight illuminated his evil face. He'd find her eventually. And when he did, she'd kill him.

# CHAPTER 64

*Laurel Springs*

Ellie stooped down beside Sarah and stroked her hand. "I'm here, Sarah. It's Detective Reeves. I'm calling an ambulance."

The woman moaned, her eyes lolling back as she passed out. Ellie felt for a pulse as she rang for help.

"911," the emergency responder said.

"I need an ambulance." Ellie identified herself and quickly recited the address. "Female, approximately thirty, severely beaten. She's lost a lot of blood, appears to have a broken arm, possible head injury." She raced to the kitchen and opened drawers, grabbing kitchen towels.

"Help is ten minutes away. Can you stay with the woman?"

"I'll be here. Am applying blood stoppers now." Her breath panted out as she hurried over to Sarah, knelt, gently lifted her head and pressed the cloths to her injury to stem the blood flow.

"Sarah, honey, hang in there. Tell me who did this to you."

The poor woman's breathing grew even more shallow, and Ellie wondered if she'd make it through the night. Needing to act, she phoned the sheriff.

"Sheriff Waters," he mumbled, his voice slurred.

Rage shot through Ellie. She thought he might have learned a lesson on the last case, but it seemed like the bottle was getting the best of him. "Sorry, butt dial." She hung up, ringing her boss instead and explained what she'd found. "Medics are on the way to Sarah Preston's house. We need to issue an APB for Ryder Rigdon and a warrant for his house. He may be armed and dangerous."

"On it," Captain Hale said. "I'll get Deputy Landrum to find out what kind of vehicle he drives. And if he has another property where he might go to hide out."

A siren wailed in the distance. "I'll follow the ambulance to the hospital and stay with Sarah to see if she can identify her attacker."

# CHAPTER 65

*Bear Mountain*

Janie mopped her forehead as heat lightning sizzled above the hills. A car had followed her for miles. She'd taken every shortcut and side street she knew, and she thought she'd escaped him.

Panic made her head swim, and she swerved into the parking lot for the gun and ammo store tucked on the corner of Bear Mountain. A shiver coursed through her.

She wasn't far from where it had all happened. Where her life and her future had been stolen.

*You have Will.*

He was her life now. Her future. Protecting him was all that mattered. She'd warned him to stay away from Katie Lee. But he hadn't listened, and now the girl was dead.

Her son would not die, though.

Nervous energy made her almost run over the curb and she barreled over a tin can. It was surprising that the parking lot was empty, but at least no one would see her make her purchase. During hunting seasons, the targets out back were occupied with hunters. She'd heard cops liked to come here to practice, enjoying the wildlife and natural setting while they fired into animal-shaped targets.

Disgust filled her at the thought of killing any live creature.

Except for *him.*

She'd been running for years now, and she'd thought she was safe. But she wasn't. She never would be unless she ended it.

Taking a fortifying breath, she threw the car into park, climbed out and hurried toward the entrance.

Her eyes scanned the road for the car, then the deserted woods beyond.

The trees suddenly shook, thunder rumbling and dark clouds moving overhead. A feral cat screeched and darted around the side of the building as she broke into a jog, pounding on the door. But no one came. She peeked through the glass window and realized the place was closed.

Panic shot through her. She had to get a gun. Tonight.

Suddenly bright lights beamed in her face, tires screeching as a truck pulled into the parking lot.

She ran toward her car, but the door of the truck opened, and a hulking figure emerged from it. She dove for her car door, but he beat her to it. Terrified, she screamed, then turned and ran toward the woods.

She heard him behind her. His boots crushing the weeds and grass as he closed the distance. His breath on her as he reached for her.

# CHAPTER 66

*Bluff County Hospital*

The plain round clock on the sterile white walls of the hospital room struck 4 a.m., the drone of the nurses' voices and footsteps in the hall echoing softly.

The head nurse had scribbled Ellie's name on the whiteboard facing Sarah's bed, and Ellie had insisted she write her own number on there for emergency's sake. But she hadn't been able to bring herself to leave.

She stretched out in the recliner beside Sarah's bed, willing the young woman to survive and name her attacker.

She thought it was Ryder Rigdon. But she needed proof. A positive ID would be the easiest way to nail the bastard.

Her eyes hurt from lack of sleep the night before and her head throbbed like a mother.

Machines beeped, oxygen feeding the battered woman air. Her arm was broken, reset through surgery and now cast. Bruises marred her face, her eye was swollen shut, her lip cut. Other injuries included three cracked ribs and a concussion. A heart monitor verified she had a pulse, although you'd never know it from the still way Sarah lay, as if death had already claimed her.

Not long ago, Ellie's own mother had nearly lost her will to live in this very hospital.

*Don't think about it. Vera made it. Sarah will, too.*

Closing her eyes, she fell into a fitful sleep. In her dreams, she was combing the trail in search of more bodies. The dead called to her. The predator's eyes peered at her through the dark cover of the trees and bushes. Sinister sounds echoed in the still air, the howl of a lone wolf. The growl of a bobcat.

The whispered hum of a killer.

By dawn, she jerked awake, overwhelmed by the sense that another woman had fallen victim to the ruthless killer. Had they left Sarah for dead and gone after another?

She rose, tiptoed over and gently eased Sarah's hair aside to check behind her ear. No hourglass carving behind the left one. Her breath tightening, she examined the other. But there was no carving there either.

Had he been interrupted before he could finish the job?

The nurse came in to check Sarah's vitals, and she moaned, but faded back into unconsciousness.

"How's she doing?" Ellie asked.

"She's in critical condition," the nurse said. "Her body needs rest and time."

"When do you think she might wake up?"

"That's hard to predict," the nurse said. "People heal at different rates. But the next twenty-four hours will be key."

Ellie glanced at the clock. She needed to get a shower, obtain that warrant and search Ryder's house. But the thought of leaving Sarah here alone, to wake up without a hand to hold or someone to talk to, made her heart ache.

Debating what to do, the answer suddenly came to her, and she called Shondra's number. Two rings, then Shondra's voicemail kicked in, and she left a message. "Shondra, I know you're having a hard time, but I need your help. Last night I found a young woman who'd been severely beaten. I'm at the hospital with her now." She swallowed, waiting, but Shondra didn't pick up. "I have to execute a search warrant for a suspect this morning, and I hate to leave her alone. When she regains consciousness, we need to question her.

Could you sit with her? You're a professional, and you understand more about what she's been through than I do."

She sighed, on the verge of hanging up, when Shondra picked up. "I heard you, Ellie. Where is she?"

Relief filled Ellie. "Bluff County Hospital. Her name is Sarah Houston. She and a man named Ryder Rigdon discovered the body at Death's Door. I went to question them but found Sarah on the floor unconscious."

"I'll come and sit with her."

"Thanks. I figured if anyone could help her, you could."

# CHAPTER 67

*Cold Springs*

Brittle twigs and weeds clawed at Janie as the man dragged her through the forest. She kicked at him and punched his legs, but he backhanded her, and stars swam behind her eyes.

God help her. She'd almost gotten loose for a moment and tried to outrun him, but he was a bear of a man and so strong that her punches didn't faze him. His eyes looked distant and dull, his movements almost robotic as he'd tied her hands together then bound her feet.

Pain stole her breath from the blow he'd delivered to her ribs and face, and sharp rocks and briars scraped her cheeks as he dragged her over a hill. The fetid scent of a dead animal assaulted her, and she gagged. Creek water gurgled nearby, then he hauled her around a tree stump, over some damp moss, and through a section of dead pine needles.

When he came to the creek, he halted. This was her last chance.

"Please let me go," she cried. "I promise I won't say anything. I'll disappear and no one will ever know."

He towered over her, his black T-shirt and jeans making him almost invisible as the dawn light struggled to penetrate the woods. The ropes around her wrists and feet dug into her skin. He grabbed her arms and hauled her into the water. She kicked and struggled with all her might, but he pressed his boot on her chest and pushed her so hard that she sank beneath the surface.

The icy water stung her eyes and cheeks, and she held her breath, kicking and flailing. Fear choked her as her lungs strained for air.

The water swirled around her, slapped at her face and seeped into her nostrils as he pushed her deeper. Her limbs felt heavy, and she tried to grab his foot, but he knelt and looked down into her face, using his beefy hands to pin her down.

Terror rushed through her. She couldn't hold her breath any longer. Frigid water gushed into her mouth and throat and her body felt as if it was on fire. Needle-like pain stabbed her eyes and ears, then she felt her lungs expanding as water filled them. Faces of strangers she'd never known blurred in front of her, then images of her son the night he was born. She'd been alone and frightened. She thought she'd found a safe place to hide and had escaped her past.

Blurred images—faces, children's, babies—floated in front of her eyes, the sound of a crying infant ripping through her mind. She made one last attempt to reach for his hands, but she was too weak and death took her.

# CHAPTER 68

A calmness overcame him as he watched her body jerk and shake, then go still. Her brown hair floated in the water, swirling like snakes around her face. Her eyes stared back at him in the shock of death, her skin blue, her mouth slack as water bubbled to the surface.

She sank deeper into the abyss, almost disappeared into the murky creek, but he wasn't finished yet. He lifted her in his arms, carrying her to the bank and laying her on the dry dirt and weeds. Pulling his knife from his pocket, he eased her head into his lap, then twisted it sideways to expose the back of her ear. Feeling with his fingers, he located the mastoid bone then pressed the tip of the blade into her skin.

The sound of the water lapping back and forth transported him back in time. The world blurred then the bright light beamed in his face, painful and hot.

Faces blended together, the soft drone of the man's voice. The screams of the girls. The flicker of the flames.

The hourglass was there, turned over, the grains of sand slipping through, counting away the minutes. *Ticktock, ticktock.*

His breathing grew ragged. Sweat dripped from his face. *Please stop*, he wanted to cry. But he couldn't move. Couldn't stop it. Could only stare into the horror.

The sound of a swooping vulture rent the air, jarring him back to his task, and he twisted the knife into her flesh. Muddy creek water dribbled from her mouth and onto his pants. With his gloved hand, he dug deeper, shaping the hourglass into her skin, smiling as the knife hit bone.

# CHAPTER 69

*Crooked Creek*

Back home, Ellie made an extra strong coffee to jump-start her fatigued body and opted to drink it black. Inhaling the rich pecan odor, she carried her mug to the glass doors overlooking her backyard. Rain clouds dotted the distance, thunderclouds gathering.

Running a hand through her damp hair, she studied the shadows, wondering if Rigdon knew they were looking for him. Was he the man torching the women's bodies? Or was another predator lurking in the hills, feeding his sickness by tormenting his victims then watching their bodies go up in flames?

Her doorbell dinged, startling her. Cord again?

She carried her coffee with her to answer the door, where Special Agent Fox stood on the other side.

For a moment, her heart stuttered. A lock of his thick dark hair fell across his forehead, his jaw set into a frown, his big body rigid. He glanced around her yard as if automatically checking for someone lurking around.

The morning heat blasted her and she opened the door. Or maybe it was how damn sexy the man was. She'd tried her best to forget that they'd slept together, but sometimes at night when her bed was cold and empty, she imagined him there warming it. Soothing her nightmares. Chasing away the demons. But none of that mattered now. *Focus on the case. You called him, remember?*

His eyes raked over her, taking in her robe, and a muscle jumped in his jaw. Her body tingled as if he'd touched her bare skin.

"Ellie, I hope it's not too early."

She tugged the top of her robe together and waved him inside. "No, I was just about to get dressed. It was a long night." She gestured to her coffee. "Want some?"

"Sure."

He followed her to the kitchen where she poured him a cup. He slid onto a bar stool at her island. "What happened?"

Ellie explained about Ryder and finding Sarah unconscious. "Deputy Eastwood is sitting with Sarah so she can talk to her when she wakes up."

His brow shot up. "Deputy Eastwood is back at work?"

"Not officially," Ellie said. "She's been taking some time off."

"How about you? That maniac attacked you, Ellie. Didn't you need some time off, too?"

"I don't have time to take off. I've got three murders to solve."

"Someone else can work the case," he said, worry in his tone.

"You sound like my father. If you're going to nag me, you can turn around and go straight back to—"

"You called me for help," he said, cutting her off. "But I'd be lying if I said I wasn't worried. You just worked and solved two major cases and nearly died both times. That's enough to warrant anyone taking a break." He exhaled. "Even the toughest law officers do it."

Heat climbed Ellie's neck. "I wish to hell everyone would stop telling me that. Let's just concentrate on finding this killer." She circled around the island. "I'm going to get dressed."

She rushed into her bedroom, quickly pulled on jeans and a T-shirt, tugged her hair into a ponytail, and jammed her feet into her boots. Her gun and holster came next, then she met Derrick back in her living room.

His face was troubled as he turned to look at her. "Does the sheriff know you called me?" he asked.

She shook her head. "I told Captain Hale."

"Waters won't like it."

"I don't give a damn." She snatched her keys. "Let's go."

# CHAPTER 70

*Crow's End*

With his eyes closed, the nightmares claimed his soul, taking him back in time. Back to where it all started.

*Red hot heat cloaked him, shimmering and mesmerizing against the darkness. Through the window he saw the stones. Tall, jagged, giant river rocks standing in a circle. Fire danced in the middle, flames flickering.*

*Cold fear made his limbs heavy and his body feel as if it had been dragged across the ground for hours. Hours without sleep.*

*Hours where he prayed the voices would quiet.*

*But they were incessant. Filled his head with images of all the ways he could take a life.*

*Filled his vision with what he had done. With the sins he couldn't outrun.*

*The girls' screams filtered through his hazy mind, the bulging whites of their eyes stark with fear as the firelight was reflected in them.*

*His hand trembled as he lit the match. He didn't want to do it.*

*But they had to die.*

Ticktock. Ticktock. *The command came again, this time more forceful. He struck the match and dropped it into the pile, then watched as the flames turned the bones into ashes.*

# CHAPTER 71

*River's Edge*

After stopping to pick up warrants. Ellie and Derrick drove to Rigdon's house. A streak of lightning shot above the mountains in the distance, thunder rumbling.

She flipped on the radio for an update on conditions. "*This is Cara Soronto, your local meteorologist. The heatwave continues, folks, with no relief in sight. In fact, today expect temperatures to soar to ninety-nine with conditions ripe for thunderstorms, which may include hundreds of lightning strikes that can ignite the dry soils and vegetation that serve as fuel for fire. Air quality is poor today, so those with respiratory and heart conditions should stay inside. In the next two days, we can expect wind gusts to pick up, possibly reaching thirty miles per hour.*"

Ellie shuddered. If that happened, the wildfires might spread rapidly, making it even more dangerous to be on the trail. People in the area might have to evacuate.

The town's Fourth of July celebration would have to be cancelled. The vendors would lose money. The children would be disappointed. All the decorations and floats would have been done for nothing.

But she pushed thoughts of the town celebration aside. How could she celebrate with people dying all around her?

"Do you think Rigdon is responsible for the burned girls?" Derrick asked.

"Hard to say right now. He and Sarah found victim number three, Vanessa Morely." Her stomach clenched. She wished she hadn't let their friendship fall apart. "Rigdon seemed distant at the crime scene, almost cold and unaffected." Ellie hesitated. "Don't killers often want to revisit the scene of their crimes?"

"They do," Derrick said. "But if that was the case, why take Sarah with him?"

"Maybe he planned to kill her there," Ellie said with a frown. "Although if that was his motive, why report the body?"

Derrick's brows arched in question.

"And then why go back to Sarah's and beat her?" Ellie murmured. "Doesn't make sense."

Arriving at Rigdon's, Ellie killed the engine and looked up at the house, which still looked dark inside.

Sunlight fought through the rain clouds and glimmered off the windowpanes, almost blinding. There were no cars in the drive and no tire tracks on the dry ground, indicating Rigdon hadn't been home at all last night.

Weapons at the ready, they approached cautiously, scanning the property around the cabin. The scent of rotting garbage swirled through the air.

Derrick pounded on the door and identified himself, then Ellie set to work unpicking the lock.

He raised another brow at that, but she simply shrugged. Her father had taught her a few tricks long before she'd attended the police academy. Pushing the door open, she stepped inside. "Mr. Rigdon, it's Detective Reeves. Anyone home?"

The sound of a ceiling fan whining echoed from the living room, a clock ticking from the kitchen. Derrick motioned that he'd go to the right, down the hall to what appeared to be the bedrooms, and she nodded that she'd sweep the living room and kitchen.

Senses alert, she inched past a hall hatstand, noting it was bare. Light from the floor-to-ceiling window in the living area spilled onto white oak floors, dust motes floating in the shards of light.

There was no evidence of anything personal in the room. No photographs, no decorations.

Trail guides, maps, and books about the Appalachian Trail lined the oak built-ins, in alphabetical order and exactly aligned. She crossed the room to the pine desk, checked the drawers and found them empty.

Moving onto the kitchen, the cupboards were bare except for one which held assorted canned goods. Just like the books, they were lined in order alphabetically and this time exactly an inch apart.

Ryder Rigdon had to be OCD. Or ex-military, with that kind of order and precision.

The refrigerator was bare, the dishes stacked neatly, all white. It struck her that there was no color in the space. Walking over to the deck, she saw it had no furniture but overlooked the thick forest leading to the river.

Derrick's voice broke into her thoughts. "Did you find anything?"

"Nothing," she said as he came down the hall toward her. "It's almost as if no one lived here."

"I agree. There were no clothes or personal items anywhere in the bedrooms."

"If he was here, he's gone." And if he was the unsub, he'd taken all evidence of his crimes with him.

# CHAPTER 72

*Crooked Creek Police Station*

An hour later, Ellie and Derrick were in the conference room at Crooked Creek Police Station.

The sheriff strode in, looking a little rough around the edges.

He took a look at Agent Fox and cursed. "What the hell?"

"I called him," Ellie said, determined not to take any bullshit this morning. The men had disliked each other from the moment they'd met. Bryce was defensive and territorial and resented the fact that Derrick was a fed. When she'd called Derrick in on the last case, he'd almost had her fired.

She offered him a saccharine smile, knowing it would piss him off more. "We have a new kind of serial killer on our hands, Sheriff, and logic insisted I find out if this perp had struck elsewhere." That shut him up. "Now, let's get started." She indicated the whiteboard with the victims' details.

"The receptionist at Raintree Family Services stated that Gillian took work files with her when she left last Thursday, which was unusual. She's trying to determine exactly which files were taken so we can explore the motive behind her murder. I'm also waiting on a list of possible disgruntled people Gillian worked with."

"Send that list to Deputy Landrum and he can follow up there," Captain Hale said.

Ellie nodded, then continued by summarizing what they knew about Katie Lee Curtis. "She attended Ole Glory Church. Landrum, did you get a copy of their parishioners?"

"I did." He consulted his computer file. "Vanessa Morely was not a member."

She sighed, disappointed that wasn't the connection. She turned to Bryce. "Any updates on the teens who found Katie Lee?"

"Nothing new. I tried talking to Will again, but he wasn't home. When I got his cell, he said he was staying with his uncle for a few days."

"So far we've found no connection between Katie Lee and Vanessa. Vanessa's daughter Mandy said she recognized Katie Lee from school, but they weren't friends. The counselor and teachers at school confirmed the same. Said Marty was protective of his sister, but she hadn't seen evidence of physical abuse. In Katie Lee's journal, she wrote that her father had nothing to do with her."

Agent Fox cleared his throat. "Psychological abuse can be just as bad," he pointed out. "Do you know what his problem was with his daughter?"

Bryce grunted. "Probably because of that church."

Derrick and Ellie exchanged a look. "We can't assume anything," Derrick said.

"Do you actually have information to add or did you just come to criticize us?" said Bryce, shooting him a venomous look.

Ellie bit her tongue to keep from defending Derrick.

"I'm here on request," Derrick said bluntly.

Bryce glared at him. "I found a lead regarding Vanessa. Ryder Rigdon, the man who found her body, knew her from the bar where she worked."

*Geez.* He was going to take credit for uncovering that even though he was too drunk to go after the guy the night before.

"He didn't divulge that when I met him and Sarah Preston at the crime scene," Ellie added, then relayed how she'd found Sarah. "Agent Fox and I searched Rigdon's house this morning but if he had been there, he's gone now."

"He drives a steel-gray SUV," Deputy Landrum interjected. "We have an APB out for him."

Ellie wiped her clammy hands on her jeans. "The killer carved an hourglass into the bone behind the ears of Gillian, Katie Lee and Vanessa. Sarah didn't have one. But it's possible that he was interrupted. Or perhaps Sarah was more personal to him and he decided to let her live."

"Or he's not our perp," Derrick added.

Ellie nodded. "Deputy Eastwood is sitting with Sarah now. Hopefully she'll regain consciousness and be able to tell us who beat her." Anxious to hear what Derrick had to say, she turned the floor over to him. "Agent Fox?"

He wrapped his knuckles on the table. "Detective Reeves asked me to check databases for any cases with similarities that occurred across the country. My preliminary search revealed nothing, but I'm still looking."

Ellie's cell phone vibrated on her hip. A quick glance at it and she raised a finger. "Excuse me. I need to take this."

Stepping into the hallway, she pressed connect. "Detective Ellie Reeves."

"It's Annalise at Raintree Family Services. I have some information for you."

"Go on."

"I'm still working on that list of files that Gillian took, but one of our other social workers said that Gillian seemed nervous lately. She also remembered seeing her stuff a file in her briefcase earlier last week. When she asked about it, Gillian got upset and said it was nothing, that it was an old case file that she needed to get rid of."

Ellie wiped at perspiration beading on her forehead. "Did she see the name on the file?"

"Only part of it. The given name on the file was Mae."

# CHAPTER 73

*Rose Hill*

The screams in Eula Ann's head were growing louder. All night a baby's wail had been shrill and eerie, reverberating like a broken record.

She jerked upright, raking her hand across the bed, shoving the log cabin quilt she'd made when she'd first gotten married to the floor as she felt for the infant. But the bed was empty, as it always was.

She'd been lost in another nightmare, one that recurred from time to time. The aching emptiness inside her sent pain stabbing at every frail bone in her body. An emptiness she'd been forced to accept when she'd learned she would never have a child.

Sweating and shivering at the same time, she threw her bony legs over the side of her iron bed, digging her feet into her worn slippers. As the fog lifted from her brain, she realized the baby's cry hadn't been a baby at all, just the screech of the ceiling fan whirring above, stirring the unforgiving hot air.

Still, the anguish was raw, and she padded through her house to the front porch, threw the door open and stepped outside. Already the temperature had to be near 100. As the sun rose, morning rays hammered down on the ground and trees, frying the blades of grass. Wilted rose petals littered the parched earth, dust swirling through the air as if the dead were carrying on down below.

Maybe the heatwave was God's way of reminding sinners what it would be like in hell when they joined the devil. Not that it mattered. Some were so lost, they reveled in their evil ways, consequences be damned.

The scent of smoke drifted to her, and she looked to the east, toward Cold Springs. Thick plumes curled above the treetops, obliterating the clouds and casting a sea of endless fog over the trail that had always held a natural untamed beauty.

A beauty that was now tainted by another killer torching bodies.

She heard the cries of the dead as if they were standing right there on her porch with her. Saw the lingering pain in the black silhouettes that hovered above the forest.

They wouldn't quiet, not until Ellie Reeves stopped the killing.

# CHAPTER 74

*Crooked Creek*

Ellie stepped back into the conference room. She was anxious about sharing what she'd just learned, but she had to come clean now as it might pertain to the case. She was just about to explain when Bryce's phone rang. He answered, alarm flashing across his face. "I'll be right there." He hung up, then headed toward the door. "Max Weatherby just called. There's another wildfire. I need to go." He turned to Ellie. "You'll keep me updated?"

"Of course."

As soon as he left, Deputy Landrum stood, excusing himself. "I'll start reviewing those police reports."

As people filed out, Derrick cornered her. "Something wrong?"

"Other than having three murders to investigate?" Ellie said dryly.

Derrick's eyes darkened. "You know you always get sarcastic when you're hiding something?"

"Do I now?" *Dammit*, she didn't realize she had a tell, and she didn't like the fact that Derrick had noticed it.

Waiting until everyone else was clearly out of sight, she explained about the phone call from Raintree. "The receptionist is trying to locate the other missing files, but one of Gillian's coworkers saw a file with the name Mae on it."

"Mae?" Derrick asked.

"The name I was given at birth," Ellie said. "Before my parents adopted me."

Derrick took a second. "So you think she was murdered to keep you from getting that file?"

"I thought that for a moment, but she disappeared before I phoned her. I'd been sitting on her name for weeks and hadn't decided whether or not to pursue talking to her."

"Who knew that you had her name and that she handled your adoption?"

Ellie struggled to think. Her head was starting to throb from lack of sleep, her eyes dry and stinging. "Just my parents."

"One of them could have phoned the social worker to give her a heads up."

# CHAPTER 75

Ellie's mind churned. If her adoptive parents had interfered in her life again by contacting Gillian, any semblance of trying to rebuild their family was over. She couldn't tolerate another lie or any more secrets.

Captain Hale poked his head back into the conference room. "Detective, Agent Fox, a 911 call just came in. Another body was found, torched like the others. This time at Cold Springs."

Four victims now. What were they missing?

"I've already called the sheriff and given him a heads-up that it's close to where that wildfire is," Captain Hale said. "I want you out there ASAP, Ellie. I'll call the Evidence Response Team and ME."

"I'll call Cord and ask him to meet us at the approach trail for the springs," Ellie said, snagging her Jeep keys and gesturing to Derrick. "I'll drive."

He didn't argue. She knew the mountains better than he did.

The hot late-morning sun pounded down on them as they hurried outside. She punched Cord's number, got his machine and left him a message. In spite of the recent crimewave, vacationers were flocking to the area for outdoor adventures, and traffic was thicker than the winter months. The parking lot for the Corner Café was packed, pedestrians clogging the sidewalks. While tourists hurried to book whitewater rafting and kayaking tours, and kids licked ice cream cones melting from the heat, they seemed oblivious to the fact that a madman was hiding among them.

Worst of all, Ellie had no idea how to warn them, because she had no idea how this unsub was choosing his victims.

"Do you know where this place is?" Derrick asked as she turned north onto the mountain road which rose high into the wilderness.

Ellie shrugged. "Generally speaking. That's why I asked for Cord."

Derrick glanced out the window at the passing scenery, and she wondered if he still had doubts about Cord and his past. In the last case, Derrick had arrested Cord as a suspect. Having been brought up by a mortician, which fit the profile of the Weekday Killer, who liked to dress his dead victims as if for burial, Cord had come under the spotlight.

But he'd been cleared. Having a dark past didn't mean he was like the people who'd raised him. He'd risen above that. His grit earned her respect and admiration, not her distrust.

While she sped around the winding road, she welcomed the acres of undeveloped land. Land she hoped would never fall into the hands of real estate developers who wanted to turn it into cookie-cutter condos and resort communities that would rob the area of its natural beauty, local culture and charm.

The Jeep ate the miles, although the blinding sunlight forced her to slow down as she negotiated the switchbacks and rounded the sharp cliffs and ridges.

Sunlight flickered through the clouds above, streaking the asphalt as Ellie parked, and gnats swarmed her windshield. Already her clothes were sticking to her, her skin itchy.

She reached behind her and snagged her bug spray to use the moment she got out. Cord hadn't arrived yet, so she pulled her phone. "You want to spray up while I make a call," she told Derrick.

His eyes narrowed, but he took the spray, opened the door and climbed out. Immediately he began swatting at the mosquitoes and flies, then pulled off the cap and began spraying his clothes and hands.

Ellie pressed her father's phone number. On the fourth ring, the voicemail picked up.

"Hey, Dad, I need to talk to you and Mom. I'm heading to another crime scene, but I'll call later before I drop by."

They could rebuild the house, the rooms, mimic the layout and color scheme, her father's office, even her bedroom, but that was just the physical structure of a house. She'd thought their home had been built on good bones, but now the foundation had been shattered.

How could they rebuild what had been inside as a family, and ensure that the memories they'd made still counted, if Vera and Randall were still deceiving her?

# CHAPTER 76

*Cold Springs*

Hill after hill, Ellie and Derrick climbed. Laney and the Evidence Response Team were close behind, along with Cord ahead, who remained brooding and silent. She'd hoped the men might shake hands and start over. But both were prideful and stubborn.

Even from a distance, the scent of smoke was nearly overpowering. She heard the loud crack of a tree as it crashed to the ground and knew the firefighters had their work cut out for them. She'd feared the fire was on top of the area where the woman's body had been left but it was about four miles away. Still, that was nothing when you were talking dry lumber, weeds and brush.

Looking to the sky, she hoped for rain, but even through the branches of the trees and the steep never-ending mountain crests, sun beat through as if it owned the sky. The ground was parched, the river and creeks so low that areas were simply dirt holes.

They passed an empty shelter on the trail, scattered with torn food wrappers and containers that indicated a bear had rummaged through the campsite. The path descended into a shallow valley with rotting vegetation and river stones that had washed up on the bank. The air smelled of pine sap, wildflowers and the choking odor of the smoke drifting through the curtain of trees.

The crack of a deer bolting through the forest was followed by the swish of Cord's blade as he slashed through overgrown vines and led them up a grassy bald. Then they wound down a narrow path carved through the canopy of trees, making the temperature cooler and giving Ellie a sudden chill.

She and the team paused to take a drink of water, then slowly negotiated a knife-edge ridge across a rocky ravine. Downed trees that had fallen during the tornado a few weeks ago blocked a gap between the hills, forcing them to go around and then down into the holler where the creek formed natural springs.

The water there was so clear you could see the bottom and although cold on the surface, below it was like bathwater.

Cord's radio crackled, and he responded, informing the ranger who was first on the scene they were near.

Ellie trudged down the hill until she spotted a gray-haired man with a scruffy beard beneath the shelter of a crop of trees. His overalls looked dirt-stained and he tore off a hunk of chewing tobacco, stuffing it in his cheek.

Cord introduced them to the other ranger. "Man's name is Homer," the ranger said, pointing to the elderly man. "Said he spotted smoke as he was about to set up camp, then went to check it out."

Ellie quickly assessed the scene. The stones encircled the woman, her body burned almost beyond recognition.

She introduced them to the old man. "Did you see anyone else out here?"

"Naw." The old guy shook his head. "Just smelled smoke. By the time I got here the flames were dying down." He spit a stream of tobacco onto the ground. "Sorry. Too late to save her," he muttered with a shake of his head.

Ellie raked her gaze over his clothing again but saw no evidence of smoke or soot. She ruled him out as a suspect. He didn't fit the profile of a methodical cold-blooded killer.

"Any significance to the area?" Derrick asked, gesturing toward the springs.

Ellie planted her hands on her hips. "The other victims were killed prior to being set on fire. With the closeness to the spring water, maybe he drowned her first."

"I'll definitely be able to tell that from the autopsy," Laney said.

Ellie checked the ground for footprints. There were at least two prints, which could belong to the ranger and the old man. The dirt appeared to have been raked in areas to cover up other tracks.

Derrick and the crime scene team remained by the creek edge while the ME began an initial exam. Laney gently checked behind the woman's ear. The grim look she gave Ellie made her stomach twist.

Anger swelled inside Ellie at the sight of the hourglass carved into the woman's bone.

# CHAPTER 77

*Pigeon Lake*

Grief clogged Marty Curtis's throat as he looked out his bedroom window. He could see him and Katie Lee playing tag in the backyard when they were little. His sister liked to run and hunt for four-leaf clovers and pick dandelions, watching the fluffy white seed heads flutter through the air when she blew on them.

She'd rescued injured birds and talked to them as if they had a secret language, and she'd stand still and let bees buzz around her as if she wasn't afraid of their stings. He used to watch them simply fly around her as if she was their queen.

One day their daddy saw it too, and he'd snatched her inside and locked her in her room. He'd said she was a witch. That he'd have to talk to Reverend Ike about her.

He'd heard his sister crying herself to sleep that night, and he'd snuck into her room and hugged her and promised her he'd take care of her, that everything would be all right.

But it hadn't been.

Tears leaked from his eyes, and he opened his window, crawled outside and down the tree to the yard. Sobbing now, he picked dandelions from the yard, climbed the tree again and took them to his sister's room.

Guilt made it hard to breathe. He should have saved her. He'd known something was wrong in his family for a very long time. Nobody talked to each other, and when they did, it was to bow down to his old man, who thought he was God himself.

Marty had been to that church every Sunday and every revival and every Wednesday night dinner since he remembered, and even before then.

"Listen to what Reverend Ike says," his father drilled into him.

Then his father had handed over all their money. He and Katie Lee had worn hand-me-downs and other kids made fun of them while Reverend Ike hoarded their money and wore a big gold ring on his finger.

What kind of preacher took from the poor to pad his own pocket? Didn't seem right to Marty.

Just like it didn't seem right to him the way his daddy treated Katie Lee.

His mama had a picture of him on her knee when he was an infant and Katie Lee just a toddler. Even in that photo, he could see the hate in his father's eyes for his sister.

He just didn't understand the reason.

Katie Lee had followed all the rules, had worked her butt off in school to make straight As, and had no social life—he'd seen her scribbling in that diary she kept to herself about wanting to get out.

When the police had showed up at their door saying she was dead, he'd almost puked his guts out. The thought of her never coming back made him go cold all over.

Then he'd thought about that book. Her secret writing. The tears he'd heard her crying at night. The harsh way their daddy had sent her to her room sometimes for no reason. The way he treated her like she was a piece of gum on his shoe.

That detective had found one of her journals. But he knew where another was hidden. The one where she kept her darkest thoughts. He'd found it once and started to read it, but she'd screamed at him and become hysterical, then their daddy had come running in and demanded to know what was going on.

He'd kept his mouth shut, and Katie Lee had told her daddy she was having cramps.

"Hush your mouth," his daddy had shouted at her. "We don't talk about those things in this house."

Then he'd locked her in her room for the rest of the night.

The house was quiet now as his father and mother were sharing spiritual time. There was nothing spiritual about the way Reverend Ike looked at the young girls in church.

Marty slipped into Katie Lee's room, laid the flowers on her faded bespread, then found the loose board beneath the window by her bed where she hid the journal.

He felt like he was betraying her as he used his fingers to pry loose the board and remove the book from its hidey hole, but maybe it would hold the answers. The floor creaked as he stepped over it, and he jammed the book inside his T-shirt then hurried back to his own room. More than anything he wanted to know who'd killed his sister.

He had a bad feeling his daddy had something to do with it.

# CHAPTER 78

*Cold Springs*

A shudder coursed through Ellie. If the latest victim had drowned, it was an especially painful way of dying. The person experienced complete disorientation, their body felt as if was literally on fire as the lungs strained for air and water began to seep in. Sometimes drowning victims dissociated from their bodies, had hallucinations and had been reported to see faces of strangers floating in front of them. Some thought they actually felt their hands moving to grab at their hearts as they exploded.

Then again, at least she'd been dead before the unsub set fire to her.

The Evidence Response Team photographed the scene and began combing for forensics.

Laney checked the woman's arms, torso and back for injuries, taking her time to magnify suspicious areas. "No gunshot wounds or stab wounds. I don't see an injection site, but I'll run a full tox screen in case she had alcohol, drugs or some other substance in her system." She gestured toward the area behind her ear. "There's the hourglass carving."

Ellie's stomach clenched.

Laney continued, "Her arm was broken. It appears her assailant grabbed her and twisted it, probably while she was fighting for her life."

"He overcame her as she was running away," Ellie said, picturing the scene in her mind. She hadn't stood a chance.

# CHAPTER 79

*Crooked Creek*

Tension stretched between Ellie and Derrick as they headed into the station, a hum of voices echoing from the bullpen.

Through the glass window of her office, Ellie spotted her parents waiting and headed there while Derrick went to the conference room to add the photos of the latest crime scene.

She rolled her shoulders and took a fortifying breath before she joined her parents.

Randall and Vera reached out her arms as if to hug her, but Ellie stiffened. "Thanks for coming."

Her father's frown intensified, crinkling his eyes and making the grooves in his skin look even deeper. Her mother twisted her hands together, looking crestfallen.

Ellie steeled herself against their disappointment.

"Why did you want us to come in?" her father asked.

Ellie squared her shoulders. "I'm sure you've seen the news about the recent deaths."

Her parents exchanged looks, then Randall nodded. A look of trepidation flashed in her mother's eyes. "What does that have to do with us?" her father asked.

Ellie pulled a photo of Gillian from her phone. "Do you recognize this woman?"

"That's Gillian Roach, the social worker we used years ago," Randall said. "Did you talk to her?"

Vera released a shaky breath. "Did you, Ellie? Is that what this is about? You found your birth mother?"

Ellie curled her fingers around the edge of her desk as she sank into her chair. "No, I didn't get a chance. Gillian is dead."

# CHAPTER 80

Ellie's father pulled a hand down his chin. "Dead?"

"That's right. The first victim we found was Gillian."

"Oh, my goodness," said Vera, gasping, "how horrible to die in a fire."

"The fire was not the cause of death," Ellie said. "She was strangled first."

"She was murdered?" Randall leaned back in his chair, arms crossed.

Ellie maintained a neutral expression. "Her body was burned to cover up the evidence."

Vera rubbed her forehead with her fingers, looking shaken.

"So again, I need to know if you talked to her after you gave me her name," Ellie said bluntly.

"What are you implying?" Vera asked, her tone shrill. "You think that *we* killed Gillian?" She lurched up as if Ellie had slapped her in the face. "How could you possibly accuse your own parents of that?"

Ellie flattened her hands on her desk. "I'm not implying anything, Mother. But you've withheld information from me before. Maybe you contacted her to give her a heads up that I might call. Or maybe you changed your mind and didn't want her to give me the information."

Her mother made a rasping sound, and her father placed his hand over Vera's.

"I don't like where you're going with this," Randall said. "We would never do anything to harm Gillian, and we put a lot of thought into it before we revealed her name. We reconciled ourselves to the fact that you needed to know the truth and that we'd deal with your decision." Randall glanced back at the bullpen. "Did Agent Fox put you up to interrogating us?"

"Are you seeing him, Ellie?" Vera asked, her voice cracking.

Ellie gave them both a warning look. "Agent Fox has nothing to do with this. He's here acting as a consultant. Working for the murder victims we've found this week."

Randall looked surprised. "Gillian's murder is connected to that young teenage girl? And to the other woman you found?"

"Yes. We also found another body today. They're all connected, and I'm trying to figure out how."

Vera fiddled with the pearls around her neck, twisting them between her fingers, and Ellie realized she was avoiding eye contact. At one time, she would have trusted Vera completely, but now…

"Mom?" she said firmly. "What aren't you telling me?"

"I'm sorry," Vera said quietly, closing her eyes. "But yes, I called Gillian." She opened her eyes with a pleading look. "I didn't mean any harm. I just wanted her to take care of you."

"Gillian was upset when she left work before she died. She took files with her that day, and another file not long before." A heartbeat passed. "One of them was my file, Mom. The one about Mae."

Guilt flashed on her mother's face. Ellie didn't have to point out the obvious, that Vera's phone call could have gotten the social worker killed.

# CHAPTER 81

Derrick stood outside Ellie's office, tense. He'd heard Ellie asking the Reeves if they'd talked to Gillian and he wanted to know the answer.

Randall thought he'd put her up to it. The damn man vastly underestimated his daughter's intelligence. Ellie didn't need him to tell her how to do her job. She was smart, savvy, and determined—he'd never met anyone with so much gumption. One day he might just tell Randall that.

Vera admitted she'd phoned the woman, and more questions plagued him. How would the killer know that Vera had called Gillian? Had he known the social worker? Had he been watching her?

"I'm sorry, Ellie," Vera said. "I meant no harm."

Randall stood and took his wife's arm. "She wasn't trying to keep you from talking to her. She wanted to make certain Gillian knew that we were okay with her talking to you."

"It wouldn't matter what you thought," Ellie pointed out. "That was between me and Gillian."

"Detective Reeves," Derrick said, "we have the identity of the last victim. We need to go."

Ellie jerked her head up, her gaze meeting his. A myriad of emotions flickered in her eyes, before she addressed her parents, "Did you actually talk to Gillian?"

Vera shook her head. "She didn't answer, so I left a message."

"Exactly when was that?" Ellie pressed.

Vera looked up at Randall, and Ellie's body went rigid. "The truth, Mom."

"Your mother called her last week after her cardiologist appointment. But she's telling you the truth, Ellie. Gillian didn't answer or return her call."

Ellie didn't respond, giving her parents a cold stare. "Don't keep anything else from me."

Her mother's face fell, and she leaned into her husband, but Ellie didn't soften. She lifted her chin and strode past them.

"You know Vera's call could have triggered Gillian's need to run or to hide those files," Derrick said as they rushed outside.

Ellie gave him a seething stare. "You don't have to tell me that." He opened his mouth to say something, but she cut him off.

"You said you knew the last victim's identity?" Ellie asked.

"Yes, Dr. Whitefeather identified her," he said. "Her name is Janie Huntington."

Ellie's breath caught. "Oh, my God. Janie is Will Huntington's mother."

# CHAPTER 82

Stomach churning at the thought of notifying Will that his mother was dead, Ellie called Bryce and relayed Laney's findings. He offered to call the uncle and have them meet at the sheriff's office.

Meanwhile, Ellie and Derrick went to the Corner Café for a bite.

Although she had no appetite, the sight of Maude Hazelnut and her gossip herd didn't help. Eula Ann Frampton was also there, sitting alone at the far end, her small frame almost lost in the shadowy corner. Maude's brood practically clucked as they passed her to get to their table, their judgmental stares rubbing at Ellie's craw.

Ms. Eula might be a recluse, but Ellie didn't think she had a mean bone in her frail little body. In fact, she sensed Eula was stronger than any of the other woman in the café.

Ellie offered her a small smile as she walked past, noting the way Eula worried the beads around her neck as she sipped the herbal tea she always drank.

Deciding tea might help her own stomach, Ellie ordered a cup and a smothered smoked turkey sandwich while Derrick ordered the chili burger that had won Lola the grand prize at the chili cook off last summer. There would be another on the Fourth. Ticket money went to the local Meals on Wheels program. Ellie had already bought half a dozen just to support them.

"So tell me about Will Huntington and his mother," Derrick said as their food arrived.

Ellie explained about Will's connection to Katie Lee. "I don't know if the mothers knew each other or if they're connected to Gillian Roach, but that might be our missing link."

# CHAPTER 83

Derrick knew this was Ellie's case, but she looked like she might break any minute.

Not that she'd admit it. She was proud, strong, stubborn, resilient and smart. That was what had drawn him to come back here.

They convened in the sheriff's office, where Will Huntington and his uncle were seated. The dark-haired kid was twitchy and smelled of cigarettes, while the uncle looked like he'd come from work. He wore a uniform shirt with the logo for an electrical company on the pocket.

Introductions were made, and the sheriff took the lead. For once, Ellie seemed glad to let him.

"Will, Eric," Bryce said addressing the son and uncle. "I'm sorry to have to inform you that Janie is dead."

Will shot up from the chair, reached in his pocket and pulled out a cigarette. He rolled it between his fingers in a nervous gesture, then lifted a lighter, but the uncle shook his head and Will stuffed the lighter back inside his pocket.

"What happened?" Eric asked, his body tense.

"She was murdered," Bryce said bluntly.

A heartbeat of silence passed.

"Do you think it was one of those losers she went out with?" Eric asked.

"Mom never dated," Will snapped, sending an angry glare at his uncle. "Never."

A second passed. "Did your mom complain about anyone bothering her?" Ellie asked.

"No, but she was upset about Katie Lee," Will said. "That's why she was killed, wasn't it?"

Derrick and Ellie exchanged looks, while his uncle glanced at him with a dumbfounded look.

"Why would you say that?" Derrick asked.

Will bounced up and down on his heels. "I don't know," he bellowed.

"Will," his uncle said sternly. "If you know something, tell the police."

Pain wrenched the boy's face. "All I know is that Katie Lee was upset about her parents. Her mama and mine were friends from college. Katie Lee thought something was weird with her folks." He gulped, wiping at his nose as he paced. "She told me she didn't think Mr. Curtis was her real daddy. She was going to find out who was."

# CHAPTER 84

Mabel pulled and yanked at the door, but they'd locked her in the room. They said it was for her own good, that she was a danger to herself.

But that wasn't true. She'd only eaten a few too many pills once or twice because she missed her baby so much.

Then they'd brought her little one back to her, and put her in her arms, and everything was all right again. Except they still kept the door locked, and the window closed. She thought it might be sunny outside, and she wanted to take her precious angel for a walk.

She rocked her daughter in her arms, crooning soft words of love and baby talk that sounded silly to her own ears. But her angel loved them, or maybe she just liked the sound of her mom's voice, even though Mabel couldn't carry a tune in a bucket to save her life. Maybe she just felt the love coming from her heart, a love unlike anything Mabel had ever known she could feel. When she'd pushed her little girl from her body, she'd been overwhelmed with emotions—the sweetest connection possible and a fear that clutched at her with sharp tentacles. That minute she'd known she'd do anything to protect her child.

Anything.

The baby quieted and she banged on the door again. "Let me out. I want to take my baby for a stroll."

She unfolded the blanket and checked the diaper, but it was clean, although where were her little booties? Her feet would get cold outside without them.

"Someone please open the door. My little girl needs her booties!"

But silence crept through the room, the only sound the lingering echo of her own voice and her breathing.

Sinking to the floor, tears spilling over, she clutched her angel tightly in her arms, then she made a tiny scratch on the wall to mark another day that she'd been here.

# CHAPTER 85

*Stony Gap*

Ellie's head was reeling as the poor kid left the sheriff's office. Will's uncle was concerned about his safety, so Bryce walked them out, planning to talk to him about taking the boy to a safe house for a while.

"Did you have any idea Mr. Curtis might not be the girl's father?" Derrick asked.

Ellie shook her head. "The family gave no indication of that. But if it's true, it might explain why Mr. Curtis was so standoffish with Katie Lee. And perhaps why he was so strict and into the church." Ellie's mind raced. "But I don't get the connection with Gillian Roach. Unless Agnes Curtis adopted Katie Lee."

"You want to drive to their house and confront them now?"

"No," Ellie said, "I want confirmation first. I'll call Dr. White-feather and ask her to run a DNA comparison between Katie Lee and both parents."

"Good idea," Derrick agreed. "Then what?"

"I say we go home for the night," Ellie said. "Tomorrow maybe we'll know about the DNA and can hit the ground running."

"All right then. I'll check in at the inn in town." He gently touched her arm. "Unless you want company for a while."

Her gaze locked with his, a seed of some emotion she didn't understand flickering. She was tempted to ask him to stop by and have a drink, but her head was hurting and she hadn't slept in days. She declined, knowing it was better not to stir up the past.

He looked slightly disappointed as she left, and she phoned Laney and explained what she needed.

Bone-weary and tormented by Will's grief-stricken face, she could hear Meddlin' Maude's accusations in her head as she walked outside. Mentally reviewing the pieces of the puzzle, she tried to make them fit. Her thoughts returned to Gillian Roach and the fact that the killer had murdered her first. What if those files she had taken related to the killer?

# CHAPTER 86

The clock was ticking. *Ticktock. Ticktock.*

The shrill sound sent a mind-numbing pain through his ear all the way to his brain, and he screamed in agony for it to cease. But the sound only grew more intense, blending with the hideous sound of the man's sinister laughter. He was enjoying this game, enjoying watching him suffer.

The bright lights were blinding him, too, sharp shards pricking his eyeballs like lasers, piercing hot and fiery. The light became hotter, brighter, vivid colors flashing through his mind and swirling in a dizzying pattern and the world spun as if he was on a tilt-a-whirl, rolling over and over, upside down, constantly moving.

*Ticktock. Ticktock.*

*Please make it stop! Make it stop!*

Then the whisper of a voice telling him what he'd done. The images came like lightning bolts, snaking through the blur that was his mind, the women lying helpless, their bodies succumbing unwillingly to what he'd done to them.

He knew it was wrong, but he couldn't stop.

The tiny grains of sand slipped through the globe of the hourglass like white powder. It was too late for forgiveness. The shadows of evil owned him.

Rising from his bed, he went outside and scoured the woods, searching for peace, for the night to steal him away. But nothing would do that except the fire.

No matter how many ways he'd imagined taking a life, it always had to end with the flames.

Pulling a lighter from his pocket, he gathered kindling and flicked his lighter. Flames sparked and shot up, the soft sound of them dancing in the wind, the orange and yellow, mesmerizing him. The embers crackled and popped as the wood caught and the flames burst to life, rippling across the ground and eating the dried brush and weeds with their fury.

# CHAPTER 87

*Crooked Creek*

Another fire raged through the wilderness as Ellie drove home. She'd seen it from her window, the bright orange ball of flames sucking the life from the trees and forest creatures. A quick call to Cord confirmed he was on his way to the scene to help with rescue efforts.

Knowing she wouldn't sleep, she stopped at Gillian's home and studied those paintings again, snapping photographs of each one of the nameless children.

Was the man torching bodies one of them? Was one of the girls Katie Lee?

Praying Cord was okay, she finally returned home, collapsing into bed. Sleep brought those children's voices whispering for justice, the screams of the torched victims. *Then the fire was raging all around her, and she was running for her life, dodging falling trees and licking flames, the heat chasing her. But she tripped, then she was falling into a well full of dead bodies, the heat below reaching for her.*

Jerking her eyes open, she dragged herself from bed. It was still dark outside, but even without the sun pouring in through her floor-to-ceiling windows, the heat seeped through, overpowering the air conditioner.

Outside, the mountains seemed quiet, the lack of a breeze creating a stillness that raised the hair on the back of her neck. Lightning danced in the distance, threatening a summer storm.

Suddenly she thought she saw a movement. Slivers of moonlight slipped through the branches and fell on a dark figure running into the woods about seventy-five feet from her back porch. Ellie's breath caught in her lungs, and she hurried to her bedside table and retrieved her gun.

Carrying it at the ready, she searched the back of her property, but the figure had disappeared. She checked the back door. Locked and secure.

Nerves on high alert, she hurried to the living room. Easing the curtains aside, she peered out into the front yard. The trees stood as still as statues. Checking the peep hole of the door, she spotted something on the porch floor.

Her heart hammered as she scanned the yard to make certain the figure hadn't woven around the side of the house, waiting to jump her.

Gun braced, she unlocked the front door. Her gaze dropped to the object on the porch.

The killer had been here. And he'd just left her a message, loud and clear. An hourglass.

# CHAPTER 88

The next morning, Ellie met the rest of the team at her office. Anger slashed Derrick's face when she showed the hourglass to him. "He was at your house."

"He was. I spotted someone running into the woods, but it was too dark, and he was too far away for me to see who it was. Although he looked tall, muscular, a big guy."

"We still haven't found Rigdon," Derrick said. "Fits his description."

"Yes, it does." She shared her theory about the unsub having possibly been one of Gillian's placement kids.

"I've tasked my partner with tracing cell phone calls for all the victims," Derrick said. "I'll check and see if he's found anything."

While Derrick called his partner at the Bureau, Ellie phoned Shondra. "Hey, are you still with Sarah?"

"Yes."

"How is she?"

"She woke up for a few minutes last night but was disoriented and frightened. I promised her I wouldn't leave."

"What's her condition?"

"She's stable now. They're going to send a victims' advocate in to talk with her when she comes to." Shondra sighed, sounding tired, but better than she had when Ellie had last seen her.

"I appreciate you staying with her," Ellie said. "It can't be easy."

"No, but it's making me get out of my own head for a while. I… I'm sorry I snapped at you."

"You have nothing to be sorry about."

A heartbeat passed. "Trouble is, I was open to therapy before. But now after being deceived by Melissa, I'm not sure I trust anyone."

"Tell me about it," Ellie said softly. "Maybe we can talk to each other."

"Maybe," Shondra agreed.

"Meanwhile, keep an eye out for that guy Ryder. If he realizes Sarah made it, he might come back to finish what he started."

"Don't worry. He'll have to go through me to get to her."

Ellie smiled as she hung up. Shondra sounded stronger already, like a mother bear protecting her cubs.

Derrick strode back in, the captain and Landrum on his heels. Laney rushed in behind them, her briefcase in hand.

"I ran an extensive background check on Rigdon last night," Derrick said, once they were all seated. "He was a former Navy SEAL."

"I suspected he had a military background," replied Ellie.

"You were right. He also did work for a private military contractor as a sniper. Has no family. Never been married. The contractor denies that he's working for them at this time."

"Like they would divulge it if he was," Ellie said wryly. Firms like that kept their work top secret.

"Being a sniper takes a certain breed of man," Derrick said. "The training, the skill, the hours and hours of being alone, studying your target. Takes iron-clad control and concentration."

"He certainly didn't have control when he beat Sarah nearly to death," Ellie pointed out.

"True," Derrick said.

Ellie gestured toward the photograph of the hourglass the killer had carved into the women's mastoid bone, then to the picture of the hourglass she'd found on her doorstep. "This hourglass is significant. He left one for me in the middle of the night. It's at the lab now for analysis. Is it his way of warning me that I'm next? Or that I'm running out of time before I find another body?"

"Could be both." Captain Hale spewed a litany of curse words. "You need a security detail."

"No need," Derrick said with a challenging eyebrow raised toward Ellie. "Detective Reeves and I will be working together until this case is solved."

Ellie's eyes widened. Working, yes. But she didn't want him around 24/7. That would be too…

Captain Hale cleared his throat. "What else do you have on him?"

Deputy Landrum glanced at the file on his computer again. "Nothing. No properties he owned, no paper trail for buying firearms, no record of arson."

"Maybe he hasn't done this before," Ellie said. "But something triggered him to attack Sarah."

"Attack, but not kill," Derrick said. "The erratic behavior doesn't fit with the MO of the other murders. Although they were violent, the killer planned them. He intentionally chose deserted areas on the trail to leave the victims and carries out his ritual with the stones." He pointed to the board. "Although parts of his MO vary, so he's either experimenting with different methods of murder to perfect the kill or he's escalating."

"He's evolving," Ellie said. "Needs to change it up to get off."

Derrick nodded. "Exactly."

"Any hits on arsonists in the area?" Ellie asked Heath.

"A couple, but both are serving time. One of those was Paulson."

The man who set fire to her parents' house. But that had been personal, an act of revenge.

"Did you check for juvenile offenders?" Derrick asked. "Often arsonists begin in their teens."

"Not yet," Deputy Landrum replied, his tone slightly defensive. "I've been busy looking at the backgrounds of the victims."

"I'll get my partner to dig into the juvenile offenders," Derrick offered. "He has access to a wider database. And a judge who can get sealed files opened for review."

"Anything on the victims' phones?" Ellie asked.

"Not yet."

"There was another fire last night. I'll run point with Max Weatherby and make sure he didn't find another crime scene," Captain Hale interjected. "And give the sheriff an update. I think he was up most of the night supervising that latest wildfire investigation. But I'm sure he'll want to speak to the press."

Ellie nodded her thanks. "With Gillian Roach being the perp's first victim, we're looking into the theory that she was killed because of her work." Ellie inhaled a deep breath. "One of those files had to do with me."

Derrick offered her a small smile as if he knew that the confession had been a bitter pill for her to swallow. Already people had died because of her. She didn't want to dive down that rabbit hole again.

"What was in the file?" Captain Hale asked.

"I have no idea," Ellie said honestly. "But I'm guessing it held answers about my birth parents' identity. I don't know what that has to do with the other murders, but we're looking for connections between the victims and also to Gillian."

Laney stood, her expression grim. "I might be able to help there."

Ellie and the others in the room grew quiet.

"I compared Katie Lee's DNA with her parents. That got interesting." Laney gestured toward the photographs on the whiteboard. "First of all, Agnes Curtis is definitely Katie Lee's biological mother."

"So she wouldn't have had reason to contact the social worker," Ellie said.

"Maybe not. But Mr. Curtis is not Katie Lee's biological father."

And Katie Lee had known as much, according to Will.

"I'm going to run her DNA against the national system," Laney said. "But that could take a while."

"We need to talk to the Curtises again," Ellie said.

Laney raised a finger. "I'm not finished." She pointed to the photograph of Vanessa Morely. "Just to cover all the bases, I ran a comparison to our other victims. And it turns out that Katie Lee and Vanessa Morely have a familial match."

Ellie stared at her in shock. "What? There's almost a twenty-year age difference between them."

Laney's brows lifted. "I know… But I ran it again to double check. And I got the same results. Katie Lee and Vanessa share the same father."

# CHAPTER 89

The possibilities ran through Ellie's mind. An affair with the same man seemed unlikely, if not impossible. There were two other options—a sperm donor or sexual assault. "Did you run that DNA through CODIS?" she asked.

"Next on my list." Like Ellie, the ME relied on the Combined DNA Index System, which blended computer technology and forensic science as a tool for linking victims. It allowed federal, state, and local forensic labs to exchange DNA profiles electronically.

Ellie ran her fingers through her ponytail. "Vanessa's sister said their mother died in childbirth, and the father was not in the picture, but I'll talk to her again. Hopefully Vanessa or their mother left some records behind." She angled her head toward Heath. "See if you can get hold of her birth certificate and if there's a father listed."

"On it." Heath turned to his laptop.

"We need to build a profile for the unsub," said Derrick, placing his palms on the table. "If the same man raped Agnes Curtis and Vanessa's mother, he would be older now."

Ellie mentally ticked away questions. "A lot of repeat sexual offenders start in their twenties. He assaults Vanessa's mother and gets away with it. Then, about twelve years later, he rapes Agnes Curtis. Mrs. Curtis would only have been eighteen or so when she gave birth to Katie Lee."

"We've been looking for similar murder cases, not rapes," Derrick said. "I'll have a run at looking back at reports of sexual assault during that time in the area. But, of course, there may be survivors who didn't come forward."

"What do we really know about Agnes Curtis?" Deputy Landrum asked.

"Not much," Ellie muttered. "Her husband barely let her speak."

"If Agnes wasn't assaulted, she might have slept around before marriage or had an affair after they were married. Could be the reason the husband got them all in that church, under his thumb," Derrick said.

"What about a sperm donor?" Laney suggested.

"I supposed that's possible," Ellie said. "Although why would Katie Lee's mother have used a fertility clinic at that age?"

"She and Mr. Curtis could have had trouble conceiving," the captain suggested.

"If that were so, it would mean both of them wanted a child. But now it seems Mr. Curtis didn't bond with Katie Lee because she wasn't his child." She pursed her lips in thought.

"We have Marty Curtis's DNA too, remember?" Laney said. "I'll check whether the Curtises are his biological parents. If they are, a sperm donor seems even more unlikely. And then what about Janie Huntington? How does she fit in all this?" Laney asked. "Her DNA was not a familial match to Katie Lee's or Vanessa's."

"Will said his mother and Agnes were friends," Derrick replied. "Maybe Agnes confided in Janie about Katie Lee's father, and the killer murdered her to keep her from talking."

Ellie mulled that over. "There's only one way to find out." She glanced at Derrick. "Let's go ask the Curtises. Then we'll have another chat with Vanessa's sister."

# CHAPTER 90

*Pigeon Lake*

Mrs. Curtis answered the door, her expression wary. An oppressive sadness permeated the air, making the stuffy room feel as if the walls were closing in around Ellie. She couldn't imagine how this woman was still standing.

Ellie introduced Derrick, earning a nervous look from the woman. Her fingernails were now chewed down to the nubs, and a bruise darkened her wrist, raising Ellie's anger. She scanned the room in search of the bastard husband.

"May we come in?" Ellie asked. "We really need to talk."

"Josiah is not here at the moment. You should come back."

Ellie jumped at the opportunity to speak to the woman alone. "Please, Agnes. It's important."

A tense second ticked by before Mrs. Curtis relented, and they followed her to the small kitchen. Ellie and Derrick seated themselves in the straight chairs at the table, while Mrs. Curtis folded her arms. No pleasantries or offers of coffee. "Did you find out who killed my daughter?"

Ellie inhaled before answering. "I'm afraid not. But we're doing everything possible to get the answers. That's the reason we're here. Is your son home?"

The woman shook her head. "He went with his father to church. The funeral is tomorrow," her voice quivered. "I... can't believe we're going to bury my baby."

Ellie's heart wrenched for her, and the fact she was going to make things worse with her questions. "I'm sorry for your loss. But we do have to ask you something."

Agnes eyes flared with suspicion. "We already answered your questions."

Derrick breathed out. "We have some new information, Mrs. Curtis."

"All right, then," Mrs. Curtis replied, then knotted her hands around her apron.

"During the autopsy the medical examiner ran your daughter's DNA," Ellie said. "That's routine. And because there have been other victims now, who died in a similar manner to your daughter, we've been searching for a commonality between them. The DNA results indicate that Katie Lee and one of those women share a familial match."

Shock flashed in the woman's dark eyes. "What? What does that mean?"

"More specifically, that they share the same father. The tests also revealed that Katie Lee's father is not Mr. Curtis," Ellie said softly. "Does your husband know?"

The woman's hand trembled as she pressed her fingers to her mouth, but she gave a small nod. Just then the back door burst open, and Mr. Curtis stormed in, his son behind him. Marty's head was down, his shoulders slumped, his eyes bloodshot.

"What's going on here?" the father bellowed.

Marty froze, eyes widening as he gripped the back of the chair where his mother sat. Her face had gone three shades whiter.

"Go upstairs, Marty."

"But, Dad—" The boy lifted his chin, and Ellie noticed that his lip was cut.

"I said *go*."

Shooting his father a nasty look, Marty darted past his parents into the hall. His footsteps pounded the wooden floor as he climbed the steps two at a time.

Ellie turned back to Mr. Curtis, barely hanging onto her temper. Derrick straightened, his stance intimidating.

"Mr. Curtis, we were just explaining that DNA results from your daughter and one of the other murdered victims we found this week indicate a familial match. We also learned that Katie Lee is not your biological daughter," he said bluntly. "You failed to share that information with us."

Pure outrage flared across the man's thin face. "My family's private life is none of your business."

Derrick didn't flinch. "It is, if it leads us to Katie Lee's killer."

# CHAPTER 91

Ellie ignored the man and addressed his wife. "Mrs. Curtis, I understand this is a difficult time, but we need your help. You do want to see Katie Lee's killer get caught, don't you?"

Agnes's eyes fluttered with turmoil.

"Did Katie Lee know that your husband was not her birth father?" According to Will, she had. But she might not have talked to her parents about it yet.

Mr. Curtis flung his hand toward the door. "Get out. Now."

"Did she know?" Ellie pushed.

Mrs. Curtis gave a tiny shake of her head, and a vein bulged in her husband's neck.

"Are you sure?" Ellie pressed. "Maybe she found out and went looking for him."

"That didn't happen," Mr. Curtis snapped. "Now stop prying into our private family business."

"If it takes prying to expose the person who killed that sweet young girl, I'll do it," Ellie said sharply. "What about the father? Who is he? Did he know about Katie Lee?"

Mr. Curtis clutched Ellie's arm in a death grip. "If you don't leave now, I'm going to file harassment charges against you, Detective."

"Take your hands off Detective Reeves, Mr. Curtis, or I'll arrest you for assaulting a police officer," said Derrick, grabbing the man's arm.

Ellie had not moved. She refused to give him the satisfaction of thinking that he'd gotten to her.

Mr. Curtis hissed, then dropped his hands and stepped away, but his look remained dangerous.

"Come on, Detective," Derrick said. "Let's go."

Ellie silently cursed, then glanced back at Mrs. Curtis. The poor woman was trembling in her thin skirt and white blouse. "If you decide to talk, please give me a call."

"She won't. Now leave us alone to grieve for our daughter."

Ellie shot him a look of contempt. He might pretend to be a doting father, but she knew better. Doting was not the word Katie Lee had used in her journal, or the way her brother had described him.

Hands knotted, she turned and strode out the front door. She would leave for now. But if it turned out he'd hurt Katie Lee; she would be back for him.

# CHAPTER 92

*Stony Gap*

"You pushed too hard with Curtis," Derrick said half an hour later, outside Vanessa Morley's house.

Ellie shot him a sardonic look. "I thought you were the hard-assed agent."

He shrugged and together they made their way to the door.

The air practically vibrated with tension, made worse by the overpowering heat and her growing remorse over not keeping in touch with Vanessa. Warm sunshine always lifted her spirits, but this summer heatwave made it difficult to breathe.

Trudy answered the door, dusting flour from her blouse. The scent of cinnamon apples wafted to Ellie, along with the heat from the kitchen. In spite of the air conditioner churning noisily, she felt like she was walking into a giant oven.

"Detective? Agent Fox?" Trudy said, her voice breaking. She wiped her hands on her apron, motioning for them to come in. A minute later they were seated in the kitchen where the scent of the pie made Ellie's stomach rumble. But sweat dribbled down her face, and she fanned it, waving away a fly who also had an appetite for the sweet dessert.

"Is Mandy here?" Ellie asked.

Trudy picked up a paper napkin and folded it in half. "She went to a friend's. I figured it was all right, that maybe it would help her. She's been so upset."

"I'm sure she has been," Ellie said softly.

"Did you need to see her for some reason?" Trudy asked.

"No," Derrick said quietly. "It's probably better we talk alone anyway."

Trudy twisted the napkin between her fingers. "Do you know who killed my sister?"

Derrick explained about the DNA, and Trudy's forehead crinkled.

"I don't understand," she said. "You're saying that Vanessa and this teenager have the same father. That would mean they were half-sisters."

"That's right," Ellie said. "You mentioned that your mother died giving birth to Vanessa. Did you and Vanessa share the same father?"

"No. Mine died overseas when I was two. I honestly don't know who Vanessa's father was."

"Did Vanessa ever search for him?"

"A while back, she mentioned having some health issues, said she needed to know about her family medical history."

"What kind of medical issues was she having?" Ellie asked.

"She didn't really explain," Trudy admitted. "Just said the doctors were asking. Said she might look for him, but if she found him, she never told me."

"Did she have any private papers here? Maybe a safe we could look into?"

Trudy glanced back and forth between them. "I don't understand what Vanessa's father has to do with this?"

"It's a link between two victims. It may not have anything to do with their deaths, but we're exploring every possibility," Ellie said. She had to. Like breadcrumbs, eventually the little pieces might lead her to the killer.

# CHAPTER 93

Trudy rocked back in the chair, stunned at the revelation. "I haven't gone through her things yet. I wasn't ready to." She clamped her teeth over her bottom lip, biting down hard. "Although I suppose I'll need to pick out a dress for her memorial service."

Ellie winced. The funeral director must not have revealed the extent of the damage to Vanessa's body caused by the fire.

"Is it okay if Agent Fox and I look around?" Ellie asked.

"I guess so, if you think it would help catch my sister's killer. And it would be better if you did it before Mandy gets back."

"Thank you," Ellie replied. "I promise we'll be respectful of her things."

"I'll look around in the living room and kitchen," Derrick said.

"I'll check her bedroom."

"What are you looking for?" Trudy asked as she directed Ellie to her sister's bedroom.

"I'm not sure," Ellie said. "Something we might have missed when we were here before."

Trudy gave a little nod. "I'm going to make some phone calls about the memorial arrangements for Vanessa."

She disappeared down the hall and Ellie stepped into the bedroom. The furniture was old and worn. Someone had made the bed up with a plain beige comforter since Ellie's last visit—the last set of bedding had been retrieved as evidence. Ellie rummaged through the drawers of the small desk in the corner. No journal, tablet or laptop. No address book. She searched for notes referencing

Raintree Family Services but found nothing except old paycheck stubs and bills. She flipped through the check log.

Most of the checks appeared to be payments for routine expenses—the power company, garbage collection, grocery store. The cursive writing was pretty, precise, as if Vanessa took great pains to form each letter. A few swirly lines suggested she might have dabbled in calligraphy. Ellie felt a tug at the thought of everything they missed out on.

She continued scrolling through the check book, stopping at a name which had been repeated. A few weeks back Vanessa had written two separate checks for five hundred dollars to a man named Patrick Grogan.

She didn't recognize the name. Curious, she googled it, finding one of the top links was to a private detective agency.

Had Vanessa hired a private investigator to find her father?

After searching the rest of the room and finding nothing else, she headed back to the living room. Derrick shook his head, indicating he'd had no luck.

Trudy looked tired and frazzled as she hung up her phone.

"Trudy, Vanessa wrote a couple of checks to a man named Patrick Grogan. There's a private investigator by that name working in the state. Do you know if she hired a PI, or why?"

Trudy's eyes widened in surprise. "I didn't know if she had." She fidgeted with the neck of her blouse. "But like I said, we weren't close lately."

Ellie thanked her, knowing their next move. Patrick Grogan might know the reason Vanessa was killed.

# CHAPTER 94

*Pigeon Lake*

Marty paced his bedroom, the detective's statement raising ugly questions in his mind.

If his father and Katie Lee's were not the same, that meant his mother had been with another man. The thought made him want to puke.

It was gross to think about his parents doing the deed. He knew they sure as hell didn't do it now, not with all his father's ranting about religion. And that was fine with him. No kid wanted to think about their parents that way.

But he wasn't stupid either.

They had to have done it sometime or he wouldn't be here. Unless the old man wasn't his real father either.

He clutched his sister's journal in his hand and skimmed several more entries. Katie Lee's writing was uneven, the lines slanting sideways, the words running together as if she'd been upset and rushing to get her thoughts down.

*I hear Mama and Daddy talking at night. Whispering. Daddy telling Mama no one can know about me. That I'm their dirty little secret.*

Marty ran a hand through his sweaty hair. It was a million degrees in his shithole of a house. The air was on the fritz again, heat bleeding through the cracks in the windows. Pigeons swooped around the ledge outside his bedroom, pecking at the glass and planting their droppings in a pile as if leaving him a present.

Another entry caught his eye. The page was wrinkled, as if his sister's tears had fallen on the paper.

*Today I asked Mama about their dirty little secret, if it was me? But Daddy slapped me and told me to shut up. Said he gave me a home and if I didn't appreciate it, I could hit the streets and see where that got me. That I'd probably end up a whore and become a drug addict. Mama cried and tried to hug me, but Daddy pushed her away, and I ran upstairs. I started to pack, but I don't know where to go. I only know that they don't want me here.*

Marty's breathing grew shallow. He'd known Katie Lee was miserable, that his father preached to her about being a *good girl*, but he hadn't known about that conversation.

He flipped the pages further to see if Katie Lee had learned the truth but found that two pages had been ripped out. The next page held another surprising entry.

*I'm going to meet Will today. We've been talking about the church. I think he might be able to help me.*

Marty heaved a breath, and turned pages, but that was it.

He had to talk to Will.

He slipped to the top of the stairs and heard his mother crying, his father's cold voice.

"You will not talk to those cops again. You will not talk to anyone."

"I didn't—"

"Shut up, Agnes. This is all your fault. I told you one day it would come back to haunt us."

Marty dug his hands into his pockets.

"Now, go and pray. Do not come out or answer the door to anyone."

His mother's sobbing grew louder, then her bedroom door closed. The key turned in the lock, and anger slammed into Marty. His father had locked her in the room.

Outrage poured through Marty. His sister had talked about wanting to leave, to get out of the house. If his father only recently learned Katie Lee wasn't his daughter, then he could have blown a gasket. He knew first-hand how volatile his old man's temper could be.

# CHAPTER 95

*Cherokee Point*

Grogan's PI Agency was located in the small community of Cherokee Point barely ten miles from where Vanessa lived, which explained her reason for hiring him. They'd driven past chicken houses on the way, and on the corner of the turnoff was a barn-like café called Goats on the Roof, complete with live goats roaming freely around the property and on the metal roof.

Grogan's office was set in a small strip mall which had fallen by the wayside. Only two other businesses were left—a dry cleaners and Inked, a tattoo parlor. The wind-beaten metal sign dangling from a post out front advertised that Grogan was also a bail bondsman.

"I hope he was cheap," Derrick said as they walked up to the frosted-glass door.

Ellie agreed. Derrick rapped on the PI's door, then twisted the doorknob and lead the way inside. Ellie followed, her gaze sweeping the reception area. Two metal chairs sat against the wall with a stack of outdated, dog-eared magazines on a center table.

The man's Georgia PI license along with a certificate for a bachelor's degree in criminal justice hung on the wall in discount store frames. A bleached-blond twenty-something, sporting a V-neck T-shirt and colorful tattoos, sat at the desk chewing gum so vigorously that Ellie was surprised she didn't crack a tooth.

"Hey," the young woman said in a nasal tone. "What can I do for you?"

They flashed their credentials. "We need to talk to Patrick Grogan."

She batted eyelashes that glittered with silver sparkles. "Daddy's on a call right now. But I reckon you can wait if you want. You here about a bail?"

Ellie bit back a smile. "No. About one of his clients. And yes, we'll wait."

"Suit yourself. I'll let Daddy know you're out here." The girl sent a text, then plugged earphones in and began to hum while she tapped the tune with her acrylic nails on the desk.

Derrick claimed one of the metal chairs and Ellie took the other. He gestured toward a print depicting Native Americans huddled around campfires in the middle of a brutal winter snowstorm. "Where is that?"

"Near here. You know the history of the Trail of Tears. Once gold was discovered in Dahlonega, the government forced the Cherokees off their land and to move west. It's said that Cherokee Point marks one of the points along the trail where many of the Native Americans died."

Derrick heaved a sigh. "That was a travesty."

Ellie nodded. She'd cried when she was ten and had first read the story with her father before one of their scenic trips. The door to Grogan's office opened, and a tall, bearded man who looked to be late forties appeared. He wore a black T-shirt with a grizzly bear on the front. Ellie couldn't help but think the man looked like a bear himself.

He extended his hand then introduced himself. "Jo-Jo said you wanted to see me."

She and Derrick accepted the handshake then showed their credentials.

"Let's go in my office," Grogan said.

Papers and notes were piled everywhere, a file-cabinet drawer stood open, which was odd since she had a feeling he rarely used it, and three coffee cups sat on the desk, all partially filled. No telling how long they'd been there.

Grogan narrowed his eyes at Ellie as he leaned back in his vinyl swivel chair. "I saw you on the news. You're that detective over in Crooked Creek who caught those serial killers."

"I am. We're here about another case now," Ellie said, filling him in.

He scrubbed a beefy hand over his thick beard, his face twisting with questions.

"Vanessa hired you?" Ellie asked.

"Yeah, she stopped by. Seemed like a nice lady."

"We believe she was murdered because she was looking for her birth father. Is that why she came to you for help?"

Indecision streaked the man's craggy face. "I keep my client's information confidential."

"That's admirable, but we're investigating her murder, Mr. Grogan. It's likely that the man who killed Vanessa also murdered three other females. One of those was a social worker named Gillian Roach."

"You know who she is?" Derrick asked.

The man heaved a wary breath. "No, but I heard about her death on the news."

"Did you find out the name of Vanessa's father?"

"No, it wasn't listed on her birth certificate and no one at the hospital knew. The trail went cold fast. Vanessa said her mother died in childbirth. But she thought that was a lie."

The hair on Ellie's arms prickled. "Why would she think that?"

"She'd done some digging on her own, asking questions at the hospital where she was born. One of the nurses said she didn't know exactly what happened to Vanessa's mother, but she'd heard that years ago there'd been a cover-up. That a new mother called Wanda Morely was okay after the birth but was later listed as having died in childbirth. Said Wanda had apparently seemed upset, though, and had told the staff that if a certain man showed up not to let him in."

"Go on."

"I tracked down some of the nurses working back then. One told me that Vanessa's mother was holding her baby when a nurse called Clara Huckabee left to take care of another patient. When Huckabee returned, the doctor was yelling for a code team—Vanessa's mother had gone into cardiac arrest."

"What else did she say?"

"Apparently, the nurse was suspicious but was ordered not to say anything because the hospital was worried about a lawsuit."

"Did the police investigate?" Ellie asked.

Grogan shook his head. "The hospital swept it all under the rug."

"Did you question this other nurse, Clara Huckabee?" Derrick asked.

"I tried to reach her, but she didn't return my calls. The whole case was on hold—Vanessa couldn't afford to keep me on it long."

Ellie and Derrick exchanged a look. "We're going to need the nurse's contact information."

# CHAPTER 96

*Peaceable Kingdom*

Derrick skimmed the file Grogan had dug from the pile on his desk, his shoulders tightening as Ellie careened around a narrow switchback. After they'd left Grogan's, they'd stopped for a quick sandwich and peek at the file, learning that Vanessa Morely had been born at Bluff County Hospital.

The delivery nurse, Clara Huckabee, had retired long ago. Grogan had tried to reach her at her home, but Derrick made a quick phone call and learned she'd moved to a small house outside of Cleveland in a neighborhood of tiny houses that had been built for seniors.

He held his breath as Ellie sped around another curve, driving way too fast for his comfort zone. The mountain ridge dropped hundreds of feet below, without a guardrail, and offered a perilous view of the brush below. Massive pines had crumbled like matchsticks into the ravine during the recent tornado.

If Ellie's search for the truth had triggered a killer, Ellie's life was in danger. His gut clenched at the thought of this latest maniac coming after her.

The Jeep bounced over a rut in the road, jolting him, and he saw the strain on her face. Ellie would never confess that she was afraid, but she had to be. She'd admit she was angry, though, and she would let that drive her. Which meant she needed protection even if she didn't want it.

Turning off the mountain road, they ended up in the retirement neighborhood called Peaceable Kingdom. On the acres of land, homes had been built among the apple orchards. There was a flower garden behind the pond, and birdfeeders were scattered along the property.

They found Clara's address, parked at the pale-green bungalow and walked up to the porch. Before they knocked, the door squeaked partially open and the barrel of a shotgun appeared.

Derrick and Ellie froze. "Ms. Huckabee," Derrick said as he held up his credentials. "Don't shoot. I'm Special Agent Fox with the FBI and this is Detective Reeves. We just want to talk."

"Go away. It's not safe to talk," the little woman shouted.

"Clara, please, I promise no one knows we're here," Ellie said. "But we need your help. It's really important."

Ellie lifted her hands to indicate she didn't pose a threat, then slowly stepped forward. "We can sit out here on your porch if that makes you more comfortable."

"No, you have to come inside. I don't want anyone to see me talking to you."

They climbed the steps to the porch, and Clara eased the door open and waved them in. She lowered the shotgun beside her and gestured toward a sitting area. The house was small, with an open concept, but neat and tidy. Ceramic kitty cats lined a bookshelf and a basket of knitting needles and yarn sat by the side of a comfy armchair.

Clara had silver hair, couldn't weigh more than a hundred pounds and clutched a shawl around her frail shoulders. She sank into the chair and propped the shotgun beside her. "You can't tell anyone I talked to you."

"What are you afraid of?" Ellie asked gently.

Clara tugged the shawl tighter around her shoulders. "I saw you on the news. Someone killed Vanessa."

"Yes, that's true," said Derrick.

"That's why we're here. Had you talked to Vanessa recently?" Ellie asked.

The little woman shook her head. "I helped deliver her years ago, but I didn't keep in touch with her or any of my patients."

"Yet you remember her?" Ellie pointed out. "Like, you said it was a long time ago. Over thirty years."

The chair creaked as Clara shifted. "Her mama died in childbirth," the woman finally said. "I never could forget that."

"Why is that?" Derrick asked.

Clara looked down at her gnarled hands. "It's not easy watching a mother die and leave her baby behind," she murmured.

"I imagine not," said Ellie, "but was there something about her death that especially bothered you? What happened?"

"That's just it," Clara said. "I don't rightly know what happened. Wanda seemed fine after she gave birth, wanted to hold her baby. Then I went to check on another patient and when I got back, Vanessa's mama was in distress. One of the doctors pushed me aside, and the baby started screaming, so I tried to soothe her. But… that woman died right there with her baby crying for her." She fluttered a hand over her white hair. "Thank goodness the grandma was around to take the infant."

"Was an autopsy done on the mother?" Ellie asked.

Clara shook her head. "Doc said it was natural causes. But… I wondered." She clucked her teeth. "Seemed like something went wrong, and the doctor just covered it up."

A strained silence fell for a full minute. "Why didn't you tell the police?" Ellie said softly.

Turmoil shadowed Clara's face as she looked up at Ellie. "This other nurse went to the chief of staff asking questions." She trembled. "Two days later, she ended up dead." Tears trickled down Clara's face. "I know I was a coward then, but I didn't want to end up dead too."

# CHAPTER 97

*Crooked Creek*

Ellie contemplated the older woman's statement as she and Derrick entered the police station. According to Clara, the doctor who'd delivered Vanessa had been killed in a housefire a few months after Vanessa's birth, so that too was a dead end.

There had also been no investigation into the other nurse's death. Records said she'd died in a car crash, but Clara seemed to think that it wasn't an accident at all.

Angelica Gomez was waiting in the station. She looked anxious, her deep brown eyes troubled.

"I'm going to look at Gillian Roach's phone records," Derrick said. "Unless you want me to handle the press."

Ellie's gaze caught Angelica's across the room. "Thanks, but I've got it."

"Can I use your office?"

"Sure."

Bracing herself, Ellie crossed the room to Angelica. Her cameraman stood ready to shoot.

"New crew?" she asked.

Angelica gave a small nod. "Barry's mother got sick a while back. This is Tom." She didn't necessarily look happy about the change.

"Is that what's bothering you?" Usually, Angelica appeared unflappable.

Angelica adjusted her mic but didn't quite make eye contact. Dark circles rimmed her eyes, and she looked as if she'd had as much trouble sleeping lately as Ellie.

"Just tired," Angelica said. "Working overtime on this story and my boss is pushing me for an interview with some local author, Preston Phelps, which is hardly a scoop, but the guy won't even return my calls."

"Have you got anything on that church?"

"The women are suppressed, just as you and I both thought. One lady said Agnes Curtis was pregnant when she and her husband joined Ole Glory. She tried to befriend Agnes, but the husband forbade his wife from socializing." Disgust laced Angelica's voice. "I don't understand why she stayed with him."

"Abusers have a way of manipulating vulnerable women," Ellie said, not ready to share the details about the familial match.

The cameraman called Angelica's name, then checked his watch. "Are you ready?"

"As ready as I'll ever be. Let's do it."

The reporter pasted on her professional face and introduced herself. "This is Angelica Gomez, Channel Five news, coming to you live from Crooked Creek Police Department where we have an update on the latest string of crimes in the area." She pushed the mic toward Ellie. "Detective Reeves?"

Ellie lifted her chin. "While Sheriff Waters and his team are investigating the wildfires raging through the Appalachian Trail, my department has been working diligently to uncover the truth about several shocking deaths this last week." She paused. "We have now identified each of the victims. Victim one, Gillian Roach, a social worker from Cleveland, Georgia was found dead at Winding Rock. Victim two, Katie Lee Curtis, a high-school student from Pigeon Lake, was found at Teardrop Falls. Victim three is Vanessa Morely, a waitress from Stony Gap. Her body was discovered at a place called Death's Door. And our latest victim, Janie Huntington, a housekeeper also from Pigeon Lake, was found at Cold Springs. While the victims vary in age, we are trying to ascertain if there is a connection between them."

"Detective Reeves, are we dealing with one killer?"

Ellie hated to stir panic, but the town deserved the truth. "We believe one perpetrator is responsible, although at this time we have no specific person of interest. We do know this, that the killer has used a different method of murder for each victim, yet for some reason he feels compelled to create a monument of stones around the bodies." She had debated on divulging that detail but decided it might trigger a witness, friend or family member to come forward about the killer. But she was going to hold back on the hourglass carving.

"Is it true that this perpetrator torches his victims?"

Ellie could almost hear the horrified ripples of shock that the information would elicit. But lying to the people she was supposed to protect would only cause more distrust. "Yes, he has set fire to the bodies, although that was done postmortem. We think he may have done it to destroy evidence." She refrained from pointing out that it could have been due to a sick perversion. Some people would draw that conclusion themselves without her planting the grisly images in their minds.

"If anyone has information regarding any of these crimes, please call the sheriff's office. And please be safe and vigilant out there, ladies. This man has no specific victim type. If you're approached by someone suspicious, get away and call the police."

She paused. "We also have a bulletin issued for another man wanted for questioning in connection with an assault case. His name is Ryder Rigdon. He may be armed and dangerous, so do not approach him, but call the police instead. Thank you."

"You heard it first hand from Detective Reeves," Angelica said. "Predators are out there, lurking in the shadows." She recited the phone numbers for the sheriff's office and then the Crooked Creek Police Department, then told viewers that a picture of Rigdon was now on screen. "Also, although police are doing their best," Angelica added, "it's never too late to learn to protect yourself. Visit our website for information on self-defense classes in the area." Ending on that note, she signaled for the cameraman to stop rolling.

Ellie started toward her office, but Angelica touched her arm. "I know you, Detective. There's more to this than you're letting on. What aren't you telling me?"

# CHAPTER 98

Ellie gave Angelica a warning look then pulled her into the corner, lowering her voice. She'd promised the reporter an exclusive and figured she might glean more information from the church members than the police. Some people were still intimidated by a uniform.

And so far, Angelica had proven trustworthy. "What I'm about to tell you is not to be aired or shared with anyone."

Angelica crossed her heart with her finger. "Got it. Now spill."

Ellie explained the familial connection between Katie Lee and Vanessa. "If we determine who fathered them, it might lead us to the killer."

Angelica's eyes sparked with interest. "I wonder if that old biddy Maude Hazelnut knows."

Ellie bit back a laugh at Angelica's description. "If she does, she won't talk to me. She hates my guts."

"How about I give it a try? I can say I'm doing a human-interest piece on the town and what they think about the recent crimewave."

"Good idea," Ellie agreed. "Someone at that church might know, too."

"I'll get on it right away." Her phone buzzed, and she grimaced when she checked the number.

"What's wrong?" Ellie asked.

"My boss again, wanting that interview with Preston Phelps. Apparently, the mayor's wife asked him to be a guest at the Fourth festivities." She sighed. "I bought a copy of his book but haven't had time to read it yet. And right now, I have more important things on my mind."

"If I know you, you won't give up until you land an interview," Ellie said wryly.

Just like she wouldn't give up until she'd found this killer.

# CHAPTER 99

*Pigeon Lake*

Marty Curtis waited until his father had been gone for an hour and checked his mother was still locked in before he snuck out. He crawled through his bedroom window, down the tree by the house until he was low enough to drop to the ground. There, he hunched down and peered around the yard and driveway to make sure his old man hadn't come back. Sometimes he'd be gone for just an hour and then other times all night.

Marty had no idea what he was doing while he was gone. His father said he was praying for all of them. But how could anybody pray for that long?

Finally deciding the coast was clear, he jogged around the back of the house and through the bushes, then hit the path in the woods that led him toward the road where Will Huntington lived. If that smartass kid knew something about Katie Lee and who killed her, he'd beat the snot out of him to make him talk, just like his daddy had done to him.

His father acted so holy, like such a God-loving man, but he'd ruined their family. No wonder his sister had wanted to run away.

Had she run into the hands of a killer?

He wished to hell he could leave himself. But he'd never leave his mama with the jerk.

They were both stuck until someone did something. Sometimes, when it got real bad, he even fantasized about killing him.

He jumped over vines and downed trees, the scent of smoke from another wildfire making his vision fuzzy as he jogged toward

Will's. Evil thoughts of hurting his father ran rampant through his head, the images giving him an odd kind of pleasure that felt wrong and right at the same time.

Night had set in, the starless sky making it seem pitch black and hard to see where he was stepping. It was so hot his clothes were sticking to him and his pits reeked like he'd just finished gym class. He broke through the clearing then crept along the riverbank until he reached the path to the run-down houses where Will lived.

It was weird that Katie Lee had turned to Will when she'd never mentioned they were friends. Then again, she hadn't shared much. She'd just kept quiet and suffered in silence, too afraid to move or talk back to their old man for fear of what the asshole would do.

He spotted Will sitting in the woods on a tree stump, throwing sticks into the river. Twigs and dry grass crunched beneath his shoes as he slowed and approached him. Before he got too close, Will looked up, an angry glint in his eyes.

Marty paused, his breath erratic as he stopped beside a tall pine.

"What do you want?" Will asked.

"I wanna know what my sister told you, why she came to you when she was upset." His defenses for Katie Lee rose. "Did you screw her, Will? Is that all the secrecy was about?"

"No way, man." Will lurched up from the tree log and lunged at Marty, pushing him so hard he knocked him to the ground. "Why would you say that?"

"I don't know, I'm just trying to find out what happened to her."

"Me, too," Will said. "Cause my mama is dead, too."

"What?" Marty staggered sideways in shock.

"Yeah, that detective we saw at Moody Hollow came by and told me." Will's voice broke. "I think it's cause your mom talked to her. Maybe it has to do with Katie Lee. Do *you* know what's going on?"

"Shit, no." Marty stood up, pacing. "I'm sorry, man."

"What happened at your house? Has your mom said anything?"

"No, Dad won't let her talk. It's so screwed up…"

Will's scowl was full of rage. "What? If you know something, cough it up."

Marty heaved a breath. "You go first. What did Katie Lee tell you?"

He and Will locked gazes for a tension-filled minute.

Will coughed into his hand, then glanced around.

"She said she heard your parents fighting, said your father said she was a whore's child and she'd end up a whore herself."

The air tightened in Marty's lungs.

"He told her she was lucky he took her in, that her daddy was the worst kind of sinner and that she had evil in her blood."

Marty swallowed hard to keep from crying like a baby. "Do you know who Katie Lee's real father was? Did my daddy tell her?"

Will shook his head no. "I don't know. She texted me to meet her at the hollow. That's why I wanted to go there that day. But that's when we found her murdered."

# CHAPTER 100

*Crooked Creek*

Doing some digging, Derrick found only one fertility clinic in the area that had been in business at the time Vanessa Morely would have been conceived. He phoned and spoke with the chief of staff, a woman named Dr. Pennybaker.

"I'm sorry, but our records are confidential," she said. "I can't release the name of a donor or patient without a warrant."

And he had no evidence to justify getting one. "I understand, but we're investigating multiple homicides which could lead back to you. If you don't want your center implicated, then we can clear it up easily. All you have to do is tell me if a patient named Morely received treatment there." He gave her the dates.

"I don't appreciate your tactics, Agent Fox," Dr. Pennybaker said.

"You can talk to me or the press. I'm sure Angelica Gomez would like to interview you."

The woman cursed. "Hang on a minute."

"Of course."

Derrick jotted the names and ages of the victims as he waited. Several minutes later, the doctor returned.

"There was no patient with the last name Morely during that time."

"Could her name have been deleted?" Derrick asked.

"Not without us knowing it. There was a case of someone hacking into records at another fertility clinic where I worked, so I installed security measures to make sure that didn't happen here."

Derrick thanked her, running a hand through his hair after he hung up, looking down at the names again.

He didn't like where his thoughts were headed. Didn't like it one damn bit.

# CHAPTER 101

A cloying sickness swept over Ellie as Derrick relayed his conversation with the doctor at the fertility clinic. Just as she'd feared, the sperm donor was a dead end. And Laney had confirmed that Marty Curtis was his parents' biological child. The hourglass the killer had left at her door was also a dead end. The lab found no prints or forensics on it.

The killer wanted her to know he was watching her. That he could get to her when he chose.

It was just a matter of time.

"So, it looks highly likely both Agnes Curtis and Wanda Morely were sexually assaulted," Ellie said. She had hoped they wouldn't have to go there. But they couldn't avoid the theory when it was staring them in the eye.

A heavy silence fell between them. "We could be dealing with a serial rapist," Derrick said. "But where does Gillian Roach come into play?"

"And Janie Huntington too. Gillian handled adoptions. What if she also covered cases where rape survivors wanted to find other homes for their babies?"

Derrick nodded. "Then Gillian was likely killed because she had information that could expose the rapist."

"And he's also committed all these murders to cover his secrets."

"And he may have been attacking women for at least twelve years."

Bile rose to Ellie's throat and she snatched her keys. "I… I have to go. We'll meet back up tomorrow."

Derrick stood and caught her arm. "Ellie, I know what you're thinking. I—"

"I said I'll see you tomorrow." She jerked away and rushed out the door, jogging to her Jeep. Derrick called her name as she started the engine, but she sped from the parking lot and raced from town, desperate to be alone and escape the glaring truth.

That she might be a product of a rape.

If she was, no wonder her mother hadn't wanted her.

# CHAPTER 102

Ellie had once found careening around the winding mountain roads a tension release. But tonight, she felt too nauseated and out of control to maneuver the switchbacks. The orange and red sky in the distance was not the sunset. It was another fire rippling through the trail.

For a moment, she considered turning the car toward Cord's. If he was home, she would tell him everything. Ask if he'd ever searched for his biological parents. Ever wondered.

How would she feel if he'd learned he was the product of a rape?

But the sting of that news was too fresh, and she wasn't ready to share it. Who was this monster who'd tormented women for over a decade? How many children had he fathered? Were the killer's targets his own children, ones who'd come looking for him?

Her head swam with all the questions.

The image of the hourglass on her doorstep floated back to her. Had the son of a bitch who'd fathered her put it there as a warning?

Back home, she went straight to the kitchen and poured herself a tumbler of vodka. The tart sweetness burned her throat as it went down.

Tears trickled down her cheeks as she carried the drink to the bathroom, grabbed a washcloth from the towel bar, and scrubbed her face, desperately trying to scour the ugly thoughts from her mind.

When she looked in the mirror, she didn't even recognize herself. A gaunt, pale face with eyes that were haunted by horror stared back.

Disgusted and suddenly dizzy, she held onto the wall as she staggered to her bedroom. She set the drink onto the nightstand

and fell backward onto the bed. The room spun and swayed, and she closed her eyes to stem the nausea.

Fear took root in her soul. Her birth mother might be better off if she didn't look for her. She probably wanted to forget what had happened to her. Or maybe she had moved on and had found peace or another family?

She bolted upright, immediately regretting it as the mattress dipped and the room blurred into a gray haze.

If this killer was cleaning up after himself, he might be planning to target her birth mother.

She pounded her fist against her chest in frustration. She had to find her. Save her.

Maybe she could even do it without revealing her identity. After all, her birth mother gave up a baby named Mae. No one except for Randall and Vera, and now her team, knew she was Mae. No one else ever had to. If she met her birth mother, she'd simply be Detective Ellie Reeves, tracking down another killer.

# CHAPTER 103

*Soulfood Barbecue Bluff County*

Derrick finished his beef brisket sandwich, not surprised the place was nearly deserted at this time of night.

The smoky meat was one of the best meals he'd ever put in his mouth, the kind that you thought about for days afterwards. He could taste the cayenne, paprika and chili powder, but it was the mesquite wood chips that added the real flavor to the beef. And the greens were cooked slow with fatback, adding to the rich flavor.

Too bad Ellie hadn't joined him. He didn't like the way she'd left the police station. He'd seen the wheels turning in her mind and knew it would lead to nowhere good. *Dammit.* She was in pain and hurting, but she'd pushed him away.

Who could blame her? He'd driven out of town when her parents had been arrested a few months ago and left her to pick up the pieces of her broken life.

He itched to go to her and comfort her. But would she want that from him?

She hadn't earlier.

The one person she might trust was that ranger, Cord McClain. Derrick hadn't liked him when they'd met, had even questioned him in the Weekday Killer murders.

The man was in love with her. Anybody could see it.

Anybody but Ellie.

What did it matter to him? His life was in Atlanta. Ellie and Cord's lives were here. Maybe they belonged together.

Silently cursing himself, he ignored the stabbing feeling in his chest and accepted the shot of Woodford Reserve he'd ordered, the only one he intended to allow himself tonight. No getting shitfaced until this case was solved and he was back in his Decatur apartment.

Alone. The way he'd been for so long.

Frustrated, he tossed back the shot, then waved the waitress over and ordered a cup of Brunswick Stew to take to Ellie. Knowing her, she hadn't eaten.

The waitress returned almost immediately, and he paid then strode outside. The minute he stepped through the door, he was pummeled by the heavy odor of burning timber in the distance and saw the gray billows of smoke rolling across the night sky. McClain and the other rangers were probably working around the clock to contain the blaze.

The fire looked close by, too, as if it might be near Ellie's.

He climbed in his car, cranked the engine and headed toward her.

# CHAPTER 104

*Crooked Creek*

*The fire danced around her, licking at her toes and searing her clothes. The hissing sound blended with the sinister whisper of his voice and the soft lilt of the sand slipping through the hourglass as time faded away. One grain at a time.*

*Ellie saw it all as the heat began to melt her clothes and her skin, raw flesh mingling with the fabric strands and puddling around her body.*

*Smoke thickened around her like a blanket of gray, smothering and heavy, sucking the oxygen from her lungs. The cackle of her cry for help was lost in the flickering flames as they crawled up her body and threaded their orange heat through her, the sizzling so intense that she opened her eyes to see if death was close.*

*Maybe it would save her from the suffocating smoke and the pain of the fire.*

Suddenly a pounding shook the house, rattling the windows. Ellie jolted awake, her head fuzzy. She always left a light burning in the bathroom but now there was only darkness.

Shaking with the sense that she wasn't alone, she reached for the lamp. But when she flipped the switch, nothing happened. A wave of cold terror gripped her.

She yanked open the drawer and pulled out her gun, bracing it at the ready.

The pounding echoed again, the sound so intense that she climbed from bed, disoriented and confused. Heart hammering,

she snatched her phone and accessed her flashlight, then froze
dead still beside her bed, her heart beating against her chest as
she took in the scene. A circle of standing stones surrounded
her bed.

# CHAPTER 105

Derrick banged on Ellie's door, the bag holding Ellie's take-out stew in his other hand. The fire seemed to be blowing this way, and he could smell smoke, but it wasn't as near her house as he'd first thought.

The lights were all off, which told him something was wrong. She always left a light burning.

"Ellie!" he shouted.

He jiggled the door and called her name again. If he had to, he'd break down the damn door. But he heard footsteps shuffling inside and then saw the peephole open.

"Ellie, it's me. Can I come in?"

The door lock turned, and she opened the door, the glow of the moon illuminating her pale face.

"He was here again," she said in a whisper.

He gently took her arm and stepped inside. Setting the bag of food on the table, he removed her gun from her fingers. "Are you hurt?"

She shook her head. Her hair was tousled, her eyes slightly dulled, her clothes rumpled. "He came in while I was sleeping," she murmured.

Derrick frowned. "Did you see him?"

"No," she hissed, her voice laced with disgust. "I didn't even hear him."

She was trembling so badly, he laid her gun on the table, then drew her against him. The fact that she'd laid her head against his chest showed her level of distress.

"I'm just glad you're okay," he said softly.

A soft sob escaped her, and she clung to him. Tenderness for her made him drop a kiss to her hair. But she suddenly pushed away and wiped at her eyes angrily. "I don't understand how I slept through him breaking in. I'm usually a light sleeper. If I'd woken up, I could have caught him."

"Ellie," Derrick said gruffly. "You have to stop being so hard on yourself. You're doing everything you can to find this maniac. You have to sleep sometime."

"Not if sleeping allows him to kill again." She gestured for him to follow her to her bedroom.

Using her phone flashlight, she shined it across the room, and his chest clenched. Not only had the unsub been in her house, but he'd stacked stones all around her bed.

"We'll get a crime-scene team out here," Derrick said. "Maybe he left some evidence behind."

"So far he hasn't. He's smart. The lab didn't find anything on the hourglass he left me."

Rage fueled his determination to catch this guy. Ellie had survived two ruthless killers before. This one was not going to get her.

# CHAPTER 106

Ellie couldn't sleep after the Evidence Response Team left her house. She wondered if she'd ever feel safe there again. The security system had been set, but the alarm had not gone off, meaning somehow the killer had gotten past it.

She arranged to have it changed immediately while Derrick went back to sleep and shower at the inn. Still shaken, she grabbed her laptop and headed to the Corner Café for breakfast.

The early morning crowd hadn't arrived yet, so she ordered her usual and claimed a booth in the back. While she sipped coffee, she heard a couple of young women talking excitedly about attending college in the fall. Will's comment about his mother and Katie Lee's mother attending the same college echoed in her head.

They hadn't met at Ole Glory. They'd known each other before their children had been born. If Agnes had been assaulted during her time at the college, maybe Janie knew the man's identity, or… had she been assaulted herself?

Her breath stalled in her chest.

Knowing the Curtises wouldn't talk to her, she called Janie's brother Eric. He sounded half asleep when he answered.

"Mr. Huntington," she began. "I have more questions about your sister. Will mentioned that Janie and Agnes Curtis attended college together. Where was that?"

"North Georgia Community College," he answered. "Why? What does that have to do with her death?"

"I don't know if it does, but we're exploring all angles. There's something else I have to ask. Who is Will's father?"

The man grunted. "I don't know. Janie refused to talk about him or tell me his name. And he never once came looking for his son."

Her pulse jumped.

"Janie must have been in college when she got pregnant. Was she happy about the pregnancy?"

"That's hard to say. She'd moved out of the house and in with a couple of other girls. By the time I learned she was pregnant, she was pretty far along."

"What about your parents?"

"They wanted her to give up the baby, even contacted some social worker and were going to set it up. But Janie wouldn't do it." His voice sounded rough. "She said she'd raise the baby on her own. One of her roommates told her about this home that helped pregnant young girls. They gave the girls a place to live, counseling and medical treatment. After Will was born, I helped her out for a while until she got a job."

"What was the name of that home?"

"I think it was called something with the word Love in it."

Ellie started furiously googling. "Was it Circle of Love?"

"Yeah, that's it."

That had to be her next stop.

# CHAPTER 107

*Circle of Love*

Ellie rolled her aching shoulders as she and Derrick stood outside Circle of Love, a large white farmhouse with a wraparound porch, flowerbeds and a vegetable garden. Heat lightning zigzagged across the sky, which held pockets of thick thunderclouds. The storm had to break soon.

"I didn't know homes for unwed mothers still existed," Derrick said.

"I think they're more progressive than years ago, when girls were sent away by their parents so no one would know they were pregnant. This one offers counseling and prenatal care as well as guidance for adoption and classes on caring for the infant." She'd bet Gillian Roach had known about this place.

"You okay?" Derrick asked.

Ellie put on a brave face, but the truth was no. The fact that she'd slept through this madman being in her house had shaken her senseless.

Derrick pushed through the door, and she led the way inside. The front room resembled a hotel lobby, with comfy chairs and a desk for visitors to sign in. To the right she saw a large living room with tables for games, a TV and a fireplace that looked homey. Windows allowed in sunlight and offered a panoramic view of the hills beyond. She spotted two pregnant teens in the room chatting with an older woman.

Ellie explained the reason for their visit to the woman who greeted them. "We need to speak to whoever is in charge here."

"That would be Ms. Bodine. I'll ask her to come to the desk."

A minute later, a woman who looked to be in her thirties appeared, wearing slacks and a white cotton blouse, her hair a brown chin-length bob. She led them into her office, which held a seating area with a couch and two club chairs as well as a more formal desk space. Books filled a pine bookcase and warm sunlight flowed through the window.

Ms. Bodine seated herself then steepled her hands on the desk. "I'm not sure what I can do for you."

Responding, Ellie laid out the facts of the investigation.

"That was a long time ago," Ms. Bodine said. "There have been a lot of girls here since then."

"We understand," Derrick replied. "But we have reason to believe that a girl who lived here had been sexually assaulted, possibly more than one."

Ms. Bodine pressed her lips into a thin line. "I still don't know what I can do," she murmured. "Our records are confidential."

"Are any counselors still around from that time?"

"I'm afraid not."

"How about records left behind?" Derrick asked.

"Our computer files only go back ten years. Funding went towards other more important aspects of our program such as counseling, childbirth and child-rearing classes and programs to acclimate the girls back into their lives after they leave here." She paused. "Again though, there are confidentiality issues."

Ellie pulled a warrant from her pocket. "I understand," Ellie said. "But we need to see those files. Do you have hard copies?"

Ms. Bodine stood, brushing her hands over her slacks. "Yes, in the basement. I can show you down there, but it's kind of a mess."

"That's fine," Ellie said. "But if one of the girls named her attacker to the counselor, we may be able to stop him before he attacks again."

# CHAPTER 108

*North Georgia State Hospital*

Mabel clutched her baby girl to her, terrified to lay her in the bed. Terrified they would come and take her.

It had happened before. So many times to the other girls. Then the girls had disappeared, too.

Her baby whimpered, and she swaddled her closer to her chest. This little girl was her heart. If they took her away, Mabel would die.

Something scraped the exterior wall and she shivered, wishing she could open the window and let the fresh air in, but it was locked. It was always dark in here, too. Felt like night when it was day and day when it was night, and she couldn't tell the difference.

Her baby whimpered, and she rocked her in her arms, pouring out all the love in her heart, her mind struggling for the words to the lullaby her mama used to sing to her.

But the words escaped her.

Frustrated, she slapped her head, hoping to jog her memory, but she'd lost that a long time ago when they'd put her in here and told her she had to behave if she wanted to keep her daughter.

But something was wrong now. She'd heard them whispering outside the room today. Seen the way they twitched and squirmed and looked away.

Heard them talking about *him.*

How he was watching. How he had eyes everywhere and he knew what they were doing.

How they had to keep quiet or it would be the end of all of them.

# CHAPTER 109

*Circle of Love*

Sifting through paper files took up valuable time. And time was the enemy at the moment.

Derrick didn't complain. He dove right in, checking the dusty boxes for dates and years.

They divided the files, the fading ink of the handwritten notations made by the counselors and staff difficult to decipher on the aged, yellowed paper.

"I found a file for Wanda Morely," Derrick's eyes narrowed as he read. "I may have something here. In one of her sessions, Wanda mentioned she was drugged at a party."

Derrick's expression grew troubled. "Later, she had nightmares of being assaulted while she was drugged. She became depressed and struggled with sleeping, even considered suicide but then discovered she was pregnant. The doctor at the college clinic referred her to Circle of Love."

"Anything about giving the baby up for adoption?"

"They offered to help her arrange an adoption, but she opted to keep her daughter."

Ellie dug through another box, her eyes sparking with interest. "This file is for a young lady named Agnes Butterfield." She showed Derrick the photograph. "That's Agnes Curtis." She skimmed through the notes the counselor had made. "Agnes described being sexually assaulted too, but not at a party." She flipped to another page. "She says she was having anxiety and trouble sleeping. Her roommate Janie—" There it was. "Janie Huntington told her about a sleep study she'd signed up for. They decided to do it together."

Ellie's pulse quickened. "Apparently Janie saw a flyer about it at the campus infirmary. They were paying a small stipend for participants to test a new sleeping medication for clinical trials."

"Jesus," Derrick muttered. "They went for help and got assaulted."

Ellie shifted, wiping more dust from the file. "A few weeks after Agnes joined the study, she started having bad dreams about being assaulted. Just like Wanda Morely, she was pregnant."

Derrick shuffled through the box, then pulled out another folder. "Janie Huntington is in here, too." He began to search through it while Ellie read Agnes's heart-wrenching description of what she believed had happened.

"Janie's account is similar to Agnes's," Derrick said. "The sleep study, then the nightmares, then the pregnancy. None of the girls came forward because they thought no one would believe them."

Derrick growled an obscenity. "We have to find the doctor who conducted that study."

Ellie glanced at the files again, wondering about her own mother. Was it possible she'd been attacked by the same man? Was her name somewhere in these boxes?

# CHAPTER 110

For the next hour, Ellie and Derrick continued studying the files, searching for the name of the doctor and the research clinic, but none of the young women mentioned a name.

The dust was making Ellie's nose itch and her eyes water, but she made a phone call to the college infirmary. A young man answered, who sounded early twenties, and she identified herself.

"Is the school associated with any research facilities?" Ellie asked.

"Not directly, but there's one nearby. Some of our grad students volunteer there," he said.

"What's the name of it?" Ellie asked.

"Mountainside Research. A couple of guys in my pre-med class did internships there."

"Was it around twenty years ago?" Ellie asked.

"Let me check the computer."

Computer keys clicked in the background, while Ellie combed through another file as she waited. Many of the young women who'd come to Circle of Love mentioned Gillian Roach. Three different young women stated that she'd stayed with them during labor and delivery, comforting them as they made the hardest decision of their lives. The names began to blur, as their stories were so similar.

Young love, hot guys, parties and alcohol played a part in some of their situations. Two young women said they'd first decided on adoption, but once they saw their infants, they'd changed their minds. Gillian had helped make arrangements for them to live in a group home, share childcare and get jobs to support themselves.

Ellie couldn't get Gillian's paintings out of her mind. The social worker had been an advocate for the young single mothers and for their children. She was the reason Ellie had wound up with the Randalls.

Now she was dead because of it.

# CHAPTER 111

*Mountainside Research*

"Detective Reeves," the young man on the phone said, bringing Ellie back to the moment. "I did some checking, and that research facility had just been formed in the area."

"It's the same one, Mountainside?"

"Sure is."

"Can you text me the address?"

"No problem."

Ellie thanked him, hung up and stood, dusting the grime from her pants. "I want to take the files from the year I was born."

"You think your mother's birth name is in here?"

"It's possible."

"Good thing you got a warrant," Derrick said.

Ellie nodded. "I'll send Landrum back to pick them up. But I'll take the ones from my birth year and leave them at the main office for him. Let's go talk to someone at that research facility."

Derrick stood, his jaw tight. "There have been cases of research experiments being tried on unsuspecting prisoners. What if someone did the same thing to college coeds?"

Anger colored his face, and her stomach swirled, but she tamped down the bile and they hurried up the stairs. She dropped the files at the receptionist's desk and explained her deputy would be back for them.

As they stepped outside, the heat lightning was intensifying, quick jolts ripping across the tops of the ridges, a thunderstorm imminent.

Lightning cracked and a dark storm cloud opened up, rain beginning to drizzle.

Fifteen minutes later, she swung the Jeep into the parking lot of Mountainside Research. The facility was a nondescript white building next to the small hospital which catered to locals and students. Tall oaks and pines stood guard outside like a fortress.

"According to the information here," Derrick said as he looked up from his tablet, "the facility is not directly connected to the college." He turned the screen toward her. "Here's a photo of what it used to look like twenty years ago. The original building was a few miles from here in a remote location, hence the 'Mountainside' name. But it was shut down when this one was built."

Ellie studied the two-story rustic house which once housed the facility. The place was set on top of a mountain ridge overlooking the valley. It looked secluded. She tried not to think about how many women had been hurt there.

In spite of the trickling rain, brutal heat engulfed Ellie as she exited the car, and they made their way to the door. Once inside, the blast of air conditioning was a welcome relief. A plaque with several doctors' names was attached to the wall. A framed certification for the clinic hung near the reception desk, and fliers were tacked on a corkboard advertising various clinical trial studies. The waiting room held several chairs, although it was empty at the moment.

Five minutes later, they sat across from a rail-thin man with a bad comb-over and freckled skin who introduced himself as Dr. Joe Sturgens.

"I'm not sure what this is about, but our patients' confidentiality is of utmost importance," he began.

It was like listening to a broken record.

"We're aware of that," she said. One by one she laid photos of the dead women on the desk. "But as you can see, we have a problem here. She pointed to Vanessa's photograph. "She was murdered."

Next was Agnes. "Her daughter was killed." Then Janie. "She was also murdered, by the same man who killed the others."

Dr. Sturgens tugged at his narrow tie. "I'm sorry to hear that, but I—"

"You can't discuss them or any studies they were part of," Ellie said, not bothering to hide her disgust. "But we need the name of the doctor who conducted the sleep study that connects Agnes Curtis and Janie Huntington." Ellie crossed her arms. "And before you justify not cooperating, be aware that this killer is not finished. He may be looking for another victim at this very minute. So let your ethics guide you into helping us. And if that's not enough, know that if this clinic is in any way involved, I will shut your ass down."

Derrick straightened, his dark gaze daring the man to argue. "Just the doctor's name."

With a huff, Dr. Sturgens turned to his computer. Keys clicked, his face puckered into a frown, but he hastily scribbled the man's name on a scrap of paper.

"Dr. Hangar," he said. "He was here during that time and worked in conjunction with a study for a new sleep medication. But he left here years ago, and I don't have any forwarding information on him." He planted his hands on his desk. "And that's the truth."

"Were you working here at the time?" Ellie asked.

He tugged at his tie again. "I came a few months before he left."

"What was your opinion of him?"

"He was serious, a hard worker. But that's about all I remember. I was new and he stayed in his office most of the time."

Leaning forward, Derrick pinned the man with a cold stare. "Did you sense anything was off about him? That he might be doing something unethical behind closed doors?"

The man's eyes widened in alarm. "What do you mean unethical?"

Ellie saw him shutting down. "I mean sexual assault, Dr. Sturgens." She tapped the photos of the women's faces. "Two of these women told their counselor they thought they'd been raped while drugged. The mother of Vanessa Morely said the same thing happened to her several years earlier. In the case of two of the women, Agnes and Janie, we believe it may have happened while they were sedated during the sleep study."

The man shot up from his chair. "I don't know what you're talking about. For the record, though, if I'd suspected one of my coworkers was unethical or improper with a patient, I would have reported him. Now, if you need to talk to me again, go through my attorney."

# CHAPTER 112

*Bluff County Hospital*

As Ellie walked down the hall to see Sarah, she couldn't help but think about the vulnerable nature of hospital patients or research study participants. They trusted their lives to the staff, who generally were caring, selfless heroes. But there were occasions when nefarious things happened, patients too disoriented on meds that they could easily be taken advantage of.

That kind of depravity turned her stomach.

Hopefully Derrick could locate Dr. Hangar and they would stop this madness.

When she reached Sarah's room, she knocked then eased open the door. Shondra sat beside the bruised and battered young woman, who was propped against the pillows sipping water through a straw. Shondra turned to her with a small smile. Her friend looked stronger than she had in weeks.

Ellie walked over and laid her hand on Shondra's back. "Thanks for staying with her. I'm sure you need to go home and get some rest."

"I'm fine, Ellie." Shondra squeezed her hand. "Seeing her like this was a kick in the butt."

Ellie gave an encouraging smile, then approached Sarah, who was watching them with pain-filled eyes.

"Hey," Ellie said. "I'm glad you're awake."

Sarah touched her swollen cheek self-consciously. "At least I'm alive."

"You're a strong lady," Shondra said. "You will get past this, I promise."

Sarah looked unsure but lifted her chin.

"Tell us what happened," Ellie said softly. "Who hurt you?"

Sarah winced as she handed the cup of water back to Shondra. "It was Ryder. I… don't know what happened. He was acting strange all day, and decided he wanted to visit places people had died on the trail."

Ellie shifted. "Was that usual for him?"

"It was weird, even though sometimes he slipped into a dark state. He suffered from night terrors, but he never explained what caused them. He was sullen after we found the body. Refused to talk, but I could tell it really got to him. I was upset, and he lost it and turned on me. When I tried to leave, he grabbed me, and I fell and…" She squeezed her eyes shut and let a minute pass before she opened them again.

"Do you have any idea where he was going when he left?" Ellie asked gently.

"No, I don't care either. I never want to see him again."

Shondra squeezed Sarah's hand, and Ellie gave her a sympathetic smile. "I can understand that. Did he mention any family or a friend he'd turn to?"

"No, he was such a loner."

"How about a second home?"

"I never even saw where he lived. He always came to my place."

"Thank you for talking to us," Ellie said. "I promise you we'll find him. He won't get away with what he did to you."

# CHAPTER 113

Ellie stepped out and saw a man coming toward the doorway.

She recognized him immediately. The dark hair, the broad face, the intense look… Ryder.

As soon as he spotted her, he turned and ran down the hall.

Ellie flashed her badge to a med tech pushing a medicine cart. "Tell security to lock down the hospital and guard the door. Now!"

The door to the stairwell flew open, slamming back. Her shoes pounded the floor as she sprinted towards it, then inside. His feet hammered down the stairs, he crossed one landing, then sped onto the next.

Her breath puffed out as she took the steps two at a time. By the time she reached the next landing, she spotted him. Jumping over the rail, she launched herself onto him, catching him around the neck. But he threw her off him, crashing against the concrete wall. Pain shot through her shoulder blades and the force knocked the wind out of her.

He growled, storming down the steps again. Dragging herself up, she caught her breath, gripped the stairwell and pulled her weapon. Darting down the next flight, she saw him rounding the landing. Speeding up, she aimed her gun.

"Stop, Ryder, or I'll shoot."

He didn't hesitate, not even for a second. She raced down, hit the landing and flew around the corner to the next level. But he was waiting in ambush, delivering a sharp blow to her arm and sending her gun flying. Then he took off again.

Shaking with anger, she struggled to regain her balance. Her arm was throbbing, but she ignored it and dashed further down in search of her gun. There it was. She snatched it, then barreled down the rest of the steps, adrenaline kicking in.

She spotted him near the exit and threw herself over the side of the landing, aiming the gun at his back. "Give it up, Ryder."

He swung around, his body moving so fast that he landed a hard kick to her stomach. She fell to the ground, her head spinning but a second later, managed to scramble to her feet and aim the gun at him.

He reached for it with one beefy hand, pushing the barrel upward. A bullet pinged against the ceiling as they fought for the weapon, going down in a tangle of arms and legs. They traded blows, fists flying, and rolled down the rest of the steps to the bottom. She lost her weapon again and heard it slide across the floor.

Pain ricocheted through her back, and she tasted blood, but the image of Sarah's battered face fueled her energy, and she crawled toward the gun. Ryder was going for it, too, but she made it first, then clenched it and jammed the barrel into his belly.

"Give it up, Ryder, I know you hurt Sarah."

He went still, his big body heaving for a breath.

Ellie took a step back, keeping the gun trained on him. "Get against the wall now."

He swallowed hard, and she braced herself for another fight, but slowly he did as she said and raised his hands in surrender.

"You put Sarah in the hospital," she said as she stood, careful to keep the gun on him. "And you killed those other women."

His wide jaw hardened and his chest rose and fell with his labored breathing. "What the hell are you talking about?"

"You led Sarah to Death's Door, to Vanessa Morely. She said you wanted to visit other places people had died." She pinned him with a stare. "Were you going to take her to the site of the murders, then kill her, too?"

Ryder's face contorted. "You're way off, Detective. I didn't kill anyone."

"You were a sniper," Ellie ground out. "You killed for a living."

His brows furrowed. "That was a long damn time ago, and it was based on orders." His voice was low, lethal. "But if you're talking about those women on the news that wasn't me. I swear it."

"Why should I believe you? I found Sarah. I saw what she looked like when you finished beating her."

His control was slipping, his edge gone as emotions took over his expression. "I… don't know what came over me," he said, his voice choking.

"Then why did you run?"

His face reddened. "I… was ashamed. Something snapped inside me when I saw that dead woman. I… came here to tell Sarah how sorry I am. I've never done anything like that before."

"All abusers deny their actions," Ellie said. "Maybe you were going to beat her to death, then carry her body out into the woods to torch just like you did the others."

"I told you I didn't kill those women," he growled. "And I certainly didn't torch anyone."

He sounded so convincing Ellie almost believed him. She slowly moved towards the stairwell exit, careful to keep a hard grip on her gun and the barrel pointed at his chest. "Get up. And if you try to run, I will shoot your ass."

He kept his hands raised and slowly stood, his gaze latched onto hers.

"Turn around," Ellie ordered.

He did as she said, his big body stiff as he allowed her to handcuff him. Once the cuffs were on, she wiped the blood from her lip with the back of her hand, then snagged her phone and called Derrick.

"Ellie?"

"Yeah," she said. "I have Rigdon in custody. I'm bringing him in now."

# CHAPTER 114

While Derrick waited on Ellie to bring Rigdon into the station, he dug deeper into the guy. He found no reports or evidence of arson in his background, and Rigdon's age also posed a problem. He was early thirties now. There was no way he could have assaulted her mother.

He made a phone call to a former SEAL who had worked for the same private company after he left the navy. Derrick had known Flint Cornwall since high school, before they'd gone their separate ways. A year ago, he'd reconnected when Flint had testified in a federal case involving a corrupt judge.

"This is Derrick," he said when the voicemail picked up. "I've got an important case and need some information. Please call me back ASAP."

After examining the files from the Circle of Love, he had nothing new to add to the investigation, but he got the sense that the staff at the home had been on the up and up. There was nothing connecting them to the research facility or mention of a fertility clinic.

He wanted to find Ellie's mother for her, but he didn't have a name. Still, he listed the women who'd given birth to cross reference with girls at the home for further investigation.

Looking for more connections, he jotted down names of anyone the girls mentioned from the home or connected to it. Gillian Roach was a common thread, always following through on her duty of care to the young women. The hair on his nape prickled as he stumbled on another name.

Reverend Ike Jones.

Skimming more files, he discovered Reverend Ike regularly visited Circle of Love to counsel the girls and pray with them. He seemed to have taken Agnes under his wing, inviting her to join a small group from his church.

Derrick turned to his computer. A quick search and his hunch was right.

Just then his phone rang. "Hey, Flint, thank you for calling me back so quickly," he said as he answered.

"You sounded like it was important."

"It is. Have you seen the news about the case in Crooked Creek, Georgia where the victims were torched?"

"I have. Is that where you are now?"

"It is. We have a possible person of interest, a man named Ryder Rigdon. Former military sniper. He worked for the same contractor at the same time you did, too."

Flint made a grumbling sound. "You know I don't like to talk about that time."

"I know, but Rigdon is a person of interest in the case."

"Burning the bodies doesn't fit with Rigdon. He was an excellent marksman. Iron-clad control. His kills were always a single bullet to the head. Clean, neat, no evidence left behind."

Derrick paused. That may have been the case once, but Rigdon had lost control with Sarah.

# CHAPTER 115

Ellie pushed Rigdon through the police station, straight to an interrogation room.

"You're wasting your time," he said between clenched teeth. "I did not kill those women."

"I'll be back." Ellie closed the door and left him to stew, debating whether she believed him or not. She'd seen the damage he'd done to Sarah, yet there was something in his vehement denial and his voice, raw with emotion, that made her question if he was a murderer. Yes, he'd been a sniper, and a SEAL. But snipers and special forces were trained to have control, to focus on their targets. To be in and out.

The crime scenes she'd witnessed didn't fit with that control and discipline. A sniper would line up his target in his sightline, wait patiently for the right moment. Sometimes he was so far away from his target he not only had to calculate the target's movement, but factor in wind speed, elevation, humidity and the parabolic movement of the bullet. When that moment came, he'd strike, usually sending a single bullet straight to his target's heart or head. Simple, clean, no mess, instant death.

Then he would be gone, like a ghost in the night.

"Did he confess?" Derrick asked, meeting her in the hall.

Ellie huffed. "Actually, he admitted to beating up Sarah but didn't cop to the other crimes. I know abusers usually apologize afterwards and can show remorse. They shower their spouses or girlfriends with gifts and flowers to make up for their behavior. But something about Rigdon seemed strange. Maybe he's a sociopath or—"

"He's telling the truth," Derrick finished.

Ellie shrugged. "It's possible. The burning of the bodies is still bothering me."

"I agree. I spoke with a former SEAL and military contractor who knew Rigdon. Said he never varied his method, single shot to the brain. In and out, left no evidence he'd been at the crime scene. Torching the victims doesn't fit."

Ellie took a breath, frustrated.

"There's more," Derrick said, explaining about finding references to Reverend Ike. "Agnes Curtis met the reverend at Circle of Love when she was pregnant."

"Interesting," Ellie said. "Why don't you take a stab at Rigdon while I talk to the Curtises again? They're hiding more than the fact that Mr. Curtis was not Katie Lee's father."

Josiah and Agnes Curtis were embroiled in this up to their eyeballs. They had kept their secrets long enough. It was time she exposed them.

# CHAPTER 116

*Pigeon Lake*

Ellie did not intend to leave until she had some answers. It took three knocks before Mr. Curtis opened the door. His look of animosity was as blistering as the heat scorching the flowers and foliage outside.

"What are you doing here again?" he barked. "My family is in mourning."

"Again, I'm truly sorry for your loss, but I have to talk to you and your wife. And I'm not going to leave until I do." She pushed past him, calling Mrs. Curtis's name as she strode inside.

"Mrs. Curtis, we need to talk." In the kitchen, she found the woman pulling a pan of biscuits from the oven, pouring more heat into the stifling room.

Agnes yelped when she saw her, burning her fingers as she shoved the pan onto the stove.

Mr. Curtis stormed in, jerking his son by the neck of his T-shirt. "Go upstairs, Marty. This is adult conversation."

Marty's frightened look made Ellie wonder what had happened in this family after her last visit. The boy ducked his head down and hurried from the room, his sneakers pounding the stairs as he climbed them.

"I have uncovered some interesting information," Ellie said. "During the course of the investigation into your daughter's death and the recent murders in Bluff County, we traced a connection between the victims." She watched as Mrs. Curtis sank into a kitchen chair and wiped her face with a kitchen towel.

"Is it okay if we discuss this in front of your husband or would you rather we talk alone?"

The woman dared a glance at her husband. "Josiah can stay."

"You need to leave," Mr. Curtis said. "My family wants to be alone."

"That is not going to happen, sir. Not until I get some answers, because whoever killed your daughter may be responsible for multiple deaths. Now, I understand your need for privacy, and I will do my best to respect it, but I now know that Agnes and Janie Huntington both participated in a sleep study where they later claimed they were sexually assaulted. Upon learning about their pregnancies, they went to the Circle of Love home." She inhaled, well aware Agnes was wilting deeper and deeper into her chair as she spoke.

"I want you to leave," Mr. Curtis snarled. He reached inside the closet, where Ellie spotted a rifle.

"Do not do that, Mr. Curtis. If you pick up that gun, I will arrest you for threatening a police officer and you will go to jail."

"Josiah," Agnes said in a muffled whisper. "Please, we don't want violence in our home."

The man's thin frame stilled, and he lowered his hands by his sides. "Why are you doing this to my family?"

Ellie licked her dry lips. "Because I want to make sure whoever killed your precious daughter is brought to justice, and I believe the assaults and the murders are linked." She relaxed slightly as he stepped away from the weapon. "I know Reverend Ike visited the Circle of Love and that you met him there, Mrs. Curtis. That someone hurt you a long time ago."

The woman's lower lip trembled, and she nodded, tears filling her eyes. "I was alone and pregnant. Reverend Ike promised to save me."

"And he did that by introducing you to Josiah, didn't he?" Ellie glanced at the husband. "You were trying to be a good man, weren't you? You heard Agnes needed someone and you met her and maybe you even fell in love."

"I did love her," Josiah said. "I… did what Reverend Ike said. And I agreed to raise Agnes's baby as my own."

"And you did. But you couldn't love her, could you? Every time you looked at her you saw the man who'd assaulted Agnes." Just as her own mother might have thought about her if she'd kept her, she thought, stomach plummeting.

"Some of the other girls gave their babies away, but I couldn't do that," Agnes said in a whisper.

"Tell me about Katie Lee's father," Ellie urged.

Agnes wiped tears from her eyes while Mr. Curtis dropped his head into his hands.

"I… don't know who he is," she choked out. "I joined this sleep study like some of my friends, but the pills did something to me. I… had dreams, hallucinations. I don't really remember things clearly."

"What happened in those dreams?" Ellie asked softly.

Agnes clutched the counter. "I… someone was on top of me. And I couldn't move or get up. But I didn't know if it had actually happened, it felt like a dream."

"Did you tell anyone what happened?" Ellie asked.

"I didn't know for sure if it was real at the time. My memory was so blurry and confused. But a few weeks later, I realized it wasn't just a dream or hallucination."

"Because you were pregnant," Ellie said.

The woman nodded, pressing a hand to her mouth.

"I'm so sorry that happened to you," Ellie said gently. "I really am. Did you consider going to the police and telling somebody then?"

Tears flowed down her face. "I was too ashamed. I… was afraid what my parents would do, so I ran away."

"That's when you went to the Circle of Love, isn't it?"

"Yes," Agnes murmured. "They were so nice to me there."

"And you met Gillian Roach there, didn't you?" Ellie asked. "She talked to other girls about adoption and offered to help you."

"I did, but I just couldn't let my baby go. But now… she's dead." Her fingers trembled as she wiped at her damp cheeks.

Mr. Curtis looked up then, past his wife and out the window as if in spite of marrying her, he still felt shame.

"That's why I'm here." Ellie pulled a photograph of Rigdon from her phone and showed it to the woman. "Do you recognize this man? Did you ever see him hanging around Katie Lee?"

Agnes rubbed at her eyes and studied the picture, confusion clouding her expression. "No… do you think he's the man who killed my daughter?"

"I don't know." Ellie angled it for the husband to see. "Mr. Curtis, do you recognize him?"

He took a quick look, his body rigid. "No, now I want you to leave. You've upset my wife enough."

"One more question," Ellie said. "What was the name of the doctor who treated you during the sleep study?"

Agnes glanced at her husband, then whispered the name Dr. Hangar.

Ellie squeezed her hand. "I know that was difficult. But for Katie Lee's sake, I'm going to bring him in. And if he killed her, I'll make him pay for what he's done."

# CHAPTER 117

"Tell me about this study," Ellie said, refusing to leave until she'd got to the bottom of this. "How exactly did it go?"

Agnes wrung her hands together. "I was having insomnia and couldn't focus on my studies, and I wanted to do well in my classes. So when Janie told me about the study, I signed up."

"It was a new experimental sleeping pill that you took?" Ellie asked.

The woman nodded. "'Z', they were calling it."

"What happened? Were you given it in the office and then monitored while taking it?"

"Yes, at first," she answered. "They wanted to make sure we didn't have any adverse reactions."

"Did you experience any side effects?"

"No, for the first time in months, I fell asleep when I went to bed. It was great. No more tossing and turning. No more counting sheep. But after a couple of weeks, it stopped working. So they altered the dosage. That's when I started having the nightmares. I dreamed someone was in my room at night and that a stranger came in while I was asleep at the clinic. I remember waking up crying and screaming. It seemed so real."

The breath stalled in Ellie's chest. "Were you alone when you woke up?"

Agnes pinched the bridge of her nose. "A nurse came in, told me I was having a reaction to the drug. That I'd been hallucinating."

"What did Dr. Hangar say?"

"He said he would document my reaction and that I should drop out of the study." She dared a glance at her husband again, whose eyes were blazing with anger.

Then she shriveled up and stopped talking.

# CHAPTER 118

*Crooked Creek*

Derrick read the message from Ellie confirming that Agnes Curtis had participated in the sleep study under Dr. Hangar. The Curtises both denied knowing or seeing Rigdon around their daughter, but that didn't mean he hadn't killed her. Someone could have paid him.

His hard-assed face in place, he set the folder containing photos of the victims on the table. The bare room with its single table, two chairs and white walls echoed with silence. Rigdon kept his cuffed hands in his lap but held his head high.

"Mr. Rigdon," Derrick began as he spread the victims' photographs on the table. "You know why you're here?"

The big man averted his gaze as if he couldn't tolerate looking at the gruesome pictures.

"Mr. Rigdon," Derrick repeated. "Do you know why you're here?"

"Yes, but I told that detective, I didn't kill any of those women." His voice thickened. "I never saw any of them before."

"You were a sniper," Derrick said. "Maybe you turned your contract work with private military firms into contract work for civilians."

Rigdon shook his head in denial. "No, I left that life behind. At least I tried to."

"What does that mean? Did someone approach you and offer you money to make these hits?"

"No," Rigdon said vehemently. "I meant I left the military and my sniper kills behind. I… wanted to have a real life, but I had nightmares about it all."

"Were you having a nightmare when you hurt Sarah?"

Pain streaked the man's dark gray eyes. "I … don't know what happened. But—"

"You think there's an excuse for beating a woman nearly to death?"

Rigdon heaved a labored breath. "No." He stared Derrick in the eyes. "I don't know why I did it. I just lost control. It was like this voice in my head yelled at me to do it and I… I didn't even see that it was Sarah. It was like it was someone else took over my body, like she was someone else."

The man's deep voice rang with sincerity.

"And who else would that be?" Derrick asked quietly.

Rigdon laid his hands on the table and looked at them. They were wide and scarred, his nails blunt. Those hands had a number of kills to their credit.

"You mentioned nightmares," Derrick said. "Are you taking any medication for PTSD?"

Rigdon went still. Shame colored his face, then he muttered he was. "I'm not proud of it, but ever since I was a kid, I had trouble sleeping. Bad dreams, night terrors, walking in my sleep. By the time I finished high school, I was only sleeping about ten to fifteen hours a week. I… thought I was going crazy."

"Go on," Derrick said.

"I was desperate, so I went to a sleep clinic. A couple of the meds didn't work for me, so they recommended a new research trial drug and I signed up for the study."

Derrick's pulse jumped.

"What was the name of the research facility?" Derrick asked, even though he already knew.

Rigdon twined his fingers together and Derrick noted the bruising where he'd hit Sarah. "Mountainside," Rigdon said. "But one of the meds only made things worse. I had hallucinations."

"Tell me about them."

Rigdon clenched his hands into fists, the handcuffs rattling. "I saw images of myself killing people. Torturing men and women. It shook me up, so I got off the drug, but still kept having them, so I signed up for the military. Decided I could use those dark fantasies to good use by taking out enemies."

"So you became a sniper?"

Rigdon nodded. "But after a while, I started having trouble concentrating. Some noises set me off and… my sergeant suggested I didn't reenlist."

Derrick showed no reaction, but his mind was racing. More than one woman in the study had been assaulted while under the influence of the drug.

Had something happened to Rigdon there, too?

# CHAPTER 119

*Ticktock, ticktock.*

The click sounded in his brain. The next name on the list. He was almost finished.

Except that detective was getting too close to the truth. And so was the fucking reporter. She was just as nosy as Ellie Reeves.

Both had to be dealt with.

Hunching in the shadows beneath the awning, he watched the people in Crooked Creek adding more Fourth of July decorations. Red, white and blue covered everything, and there were at least five floats in the vacant parking lot of the feed store that had gone out of business three years ago.

One frilly float held a small throne and a larger one boasted signs for Miss Teen Bluff County and Little Miss Bluff County. He'd watched the mothers fuss over their little girls in their frou-frou dresses, wearing makeup not fit for kids their age, and sporting bows that were almost as big as their heads. The mothers were clucking around like hens, darting furtive glasses at the other darlings and their moms, their determination to win evident in their cutthroat whispers.

The gossipy group he'd heard talking about Ellie and her family had gathered to set up a stage for the teen talent show and the food vendors were in place.

At one end, little kids, ten and under, were taping streamers, plastic flowers, gemstones and whatever else they could find to dress up their bikes.

The parade was the perfect place to claim his next victim.

While everyone was busy enjoying the festivities, stuffing their faces with hot dogs, funnel cakes and snow cones, cheering noisily as the parade carried on, he could slip away with her and no one would know.

Before the high school band finished playing the Alma Mater, and Miss Teen and Little Miss Bluff County were announced, they would be far away in the woods where no one would find her.

Except for the detective. He'd lure her there. Make her think she could save the day.

But it was too late for both of them. Soon their bodies would turn to ash. And then he could finally escape and put all this behind him.

# CHAPTER 120

*Somewhere between Pigeon Lake and Crooked Creek*

Ellie couldn't shake the image of a young Agnes from her mind. A girl who'd been taken advantage of. A girl who'd learned she was pregnant but had no idea who'd fathered her child. A girl so terrified of what her parents would think that she'd run away. A young woman so vulnerable that she'd been susceptible to Reverend Ike and his agenda.

There was a tiny chink in her anger for Mr. Curtis. It sounded as if he might have really cared for Agnes when they'd met, that he'd meant to do right by her and Katie Lee. When had that compassionate person turned into a controlling, condescending, hard man? Had Reverend Ike and his teachings changed him?

The storm clouds accumulating made it feel later than it was, and fog enveloped the road ahead. Two cars whizzed past her heading the opposite direction, and the sound of an engine roared behind her as a car sped up. Tires screeched as the driver rounded the curve too fast, and she tensed, glancing back to make sure he didn't run off the road.

His brakes squealed and he slowed, but she kept a steady grip on the steering wheel, and adjusted her fog lights, hoping the driver stayed back.

No such luck. The vehicle's headlights nearly blinded her as he ramped up his speed again. She pumped her brakes, hoping to send him a warning, but he accelerated, weaving over the center line, then closing in on her tail.

She swerved sideways then veered toward a side street to let him pass. Instead, he steered around the curve and spun up behind her.

This wasn't just some overzealous joy rider. He was following her.

Whoever it was wasn't hiding the fact either.

She squinted to determine what kind of vehicle it was, but the lights and fog made it impossible to tell. Maybe an SUV of some kind. The muffler sounded loud though, as if the vehicle was older, on its last legs.

Flooring her Jeep, she picked up speed. His tires screamed as he careened onto the road behind her. She slowed and waved him around just to see if he would pass her, but he was going so fast he slammed into her rear bumper.

Cursing, Ellie spun sideways, grappling for control as her Jeep skidded toward a boulder. On a wing and a prayer, she managed to control the car, shrieking to a halt. The SUV had bounced back then skated sideways toward the ravine.

Breath panting out, she yanked her gun from her holster as she slid from her Jeep. Dust swirled around her face, rising from the earth like a sea of ashes. She scanned the area quickly and noted the driver hadn't gotten out yet. The front end of the SUV, a gray Pathfinder, hung precariously over the edge of the ravine, rocking back and forth.

Inching slowly toward him, she kept a look out in case the driver wasn't alone. Hell, he might be hurt, or he might be watching, ready to ambush her.

Coughing at the dust, she inched toward the driver's side. Suddenly she saw movement inside. The driver was trying to open the mangled door. But when he did, it became wedged in the ground.

Ellie eased to the opposite side and snuck up on the vehicle, bracing herself for a weapon to appear as she peered inside.

Instead, Marty Curtis was wiping blood from his forehead. He looked dazed and disoriented, but she didn't see a gun.

She rapped on the window, and he turned toward her, his eyes filled with terror. She gestured for him to stay still, then she gently tugged the passenger door open. The Pathfinder wobbled unsteadily, and Marty yelped in fear.

"Stay calm," she mouthed, reaching out her hand in offering. He made a strangled sound but slowly eased across the seat. Another wobble of the car and the front jerked, scraping rock.

She snatched his arm and screamed for him to jump as she pulled him from the vehicle. A second later, the Pathfinder shook and rocked again then teetered over the edge and plunged into the ravine.

Marty fell against her and they both hit the ground, dirt and rocks flying. Ellie's chest ached for a breath as she dragged him further away from the overhang. When they reached a tree, she let go of him and turned to him, arms crossed.

"What the hell were you doing chasing me like that? You could have gotten us both killed."

The boy's chin quivered, then he made a mewling sound. "I'm sorry. I… just wanted you to stop."

"You could have called me," Ellie said, sweat pouring down her neck and back. The height of the ravine was making her dizzy, and her chest ached from struggling to breathe. She forced herself not to look down.

"I couldn't, Daddy took the phone," Marty said, his voice shaky.

Ellie willed herself to calm down. "I'm sorry, Marty. Tell me what's on your mind."

He ran his hand over his buzz cut. "After you left, my old man went crazy. He accused Mama of telling people about Katie Lee, that she wasn't his. I've never seen him so mad, like he might hurt her. I… thought you could stop him."

Ellie cursed herself. She'd stirred up a hornets' nest in that house and this teenage boy was being stung by it. "I'm sorry, Marty. I'll go back and make sure she's all right."

"I've never seen him get so rough. What if he kills my mama?"

"He won't," Ellie said, "I'll make sure of it. Come on, I'll drive you back and make sure things have settled down."

"What about my car?" His voice splintered. "Daddy will be furious."

"You had an accident," Ellie said, willing to forgive the fact that he'd chased down a police officer, and could have gotten them both killed. "I'll make sure your father knows that," Ellie said. "And if he has insurance, it should cover it."

He nodded, although he was trembling as he followed her to the Jeep.

When she climbed inside, she pressed Shondra's number. Her friend answered on the second ring. She quickly explained that Rigdon was in custody and asked Shondra to meet her at the Curtises. "I need your help," Ellie said. "Rigdon confessed to beating Sarah, but not to the murders. But for now, Sarah is safe."

# CHAPTER 121

Derrick studied Rigdon's body language. The man was growing more agitated with every second.

"Do you still take any sleep medication?" Derrick asked.

Rigdon made a sound of disgust. "I still take the same damn pills, despite everything. I surrendered them when I was booked."

Derrick strode to the booking desk and retrieved the bottle. When he pulled it out, he read the label—Z. A doctor named Frankenson had prescribed it. He hurried back to the interrogation room. "Is this the doc who originally conducted the sleep study?"

"No, a new primary care doctor."

"Do you recall the name of the doctor who first prescribed it?"

"I'll never forget it," Rigdon said. "Dr. Lewis Hoyt. He and this doctor named Hangar ran the study. When I talked to them about the nightmares I'd had while on the sleep medication, Dr. Hoyt brushed me off. Said I could go off them if I wanted. But…"

"But you're hooked on them?" Derrick asked.

"I guess so. I tried a few times to kick them, but then I literally wouldn't sleep for a week. Then I'd get so anxious and jittery and sometimes I… just exploded."

"Like you did when you beat up your girlfriend."

Rigdon closed his eyes, emotions overcoming him as he collapsed back into the metal chair. "I don't even remember doing that. But when I saw those standing stones, I… had these flashbacks of that study."

"What was it about the stones?"

"I… think they were there. I remember seeing stones like that through the window when I was in that room. Then the hallucinations started."

"Can you describe the place?"

Rigdon closed his eyes. "There were different rooms," he said in a low voice. "I was strapped down and given the drug. Then this bright light was shining directly in my eyes. The room was cold and a clock was ticking. Over and over, it was so loud it hurt my ears and the light hurt, then I heard screaming." He opened his eyes, his pupils flared. "And then… I don't know what happened exactly. But… I… I know it was bad."

Derrick gave him a moment. "That memory triggered you to hurt Sarah?"

Rigdon looked down at his scarred hands. "I think I was trying to escape, to get away… and it was like she was them, the ones in the hallucination who wouldn't let me go…"

Derrick heard the anguish in Rigdon's tone. Not only had the young women in the study been sexually assaulted, something had happened to the young men.

What exactly were those doctors doing in that study?

# CHAPTER 122

"Stay here, Marty," Ellie ordered, as she met Shondra outside the Curtises house. "I'll let you know when we defuse the situation."

He rocked himself back and forth, and she reached inside, laying a hand on his shoulder. "You did the right thing coming to me. We'll make sure your mama is safe. I'll be back."

Marty nodded, although the poor kid was battling tears. Ellie glanced at Shondra, who wore her sympathy like her badge, even though Ellie knew she was as tough as they came.

They silently rushed towards the house, creeping along the bushes and crouching low so as not to draw attention. As they approached, she and Shondra scanned the property, pausing to listen by the windows. The heat clung to every pore in Ellie's body, the silence from the woods and mountains ominous as pigeons flocked the backyard. Ellie motioned for Shondra to cover the front door, and she inched around to the back. She peered inside the windows, but the curtains were drawn as if intentionally shutting out the world.

She inched up the three steps to the back stoop and looked inside the kitchen. A pot was boiling on the stove, but she didn't see either of the Curtises.

She jiggled the doorknob, and the door opened. She crept through the room, pausing in the hallway. The couple's bedroom looked to be at the end of the hallway upstairs, but it was dark. Still, she swept through the upper floor with her flashlight, but no one was there.

Back into the hallway downstairs, she met Shondra, who signaled the living room was clear before gesturing toward a door that led downstairs to a basement.

The hair on the back of Ellie's neck prickled as she slowly turned the knob.

The minute she did she heard Mrs. Curtis scream.

# CHAPTER 123

Ellie kept her weapon at the ready and slowly tiptoed down the steps. Shondra had her back.

The stairwell was dark, the sound of dripping water echoing like a torture chamber. Mr. Curtis's sharp voice shouting at his wife and his shoes pounding on the concrete floor floated towards them.

It was dark, except for candles lit in a circle around a chair where Mrs. Curtis sat hunched over, her spirit broken.

Reverend Ike stood over her, condemnation glowing in his eyes. A metal tub large enough for a human sat to the right, filled with water. An odd, bitter odor permeated the room.

Then she spotted the source of the smell, a pot brewing on a hotplate. Judging from the dazed look in Agnes's eyes, it was some kind of tea, probably laced with psilocybin or another hallucinogen.

The reverend must be drugging his parishioners to brainwash them.

"I promised you redemption," the reverend said. "Agnes, your husband made you respectable by marrying you. He offered you a haven for your illegitimate child. But you have disobeyed."

"You should have kept silent, Agnes," Mr. Curtis said. He was cradling a shotgun. "Now my son and I will have to live with your shame."

Agnes lifted her pale thin face, gaunt with fear. "You know what they did to us, that I was drugged," she finally said to her husband. "And you're doing the same thing now."

"I gave you a home and a respectable life," Josiah said angrily.

As Agnes turned to the reverend, tears swam in the depths of her eyes. "Did you know what they were doing back then? Were you part of it?"

"I heard the ramblings of some wayward girls who denied they'd been sleeping around."

"We didn't do anything except trust the doctor at that clinic," Agnes said. Finally, a hint of some fight left in her. "And he took advantage of us."

"Your memory is foggy because you choose not to admit your mistakes," the reverend said.

"My mistake was listening to you and not going to the police. If I had, my daughter might still be alive."

"Shut up," Josiah shouted.

"You hated Katie Lee more every day. Did you kill her?" Agnes cried.

"Of course not," Josiah snapped.

The reverend took Agnes's arm and she swayed as she stood.

It was time to act. Ellie took two more steps, the staircase creaking. She felt Shondra behind her. "Step away from Agnes," Ellie ordered. "Both of you."

The two men looked up, stunned.

"You're trespassing," Mr. Curtis said, turning the shotgun on Ellie. "Get out or I'll shoot you and tell the sheriff I thought you were an intruder."

"You're going to kill me and keep covering for Katie Lee's killer?" Ellie replied as she aimed her own weapon at him.

"Yeah, Dad, are you?" Marty yelled.

Ellie tightened her fingers around her weapon, "Stay back, Marty."

But he didn't. His shoes pounded the steps, rushing toward them. "Did you kill her, Dad?"

Mr. Curtis shook his head in denial. His hand was trembling, the shotgun wavering. "No, son. I swear I didn't."

Ellie eased toward him.

"Then who did?" Marty screamed. "You know, don't you?"

As Mr. Curtis shook his head again, Ellie took advantage of the moment and shoved the gun upward.

The reverend pushed Agnes into the tub of water. The drugs must have taken effect now, because she collapsed without a fight. Her dark hair swirled around her face as she went limp.

Shondra raced toward the reverend, her gun on him, and Marty ran to his mother. As Ellie wrestled with Josiah, Mr. Curtis dropped down, knocking over the candles. They fell over, hot wax pouring.

"Do you know who killed your daughter?" Ellie yanked him around and handcuffed him.

"I didn't do it," Josiah stuttered.

"Mom! Mom!" Marty helped his mother from the water, while Shondra called for an ambulance and restrained the reverend.

Ellie pushed Josiah against the wall and into a chair.

The flames from the candles were starting to spread, creeping along the floor and catching as they found cardboard boxes and a stack of old church bulletins.

"Let's get out of here," Ellie shouted.

Marty put his arm around his mother's waist, and she staggered, opening her eyes. "Come on, Mom," he said as he helped her cross the room.

The flames burst higher as Shondra dragged the reverend forward and Ellie pushed Josiah toward the steps, battling through the thickening smoke as they raced upstairs.

# CHAPTER 124

Minutes later, Ellie's heart ached for Marty, who stood beside the ambulance shaking while the paramedics examined his mother and firefighters ran into the house to extinguish the blaze.

Angelica and her crew showed up seconds later. The reporter jumped out and hurried toward Ellie.

"Keep that camera off the family," Ellie ordered.

"Tom, do as the detective says," said Angelica, motioning for her cameraman to lower his lens. Angelica halted, her expression concerned as she zeroed in on Marty.

Marty's hair stood on end—he'd run his hand through it a dozen times. The poor kid had been through a lot. Losing his sister, then trying to protect his mother.

Deputy Landrum read Curtis and the reverend their rights, then shoved them in the back of his squad car while Ellie spoke to the medics. "Mrs. Curtis needs to be treated for trauma and to be evaluated by a psychiatrist. Also run a tox screen. I believe she was drugged, possibly with a hallucinogen."

"Will do. What about the son?"

"Physically he's okay, but emotionally, I don't know," Ellie said. "He needs to be with his mother right now."

Unable to bear the agony on Marty's face, Ellie had to say something to Agnes. She gripped the woman's hand. In spite of the heat, she was shivering from the ice bath. Her damp hair was tangled around her milky-white face, eyes swimming as if she couldn't focus.

"I know you're in shock and hurting, Agnes. You're grieving for Katie Lee and I can't bring her back. But I promise you, I will find out who killed her and put him away." She paused. "But your son is still here, and he needs you more than anything. He needs you to take care of him, to teach him how to be a good man, the kind of man who would love a woman and treat her with respect."

Agnes's eyes fluttered, then she looked at Ellie, frowning, but slowly she seemed to comprehend.

"Deputy Eastwood is accompanying you and Marty to the hospital and will see that you receive the help you need."

Agnes slowly nodded, tears running down her cheeks.

"You can do this," Ellie whispered. "Do it for Katie Lee and your boy."

Shondra pulled her keys from her pocket. "If it's okay, I'll drive him to the hospital to be with her and stay with him."

Ellie squeezed Shondra's shoulder. "I'm sure Marty could use a friend. Someone who understands and can guide him through the process."

"It's nice to be back, working together with you," Shondra said.

Ellie gave her a quick hug. "It's nice to have you back. Better guard Agnes. If Janie was killed because she could expose the man who assaulted her, then Agnes might also be in danger."

"Don't worry. I'll keep her safe." Shondra gestured toward Deputy Landrum's car. "What about them?"

She'd like to stuff them in that tub of water, push them under and let them see how it felt. "We can charge the husband with spousal abuse and threatening an officer. We'll investigate the reverend for the drugs."

Shondra smiled sympathetically at Marty. "I'll do my best to convince the mother and son to enter a shelter."

Ellie saw Angelica watching. Knowing she had to answer to the public, she crossed to her.

"Can we record?" Angelica asked.

At Ellie's nod, Angelica motioned to Tom to film, then introduced herself. "We're here with Detective Ellie Reeves. Detective can you tell us what happened here today?"

Ellie stared into the camera. "We responded to a domestic situation at the home of Agnes and Josiah Curtis, the parents of Katie Lee Curtis, who was recently murdered.

"At this point I can't divulge specifics of our investigation into the teenager's death, but we are investigating Mr. Curtis for spousal abuse and bringing Reverend Ike Jones in for questioning. Again, I'm reaching out to the public for information regarding Katie Lee's murder and for any information regarding the Ole Glory Church and Reverend Ike Jones." The ambulance was pulling away, lights twirling against the night sky. "Excuse me, I need to go."

Angelica looked disappointed. "Detective—"

"I'm sorry, that's all I have for now. I need to question Mrs. Curtis."

Derrick called just as she got in her Jeep, and Ellie explained what had happened. "Once Agnes is treated, maybe she can fill in the blanks about the church, and that research facility."

"Good work, Detective." Derrick paused. "I have something, too. Rigdon gave me the name of the docs who ran the sleep study. Dr. Hangar and Dr. Hoyt."

She knew the name Hangar. But Hoyt was a new name to her. "Find them. They might be the key to everything."

# CHAPTER 125

*Crooked Creek*

Angelica Gomez tried not to feel disgruntled as she and Tom drove toward Crooked Creek. Her boss insisted they cover the Fourth of July festivities and see if she could connect with that author, but Angelica wanted to be working the bigger story. The murders.

She itched to chase Ellie down and make her tell her everything she knew. The detective was holding back, she was sure of that.

But then again, so was she. She thought she might have a lead on the case, but she wanted proof before she went to the detective. Had to check her facts. The last thing she wanted was to lose Ellie's trust.

Lately she'd felt as if someone was watching her. Then the phone calls started. Phone calls in the night with no number listed. Heavy breathing on the line when she answered.

Signs that her own investigation might be leading her close to the truth.

As they approached the center of town, traffic thickened. Main Street was blocked off and so were several side streets. The bad weather they'd feared had held off, but the parade had been delayed. It would start soon, followed by fireworks later. People were flooding the sidewalks, setting up lounge chairs and crowding in fronts of stores to grab a view. Several floats were lining up at the high school and she spotted the fire engine from Max's house.

Floats, cars and trucks were decorated with streamers, papier-mâché flowers and animals waiting to entertain the eager spectators. The lead float featured a giant bear that had been constructed from wire to resemble the school mascot, symbolic of Bear Mountain. Kids who'd decorated their bikes for the Fourth gathered to line up while clowns began to do tricks on the sidelines, giving out balloons and candy. Horns honked and locals shouted greetings as they finished setting up the arts and crafts booths.

Still, a shudder rippled through Angelica as she scanned the streets. Was the killer lurking among them, waiting to abduct another woman?

# CHAPTER 126

Derrick sped down the highway, rain clouds moving across the sky, low and ominous.

"I haven't been able to locate Dr. Hangar. The man virtually disappeared. No record of him practicing anywhere, relocating or renewing his driver's license. Also, no death certificate on file." He took a breath as he steered his car south of the county line. "It was Hoyt who spearheaded the research drug they used in that sleep study. I'm on my way to see him now."

"I'll ask Agnes about them," Ellie said, her voice muffled over his car's speakers.

"Two years after the trial Rigdon was involved in, the sleep medication was approved and was picked up by a major pharmaceutical company affiliated with one of the lead research and teaching hospitals in Atlanta at the time," Derrick continued. "Hoyt made a fortune. If he was a party to the sexual assaults, he wouldn't want that to come out."

They hung up, and he slowed as he approached the man's address. He was still in the country somewhat, but this was not poor rural Georgia. He'd done his homework before the drive. Hoyt lived on a twenty-five-acre estate on the Chattahoochee River with its own tennis, racquetball and golf courses. The two-million-dollar Georgian house had even been featured in *Southern Living*.

As Derrick reached the end of the two-mile drive, which had been lined with live oaks draped in Spanish moss, he saw a broad-shouldered man, about five-nine, hurriedly rolling a suitcase to a waiting limo.

Derrick accelerated, swerving in front of the limo to block it.

He shifted his car into park and climbed out. "Dr. Hoyt?"

The man instantly threw his shoulders back. "Excuse me, but I have a flight to catch."

"You're not leaving town anytime soon."

"I have to. I have business to attend to."

"I bet you do." Derrick flashed his credentials. "Special Agent Fox. And you, sir, are coming with me."

Anger shot across Hoyt's angular face. "What is this about?"

"The recent murders in Bluff County." He named the victims as he grabbed the man's arms and forced him to turn around. "You are under arrest. You have the right to remain silent—"

"I want a lawyer," Hoyt bellowed.

Derrick grabbed him by the collar of his button-down shirt, spun him around, pressing his face into the man's.

"You want a lawyer so you can protect yourself from the fact that you drugged and raped numerous women over the years. And now you're killing those same women to cover your ass."

"I didn't kill anyone," Hoyt snapped. "And I certainly didn't rape anyone."

"I don't believe you." Barely holding onto his control, Derrick shoved him in the back seat of his car and slammed the door.

# CHAPTER 127

*Bluff County Hospital*

Ellie was rushing through the hospital, anxious to question Agnes. Without her husband present, maybe she could finally tell the truth.

The doctor exited the exam room, and she stopped him. "How is Mrs. Curtis?"

"Resting," the doctor replied. "The tox screen showed she drank tea laced with hallucinogenic mushrooms. Thankfully she didn't ingest much of it so it should work its way out of her system quickly."

"Can I see her now?"

"Yes, but for just a few minutes. She's pretty traumatized."

Murmuring that she understood, Ellie slipped inside the room.

Marty hovered beside the bed, looking shaken. Shondra sat in the corner, a quiet force of calm.

"Hey," she said softly to Marty, placing a hand on his shoulder. "Why don't you grab a soda and a snack with Detective Eastwood while I talk to your mama?"

"I don't want to leave her," Marty said in a protective tone.

"I promise she'll be okay. I'll be right here."

Shondra stood. "Come on, kid, I'm starving. They have pizza in the cafeteria."

"I'll stay with her until you're back," Ellie said.

He reluctantly agreed and followed Shondra. Ellie approached the bed, easing up beside the fragile woman. "Mrs. Curtis," she said. "Can we talk?"

The woman opened her eyes and murmured yes.

"I'm sorry for what you've been through today. But I need some more help from you. Do you know who assaulted you and the other women?"

A fresh wave of agony washed over her face. "My memory's so fuzzy, but I'm pretty sure it was one of the staff. One of the doctors conducting the study."

Ellie showed her a photograph of Dr. Hoyt. "This man?"

Agnes squinted as she studied the picture. "I don't know… the drug made me so messed up. I can't even remember his face clearly, just that he was… on me."

Which was exactly what the bastard wanted.

The sound of someone arguing echoed from the hall, and Ellie closed the door to drown out the sound, but Agnes startled. "I… I remember a woman arguing. Yelling at the doctor. The older one who was in charge of the study."

"Was his name Dr. Hangar?"

"I… I think so. The woman… it was his wife. He called her Eula."

# CHAPTER 128

*Rose Hill*

Ms. Eula stared at the wilted roses in her garden. Everything was unraveling just as the threads of her afghan had. The scent of evil floated through the air as strong as the acrid odor of the charred bodies.

She saw the innocence and the terror in the faces of those girls in her mind and the guilt weighed heavy on her heart. She'd kept her secret too long.

It was all going to come out now.

She stepped on one of the wilted roses, crushing it beneath her shoe as if she was crushing the evil that lay below. She was getting to be an old woman, and if it helped save lives, what did it matter if the truth was revealed?

When the bodies had first started piling up on the trail this time, she hadn't understood. Hadn't known what it was all about. Only that the devil had crept through the forest one more time.

A slight breeze stirred the leaves, a breeze she hadn't felt in days. Yet it brought a chill of foreboding just as the crows that had taken root on the awning of her front porch brought their sinister message.

Eula crushed another row of dead roses with her boot, then another and another, then scooped up a handful of the wilted dry petals, lifting her hand to the breeze. It scattered the petals across her yard like black snowflakes, the wind picking them up and swirling them in a circle around her head and dropping them back to the ground like ashes.

# CHAPTER 129

*Crow's End*

This is where it had all started for him.

Crow's End. Thirty miles north of Crooked Creek and buried so deep in the mountains it wasn't even on the map.

*Ticktock. Ticktock.*

Sweat soaked his shirt and neck as he shuffled through the overgrown, brittle weeds. He paused, the bright evening sunlight a reminder of the searing light that had burned his eyeballs.

The old building that had been a monster in his eyes still stood, the paint chipped and faded, the front porch sagging, the pillars rotten.

So many dark days he'd spent in there. A place where he'd come to heal.

A place that had stolen his soul.

Gripping the sledgehammer in his hands, he swung it against the posts that held up the porch and watched the wood crack and splinter. Over and over, he attacked the building that had been their hiding place. The monsters who'd promised to help had worn disguises. But they were still monsters.

Another few bangs and the side began to crumble. It was falling down already. The tornado a few weeks back had ripped the roof off, shattered windows and torn the back rooms completely off.

He had two hours until the parade began.

He breathed out, the scent of smoke lingering on his skin, enticing.

Two hours until he could finish this nightmare and finally sleep again. Two hours until he could go after Ellie Reeves. The one who'd started the chain of dominos falling…

# CHAPTER 130

*Rose Hill*

Ms. Eula sat in her rocking chair on her front porch, gently swaying back and forth, a calmness descending over her. Rays of evening sunshine glinted across the wood rails of the porch, hints of a thunderstorm flickering along the fog over the ridges. A sudden wind whipped through the trees, sending dried leaves to the ground.

The sky was at war, Mother Nature caught between the chill of the dead and the wicked heat of the devil as he lingered in the foothills.

She'd seen the news. Heard that girl Ellie Reeves promising to get to the bottom of those murders.

Resignation settled inside her, bringing a small sense of relief that the lies would finally be told. No telling what would happen to her, but she'd lived a life full of ghosts and shadows, and maybe it was her time to settle up with the one who saw all.

Katie Lee Curtis's sweet young face tormented her. Her spirit floated in front of Eula as if she'd come to sit a spell. Maybe it was to condemn her, to say she was a fool for not being able to see what was in front of her very own eyes back then.

Or maybe it was to thank her for what she'd done when those tired eyes had finally opened to the truth.

After all, she'd done it for Agnes and the others.

But now Katie Lee had been killed because of it.

She could practically hear Ernie's bitter laugh rippling in the heat lightning as he'd ordered her to keep silent. To protect him.

He thought she would obey like she had before. Like that Reverend Ike touted.

But she'd lived in denial for too long. She remembered his hands on her, pushing her to the floor, telling her she was no good, that she was less than a woman. That she couldn't satisfy him.

Her hand hovered over her stomach. She couldn't give him a child either. Not that he'd wanted one. But she had. Oh, lord, how she'd wanted a baby.

That made what he did even more heartbreaking.

Tears burned the backs of her eyes at the memory of his humiliating comments. Tears she'd refused to shed until *that* day.

She hadn't cried for herself. But the screams coming from Ernie's office had sent her running inside.

Then everything had changed.

She didn't regret what she'd done, not for a minute.

# CHAPTER 131

*Crooked Creek*

He watched from the cover of the live oaks near the park as Angelica Gomez and her cameraman discussed where to set up. Her ebony hair draped her shoulders, her lips painted a bright red, her cheeks glowing. She looked impeccable on camera.

She would be beautiful in death as well.

The reporter had gotten too close to the truth. He'd known she was relentless in pursuing a story, but he'd underestimated her drive and determination to get answers.

That had been his mistake.

The second was getting to know some of the people in this small town. For years, he'd been able to live without being noticed. To hold a job *and* hold onto his sanity. To fit in.

Sometimes he wanted that more than anything.

Then the call had come. The clicking sound, the chime of the clock, then the voice ordering him what to do.

It was too late for redemption. The past had been written eons ago, and although he'd fought it, he'd been weak and his fate was sealed.

He carried the shame with him, the heaviness a constant weight on his shoulders, but he couldn't turn back time. The instinct to survive burned hot through his veins.

The reporter. Then Ellie Reeves. And maybe… one more, although he didn't think she posed a real threat. Her mind had been stolen from her just as part of his had, only she had never found her way back to reality. Still, he couldn't leave loose ends.

Angelica's cameraman walked back to the van to get the camera equipment from the back while the reporter stood looking at the crowd gathered for the Fourth of July as if studying how best to capture the story.

Only her story would end today.

His breath puffed out as the sound of excited children's voices filled the humid air. The tower clock in the middle of the square chimed.

*Ticktock. Ticktock.* Time to say goodbye to Angelica.

The crowd was the perfect place to hide.

People scrambled to their viewing spots before the parade began.

Music erupted and the crowd cheered. Grateful for the noise and distraction, he called Angelica's number, tapping his foot on the ground as he waited. She answered immediately.

"I know who killed those women. Meet me at the gazebo."

Anticipation built inside him as she pivoted to scan the park, hesitating. Debating. Wondering if the call was a trap.

She came anyway, just as he knew she would.

His car was parked a few feet away, out of sight and far away from the main crowd.

She carefully picked her way across the grass, her heels grappling with the sand and uneven soil as she drew closer. Her body was tense, eyes peeled for trouble, and she gripped her phone as if it was a weapon that could protect her.

Still and quiet, he waited. Watched. Not breathing.

When she reached the trees near the fence, he slipped up behind her. She startled, but he grabbed her around the neck before she could turn, then shoved the rag of chloroform over her mouth and nose. Seconds later, she collapsed against him, unconscious.

Her long hair fell across his arm as he picked her up, carrying her into the nearby warehouse, a holding ground for granite and stone, a big business in the area.

The need to end it here burst inside him, to light the fire and watch her body go up in flames.

But he had to wait until the timing was right.

He tied her up and dumped her between the giant stone slabs, satisfied that if she came to, no one would hear her for the sound-proofing of the granite and concrete markers inside.

Then he walked back to the parade, smiling as he went to take his place among the locals.

# CHAPTER 132

*Rose Hill*

Ellie's gaze was drawn to the wilted and crushed rose petals on the ground by Ms. Eula's house. When she'd visited the older woman before, the roses had been blooming such a brilliant bright red that you could see them from the dirt road leading to the house.

Now the red had faded, the dead flowers resembled the color of dried blood.

The pungent scent of life was gone and it its place, the rotten odor of death permeated the air.

"Come on, up, Ellie," Ms. Eula said. "I've been expecting you."

Ellie raised a brow and climbed the steps. "You knew I was coming?"

"Just a sense." Ms. Eula laid a hand on her heart, her wrinkled hand starting to show the strains of arthritis. "It's time, I suppose."

Ellie sank into the second rocker, surprised at the breeze fluttering through the trees.

"It's the ghosts whispering for me to tell," Ms. Eula said.

"Tell me what?"

Sighing wearily, Ms. Eula turned to face her. The woman's stare sent a shiver through Ellie.

"How much do you know?" Ms. Eula asked softly.

Ellie curled her fingers around the arms of the rocking chair. "That you were once married to a man named Dr. Ernie Hangar. That he disappeared a few years back."

Ms. Eula gave a resigned nod. "The rumors say I killed him and buried him in the garden."

"I've heard that. But I want to hear what happened from you."

Pulling a lace hankie from the pocket of her housedress, Eula dabbed at her eyes. "It was so long ago, it doesn't seem real now. But when you started finding these women murdered, I knew it was time for the story to come out."

"Your husband worked at a research clinic?" Ellie sat patiently, giving the woman time to tell it in her own way.

"He did. His good friend Dr. Hoyt was excited over developing a sleep medication. Ernie agreed to run a sleep study to test the medication."

Nausea rose in Ellie's stomach. "What was the purpose of the study?"

"He said they wanted to help folks with anxiety and sleep disorders like insomnia and sleep apnea. That lack of sleep can literally cause people to lose their minds. But that's not all he was doing." Pain laced Ms. Eula's voice. "I was such a fool, I was blind to what was happening. Blind for a long, long time. But one day I figured it out."

"Figured out what?" Ellie both needed to hear Ms. Eula say it and dreaded it at the same time.

Ms. Eula closed her eyes, the shame and agony of the memory gripping her. "Ernie took advantage of those young girls while they were sedated." Her breath wheezed out.

"How did you find out?" Ellie asked.

"One day I went to the office to drop off some muffins. As usual, I was trying to please him, be the good wife." Self-disgust laced her voice. "The receptionist was gone, and I heard voices from his office, so I went in and this girl was there. She... was crying, said she thought she'd been molested during the study, that she was pregnant, and she had dreams about a man being on her while she was in the lab."

Ellie released a shaky breath. "How did your husband respond?"

Ms. Eula's eyes were rimmed with tears. "He denied it, said the drug was causing hallucinations in some people and that she'd probably gotten drunk and slept with someone and wanted to blame the study. But the girl said she had been a virgin."

"Who was the girl, Ms. Eula?"

Lightning streaked her anguished face. She looked as if she was a million miles away. "Agnes Butterfield… at least that was her name back then."

"She's Agnes Curtis now."

Ms. Eula nodded. "I know. That poor child of hers. She was a sweet little girl."

"What happened then?" Ellie asked, drawing in a labored breath.

"I went home, was in denial. But then I started thinking about the way he acted sometimes. How uptight he was, how distant. On the days of the sleep studies, he came in and went straight to the shower, as if he was trying to wash something right off him." She tugged the worn afghan around her shoulders. "But that night… that night I got hit hard with the truth. That night I got blood on my hands." She lifted her wrinkled hands and stared at them as if she could still see the blood on her fingers.

# CHAPTER 133

Blood stained Eula's soul just as it had her hands that night.

She was bone tired of keeping quiet. Her frail legs had walked miles and miles down the path of darkness, aching and determined and blundering along. She'd lost her way so many times she reveled in it. Hovering between worlds where she could speak to the dead, hold hands with the in-betweens, and mourn the past that never should have happened.

But all that was coming to an end, like a well-tended vegetable garden after harvest. The good had been picked and all that was left were the weeds, dried seeds and soil that needed tilling again.

"Ms. Eula," Ellie said, drawing her out of her thoughts. "About that night?"

"Yes, dear, please forgive an old woman her musings." She rubbed her fingers over the worn threads of the blanket, lost in the tragedy and horror. "I was so distraught. Afraid what would happen when Ernie came home, that he'd raise his fist or call Reverend Ike. They were buddies back then, had been for years. Ernie bought his malarky hook, line and sinker. They met at college. It was the late seventies, and everyone was experimenting with LSD, cocaine, heroin and marijuana. Ike discovered he could use it to get people to follow him. He and Ernie thought they were gods."

"Ike is still using drugs to make his followers submissive," Ellie said.

Eula nodded gravely. "I would believe that… That night, all those years ago, I went home feeling sick inside. Ernie had this home office that he kept locked, forbidding me from going into it. Said a man had to have his privacy." Her voice warbled. "But I couldn't get Agnes's words out of my mind. Her voice, her fear, her accusation." The rocker moved back and forth, comforting as the wind picked up, swirling the humid air around her as the memories came to life again.

"I broke into that room like a madwoman, throwing things around, digging through drawers. Finally, I found a key to the safe in his closet." She closed her eyes, reliving the moment in vivid clarity. "I opened that safe and there it was."

"There what was?" Ellie said.

"Pictures of those girls. While they were sleeping in that cold sleep lab, he stripped them naked and took advantage of them."

"Photographs of him assaulting the women?" Ellie asked.

Eula pressed her hand to her chest with a nod. "It tore me up. I… for a few minutes, I couldn't believe what I was seeing. When I first met Ernie, he was so smart. Ambitious. Talked about becoming a doctor to save lives." That was the day Eula had fallen in love. "I had stars in my eyes. Came from a family who never amounted to anything. Ernie was so handsome and charming. I couldn't believe he wanted to be with me." Shame filled her for being swayed by his false charm. "When he got into med school, I took a job at the sewing plant to help pay our bills. And when he finished and started to practice, I thought our life would always be good." Her bones cracked as she shifted in the rocker. "Damn fool, that's what I was."

"You wanted to believe the best in him," Ellie said. "What happened to change things?"

"I wanted a baby." She laid her hand over her stomach and shook her head sadly. "But it didn't happen. God didn't bless me that way."

"I'm sorry," Ellie murmured.

"So was I. Ernie got frustrated. Blamed me. Started saying I was worthless. Started staying out late and smelling like other women. He'd hang around the bars, chasing coeds I thought. I knew he was cheating, but I stayed. Thought it was my fault."

"That's what he wanted you to think," Ellie said.

"I know that. And it worked for a while. We said vows," she said, her heart breaking all over again. "Back then, with the way I was raised, that meant something."

The sound of her own erratic breathing blended with the wind rustling the flowers in the yard. Or maybe it was the ghosts of the dead remembering Ernie.

"But then I saw the cold hard truth in those pictures, and I couldn't deny what he was, a monster." Her voice rose as the anger took root again. "I didn't make him do that."

"No, you didn't," Ellie said.

The rocker moved back and forth. "Lordy, I was in such shock that I didn't hear Ernie come in until he was standing above me." The memory of his firm hand on her shoulder and his enraged voice struck her as if it was yesterday. "He was furious that I violated his privacy." She looked at Ellie then, back in time as she spoke, "Now ain't that something? He was taking advantage of young girls and lying to me, and he was angry at me."

Ellie reached out, taking Eula's hand in hers and stroking it. "That must have been horrible."

"For a minute, I was so upset I went plumb out of my mind. I shoved the pictures at him and told him I was going to the police. He grabbed me and threw me against the wall," Eula said. "My head hit the side table and then I was bleeding. He came after me and tried to strangle me." Her hand went to her throat as she recalled the pressure of his fingers against her windpipe. "But I heard Agnes's voice in my head and then these other voices. Ones I didn't know but girls screaming that he'd done the same thing to them, and I grabbed the lamp on his desk and flung it at him. I ran to the kitchen, was going to get the keys and drive to the sheriff's office." Her pulse hammered as the details flooded her mind, yet a sense of peace at finally telling her story bled through her. "But he caught me. Dragged me backwards by the hair. And I yanked the butcher knife from the counter and swung it at him. He laughed, said I was too weak to kill him." A bitter chuckle rumbled from deep inside her. After all the times he'd used his brute force on her, she'd snapped. "But he was wrong. If I kept quiet about what he'd done, he'd keep on doing it. And I couldn't let that happen."

Ellie stroked her hand. "I'm so sorry, Ms. Eula."

"Don't be sorry for me. That was the first time in my life that I showed some courage." A smile tugged at her lips as she remembered the shock on her husband's face. "Oh, it wasn't easy, mind you. We fought and struggled, and he beat me half to death, but I managed to push him off, grabbed that knife and crawled over by the stove. He thought he had me and lunged at me, but I hit him in the head with the cast-iron skillet, then stabbed him straight in the place where his heart should have been." She couldn't help herself. She laughed, her chest heaving as she looked down at the rose garden.

"He died then?" Ellie asked, eyes widening.

"Not right away. I put that knife to his throat, and I made him admit it." Her chest heaved up and down. "He did, too. Told me it all started before he met me. He drugged a couple of women before. He was afraid he'd get caught, so he married me and tried to stop. But he started again a few years after we married, when I just thought he was out sleeping around. He was a doctor by then, researching pharmacology, knew what to use. Or at least he thought he did—one girl had a psychotic break after he attacked her, so he stopped again. He and Hoyt had been buddies forever. Hoyt was working on the sleeping drug and wanted to do experiments with it."

"And they teamed up to do a clinical trial study," Ellie filled in.

Eula nodded. "At the place by the community college."

"That's where Agnes Curtis and Janie Huntington got involved."

"It was."

"Ms. Eula, do you want a lawyer?" Ellie asked softly.

The old lady shook her head. "No, darlin', I want it all told. I want those poor girls to know that I killed that bastard. Then I cleaned up all that blood and dragged him outside. He was mighty heavy, but I figured he wasn't worth a casket." A cackle escaped her. "So, I dug a hole, put his sorry ass into the cold hard ground with that skillet and covered him with dirt, cause that's what he was made of."

# CHAPTER 134

*Crooked Creek*

Angelica roused from unconsciousness long enough to remember that someone had jumped her from behind. Anger at herself for getting caught off guard fueled her adrenaline and she tried to get up. But her wrists and ankles were tied, a gag stuffed in her mouth. Struggling against the bindings, she fought to undo them as she wiggled her body to the side. But she couldn't turn over. Couldn't move. *Dammit.* She silently screamed. The space was too tight.

Fear choked her as she realized she was trapped. Inhaling to calm herself, she lifted her fingers in search of a way out, but they connected with smooth, slick cold stone that seemed to rise on all sides of her, surrounding her and shutting her in.

For a moment, she thought she might be in a cave, but the stones felt smooth.

Panicking, she clawed at the stone to pull herself up. But the mountainous rocks rose above her higher than she could reach and she couldn't get any traction.

The air was stifling, smothered with dust, and she felt like the concrete was caving in on her from all sides. Pretty soon she would be crushed.

Collapsing, she forced herself to lie still and listen.

She had to think. Be smart. When he came back, she'd pretend to be unconscious. Then she'd fight like hell.

Until then, she maneuvered her hands to her mouth and tugged out the gag. She pulled at the ropes with her teeth. The rope strands frayed but didn't budge. Spitting them out, she wiggled her wrists to loosen her hands, but the ropes were tied so tight that they cut into her skin and blood dripped down her arms.

Frustrated, she banged and pushed the stone, hoping to move one of them, but they were so heavy she lost her breath and gave up.

The dark space closed around her, and she screamed, praying someone could hear her. But her cries died between the concrete walls.

# CHAPTER 135

*Rose Hill*

Ellie stared at the bed of roses where Eula had buried her husband. "Why roses?" she asked.

"There was so much blood," Ms. Eula whispered. "Ernie was a bleeder. All over the linoleum floor, spattered on the walls, all over my hands." She lifted her hands, her fingers gnarled. "I had a hard time scrubbing it out from under my fingernails. But once I had Ernie in the ground and covered, I came back inside and took the bleach and started cleaning." She laughed softly. "Took me hours to wash up all that blood. Thought I'd pass out from the bleach fumes, but I wanted to scrub his dirtiness from my house and my soul. That's when I decided to plant the roses. Blood-red roses to remind me of the blood that flowed from that man, freeing the evil inside."

Ellie didn't know what to say. Then again, she sensed she didn't have to say anything, that Ms. Eula had needed to unburden herself for a long time.

"Ms. Eula, I think my mother might have been one of Ernie's victims," Ellie said, the words causing a sour taste in her mouth. "I'm adopted. And my file was with Gillian Roach, the social worker who handled some of the adoptions of the babies born from the assaults. Do you know anything about her? Maybe my mother's name?"

A deep piercing sadness darkened Ms. Eula's eyes. "I'm afraid I don't, darlin'. But I... may know where the answer is."

"Where?" Ellie asked, pulse jumping.

Ms. Eula stood, her knobby knees cracking. "I kept those pictures and those files of Ernie's. I don't know why," she said under her breath. "I guess as punishment." She wrestled the afghan around her shoulders and reached for the screen door. "Or maybe because I knew that someday someone would come looking for them."

Ellie gave a nod but remained in the porch rocker, looking at the roses, her mind churning as Ms. Eula hobbled inside to retrieve the files.

She was a by-the-book cop. Had to answer to the people of Bluff County. She should take Ms. Eula in.

But… that didn't feel right.

Still, she had to update Derrick. Dr. Hangar's death meant someone else was cleaning up after his crimes.

# CHAPTER 136

*Crooked Creek*

Derrick grabbed a cup of coffee while the forensic psychiatrist evaluated Rigdon.

His phone buzzed with a call from Ellie.

"Derrick," she said, her voice breaking as if they had a bad connection. "I have information. I tracked Dr. Hangar to Eula Ann Frampton. She admitted that her husband Ernie assaulted women in that sleep study, and for decades before it."

"And she covered for him?" Derrick bit out.

"No. When she discovered what he'd been doing, she intended to tell the police. They fought, he attacked her and she killed him."

"How do you know she's telling the truth?"

"Because I just do," Ellie's voice quivered. "I saw his grave."

"If he's dead, who's covering it up now?"

"I don't know. Maybe the other doctor, Hoyt. Angelica left a message for me to meet her in town. Maybe she uncovered something."

"Hoyt is here now, but he lawyered up. I'll use this to push him to talk." He set the coffee on the table. "Are you bringing Ms. Frampton in for booking?"

A tense heartbeat passed. "I thought we could talk about that. There were extenuating circumstances. It was self-defense."

Derrick took a breath. Ellie hadn't been one to cross the line professionally. He'd just have to trust her.

"Okay. We'll discuss it later."

They agreed to stay in touch, and he left the office to interrogate the doctor again.

Hoyt's lawyer was seated with him, the two of them in deep conversation.

Striding in, Derrick seated himself across from them, anger hardening his tone. "Dr. Hoyt, I've just learned something very interesting."

The doctor glanced nervously at his lawyer.

"I have a witness that confirms that Dr. Hangar, who you worked with on the clinical trials for your sleeping pill, Z, sexually assaulted several women during the course of the study." Derrick laid the photographs of the recent victims on the table again. "We now know that Janie Huntington was herself a rape victim. In the cases of Katie Lee Curtis and Vanessa Morely, the victims were their mothers. Indeed, their mothers were attacked by the same man. Gillian Roach was a social worker who worked with young women, including sexual assault survivors. She worked with Janie Huntington, Agnes Curtis, and Wanda Morely, Vanessa Morely's mother. We believe she was murdered because she had recognized a link between these women and other adoptions she'd handled."

Hoyt's breath quickened, and he shifted restlessly. "If Dr. Hangar assaulted them, I knew nothing about it."

"I find that hard to believe," Derrick said coldly. "It was your sleeping pill. You worked with him to organize the study."

Plastic crinkled noisily as Hoyt's fingers dug into the water bottle Derrick had left him. "Listen, I supplied the sleep medication but the staff there handled the actual study. I simply analyzed the data they collected."

The lawyer cleared his throat. "It seems Dr. Hangar is the man you should be questioning, not my client."

Derrick narrowed his eyes. "I would like to do that, but unfortunately that's impossible. Dr. Hangar is dead and has been for years."

Hoyt's eyes widened in shock, and the lawyer squared his shoulders.

"You see why I have a problem. We believe these women were murdered to cover up what happened during that sleep study and its links to earlier cases. And with Dr. Hangar dead, that means someone else is cleaning up the mess."

"I… you can't think it's me," Hoyt stuttered.

"Be quiet," the lawyer snapped at Hoyt. He addressed Derrick, "My client has already stated his innocence. Now, if that's all?"

"No, it's not. I think you knew exactly what Hangar did and you let it slide because you wanted to make money off that drug. Hangar might have been a rapist, but he was a great research partner, right? The assaulted women were casualties, and now they're collateral damage. Besides," Derick continued when the lawyer started to protest again, "you're lying about simply supplying the drug. You conducted your own studies, experiments on men. I have a witness who claims he experienced hallucinations while restrained."

"I have alibis," Hoyt protested.

The lawyer placed a hand on Hoyt's arm. "I told you to be quiet."

Fear flashed in Hoyt's eyes. "But I do. Give me a piece of paper and I'll write down where I was and who I was with during the times those ladies died."

"You may well have alibis," Derrick said, earning a glare from the attorney, "but if you knew what Hangar was doing, you're responsible and you're going to jail. And that's before we dig deeper into the later trials on men."

"I didn't know," Hoyt shouted. "I swear I didn't. There were other docs at that research facility. Maybe one of them did."

"I want names. Names of anyone who worked with your drug at that stage, even if it was at another clinic." He leaned forward, eyes glaring. "And don't leave anyone off that list."

# CHAPTER 137

Ellie had rung Angelica repeatedly, but there was no answer. It wasn't like the reporter to miss a call or a chance for a good story, so her senses were on high alert. She was claustrophobic just looking at the crowd lined up for the parade. Slowly, she began to weave toward the center stage, where the press would be set up to highlight the festivities.

Main Street and several side streets had been roped off for the parade route, the sidewalks filled with excited children, locals and tourists. Balloons bobbed up and down, between flags, streamers and other decorations. People were decked out in Fourth of July T-shirts and hats, some waving party favors and banners.

Mayor Waters's voice boomed on the speakers from the stage as he introduced his wife.

"It's time to crown our Little Miss Bluff County and Miss Teen Bluff County," Mrs. Waters said.

Ellie glanced at the stage as she veered around a group of spectators and saw five little girls prancing on stage wearing frilly dresses and bows in their hair. Vera had always wanted Ellie to dress and look like that, but she'd never gotten her wish.

Mrs. Waters announced each child, and applause sounded. "While all our contestants are worthy of the title, our committee had to make a choice. Our runner-up for Little Miss Bluff County is Sadie Simpson." More applause, then Sadie was draped with a big ribbon. "And this year's winner is Lily Whiting." The little girl's mother squealed while Mrs. Waters crowned the child.

Ellie tuned out the crowning of Miss Teen Bluff County, although she didn't miss seeing Bryce puffing up his chest as he joined his mother on stage to make the announcement.

As soon as the pageant finished, the high school band began playing and shouts echoed from the crowd.

Another stage in the square had been set up for the musical guests, Fiddlin' and Pickin', and for the Mountain Laurel cloggers to perform later.

Meddlin' Maude and the ladies from the garden club were setting up the baked goods table for the cake walk. Even Lola at the Corner Café had a booth with iced coffee, pies and funnel cakes.

As the band marched down Main Street, she scanned the sidewalks and stages in search of Angelica. Instead, she saw Max Weatherby in full firefighter's gear on a float with his squad. He was too far away to ask if he'd seen Angelica, but her cameraman, Tom, stood on the sidelines filming the parade, so she made her way toward him.

In spite of a serial killer stalking the trail, the overpowering heat and the storm clouds looming, everyone was in full celebratory mode. Someone bumped her as the boy scouts and girl scouts tossed candy from their floats and kids scrambled to snatch it.

She finally reached the cameraman, but Angelica wasn't beside him.

She nudged his arm. "Tom, have you seen Angelica? She left a message asking me to meet her here. Said she had something important to tell me."

The crewman ran a hand through his wiry hair. "I don't know where she is. We started to set up, but then she just disappeared."

"What do you mean, disappeared?"

His brows bunched together as he frowned. "I was getting the camera equipment from the back of the van, but when I turned around, she was gone."

Ellie's heart thundered.

# CHAPTER 138

"It's not like Angelica to ditch a story," Tom said. "Even if the parade wasn't top of her list. I wanted to look for her, but my boss would lose her mind if I didn't get at least some parade footage. That'll do it, though." He lowered the camera and led Ellie back to the news van.

Ellie scanned the area and saw drag marks in the dirt, leading to the park. "Do you have any idea what she wanted to tell me?"

"Are you kidding?" He harumphed. "I just follow her around. She doesn't tell anyone what she's working on until she has something good."

That was what made her a good reporter and earned trust from informants.

"Look back at the footage you've taken so far. See if you spot her or someone suspicious."

Ellie let Derrick and her boss know about Angelica, and Captain Hale responded immediately that he'd get Sheriff Waters's deputies looking for her.

Even from a distance, she saw Bryce waving to the crowd from the stage as if he was the big hero in town. Through the speakers, Mayor Waters's wife Edwina was announcing that Preston Phelps, the author of the book *Mind Games*, had left signed copies at Books & Bites, the local bookstore.

After booking Josiah Curtis and Ike Jones, Deputy Landrum was now working security, so Ellie called him. Static echoed, blending with the crowd noise as he answered.

Ellie quickly explained what had happened. "Keep an eye out for Angelica and start canvassing the crowd to see if anyone saw her."

"On it," he said.

Ellie hung up, pulled up a photograph of Angelica from her phone, then rushed from one person to the next asking if anyone had seen her. Remembering that Angelica wanted an interview with the author of that book, she navigated her way through the throng of people. The bookstore was pretty deserted except for Winnie Bates, the owner, who was arranging copies of the book on a display table.

"Hey, Winnie, have you seen that reporter Angelica Gomez? She was trying to get an interview with Preston Phelps."

Winnie toyed with the silver hoop earrings dangling to her shoulders. "She hasn't been in here. And that author never showed either. Called and said he was sorry but he wasn't feeling well and couldn't come." She pursed her lips.

"Okay, thanks."

The clock on the wall ticked away the hour, and she hurried back outside. If Angelica had been abducted by the unsub, she might not have long to live.

Pulling her flashlight, she shined it into the store windows as she raced along the sidewalks. Most of them were locked up and dark while the parade was on.

She passed the stone warehouse, shined her light at the windows, but they were closed tight, and the interior was dark.

Still, she banged on the door with her fist. It was padlocked and secured with a chain. She shouted Angelica's name and jiggled the lock, but she'd need a crowbar or bolt cutters to get inside, and she didn't have time.

So she moved on, running. But she feared she was already too late.

# CHAPTER 139

Angelica gasped for a breath, her lungs straining as she screamed and banged at the heavy stone. Her voice was hoarse and raw, her fingers bloody.

A flicker of light seeped through the closed windows, which were so high she couldn't see out of them even if she could stand. The air was growing thicker, making it hard to breathe. The suffocating heat made her feel nauseous.

"Help me! Someone, please help me!"

But her voice died in the thick slabs of concrete and stone. And a dizzy spell overcame her. Fear began to override her hope.

Did anyone even know she was missing?

# CHAPTER 140

Ellie pushed through the crowd, the noise growing as the revelers cheered and clapped. She climbed the steps to the stage and nudged Tom, who was back filming.

"Did you find her?" he asked, barely glancing at her.

"No. Did you notice anything on the tapes?"

"Not a thing," he muttered.

"Did Angelica take notes on what she was working on?"

"She had a tablet but it's password protected, and no one can get in. She didn't trust anyone at the station with her contacts and refused to share the scoop until she verified facts." He shifted. "But she did carry a pocket notepad that she scribbled in. She might have left it in the van."

"I need the keys."

His frown deepened, but he handed her the van keys, and Ellie bolted down the stairs and jogged through the back street to the parking lot. She unlocked the van then ran her hands over the seat. She didn't see a notepad anywhere.

Frantic, she checked the back of the van and found an extra camera and tripod, but no notepad. Hurrying to the passenger door, she lurched it open. She raked her hand across the seat again, but it was empty. Moving beneath the seat this time, her breath quickened as her fingers brushed a pocket spiral notepad. Tugging it out, she flipped through the pages. Frustration knotted her stomach as she realized Angelica used a shorthand.

A noise suddenly erupted, and Ellie looked back at the town center. It almost sounded like an explosion.

Jamming the notepad in her pocket, she raced in the direction of the sound. A car alarm had gone off and was trilling so loudly it pierced her ears. Blinking lights and a smashed window on a nearby Toyota looked like a break-in.

Pulling her gun, she slowed, surveying the car and parking lot as she approached.

Smoke oozed from the front hood. A sizzling sound filled the air. Heat rose from the vehicle, sparks of fire shooting. And then the gas tank blew, throwing Ellie to the ground.

# CHAPTER 141

Ellie threw her hands up to break her fall, but she hit the pavement face down. Pain shot through her extremities, her shoulder wrenched, and she tasted blood.

The sound of the explosion reverberated in her ears, fire crackling and popping as the metal burned and glass shattered. Lifting her head to see if anyone was hurt, she saw footsteps running toward her.

Struggling to catch her breath, she pushed to her hands and knees. Her wrist felt as if it was sprained, and her right knee throbbed.

"Ellie!" Cord jogged to her, helping her up. Stunned from the force of the explosion, she staggered, but he slid his arm around her waist and they raced away from the flaming car.

Voices filled the air, and the blare of a siren as a fire engine screeched up.

Cord urged her to sit on the ground then stooped down beside her and cupped her face between his hands. "Are you okay? Where are you hurt?" He pulled a handkerchief from his pocket and gently wiped the blood from her lip. "Ellie, talk to me," he said gruffly.

She finally managed to find her voice. "I'm okay, just… I don't know what happened."

"The car exploded," Cord said, his voice hard. "The medics should be here soon."

"What are you doing here?" Ellie asked.

"A couple of the rangers and I volunteered to help with crowd control. Deputy Landrum told me you thought Angelica was missing so I was looking for you." He exhaled. "Did you hit your head?"

"No." She held up her hands and glanced at her palms, which were grazed and scraped. Her jeans had a hole in the knee, where she could see a pool of blood.

Cord dabbed blood and dirt from her palms then examined her knee, moving it around to check it. "Does that hurt?" he asked.

Ellie winced. "A little but I think it's just bruised."

Suddenly there were more voices, and Ellie's parents raced over. Her stomach pitched at the terror in Vera's eyes.

"Dear God, what happened?" Randall asked.

"A car alarm went off and I went to check it out. But the car just exploded."

Vera's hand went to her chest. "My heavens. You could have been killed."

"Was anyone in the car?" Randall asked.

"I didn't see anyone."

The ambulance appeared, and two medics sprinted to her while the firefighters were working to extinguish the blazing metal. Black fumes and the heavy scent of gas permeated the air, smoke billowing into the gray skies.

Cord squeezed her arm gently then stepped aside while the medics examined her.

The sound of more cheers from the parade echoed over the noise of the burning metal.

Randall went to talk to the firefighters while Vera huddled by Ellie in horror.

"Go back to the parade, Mother," Ellie said as the medics cleaned her up and applied a bandage to her knee and wrist. "I'm fine. Just a few scrapes."

Her mother folded her arms across her chest. "I can't help but worry about you."

"You don't have to," Ellie said. "I can take care of myself."

Vera gave her a look of disdain. "You never would let me mother you."

Pushing to her feet, Ellie walked over to Cord, who stood talking to one of the firefighters. "What do you think happened here?" Cord asked the fireman.

"Looks like a pipe bomb inside the vehicle," he said. "I saw pieces of a watch, so it could have been set on a timer."

Cord's look darkened as he took Ellie's hand. "Did you hear that? Ellie, it might have been meant for you."

Ellie nodded, her teeth grinding together. "It was a diversion. He set off the fire to distract me so he could get away with Angelica."

# CHAPTER 142

*Somewhere outside Crooked Creek*

Angelica roused from unconsciousness, the world spinning. Her head throbbed as she opened her eyes to orient herself. Darkness engulfed her. The sound of a motor rumbling. The smell of gasoline.

Then it came back to her. She'd been attacked from behind. Hadn't even seen her attacker's face. And she'd been locked in that room, surrounded by stone, like some kind of grave.

A sudden movement sent her slamming against something hard, and she realized she was in the trunk of a car. The vehicle bounced over a rut, jarring her teeth and making bile climb her throat.

Swallowing to tamp down the nausea, she ran her fingers along the interior in search of a release button for the trunk. The reports of the other women taunted her. They'd been murdered. Their bodies burned to ashes.

Cold fear caught in her throat. She'd just turned thirty-one. Had worked so hard for her career that she'd made sacrifices in her love life.

And now she'd met Max… He was charming. Attractive. A man who saved lives. A man who made her stomach flutter.

If she survived, maybe they could have a future.

But she had to let go of the past to do that.

Two months ago, she'd resolved to give up her search for her birth mother. To accept that she might never know what happened with her.

And then this case had broken. The minute she'd learned Gillian Roach had been murdered, she'd wanted the story. Had known that if anyone could uncover the truth, it would be Ellie Reeves.

They might have clashed when they'd first met, but she admired the detective for her perseverance. If only she'd done that tell-all she'd been after, maybe Angelica could have put things together sooner.

Tires squealed as the driver sped around the winding road, and Angelica felt her stomach rising to her throat again. She couldn't find the release lever, so she ran her hands across the floor of the trunk in search of something to use as a weapon.

Nothing. Not at first. But she managed to turn herself sideways. The spare tire. The tire iron.

She wiped her clammy hands on her dress then tugged the tire iron from its holding spot. Gripping it tightly, she ordered herself to be brave.

The minute he opened this damn trunk, she would hit him with it.

The car bounced over another pothole, and her head banged the side of the trunk. Tears filled her eyes, and she cried out as the driver swung a sharp right. They were climbing now. She felt it in the chugging of the tires. In the almost figure eight-like switchbacks. In the pressure building in her ears.

The sound of another car passing jolted her into action and she beat at the trunk, screaming. But the vehicle raced by, and she sagged against the floor again.

Another quick turn, then the tires ground over what sounded like gravel. Seconds later, brakes screeched, and the car skidded to a stop. Angelica tightened her fingers around the tire iron.

Footsteps crunched the gravel, then she heard the trunk pop.

A second later, he lifted the trunk door. Shadows from the surrounding pines flickered around him, a sliver of light framing him as if he was a ghost.

Then she saw his face and shock momentarily immobilized her.

His sinister laugh echoed in the tepid air as he reached for her.

Anger and adrenaline shot through her, and she used all her force to swing the tire iron at his head. But he was fast, his arms beefy and muscular, and he jerked it from her. She threw a hard kick toward his gut, but he dodged the blow, then grabbed her arms and hauled her from the trunk.

She jabbed at his eyes, but his fist slammed into her throat and she choked, gasping for air as she sank into the dirt. Denial screamed in her head as she collapsed into the darkness.

# CHAPTER 143

*Crooked Creek*

"Ellie, let me take you home," Cord offered.

"I can't go home," she said. "Angelica's missing. I have to find her. Contact Max and tell him to let us know if another wildfire starts up. That might lead us to Angelica."

Ellie headed toward the police station, hoping Derrick had some answers. His eyes widened in alarm when he saw her.

"What happened to you?" he asked, his tone grim.

"I'm fine, but there was a car explosion a half-hour ago. I was close by."

Derrick's eyes raked over her. "Do you need a doctor?"

She shook her head. "I'm fine. I think the fire was a diversion so the killer could get away with Angelica. Deputies are combing the town."

She pulled Angelica's notepad from her pocket. "I found this in the news van. It's mostly shorthand, but I'm hoping there's a clue in here. Any luck with Hoyt?"

"He denies knowledge of the sexual assaults, but he could be lying. His alibis check out and he said there were other research docs at that clinic, so one of them could have worked with Hangar and known what he was up to." He tapped the legal pad on the desk. "According to the forensic psychiatrist who interviewed Rigdon, he suffered from night terrors and nightmares as a child. He signed up for the sleep study to help with that but got hooked on the medication. It's an initial assessment, but the doctor believes he was brainwashed, that he was the subject of mind experiments."

"That could be the answer," Ellie said. "Hoyt may not have committed the murders, but he could have manipulated someone else into doing it."

"I was plugging the doctors' names in for background checks and locations to follow up."

"Let me look through Angelica's notes."

Ellie sank into the chair at the round table in the corner and began to flip through the notepad.

There were dates, initials and places which made no real sense, although she assumed they referred to appointments or meetings. Three-quarters through, she saw her own initials and realized the times recorded were probably when Angelica had contacted her.

On another page, scribblings noted the deaths of Katie Lee, Vanessa and Janie. Question marks dotted the pages, as if Angelica was tossing her own theories around in her mind.

The last entry was devoted to a page with the word *Mind Games* scribbled on it, the book written by the local author. Below it, she'd jotted the author's name.

Then the words 'pen name'. Then a question mark and a line to the words 'torch victims'.

Ellie's thoughts raced. Many authors used pen names, but why would that interest Angelica? And what did it have to do with the murders?

The fact that this was Angelica's last notation might not be significant. But she snatched her laptop and plugged in the author's name. It came up immediately, along with a display of the book cover and an author bio. According to the blurb, the novel was about a doctor who conducted mind-games research on prisoners. The bio did not list the author's real name.

Ellie sat back, tapping her foot as she contemplated the implications. "Angelica made a note about that local author, Preston

Phelps," she said to Derrick. "He was supposed to be in Crooked Creek for an appearance at Books & Bites but didn't show. He wrote under a pen name." She explained what his book was about, and interest sparked in Derrick's eyes.

Ellie tracked down the name of the author's agent online and reached for her phone. It took several back-to-back calls to get an answer—it was a work cell phone and this was a holiday after all—but once she got through and emphasized that she was investigating a multiple homicide, she got the agent's attention.

The agent hesitated. "I don't understand why you're asking for his real name. Or why that nosy reporter did. The author simply wants his privacy."

Angelica must have thought something was off if she'd persisted. "Just answer the question, please," Ellie said as she glanced at the clock. "What's his real name?"

"You won't reveal this?" the woman replied. "It could affect our promotional plans."

"I do not give a rats' ass about your promotional plans," Ellie snapped. "Four women are dead and another's been abducted. What is his real name?"

The woman's shaky breath echoed back. "Lewis Hoyt. The bio is actually his. But he's a research doctor—"

"I know who he is." Ellie lurched up from her chair, slamming it backward. "I have to go."

# CHAPTER 144

"Hoyt is behind the book," Ellie told Derrick. "He may be behind the murders, too."

Derrick's eyes clouded. "If he conducted mind experiments and he knew what Hangar was up to, he wouldn't want that information to be made public. So why publish a novel on that topic?"

"Money. Fame. He's an egomaniac," Ellie said. "He thought he'd gotten away with it and he had for years. So he decided to fictionalize it and thought no one would ever figure out it was based on truth."

"But someone did," Derrick said. "Maybe Gillian?"

"Or Josiah Curtis," Ellie said. "Or Angelica's call to his agent triggered him to realize he'd made a mistake in publishing the book."

"So he decided to clean up everyone who could expose him," Derrick said.

"He's not getting away with it." She lurched up from her seat. "Let's have another talk with him."

Ellie led the way to the interrogation room, where Hoyt's lawyer buttoned his suit jacket and stood. So did Hoyt. "You've held my client long enough," the lawyer said. "We're leaving."

"You aren't going anywhere," Ellie said. "Sit back down, Dr. Hoyt. Or should I call you Preston Phelps?"

Derrick stepped toward the man. "We know who you are, Hoyt, and we know why you murdered these women."

Panic shot through Hoyt's eyes. "I didn't kill anyone."

Ellie pinned him with her stare. "You conducted research using your sleep medication on unsuspecting coeds. While Hangar sexually assaulted the females, you conducted mind studies on the male subjects." She leaned closer. "You're so arrogant you even wrote a book about it. But that ego of yours was your big mistake."

"That's ridiculous," Hoyt snarled.

The lawyer lifted a hand to stop Ellie from further questions, but she flipped her phone around to reveal the website for his book. "*Mind Games*," she said. "We know you wrote it under this pen name Preston Phelps."

"You're at the pinnacle of your career," Derrick cut in. "Drug making money for you. Book about to explode. You're getting all this attention."

"Only Angelica Gomez called you for an interview," Ellie said between clenched teeth. "And you knew if she uncovered your identity, the truth would come out."

"I didn't kill them," Hoyt said, his voice low and lethal.

"But you know who did," Ellie said. "Because you used mind manipulation to force another man to do your dirty work." She narrowed her eyes. "He has Angelica now. If she dies, that's one more murder you'll be held accountable for."

Hoyt's lawyer shifted restlessly. A muscle ticked in Hoyt's jaw.

"Where is he?" Ellie asked.

"I don't know," Hoyt said. "I don't know details of anything."

"That way you can plead innocence," Ellie said, rage sharpening her tone. "But that's not going to fly in a courtroom. Rigdon has already described what you did to him. Who else was in that study?"

She was so angry she could barely breathe. No telling what Angelica was enduring now. If she was even still alive.

Ellie inhaled sharply, then took the folder of the crime-scene photos and spread them on the table. "Look at these," she said. "Look at the brutality. He uses different methods to murder the women. Then he sets fire to them."

Hoyt made a pained face and looked away.

"Look at them," Ellie pushed. "The methods are different, but the fire and the standing stones he places around the body are the same. He also carves an hourglass behind each victim's ear." She stabbed the picture with her fingernail.

Perspiration beaded on Hoyt's forehead and neck, and he scrubbed a hand over his face.

"What does it all mean?"

Hoyt's jaw tightened.

"Where would he take her?" Derrick growled. "Think, dammit. Is there a place?"

Hoyt's lawyer touched his arm, then murmured something in Hoyt's ear. When he finished, his client looked tormented. "The stones… the place where we originally conducted the studies. There were natural standing stones there that resemble these."

Ellie's breath quickened. "Where is it?"

The lawyer nudged him again and, finally, Hoyt told them.

# CHAPTER 145

*Crow's End*

*Ticktock. Ticktock.* His clock chimed. The voice in his head grew louder.

Angelica moaned and struggled as he carried her up the hill, but the drug had weakened her. Powerless against him, she lost the fight and faded away again.

Memories swirled around him like a foggy night as he neared the top of the mountain's edge. He was nineteen again, locked in the room with the lights and the hourglass and the clock ticking relentlessly on the wall. Back in the nightmares.

As the minutes ticked by and his chest seized with panic, he saw the standing stones through the window. The circle of stones represents the circle of life. The mourning would begin.

The five-foot stones stood like giant boulders, creating a fortress around the old building. This was where it all started. Earlier, he'd destroyed the walls and torn down the structure in his rage, and now he had to lay Angelica to rest. He gently laid her in the middle of the circle, his fingers brushing over the silky strands of her long dark hair. She was so beautiful, exotic, with her creamy caramel skin and those full lips that begged for a man's kiss.

Yet her mouth got her in trouble. She was sassy and smart and didn't back down from asking the tough questions.

That was her downfall.

His was getting to know her.

He hardened his heart. He couldn't let his emotions interfere. He had to finish this.

Leaving her tied and lying in the dirt, the moonlight broke through the gray clouds and illuminated the ground as he gathered sticks and timber from the building he'd demolished. This was the place where the nightmares had turned him into a monster.

The place where it had to end.

# CHAPTER 146

*Somewhere between Crooked Creek and Crow's End*

Knowing they might need a guide to search the woods for the old research facility, Ellie picked up Cord. Black storm clouds thickened overhead, rain falling at the higher altitudes, a misty fog hovering over the mountain.

"I don't understand," Cord said. "You think this doctor had something to do with all these murders?"

Ellie explained about the sleep study. "We believe the male subjects were exposed to mind games, manipulation, brainwashing. One of them is cleaning up for Hoyt."

The Jeep ground the shoulder as she made a turn and raced over the graveled road toward the mountaintop. She bumped over debris in her way, then screeched to a stop at the sight of a tall pine that had fallen across the road, probably in the tornado a while back. The road was so remote it hadn't been cleared yet.

"There's no car here," Derrick said.

"He could have taken another back road."

"There's smoke," Derrick said, dragging her attention to the hills, where smoke rose above the wiry branches.

Ellie's pulse jumped. "He's up there with Angelica. The wildfires have been a diversion."

"I'll call in the fire," Cord said, then proceeded to make the call.

Ellie checked her weapon and climbed out. Derrick followed.

"The fire crew is already on the way." Cord's phone dinged and he checked an incoming text. "That's Weatherby. He wants me to meet them at the scene. This one is spreading fast and some campers were spotted not too far from there."

Ellie pulled her compass from her pocket. "Then go, Cord. Derrick and I can find our way. Radio me if you see or hear anything suspicious along the way."

"Copy that." Using his compass, Cord headed toward the heart of the fire. For a brief second, fear for the ranger seized Ellie. But she reminded herself that Cord knew what he was doing.

Her job was to find Angelica.

# CHAPTER 147

Anxiety needled Ellie as she led the hike up the hill. Every nerve cell in her body screamed with tension. What if she was too late?

Dusk had long fallen, the dark clouds above making it even darker and more difficult to find her way. Using her compass and flashlight to guide her, she wove through rows of pines and cypresses, over one hill and then another, each ridge similar to the next except for the varying heights, and clusters of foliage and stones. Derrick stayed close on her heels.

Up above, dark clouds formed shapes resembling animals, reminding her of the game she and Vanessa played as children. She was doing this for Vanessa, she told herself. The sound of the river water gurgling indicated she was on the right track.

They passed a wooden post with directional arrows pointing toward various sites along the trail. One led to Cathead Creek, another toward Hangman's Bluff and another was marked Standing Stones.

Ellie hesitated, the name on the sign sinking in. *Standing Stones*—the stones hadn't represented the ones at Ole Glory, but they symbolized this place.

"This way." She pushed forward, following the trail. The scent of smoke drifted towards her, and she pulled a bandana from her pocket, tying it around her mouth and nose. To the north, exactly where she was headed, thick smoke clogged the air, swirling above the treetops in a black-gray haze.

Heat suffused her, perspiration turning to rivers of sweat as she plunged deeper and deeper into the woods.

The heat sucked her energy, and she stopped to take a drink of water.

One foot in front of the other, the images of the torched women taunted her. Katie Lee, just a teenager with her whole future in front of her, a girl who'd suffered because of her family's dark secrets. Gillian Roach, so tormented by the children she tried to help that she had no one to love. Vanessa, who'd sought the truth about her own mother, and Janie who'd only wanted to protect her son.

Then she thought of Eula Ann Frampton. A woman who'd punished herself for her husband's sick crimes by tolerating rumors and imprisoning herself on the hill where she'd killed and buried her monster of a husband.

The sound of brush crackling in the fire boomeranged through the air, a tree falling in the distance, red, orange and yellow flames shooting into the black sky.

Coughing, Ellie glanced at her compass, making a slight right and sprinting ahead. The woods were burning around her, her hiking boots grinding the scorched ground, the heat searing the soles of her feet through her shoes.

Spotting flames shooting up about a hundred feet ahead, she took off at a dead run. She heard Derrick's breathing as she raced behind her, then a crashing sound.

They finally reached the hilltop, where she spotted the remains of an old building that had been torn down.

Large boulders resembling giant arrowheads formed a circle around what appeared to be a fire pit.

In the middle lay Angelica, fire dancing around her, the flames reaching for her hair.

He was going to feed her to the fire.

A noise on the other side of the building grabbed her attention.

"Go after him," Ellie yelled. "I'll get Angelica."

Derrick jogged past the circle of fire and the broken-down building. A gunshot sounded, and she lost sight of him, terrified he was hit.

Angelica's ashen face sought out Ellie, her scream rising above the roar of the fire. Inching towards the flames, heat scalded her face and body.

Gravel crunched behind Ellie, and she spun around. Shock slammed into her as hard as a man's big hands grabbed her.

It was Max Weatherby.

"It's him, Ellie!" Angelica screamed.

Ellie pushed at him, reaching for her gun, but he yanked her arm upward with such force it knocked the breath out of her. She stumbled, off balance, and he lunged at her then, punching her in the face and closing his hands around her throat.

Ellie jerked her knee up and hit him in the groin, and he grunted but didn't release her.

Angelica screamed again, and Max shoved Ellie backward toward the fire. Her back felt hot, the sizzle of the embers popping into the dark night. Summoning all her strength, she jabbed at his eyes, but he deflected. She reached for his hands, digging her fingernails into him, clawing at him to release her.

"Sorry about this, Detective," he said, his eyes cold and hard. Distant. "But you and the others have to die."

Ellie went into full fight mode and stomped at his ankle, then tried to knee him again. But his hands tightened around her throat, and the world spun in a blinding rush as his fingers pressed into her windpipe.

*Fight, Ellie, Fight. Angelica needs you.*

Raising her elbow, she jabbed him in the chest, tried to wrap her leg around his and pulled at his arm in an attempt to flip him to the ground. She managed to throw him off, and they fell to the dirt, rolling and fighting. Wood hissed, spewing sparks that landed beside her head. Flames licked at her hair and she shoved his chest in an attempt to throw him off her.

But he straddled her, holding her down, then punched her so hard that everything went black.

# CHAPTER 148

Derrick had fired his gun when he thought he'd seen someone running through the woods. But the man disappeared and then a blast sounded. Smoke choked his lungs and stung his eyes as he set off in pursuit, a thin pine crashing in front of him in a blaze.

Flames rippled along the forest floor. The lack of rain turned the trees and brittle foliage into fuel for the wildfires. If they didn't save Angelica and get out of here, they'd be caught in the inferno themselves.

A wave of heat hit him as a section of trees a few feet away burst into flames. Then another boom in the opposite direction and lightning streaked across the tree tops.

Ellie was right. The killer was setting the fires as a diversion. He must be using a timer or be close by to activate the explosions. Brush rustled as deer raced through the gray haze.

A shout from somewhere in the distance drifted through the loud noise. Above the trees, he heard a plane soaring, dumping water on the blaze.

His boots skidded on the grassy slope as he descended the hill, reaching a ravine. He hated heights and screeched to a stop. Sweat coated his skin, and he could taste the burning brush.

The shout came again. Almost lost in the noise, but it was closer this time.

Inching toward the ledge, he plastered himself against the rocky wall and moved one foot at a time, inch by inch. Stones tumbled downward into the ravine.

Wiping his clammy hands on his jeans, he released the breath he'd been holding and made it to the other side of the ledge. Something moved from down below.

He pulled his gun at the ready and crept closer.

"Down here!"

Derrick froze as he spotted Cord lying in the thicket below, blood on his forehead, his foot twisted at an odd angle.

# CHAPTER 149

*Crow's End*

Heat seared Ellie's face as she roused from unconsciousness.

Angelica's terrified scream reverberated over the blaze surrounding them. "Ellie, hurry! The fire's closing in!"

Ellie's head throbbed, nausea bubbling in her throat. She pried one aching eye open and heat seared her face. Orange, red and yellow shot up all around her. Max was nowhere to be seen.

"Hurry, untie me!" Angelica shouted.

Slowly Ellie turned her head. She lay on the ground in the center of the tall stones. She was next to Angelica, who was frantically trying to get up, but her hands and feet were bound tightly. Ellie tried to sit up, but she was constrained as well, and her body felt so heavy she could barely move.

Dust flew in Ellie's face, and she tasted burned wood and realized Angelica was kicking at the dirt wildly to try to free herself. Panic brought Ellie back to life, and she scooted toward her.

"Roll and put your back to me," Ellie said. "Now." She dragged herself closer while Angelica thrust herself onto her side. The heat was smothering, smoke clogging her lungs. Angelica trembled as she maneuvered her body so they were back to back.

Ellie wiggled her hands and stretched her fingers, trying to reach inside her pocket for her knife. But she couldn't reach it.

Breath puffing out, she gave up on the knife and used her bare fingers to loosen the rope around Angelica's wrists. Angelica's breathing became slower, her cries lower. She was struggling to stay conscious. The smoke was getting to Ellie, too.

Flames crawled toward them, closing in. Time was running out.

She pulled and tugged with all her might, and finally felt the rope loosen.

Her hands and wrists were slick with sweat and she fumbled with the frayed ends and managed to unravel the knot. She pulled it all the way through, kicking at the flames nipping at her feet.

"Angelica, hold on!" Rolling over, Ellie scrambled to untie Angelica's feet. "Come on, I need you to help me."

The fire caught higher, growing more intense, and she realized the reporter had passed out. Panicked, she shook her, hard and urgently, and Angelica finally roused.

"Angelica, untie me now!" Ellie shouted over the blaze as she shook Angelica again.

Angelica moaned and Ellie beat at the flames nipping at Angelica's hair. Pulling her legs up, Ellie tried to reach her ankles and untie them. Sweat poured down her face and back as she yanked and pulled at the bindings, desperate to escape the flames diving for her.

Time was running out.

She shook Angelica again. "Come on, Angelica, get up and help me out of here!"

Her words finally sank in. Coughing and groaning, Angelica pushed up to her hands and knees. Realizing her hands and feet were free, Angelica untied Ellie's ankles, grabbed her arm and helped her to stand. They both swayed, dizzy from the smoke, but stumbled forward. Flames sucked at Ellie's shoes and were shooting up in a wall all around them.

"Let's go!" she shouted.

Angelica held her arm and together they ran through the blaze.

Hot air and fire engulfed Ellie, and the tail of her shirt had caught aflame. She stumbled, hanging onto Angelica with all her might. Even when they crossed through the ring of fire, the smoke was so thick you could barely see the trees.

Angelica staggered, and Ellie coaxed her away. They ran until they escaped the blaze and Angelica collapsed on the ground, with Ellie sinking down beside her and snuffing out the fire that had caught her shirt.

"Angelica, reach in my pocket. Get my knife."

Angelica coughed, her body shuddering with spasms, but she did as Ellie said. Her hands trembled as she removed the pocketknife, but she flipped it open and sawed at the ropes around Ellie's wrists.

"Did Weatherby say where he was going?" Ellie asked.

"No," Angelica said in a hoarse whisper. "Just that he had one more person on his list, the last one who could expose him."

Who was he talking about?

Finally free, Ellie dragged herself up, grasping the tree to stay on her feet as she searched the smoky haze for Derrick.

# CHAPTER 150

"McClain!" Derrick yelled. "Can you hear me?"

Slowly, Cord lifted his head. "Call for backup. I think my ankle is broken and my shoulder's dislocated."

"Are you hurt anywhere else?" Derrick shouted.

"Maybe cracked ribs," Cord yelled back. "I dropped my phone in the fall. Call the ranger station. I don't think I can climb back up."

"On it." Smoke wafted in thick waves across the sky as Derrick made the call and gave them the general location. "What happened?" he asked the ranger as he hung up.

"I was ambushed," Cord said, his voice gravelly with pain. "Didn't see his face. But he hit me in the back of the head then pushed me over."

Derrick's phone buzzed and he connected. "Ellie?"

"Yeah, I'm okay. But he got away," she said her breathing shaky. "Angelica needs an ambulance. Where are you?"

"I found McClain. He was assaulted and pushed over a ledge."

Ellie gulped. "Is he all right?"

"He will be. I've already called for help. I'll call medics for Angelica and for you."

"Thanks," Ellie said, her breath erratic. "I'll phone Captain Hale and ask him to issue a bulletin for Max Weatherby."

Derrick went still. "The arson investigator?"

"Yes," Ellie said. "He's the man we've been looking for."

# CHAPTER 151

The next hour passed in a blur. Derrick waited with Cord while the SAR team extracted him, and Ellie rode with Angelica to the hospital.

Angelica was being examined and treated for smoke inhalation, but the medics said her condition was stable.

She paced the ER waiting room, anxious to see Cord. She wouldn't rest until she saw for herself that he was all right.

The sheriff rushed in, his expression concerned as he approached her.

"Ellie, are you all right?"

"I'm fine, just pissed that the killer escaped." She winced as she rubbed her bandaged hands on her jeans. Her skin felt raw all over, her body throbbing.

A muscle ticked in Bryce's jaw. "The captain said Weatherby is behind all this."

"Not exactly. Hoyt is the mastermind. He conducted mind experiments on Rigdon and Weatherby and turned Max into a hit man. But Weatherby's still out there, Bryce. He's planning another kill right now."

"We've issued a bulletin and I've contacted bus and train stations and airports. We'll get his picture out there, too."

The doors to the ER opened, and the medics rolled Cord in. Derrick was behind him, on the phone.

Ellie rushed to the ranger, her breath catching at the sight of the blood on his forehead. His expression was stone cold, his jaw clenched, his eyes so dark that Ellie saw the pain he tried to hide.

The medics rattled off his stats to a nurse who was taking over, and Ellie squeezed Cord's hand. "Hey, you okay?"

Cord grunted. "I feel like a damned fool, having my own men carry me out."

A small smile tugged at Ellie's mouth, and she raked his sweat-soaked hair from his face. "I get it," she said softly. "I'm just glad you're all right."

He coughed through the pain. "I can't believe I worked with that bastard and he was starting the fires and murdering without me realizing it."

"He had us all fooled," Ellie said, mentally kicking herself too.

"We're ready to take him back," the nurse said.

Ellie looked at the plump woman. "You'd better take good care of him."

The nurse smiled and rolled the gurney toward the exam room. When she looked up, Derrick was watching her, his eyes intense.

The nurse in charge of Angelica appeared and motioned to Ellie. "Miss Gomez is asking for you."

Ellie headed through the double doors to Angelica's room. The reporter looked weak, her hair was a tangled mess, and she reeked of smoke. An oxygen tube fed air to her and an IV pumped fluids into her body.

"How are you feeling?" asked Ellie.

Angelica shrugged. "Grateful to be alive. Thanks to you."

"No problem," Ellie said, her throat thickening with emotions. "I found your shorthand note and we have Hoyt in custody. He admitted to Special Agent Fox that he wrote that book which was based on mind experiments he'd conducted on unsuspecting patients. I suspect he brainwashed Max into cleaning up after what he and Dr. Hangar did."

"There's something else, Ellie. It's about Gillian Roach." Angelica began to cough again, and Ellie handed her the cup of water on the nightstand, waiting while she sipped through the straw. "I always knew I was adopted," Angelica said. "When my adoptive mom died last year, I decided to look for my birth mother. An aunt told me about Gillian Roach, so I contacted her."

Ellie's breath stalled. So Angelica had called Gillian about her own adoption, not about Ellie's.

"Gillian said she met my mother when she was pregnant, that her name was Isabella, that she claimed she was drugged and sexually assaulted by a doctor she worked for."

"The same thing happened to Vanessa's mother," Ellie told her. "Dr. Hangar's wife confessed that her husband had been date-raping girls since college. There were several in the eighties. One was Wanda Morely. Another... I think was my mother." Ellie hesitated. "Did you find yours?"

"She died when I was a baby. The report I found said it was suspicious but that's all I found. But that's why I kept asking you if you were looking for your birth parents."

Ellie gasped as she mentally maneuvered the pieces in her mind. "If your mother and mine were both sexually assaulted by Dr. Hangar, that means—"

"That we're half-sisters," Angelica said in a raw whisper.

# CHAPTER 152

Ellie and Angelica stared at each other for a long moment. They'd have to check DNA to be certain, but Ellie's mind couldn't help wondering…

She had always wanted a sister growing up. A friend.

Maybe Angelica could be both of those things to her.

Derrick rapped on the door and poked his head in. "Miss Gomez, how are you doing?"

"I'll survive. Any word on Weatherby?"

Shaking his head, Derrick glanced at Ellie. "McClain is okay. A broken ankle which they're setting, sprained wrist, dislocated shoulder, three cracked ribs. They're going to keep him overnight at least."

"Good," Ellie said. "Meanwhile, we have to find this bastard."

"Go, Detective," Angelica murmured. "Find Weatherby so he can't hurt anyone else."

Ellie squeezed Angelica's hand, a silent moment of understanding, hope and friendship passing between them. "Get some rest, Angelica. I'll keep you posted."

On the way out, they stopped by Cord's room. The ranger looked groggy and was propped against the pillows. To her surprise, Lola from the Corner Café was sitting beside him, holding a water cup.

For a second, Ellie's heart stuttered. Lola pivoted and waved up at her. "Hey, Ellie. I heard Cord was hurt and wanted to check on him."

Cord blinked and looked past Lola, the drugs and pain fogging his eyes. "El?"

"Get some rest, Cord. We'll talk later." She turned and hurried back down the hall, trying not to think about the tiny stabbing pain in her chest.

"You okay?" Derrick asked.

"Angelica said Weatherby was going after someone else. We have to work fast."

Derrick sucked in a breath. "He's coming after you?"

"Maybe. But he mentioned something about the last one who could expose him. That could mean another rape victim. I think it might be my mother."

"Do you know where she is?"

Ellie shook her head. "Before I left Ms. Eula, she gave me a box that belonged to her husband. I want to look through it. Maybe Hangar left the answers in there."

"You look like you need a hot bath and some rest right now. In the morning?"

She needed exactly that. And maybe some Epsom salts. But killers didn't wait for the cops to go home and sleep.

"No, tonight."

"Then let's pick up some food and get to them."

Ellie murmured her agreement, her mind already racing as she and Derrick went outside to her vehicle.

He pulled out her keys, and she didn't argue. She slid into the passenger seat, her earlier adrenaline rush quickly dissipating.

But she couldn't turn off her mind. She had to find her mother.

# CHAPTER 153

*Crooked Creek*

Derrick's anger threatened to take hold as he looked at Ellie's battered face.

"Let me take you home and you can shower. I'll go question Hoyt again and then pick up food."

"The shower can wait," Ellie said. "I'll look at the files while you question Hoyt. If he manipulated Weatherby's mind, maybe he knows who's next on the hit list."

The parade and festivities in the town were winding down, the vendors packing up for the evening, yet the fireworks show remained. Night had set in, people parking on the lawn in lounge chairs in anticipation of the fireworks and the concert on the square.

Pulling into the parking spot in front of the police station, Derrick was determined to take care of Ellie. She might be right about Weatherby coming for her mother. But he might be coming for Ellie instead.

Together they entered the police station, and Ellie stopped to speak to Deputy Landrum who'd been tasked with babysitting the station while everyone else worked the case.

Snagging the keys to the cell, Derrick walked to the holding cells while Ellie went to her office.

Rage at Hoyt fueled him, and he hurried to the cell. The lights were dim, and there was the sound of something rhythmic, like a tapping against the wall.

Since Rigdon had been moved to the psych hospital for evaluation and treatment, Hoyt was in the back alone. Derrick's boots sounded on the concrete floor as the scent of sweat and piss wafted toward him. When had the damn cells last been cleaned?

The quiet was almost eerie, as if the place was empty. But as he reached the cell, he saw the source of the sound.

Hoyt hanging from the bed sheet, his body swinging back and forth, banging against the wall.

# CHAPTER 154

Ellie opened her desk, removed a bottle of painkillers, popped two in her mouth and washed them down with a big chug of water. She set the box Ms. Eula had given her on the table in the corner and perched on the edge of the loveseat to study the files.

Just as Ms. Eula claimed, there were sordid snapshots of her husband, much younger then, engaged in sex with young women who appeared to be drugged or asleep. Sickened at the sight, she had to inhale to keep from getting sick.

She spread the photographs out, narrowing her eyes as she identified Agnes Curtis and Janie Huntington. She found a file on each woman detailing the sleep study, their reactions to the medication, with Hangar's scrawled writing describing that he'd chosen them because they were most susceptible to the drug.

*It was like lightning had struck when I teamed up with Lewis Hoyt. The sleep study was the perfect venue for what we both wanted.*

*It all started years ago, though, when I met Mabel. Mabel was so beautiful, with her sandy blond hair, big green eyes and curves that would take your breath away when she walked into the room. She lived in an apartment next to campus. I used a college lab for my research and would scour campus for suitable young women. I couldn't help but watch her. She was so young and beautiful and kind to everyone. She had everything Eula had lost.*

*One night at a bar, I saw the sparkle in her eyes when she looked at me and thought she wanted me. But when I tried to kiss her, she shoved me away. I thought she was just playing hard to get, that she needed to loosen up, so I slipped a drug into Mabel's drink and watched as it took effect. Then I walked her home.*

*But she didn't take well to the drug. She started hallucinating. I just meant to calm her, to soothe her fears, but once I touched her, I couldn't stop myself. I'd wanted her for so long.*

*Three weeks later, she was still hallucinating. And she was pregnant. That's when I knew I had to do something. I didn't think anyone would believe her, but I couldn't risk that chance.*

The notes stopped abruptly, but there were more photos—older, faded, not taken in a clinic. She was sure one of them was of Wanda Morely. There was also a young Hispanic woman. Isabella, Angelica's mother?

Ellie's pulse clamored as she searched the box for more pages, for some sense of what had happened to Mabel, but there was nothing until, right at the bottom of the box, she found a picture of woman that matched Mabel's description. And Ellie's own. Furious, she snatched up the photographs, rushed from her office and through the double doors to the jail cell.

She was damn well going to make Hoyt talk.

# CHAPTER 155

Mabel clutched her baby girl to her, shushing her as she rocked her in her arms. She'd known he would come for her one day. Come back and try to take her little girl away.

She would die before she let that happen.

Tonight, just as she'd tried to get the baby to sleep, she'd seen him. It had been years, but she recognized that dark evil look in his eyes.

The door squeaked open and the nursing assistant appeared with her night pills and water. Mabel gently laid her infant in the crib, dug the two pills from the cup and popped them in her mouth. She made a show of swallowing hard, then stuck out her tongue for inspection.

"Good girl," the nursing assistant said. "Sleep tight, Mabel."

Mabel faked a yawn and closed her eyes, grateful the woman hustled from the room to finish her rounds. As soon as the door closed, she spit the pills into her hand, then carried them to the toilet and flushed them. Quickly, she retrieved the thin piece of metal she'd pried from the broken springs in her mattress, crawled in bed and waited.

*Ticktock. Ticktock.* That damn clock drove her insane. But sometimes it was the only way she knew if it was night or day. She begged to take her little girl out into the gardens for a stroll, and sometimes they obliged. It was a reward for taking her meds.

Other times when they found she'd spit them in the toilet or the plants in the solarium, she was punished and locked inside the room for days.

*Ticktock. Ticktock.* The clock struck ten o'clock. Time for all the lights to be out. Time for the crazies to sleep, the workers to gather in the break room and eat doughnuts and Little Debbie cakes and make fun of the patients.

She watched the clock, waiting, waiting, counting the minutes. By eleven, it was quiet in the halls.

Slipping from bed, she quickly dressed then jammed the tip of the metal wire into the door. She wiggled and twisted, but the lock didn't budge. Blowing hair from her face, she stooped to her knees and tried again. It was hard seeing in the dark, but she didn't dare turn on the light. That would bring the nurse back, or worse, one of the guards.

She bent the tip of the wire again and tried once more. She pricked her finger and blood dripped from the tip, but she wiped it on her clothes and jiggled the door as she twisted the metal and maneuvered it in the lock.

Finally she heard the sound of a pop.

She held her breath, listening to make sure no one was outside. Thankful for the silence, she hurried to the crib, scooped her daughter into her arms, then slowly opened the door, peering left and right. Empty.

A voice echoed down the corridor, and she froze, praying as she waited. Finally, the footsteps faded, indicating whoever it was had disappeared down the hall. She tiptoed down the hall in the opposite direction, then around the corner, stopping at every turn to make sure the hall was empty.

She'd seen the custodian's entrance and exit on one of her walks to the treatment room—she shuddered at the memory of that—and she made her way there. Easing into the stairwell, she pushed at the door, rushing outside.

An alarm trilled, sending her heart racing, and she began to run. The hot night air blasted as she hurried down the steps. The parking lot was on the opposite side of the building. Maybe she could make a break for it. Someone might have left their keys in their car.

But there were cameras out there. And if she set off one of the car alarms, they'd catch her.

The woods were her only choice. Shivering at the thought of getting lost in the thickets of the forest, she hesitated. But she didn't have an option.

# CHAPTER 156

*Crooked Creek*

"You are not going to take the fucking easy way out," Derrick growled as he jumped onto the prison cot and grabbed Hoyt's body to pull him down.

The man struggled, kicking at Derrick and coughing as he tried to tighten the knot around his neck. "Let me go! I'm not going to prison."

Ellie came barreling down the hall. "What the hell?"

"Help me," Derrick shouted. "There's a knife in my pocket."

No matter how hard Hoyt kicked out at him, Derrick held tight.

Ellie raced into the cell, dug in his pocket and pulled it out. While he kept Hoyt steady to keep him from choking, Ellie cut the sheet and ripped it away from Hoyt's neck.

The man coughed and struggled, his arms flailing as Derrick dragged him down. They fell to the floor, Hoyt still trying to resist, but Ellie shook him.

"Give it up, Hoyt," Ellie yelled. "You can still do the right thing here."

He finally went still, his breath sputtering out as he gasped for a breath.

# CHAPTER 157

Hoyt looked at Derrick in panic. "She's crazy. You're not going to let her force me into confessing to something I didn't do, are you?"

"Innocent men don't try to hang themselves." Derrick gave him a cold stare. "If I were you, I'd talk."

"I want my lawyer," Hoyt screeched.

"Your lawyer can't save you," Ellie snapped. "It's over, Hoyt. We already know most everything. You and Dr. Hangar worked together on the sleep study." She shoved him against the wall. "He raped several women while they were under the influence of the drug, and you conducted mind experiments. Rigdon and Weatherby were both susceptible," she continued. "Just what were you trying to do with that study?"

"It was for the military," Hoyt spat, finally relenting. "We were trying to create men who could kill without remorse."

"And it worked. Rigdon became a sniper. What about Weatherby? He's a fireman."

"Not back then," Hoyt admitted. "He was military also. When he got out, he decided to join the fire department."

"And he became your hitman," Ellie concluded.

"You have no proof of that," Hoyt barked. "They don't remember anything that happened. I made sure of that."

"What triggers Weatherby to kill? Does he have a hit list?"

Hoyt shifted then nodded. "His smart watch. I call it and when he hears the sound of the clock ticking, it's his cue. I… also planted suggestions, memories in his head so he believes that he took part in the sexual assault. At the time, it was cutting edge."

Ellie jerked him by the collar, sickened by his depravity. "He's still out there and going after someone else. And this is personal to me."

"What do you mean personal?"

She leaned forward, her voice filled with calm rage. "One of the women he assaulted was my mother." One by one, Ellie picked up the photographs Hangar had kept, naming them. "Wanda Morely. Agnes Curtis. Janie Huntington." Her breath puffed out angrily. "And then there's Gillian Roach. You see, she handled my adoption. Worked with all these women."

She swallowed hard. "But why Katie Lee? And how did you know that any of them contacted Gillian?" The man looked away. Ellie gripped his collar tighter. "If you want to be saved from the death penalty, you'd better talk."

He scrubbed a hand down his face. "All right, all right. I kept tabs on all of my subjects and Hangar's victims just to be on the safe side. Ike told me that Josiah mentioned that Katie Lee was asking questions. We both knew his wife Agnes didn't have the guts to come forward, but her daughter was nosy. And she and Janie Huntington's son were friends, so they were stirring up a hornets' nest. So was that reporter who started it all by contacting the Roach woman."

"Reverend Ike was part of this?" Ellie asked.

He nodded. "The three of us went way back."

"What about Gillian?"

"I don't think she knew at the time what had happened, but when Vanessa Morely reached out and Angelica called her, she got suspicious. She called me asking questions."

"So you had to silence her." Ellie was going to nail Reverend Ike's ass to the wall and enjoy doing it. Another nod. "What about Vanessa's mother? She died suspiciously in childbirth."

Hoyt hung his head. "That was Ernie. When she decided to keep her baby, he panicked. Decided he had to do something. His entire career would be ruined if he was exposed."

Ellie shoved him backward and slapped her hands on the table. "As it should have been! But you and Ike and Hangar thought you were above the law and entitled. You are disgusting, and you and the good reverend are going to rot in prison."

Furious, she showed him another picture. This one was old and grainy, of a young dark-blond woman, taken in a bedroom. "I think this is my mother and that she was one of Hangar's victims. That's why Gillian Roach took files from her office. And you found out. Now tell me her full name."

Hoyt started to protest, but Derrick folded his arms across his chest. "You ordered hits on these women and Gillian Roach just to save your reputation. And this woman is next on the list, isn't she?"

Ellie pulled her gun and placed the barrel between the man's eyes. "Tell me her name."

"Mabel M-Morgan," he finally spat.

"Where is she?" Ellie growled.

"She went crazy," Hoyt said. "I never knew her, but Hangar talked about her. Said he'd watched her for weeks. He met her at a bar and thought she was into him, but when he made an advance, she pushed him away. He thought she was playing hard to get so he drugged her and… then she got pregnant."

"She's still alive?"

Hoyt gave a short nod, his breathing raspy.

"Where is she?" Ellie asked again.

"She had a psychotic breakdown and he had her admitted to the state hospital. She had the baby there, and the state put the child into foster care.

"What was the baby's name?"

"Mae," Hoyt said. "She was named after her mother."

# CHAPTER 158

*North Georgia State Hospital*

Hoyt finally admitted that he'd overseen Mabel's care while at the hospital to make sure she never remembered what had happened. Ellie wanted to kill him. But making him suffer in prison for the rest of his life would have to do.

A call to the facility and she learned Mabel was alive.

Fury at Dr. Hangar and his cohorts made it difficult for Ellie to breathe as she looked up at the mental hospital where she and Derrick had been on a previous investigation. The ancient stone structure looked like a gothic castle straight out of a horror movie.

As they walked up the stone path to the door, they both scanned the property. Max Weatherby had a head start on them. If he was after Mabel, he might already be here.

They went straight to the security desk when they entered, the chilling concrete walls a reminder that patients were locked inside like a prison. Mabel had been stuck here for life, all because of Hangar.

She hated him with every fiber of her being.

Ellie introduced herself and Derrick at the desk. "As I explained over the phone, Mabel Morgan may be in danger. Where is her room?"

The guard and desk nurse exchanged nervous looks.

"What's going on?" Ellie asked.

"The alarm at the custodian's exit went off. We're trying to reach him to see if he forgot to use his key card."

Ellie's pulse jumped. "Can you show us Mae's room?"

The nurse clenched her phone. "There's a night-shift doctor, but I'll also call the doctor in charge of Mabel's care."

"Of course." Impatience nagged at Ellie as she waited for the nurse to make the call. Seconds ticked by. The building seemed unusually quiet tonight, but Ellie knew the walls were soundproofed to drown out the screams and cries that could haunt this place.

"Dr. Buckley is twenty minutes out," the nurse said. "She can meet you here in the morning."

"We can't wait until then," Ellie said. "We need to make sure Mabel is safe tonight."

The nurse still seemed hesitant but gestured to the guard to escort them to Mabel's room. The walk through the dimly lit, high-ceilinged halls gave Ellie a chill. The guard led them through a set of locked doors then down another hall until they reached room number 2121.

Ellie's chest ached at the thought of Mabel Morgan being drugged and assaulted, then being shut in this facility for most of her life. Mabel had been a victim, and no one had even known.

Pulling keys from his belt, the guard went to unlock the door, but the moment he touched the knob, the door creaked open. Alarm shot across his face as he stepped inside, and Ellie looked past him to see that the room was empty.

# CHAPTER 159

Mabel ducked behind a tree, searching all around her as she hugged her baby in her arms. The moon slanted through the treetops and across the woods in a soft glow. Leaves rustled, and twigs snapped as something darted through the forest. Thunder popped in the inky sky, raindrops splashed her.

Terrified the man had come for her, she hugged her daughter tighter to protect her from the wind. Tears filled her eyes, trickling down her cheeks as panic seized her.

*You're so stupid, Mabel. How can you get away when you have no idea where you are?*

But what else could she do except run? No one in the hospital would believe her if she told them she thought someone was after her. They never had before.

She couldn't give up. Clenching her daughter to her, she dashed through the woods. If she made it to the river maybe she could find a boat somewhere to take her downstream.

She hadn't been past the gardens since she'd come to live here, though, and had no idea which direction the town would be. And she'd heard others talking about the electric fence and barbed wire surrounding the property.

A noise sounded behind her, and she glanced around. There was a movement in the thickets.

It was a man. He was big, tall, a hulking figure. Danger emanated off him. He halted in the shadows and looked straight toward her as if he could see her in the dark.

Terror-stricken, she sprinted toward the sound of the river, her lungs straining for air as she ran.

She couldn't let them take her baby away again.

# CHAPTER 160

Ellie raced into Mabel's room, hurrying to the bed, but it was empty. The crib in the corner confused her. It was empty, too, and the guard radioed for security to lock down the hospital.

"Have them search the parking lot, the cars, the hospital inside and out," said Ellie. "She could be hiding somewhere inside this place."

The guard gave a quick nod. "I'll get someone looking at the security footage. If she's here, we'll find her."

"While your people cover the inside, we need to start a search around the perimeter of the building." She glanced at her watch. "When was the last time someone checked on her?"

"Ten," the guard said as he gripped his radio. "We do bed check and last meds then. The nurse assistant would have reported it if there was a problem."

"Could she have gotten into another patient's room?" Ellie asked.

"Not without a master key," the guard stated. "And that would be difficult to obtain."

"Have your people search every single room. We'll start outside. Where is the closest exit from here?" Ellie asked.

The guard stepped to the doorway. "The staff exit down the hall. It's the door that triggered the alarm."

Ellie and Derrick raced out, surveying the hall as they passed closed doors to patients' rooms. As Derrick pushed open the exit, they covered each other as they crept outside.

Pulling her flashlight from her pocket, Ellie shined it across the treeline, searching and listening for movement.

She spotted some brush that had been trampled and took off toward it, Derrick on her heels. Body tense, she wove through the rows of thick trees, sweeping the area as she jogged over fallen tree stumps and dry weeds. The sound of the river in the distance echoed. Mabel might head that way.

She gestured toward Derrick and they separated, spanning out to cover more territory. Perspiration beaded on her skin, and thunder rumbled, the thick trees shrouding the gray skies. Brush crackled beneath her shoes and a tree branch slapped her cheek as she shoved her way through the denser areas.

Then a scream broke the silence.

Ellie hurried past a section of hemlocks, climbing over rocks as she neared the river. Her torch illuminated a patch of weeds, then she spotted a figure in dark clothing dragging someone toward the edge of the cliff above the river.

"Stop! Police!" Ellie aimed her gun at the man's back, creeping closer.

He turned and looked at her, the feral look in his eyes cold and hollow. Dear God, the woman was holding a baby. And Max had her by the throat.

"Let her go!" Ellie ordered.

It was almost as if the man didn't hear her. He pushed the woman toward the edge, and Ellie raced toward them. The woman's stringy dark-blond hair hung past her shoulders. But when she looked at Ellie, her face looked familiar. She had the same color eyes. And that pointed chin.

Inhaling, she shouted, "Let her go, Weatherby, It's over."

"Listen to her," Derrick shouted from the opposite direction.

Weatherby froze, finally registering their voices. But he grabbed Mabel by the arms and pushed her toward the cliff. "Don't do it! She's innocent. Just like you were. Let her go," Ellie said between clenched teeth.

But his blank look indicated he was in the throes of whatever had happened in those mind-control experiments. "I said let her go," Ellie hissed.

"Don't hurt my baby!" Mabel screamed.

"Please," Ellie said in a whisper as she inched toward them.

"Mae didn't do anything," Mabel cried. "Please don't take her away."

Ellie froze, the breath leaving her lungs.

Max pulled a lighter from his pocket and flicked it on, the flame illuminating his sinister expression.

"Let the woman and baby go," Ellie said. "We know you didn't mean to do this. We know what Dr. Hoyt did to you and the others, but we've arrested him. It's over. It's time for it to end."

Dr. Hoyt's name brought a reaction, and Max stiffened. Emotions flashed across his face, before his shoulders slumped. Then he looked down at Mabel and the baby, giving them a shove.

Ellie's breath wheezed, watching it happen in slow motion. Derrick fired and hit him in the chest, and his body bounced backward over the ridge.

Heart hammering, Ellie raced toward Mabel, who was screaming and barely hanging onto a tree branch as she struggled not to slide over to her death. Dropping to her knees, Ellie grabbed Mabel by the shoulders, dragging her up over the edge.

The woman collapsed to the ground, crying and hugging the bundle to her. "Get away from me! You can't have Mae."

Tears clogged Ellie's throat as she realized the bundle was a doll. "Mabel," Ellie said softly. "I'm Ellie. You're safe now. And so is Mae."

Mabel collapsed into Ellie's arms and she wrapped her into a hug. Tears stung her eyes. She'd finally found her birth mother. She didn't know what would happen next, but she would make sure Mabel got the proper treatment and would know that she hadn't lost her daughter.

# CHAPTER 161

Ellie comforted Mabel while Derrick coordinated with the guards and staff at the hospital, then called a rescue team to recover Weatherby's body.

She desperately wanted to explain everything to Mabel, but shock had set in and the woman lapsed into a catatonic state. By the time her doctor arrived, Ellie had put everything together in her mind and explained what had happened.

"I want a specialist in trauma brought in," Ellie told the doctor. "We're going to get Mabel well and off the damn drugs she's been taking. Then I'll explain everything to her and make sure she finally has a chance at life."

The doctor looked harried and worried but agreed.

"I was just following Dr. Hoyt's direction," the doctor assured her. "And I promise you we'll figure out what's best for Mabel. Now that I know the story and background, I think we can treat her, and her condition will improve."

Hope filled Ellie as the doctor explained that Mabel would be transferred to another hospital, where she would be treated more like a patient with a future than a prisoner sentenced to life within these walls.

By the time the rescue team recovered Weatherby's body, exhaustion had intensified her emotions.

Derrick's dark eyes skated over her, a mixture of tenderness and concern in his voice. "Come on, we've done all we can for the night. I'll drive you home."

He took her hand and coaxed her toward the car.

Ellie felt like she was in a fog as Derrick drove them back toward town. The case was done. Hoyt was in prison and Weatherby was dead.

Angelica was safe. They'd run the DNA, but she felt certain it would prove that Mabel was Ellie's mother. And that she and the reporter were half-sisters, and half-siblings of Vanessa Morely, Katie Lee Curtis and Will Huntington. They were all the products of violent acts.

How was she supposed to feel about that? And Will—he had to deal with his mother's death. She couldn't blow up his entire world by telling him the truth.

She barely realized it when they reached her house, but Derrick parked and she climbed out, moving on autopilot.

"Take that shower now, Ellie," Derrick ordered softly. "I'll make you a drink."

She nodded, lost and on her last leg. Shuffling forward, she went to her room, undressed and climbed in the shower. The tears fell, hard and fast, and she doubled over beneath the hot spray as Mabel's pitiful cries echoed in her ears. Would her mother ever be normal again? Would they have a relationship?

She sobbed until her cries dissipated, then she washed them away, her determination setting in. She was no quitter. No doomsday girl.

Randall and Vera were rebuilding. She could build something with Mabel, too.

Finally, the hot water assuaged her aching muscles and helped wash away the stench of the night.

She towel-dried her hair, pulled on a tank top and pajama shorts and padded to her living room. Derrick stood in the kitchen, the moonlight silhouetting his handsome, strong face, his eyes so dark and sexy that she almost lost herself inside them.

He offered her a drink and poured himself one as well and then he took a sip. "Do you want to talk about it? About Mabel?"

The tenderness in his eyes made tears clog her throat. She tossed back the vodka, determined to hang onto her control. "Not now. I just want to be alone."

Derrick's gaze connected with hers for a long minute, questions and worry darkening his eyes. "Are you sure?"

No, she wasn't. She wanted him to hold her. But she was too vulnerable tonight. So she gave a nod.

He didn't push her. Instead, he gave her a quick hug and said goodbye.

His taillights had just disappeared around the corner when Shondra arrived. Ellie remembered Shondra pushing her away after she'd been rescued from the Weekday Killer and considered doing the same thing now. But Shondra had cartons of ice cream with her and a bottle of vodka, and Ellie knew that she couldn't turn her friend away.

"Are you okay?" Shondra asked, as Ellie let her in.

"I don't know," she said honestly. "But I'm glad you're here."

Shondra hugged her then pushed past her and went for spoons in the cabinet. She poured herself a drink and refilled Ellie's, then they carried the ice cream to the back porch. It wasn't far off dawn now, but the drink and sugar were sorely needed after the day she'd had.

As they inhaled the dark chocolate ice cream filled with peanut butter swirls, Ellie filled Shondra in on what had happened with Mabel and Mae.

"We're a pair, aren't we?" Shondra said wryly.

"Yeah, I guess we are," Ellie murmured.

"I can't work for Bryce anymore," Shondra said softly. "I put in for a transfer to Crooked Creek."

"Good. I need a partner."

They toasted Shondra's decision, then sipped their drinks in silence.

Birds twittered and cicadas began to sing. A breeze picked up, and for a moment Ellie thought she heard Vanessa's childhood giggle floating in the wind as she pumped her legs on the swing in the park. She could almost see her hair blowing behind her as she darted through the trees, the two of them rolling down the grassy bald into the creek below it, splashing and kicking and laughing.

Vanessa's daughter's pained face taunted her. Mandy had lost her mother. Ellie knew all about that. Maybe she could make up for not reconciling with Vanessa by being a friend to the girl. She could tell her stories about the images they'd seen in the clouds and their camping trips.

And how once upon a time, before the monsters came, they'd dreamt of rainbows and unicorns and made mud pies in the forest.

# A LETTER FROM RITA

Thank you so much for diving into the world I've created with Detective Ellie Reeves in *The Burning Girls*! If you enjoyed *The Burning Girls* and would like to keep up with all of my latest releases, you can sign up at the following link. Your email address will never be shared, and you can unsubscribe at any time.

*www.bookouture.com/rita-herron*

I'm thrilled to bring you the third installment in this series! The small town and quirky characters of Crooked Creek, along with the folklore and danger surrounding the mountains and Appalachian Trail are once again ripe with mystery, suspicion, secrets and murder.

I've always been fascinated by people's differing reaction to trauma and adversity. Some people let it break them while others use that hardship to make them stronger. Some dwell on the past while others move forward and rise to the challenge.

I hope you enjoyed Ellie's journey in *The Burning Girls* as much as I enjoyed writing it. If you did, I'd appreciate it if you left a short review. As a writer, it means the world to me that you share your feedback with other readers who might be interested in Ellie's world.

I love to hear from readers so you can find me on Facebook, my website and Twitter.

Thanks so much for your support. Happy Reading!
Rita

f ritaherron

🐦 @ritaherron

💻 www.ritaherron.com

# ACKNOWLEDGMENTS

First of all, a huge thanks to Christina Demosthenous for seeking me out. When she suggested I write a detective series, I had this one in the works and was thrilled to send it over. Her insight from day one, suggestions and edits helped shape it into a much better series, with twists I hadn't originally even dreamed of. I also want to thank the Bookouture team for the great cover and title. And a big thanks to Fraser Crichton for catching my mistakes in the copyediting stage!

Also, thanks to my agent Jenny Bent for her unfailing support and guidance.

Another thanks to my long-time critique partner and writer friend Stephanie Bond for brainstorming and encouraging me from the get-go with this dark mystery series.

Made in the USA
Coppell, TX
27 March 2024